SPIRIT

SPIRIT

The Sarah Midnight Trilogy

Book 3

Daniela Sacerdoti

BLACK & WHITE PUBLISHING

First published 2014
by Black & White Publishing Ltd
29 Ocean Drive, Edinburgh EH6 6JL

1 3 5 7 9 10 8 6 4 2   14 15 16 17

ISBN: 978 1 84502 540 3

ALBA | CHRUTHACHAIL

Typeset by Iolaire Typesetting, Newtonmore
Printed and bound by Grafica Veneta, S. p. A. Italy

This book is for Edo

Acknowledgements

My heartfelt thanks go to Janne Moller, Kristen Susienka and Rachel Reid, my wonderful editors and friends. I am forever grateful I had the chance to work with you. Many thanks in particular to Rachel for being the first to believe in Sarah. Thank you from the bottom of my heart to Charlotte Robertson, for being the agent to end all agents! My gratitude goes also to Lindsey Fraser and all her precious advice, to Campbell Brown and Alison McBride at Black & White Publishing for overall wonderfulness, and to Stuart Polson for the covers of all three books. Thank you, thank you, thank you to Roy Gill and Phil Miller for writerly talks and for your generous support, not to mention beautiful writing to inspire me. To those who soundtracked the trilogy – Manran and the amazing Norrie McIver, Julie Fowlis, Clannad and Duncan Chisolm – thank you for endless inspiration.

Thank you Ross for your belief in me and for providing endless cups of coffee! Thank you to my wonderful mum, Ivana, and to my mother-in-law, Beth, for being such amazing mothers and grandmothers. And more than anyone, more than ever, thank you to my little writer and artist, Sorley, and to my little hero, Luca: everything I do and everything I am is for you.

Contents

CONTENTS

Prologue
The Sleeping Girl

A dream on the water
A city of plague and laces
Steps in the night
Echo my call

Venice, Italy

Nobody saw the slender, amber-skinned girl walking on the water of the Grand Canal, placing one foot slowly in front of the other, the moonlight reflected on her cropped black hair and the hem of her gown dripping with every step she took. To either side of her, tethered boats and gondolas swayed on the murky waters, the canal's foulness a contrast to the beauty of the palaces. The city itself was rotting quietly, year after year, crumbling and dissolving in a dream of splendour and decay.

Micol walked on, straight-backed and solemn and silent, worn from the effort of staying afloat on the water and still unable to stop, because when she stopped she would have to go home, her new home. And to go back to Palazzo Vendramin, where the sleeping girl seemed to steal the air from her lungs, where the Ailment had slowly eaten one of her brothers' bodies and the other's mind – to go back was just unbearable.

But she had to. There was no other place of safety, and to be out alone at night – or any time, really – was almost certain death.

Still, for a little while longer Micol would walk under the moonlight, the sound of lapping water in her ears, the slow *swoosh* of her gown sending rats scurrying along the walls of the palazzos. Micol gazed at a little pack of them, fat and black and fearless, climbing down a gilded façade and into the water, and then she looked up at the black sky still dotted with stars, slowly turning orange in the east. She longed for freedom and purity and wished herself far, far away from this dying city.

But she knew that the plague would get her too, one day soon. Like it came for her brothers, Tancredi and Ranieri. For her, a quick demon death would be preferable to the Azasti. So Micol had made her decision: as soon as she spotted the first signs on herself – the blue nails, the constant exhaustion, the bleeding at the slightest cut, the slightest bruise – she'd go out and walk. Just walk.

And when they attacked, she would not defend herself.

A glimmer of light danced on Micol's bare feet. Dawn was breaking, and the city would soon awaken. She couldn't delay any more. She had to go back and let those mad Vendramins lock her up for another day.

Micol shuddered as she lifted herself up onto the street, her hands struggling to find a grip on the algae-covered bricks. She sat on the pavement for a moment, her wet feet freezing in the winter air, and then forced herself up. What she would give not to see Lucrezia, the sleeping girl, again. Not to hear her screams ever again for as long as she lived.

Micol tiptoed along the *calle* until she reached the palazzo. She lifted her dress and tied it in a knot at her hip, and then she started climbing the ivy-covered wall, her slim limbs strong and supple, her grip firm like someone who'd been climbing trees every day of her fifteen years of life. In no time at all, she'd scaled the wall and jumped into the Vendramin garden, making no noise as she fell to the frosty grass. In one graceful movement she lifted her arm, fingers extended, and murmured a few words in the Ancient language. A lightning bolt danced from the sky and hit her index fingers, travelling through her body and discharging into the earth. One of Vendramin's demon traps – she knew them all. Or at least, she hoped so. Maybe one day, returning from one of her night water walks, she'd find herself skewed or electrocuted by a trap she wasn't aware of, or eaten alive by some new Elemental she had no control over. And still, as dangerous as it was, she couldn't stop going out at night. If she had to spend her nights locked up with those crazy people who were sheltering her now, she'd go crazy too. Like Lucrezia. Often in her dreams, Micol saw herself lying beside Lucrezia, in an equally tormented sleep, without ever being able to wake up.

A throaty growl interrupted her thoughts. She turned around to see a night-black beast looking at her, eyes narrow, its incisors too big to fit into its mouth, saliva dripping down its neck and onto the grass. The creature bent slightly to give itself momentum, and then pounced.

"Ouch! My legs, you silly beast! Oh, come here. You happy to see me? Me too. Good bo—" She didn't have time to finish the sentence when an arrow hissed in front of her nose and buried itself into the brick wall behind her.

"What did you do that for?" she whispered, too angry to even articulate properly. A young man stood a few feet from her, a furious look in his eyes. He clutched a bow with both his hands, and there was another arrow in it, ready.

"I'll kill *you* before you get us all killed. Do you understand me?" the man said, and something in his voice left Micol in no doubt that he meant it.

Raging, Micol strode through the manicured gardens, in between a row of stone statues and one of the palazzo's exquisite rose bushes. The young man followed her closely.

"If you kill me, your dad will kill you, Alvise."

"You're not that precious, Micol. Stop fancying yourself as some kind of princess."

Micol stopped suddenly and turned around to face Alvise. "Yes, well, stop fancying yourself as some kind of hero, because you have no powers and a Secret heir with no powers is good for no—" Her words were again interrupted, this time by a slap so swift and strong that it made her head twist sharply to one side. She tasted blood on her lips.

Micol saw red. She narrowed her eyes, and static raced over her arms. Her short dark hair began lifting slowly.

"What do you think you're doing, little girl?"

Guglielmo Vendramin was standing in front of her. Without ceremony, he grabbed her by the shoulder and dragged her inside. As soon as they stepped into the hall, with its ornate ceilings and its arched windows, he threw her on the floor.

Micol sobbed in anger. She was furious. Soon her brother

would come back and take her away from here. She focused on the mosaic tiles on the floor, following their patterns, their colours. She wasn't there. Her body was there, but not her mind. She would not let them win.

She studied the floor, a mosaic of swirling colours. A lion on fire, devouring the sun. The symbol of the Vendramin. Brutal, like them. And mad. They all were.

Suddenly, a strong hand curled around hers, and lifted her to her feet.

"Micol. You don't seem to understand the situation," hissed Vendramin. His silver hair and beard glinted in the rays of the rising dawn, the lines on his face deep and his eyes etched with worry. "The Secret Families are dying. Because of the Azasti, because of the demons closing in on us. And you run away like a little girl. You render traps around the palace useless, as if this were some kind of joke!"

"She'll get us all killed, Father," the young man reiterated. Vendramin gazed at his son. His strong features, the sharp cheekbones, the white-blond hair. He was the double of his mother. Only nineteen, and so much on his shoulders already. Every morning Vendramin checked him for signs of the Azasti that was devouring so many Italian Secret Families, but for now, their family had been spared.

"She won't," Vendramin said unexpectedly. There was a hint of fatigue in his voice, a weariness that clashed with the man's proud demeanour. "She's learnt her lesson. Haven't you, Micol?"

Micol lowered her eyes. She hated him. She hated them all and she wanted to go home. But she knew they were right. She knew that what she was doing was foolish. She'd have to survive being locked in with all these sick people, these mad people.

At that moment, a scream pierced the silence, followed by a shuffle of feet and a tapping of heels. It was the sleeping girl screaming out a nightmare, and Cosima, the chief maid and Lucrezia's main carer, running to see to her.

"If she doesn't toe the line," Vendramin continued, his eyes on Alvise's face but his words clearly directed toward Micol, "she knows what will happen to her."

Micol felt nauseous.

Yes. She knew.

1
On the Edge

You are our dark heart
Black reflection
Of what we fear we are

Germany–Poland border

A trickle of sweat ran down Sarah's back as the soldier beckoned her out of the car. Why had he singled her out, out of all the members of their group? Why now? They had travelled through half of Europe, from Islay all the way to the Polish border, without ever being stopped. They had been lucky. Their passports were kosher, of course, except for Nicholas', who had a completely forged identity – but he had reassured them it was watertight. There had been no time to create new identities, new passports after leaving Islay, and they had got from place to place by sheer luck. But finally, it seemed their luck had given in.

The soldier, a young blond man with enormous hands

and suspicious eyes, said something in Polish. It didn't sound friendly. Sarah couldn't speak Polish, but the meaning of his gestures was clear enough. She obeyed and stepped out of the car, joining Sean under a fine, frozen drizzle that chilled her to the bone. Even though she had on a heavy black jacket and fur-lined boots, she was still freezing in the harsh Polish winter. They all were, after days and nights outside without daring to light a fire.

Nicholas' ravens – the Elementals he had under his control – were circling above them, black wings against the white sky, cawing. They were guiding Sarah and her friends to the Gate of the Shadow World. Their cawing said that this unscheduled stop was not welcome.

Sarah's breath congealed in little white clouds as she stood, waiting for the soldier to speak. The soldier fixed his eyes on Sarah. He was studying her face, she realised. As though he'd seen her somewhere before, like the memory was about to click in his mind – or was she being paranoid? Her stomach churned. Her biggest fear throughout the journey had been that someone, somewhere – the Midnight housekeeper on Islay, or the family and friends Sarah had left behind in Edinburgh – would decide to issue a missing person alarm over her disappearance. Her face would be passed on to the police and plastered inside petrol stations and rest stops all over the world. When she had phoned her aunt from Islay, she hadn't thought of asking her not to do that. She'd been too astonished to find out her aunt was alive, after the wildcat attack that had left her for dead. Sarah believed Aunt Juliet had understood that involving the police wouldn't help – the opposite, in fact – but she couldn't be sure. Contacting her again would have been too dangerous.

"Is there a problem?" Sean asked the soldier, sounding calm and unconcerned. She looked at him from the corner of her eye. His self-control never ceased to amaze her. The more danger they were in, the more he seemed to keep his composure.

"No problem," the man replied in heavily accented English. His eyes were still narrowed, still studying Sarah's face. "I go inside for a moment," he said, shifting his rifle towards the concrete cabin at the side of the road. "Lont!" He beckoned to a young man with black eyes and a thin, barely there moustache.

As Lont saw Sarah, something passed over his face – a flicker of recognition – but he didn't say anything. The two soldiers had a brief conversation in Polish. Sarah gathered that Lont was supposed to keep an eye on them while the blond soldier went inside the station. Her heart was pounding against her ribs. What was he going to do, once inside? Was he going to call someone? Check her face against a database of missing person's alerts? Her mind was racing. She met Sean's eyes and something unspoken flew between them.

Sean looked over at Niall, who was just behind them, leaning against Nicholas' car door, waiting. Both nodded imperceptibly. The message was clear. They had to run. Sarah gazed around her. There were soldiers everywhere, with rifles and a look on their faces that said they were not afraid to use them. It was like some war film, she thought, exasperated. Her hands were already flooding with Blackwater – the power to melt and dissolve skin and bone – when Lont took a step closer. In the blink of an eye, Sean's hand was on his *sgian-dubh*.

"Sarah Midnight. It is you," whispered Lont. Sarah gaped

9

at him. How did he know her name? He hadn't seen her passport; the blond soldier had taken it inside with him, and as they spoke he had not picked up on her name. For a moment, she was too shocked to speak. Sean was holding his *sgian-dubh* low against his stomach so that nobody would see. He had already begun tracing his runes.

Lont's gaze fell on the blade, and he put a hand up. "No use the runes, Midnight Gamekeeper," he whispered in broken English. "Listen to me. I am Gamekeeper too. You go. Now."

It took a split second to take in the soldier's words, but then Sean nodded, and made a gesture towards Niall to tell him to get back into the car. Lont released the barrier, shouting something in Polish towards the other soldiers, who were standing in little clusters along the border. And then, to Sarah: "Go!"

She didn't have to be told twice. Praying that the blond soldier in the station was not aware of Lont's betrayal – yet – they climbed back into their cars. As Sean drove away as fast as he could, but not too fast – in case the other soldiers thought they had something to hide – Sarah met Lont's eye for a moment. *Thank you*, she mouthed.

Sean calmly raised his hand in greeting towards the soldiers and nodded briefly. Sarah could not believe how calm he was. She wanted to look as composed as Sean, but she couldn't help turning back and gazing into the mirrors, imagining army vehicles or police cars following them, a car chase like in an action movie. As if the demons weren't enough to deal with. She switched on the radio and started messing with the stations. "Do you understand Polish at all? In case we're in the news."

"Not a clue, sorry. The only word I could make out was

your name. I hope the Gamekeeper is okay," Sean replied. "How on earth did he know?"

"I have no idea. I suppose there must still be a few people left in the network, looking out for the Secret Families." Sarah took a deep breath. Her mouth was dry. "We'll never know, I suppose. Not until all this is over and we can try to find out how many of us are left."

Sarah's words hung between them. They both had finished the sentence in their minds: *if we're still alive.* They were quiet for a while, the drizzle turning into tiny snowflakes again, falling white and silent on the road and on the fields around them. And then Sean braided his fingers with Sarah's and squeezed her hand for a moment, a moment that ended too fast. He returned his hand to the wheel, leaving Sarah with a melted heart and a racing mind.

It was the first time he'd touched her since they'd left Islay. The feeling of his skin on hers brought on a sea of emotions she didn't know how to handle. She swallowed, wrapped her arms around herself, and sank deeper into her seat.

I love you, she said in her mind over and over again. The same words she'd whispered in his ear on the beach back on Islay, with only the sea and the wind to hear.

Sean. Her Sean.

Sarah caught a glimpse of his profile as they were driving on. His handsome features were tense, tight, but underneath the fear and tension, Sarah could truly see him, his essence – eyes clear as a summer morning and the golden skin of someone who'd grown up in a sunny place, still not faded after months in Scotland and now through the European winter. An image formed in her mind: she and Sean in each other's arms, alone, in the darkness. But immediately, she chased it away. What was the point, if Sean was convinced they couldn't be together?

Her feelings for him had been a galaxy of mixed emotions, from diffidence when he first stormed into her life pretending to be Harry Midnight, to affection tinged with something forbidden — she had been told they were cousins — to the first flickers of love. And then anger when she discovered his lie. Forgiveness had come eventually, and a need for each other that they could not deny.

And then, the terrible revelation: they could never be together. Another consequence of her curse, because that's what Sarah had decided being a Secret heir was: a curse. It all came down to a lottery of blood, and she had lost. Big time.

Children of a Lay man — a non-Secret — and a Secret woman carry no powers, and Sean, loyal to the oath he'd made to the Secret Families, could not allow the Midnight powers to be lost. Sean was a Gamekeeper, and he had sworn to serve the Secret Families with all he had. His oath was his whole life. He would never break it.

If she survived all this, Sarah knew she'd have to marry another Secret heir and carry children with pure Secret blood, keeping the net of protection alive around the world. Made to breed like a thoroughbred horse, not like a woman with a heart and soul.

Once again, as they drove along snowy fields under a white sky, Sarah contemplated the full extent of the destruction her Midnight blood brought her and those around her. She was locked in a life of violence, she was denied the love of her life, and what was worse — infinitely worse — she'd hurt those dearest to her. She thought of her aunt Juliet, miraculously alive after a terrible attack. She'd believed her dead for weeks, until she heard her voice in a quick, heart-rending phone call she'd made from Islay before leaving for her final quest. She remembered her heart stopping as she heard her aunt's voice, like an echo from the afterlife.

The images of her loving aunt being torn apart by a demon tormented her every day, every night. The Midnights brought devastation on everything they came in contact with, on everything they loved. Was Aunt Juliet really safe? And Bryony, her best friend? Had the demons got them, since the last time they spoke? She had no way of knowing. She didn't dare call them again, in case it would bring danger on them, and herself and her friends.

"Are you okay?" Sean asked her, interrupting her thoughts. Sarah couldn't stop her lips curling slightly. *Are you okay* was his favourite question, and had they been in different circumstances, it would have been followed by the offer of coffee. For such a fearless warrior, strong, often ruthless, Sean had a soft, domestic side to him that always made her smile.

Sean smiled back. "I know, I know. I ask you all the time."

"You haven't asked me in a while, actually," she said.

"I still kept an eye on you. Always."

"I know."

There was a moment of silence, and Sarah hoped he'd take her hand again, but he didn't. She wondered when, if ever, she'd feel his skin against hers again. She watched the snowflakes land on the car window, tiny and perfect and intricate like lace, and the wintery landscape around her mirrored the bleakness in her heart.

2
Guilt

The North
Gives us refuge

Micol lay on her bed, alone in her room in the heart of Palazzo Vendramin. Nothing unusual there, she did that a lot. There wasn't much else to do, given she wasn't allowed out and her wandering around the palace wasn't exactly welcomed by the million servants the Vendramin Family seemed to have.

She studied the frescoed ceiling: a blue sky with gentle, white, fluffy clouds and fat baby angels sitting on them. The place looked like a museum. The whole of Venice looked like a museum. Before long, her thoughts began to wander to her brothers, when they had first come to the palazzo, and the months that followed.

They'd arrived by boat, in the middle of the night. Micol had been enchanted by the lights on the water and the web of canals they had had to negotiate to get to the palace. In spite of their desperate situation, she had been speechless with the beauty of the city they'd taken refuge in.

But then dawn rose, and she could see the decay in the buildings, and smell the foulness of the water, and feel in her bones how everything was rotting, how everything was falling to pieces. She decided she hated Venice. "The most beautiful place in the world," Vendramin had said around the breakfast table, and her brothers had agreed – because they had to be polite, Micol guessed.

She had wanted to be back home so badly. The Tuscan countryside, with its sun-baked hills and the scent of greenery, and not a black canal in sight. She had sat at the huge antique table with a piece of bread and jam in her hands, not wanting to put it down in case Tancredi fretted she wasn't eating, but unable to bite into it. She couldn't cry, of course, though she had wanted to.

Just at that moment, Ranieri had started raving about how the whole city was beautiful now but one day it would be filled with oil and lit up by fire-breathing rats. The onset of his delirium was always sudden, unexpected. The first time it happened was in church. Afterwards, their mother had cried. Micol saw that her mother knew what the episode meant, that the Azasti had begun in her eldest son's blood, and there was no way to stop it.

His crises were short-lived, but horrible. It was so strange to see her sensible, wise, strong brother shout nonsense, and in the worst moments, scream and cry and rip his hair out. Of all the scary symptoms he was suffering – the blue nails, the copious bleeding from every little cut, the weight loss that had wasted his muscles and turned him into a shadow of himself – the madness was the worst. It felt like her brother was vanishing, leaving a stranger in his place.

Tancredi had begun coaxing Ranieri towards his room. As they stepped out of the dining room, Vendramin said a servant would knock on their door later with something to calm him down. Micol had gasped silently. What were they going to give him? Some evil medicine? Maybe that was why Lucrezia was that way, the silent girl she'd only caught a glimpse of when they had arrived the night before. She had lay on her bed, pale and immobile, her lips moving in quiet, indiscernible whispers. They'd been told Lucrezia was ill, but was it her family who'd made her that way, or something else? They knew little about the Vendramins, after all. They had been brought together by the culling of the heirs, but they had never met before. And although the Vendramins had come to their rescue, Micol didn't trust them.

Left alone at the breakfast table, she had looked around from beneath her eyelashes. Alvise, Lucrezia's older brother, sat across from her. He seemed quiet, and his face was unreadable. He looked like he carried a heavy burden. But then, what Secret heir didn't these days? Ranieri and Tancredi seemed to like him, or at least they spoke about him with respect. But, Micol thought, maybe it was because they had nowhere else to go, and nobody else to ask for help but the Vendramins.

Micol could still smell her family's burning house. She could still see the flames dancing out of the windows as they ran. She remembered the soil demons grabbing her ankles, and Tancredi cutting their white, muddy hands off with his sharp claws – and the demon slaves, the dogs with human faces, hounding them all the way to the hideout her family kept at the edge of the lake. They remained there for a day and a night, listening to the growling and scratching outside, until the Vendramins' Gamekeepers came to help. It was a miracle they had escaped.

"You must eat something, Micol," the housekeeper said, kindly enough. But her stomach was in a knot, Ranieri's delirious screams coming from upstairs upsetting her.

The palazzo was huge, but the acoustics were strange. You could hear almost everything from anywhere in the house. Micol wondered if it had been built like that on purpose, to enhance security. She already knew that the Vendramins were paranoid. Apparently, there were traps all around the palazzo. They were meant to keep the Surari out, but Micol suspected they also fit another purpose: to keep her brothers and her in.

"Sorry, I'm not hungry," she responded, pushing her plate away and standing. "I'm going to my room." She wanted to be alone.

As she sat on the sumptuous bed, the tears she'd kept inside finally fell. She buried her head in the fine silk of her dress – she had brought nothing with her, obviously, and was given Lucrezia's clothes to wear. No jeans and T-shirts in sight, nothing normal, just long dresses that seemed to have sprouted from an evil fairy tale.

Micol cried for a long time, her shame in acting weak and vulnerable overcome by grief and fear. She hadn't even had time to cry for her parents properly, she thought as a fresh bout of sobs broke her. They were barely cold in their graves when everything else had been destroyed.

Suddenly, there was a soft knock at the door. "*Sorellina?* It's me," a voice said. It was Tancredi.

"Come in," Micol replied, in a tone that she hoped was steady enough. Tancredi had enough on his mind without worrying for her too. She had to be strong. She dried her tears the best she could, leaving dark patches on the sleeves of her dress.

"Hey, you've been crying . . ."

"No. I haven't. I just washed my face," she said lamely.

Tancredi sat on the bed beside her and wrapped her in his arms. She snuggled in, and to her dismay, tears started flowing down her cheeks again.

Ranieri was the strong one, the one they all relied on. He was brave and generous, but a bit distant, a bit more like a father than a brother. Tancredi, instead, was her best friend. There were over ten years between them, but they were so close that the age difference didn't matter. The love she felt for him squeezed her heart. Ranieri was so sick; now it was just Tancredi and her, like two castaways in the middle of a hostile ocean.

"It's okay, *sorellina*. You'll see. We'll be fine. We'll find help for Ranieri and go home soon. I promise."

Micol didn't believe him.

In the weeks that followed, Micol remembered now, still staring at the ceiling, Tancredi had started hiding his hands from her. He'd even taken to wearing riding gloves whenever he could. But it was no use. Micol had seen his blue nails, and knew that the Azasti would come to take her second brother too.

18

3
White Is the Colour of Death

Orbiting in deepest, coldest space
Say one word, and I shall be saved

Poland

"What are they doing?" grumbled Sean, tossing the remnants of his sandwich into the bin beside the petrol pumps. Niall and Winter had been inside the little shop for some time – too long. They couldn't linger anywhere. They never knew who'd spot them, especially after the incident at the border. There in the heart of Europe, besieged by demons, on their way to the Gate of the Shadow World, there could be no respite, from demons or from humans.

"No idea, but they need to come back now," Sarah replied, looking around her anxiously. She surveyed the scene, checking possible threats. There was an elderly couple hovering around their car, and a mother and child holding hands, heading for the shop. People made Sarah nervous. People could get hurt, or hurt them.

She'd had a dream the night before – a confused vision of something huge with flailing limbs towering over her, and blue flames everywhere. It had been too blurry a scene to make out exactly what was happening, but she was sure an attack was imminent. Sarah was a Dreamer, and her dreams were supposed to guide them all towards the demons they were supposed to destroy, and warn them of dangers, but these days they were a phantasmagoria of terrifying visions. They were no use. Maybe she wasn't getting enough sleep. Maybe her sleep was too troubled to go to the place in her mind where the dreams happened. Or maybe Nicholas was messing with her mind again. There was no way to know for sure.

She slipped her hand into the glove box of Sean's car and took out her scarf. She tied it around her neck twice, like she always did. It was so cold that she was shivering already.

In the parking space beside them, Elodie unbuckled her seatbelt. "I'll go get Niall," she said, stepping out of Nicholas' car.

Nicholas shifted his weight uncomfortably after the car door slammed shut. He didn't like it when Elodie left him. He wasn't used to being blind yet, and he feared the complete darkness, the loss of balance, the sense of not knowing what could be lurking around him. On the roof of the petrol station, Nicholas' ravens perched and waited to resume the journey. Without them, Nicholas would have been unable to guide Sarah and her friends to the Gate. Although he knew the Shadow World like the back of his hand, the loss of his sight had made it impossible for him to orientate himself. The Elementals now saw for him.

Sarah blew on her hands and rubbed them together. There were dark shadows under her eyes, and her hands kept closing and opening, as if getting ready to summon the Blackwater, even if they weren't in a combat situation. She was too terrified to switch off, even in her sleep – especially in her sleep, when the jumble of confused, cruel visions made her toss and turn and wake up screaming.

"Are you okay?" Sean's question made her jump.

"Sort of. You?" she said, stopping herself from resting a hand on his arm, from stepping closer to him.

He shrugged. "I haven't slept in a week. Apart from that, I'm great." Their eyes met, saying so much more than words ever could.

"Hey!" Nicholas' deep voice came through the open car window.

"What do you want?" growled Sean in reply. He had accepted Nicholas' presence: he knew they needed him, but he didn't trust him, and left to his own devices, he would have gladly given him a piece of his mind – with his fists. Just to remind him where they all stood. But Elodie wouldn't have let him, for some reason that was known to Elodie alone.

Nicholas stepped out of the car slowly, leaning heavily on its door. His obsidian eyes, cloudy and sightless, turned towards Sean's and Sarah's voices.

"We need to go," he said, and the ravens cawed in reply, once, twice.

"Yes, we know that," replied Sarah, her voice icy.

"I mean, we need to go now. Trust me."

"Ha!" Sarah turned around, her eyes blazing green with the Midnight gaze. It couldn't harm Nicholas because he couldn't see her. Had he been able to, it would have hit him like a blade between his eyes. "We *are* trusting you, Nicholas, otherwise we wouldn't be here," she spat.

"Here they come," said Sean with a sigh of relief. Sarah followed his gaze and saw Elodie, Niall and Winter leaving the petrol station.

"What took you so long, Niall?" she snapped as soon as he was close enough to hear.

"The man in there had a story worth listening to," he replied in his cheery manner.

"A story?" she hissed. Of course, Niall would choose this time to listen to stories, possibly with a drink in hand. Niall was a strong fighter and loyal to a fault, but sometimes he tended not to grasp the gravity of situations.

"They saw something around here," Winter explained, gesturing with one hand towards the petrol station. Her other hand held Niall's.

They all turned to follow her gaze, and from the shop window a bald man with a black moustache, sitting at the till, met their gaze.

"Something big and white. Very big," Niall continued, running a hand through his light-brown hair. "They called it a golem."

"Shit. Demons," he said in a low, urgent voice. "Let's just go. Are we still far, Nicholas?"

"No. Not far. But let's hurry," he said. Something in his tone made Elodie's lips turn ever so slightly blue, as the poison that was her family's power began spreading in her body, ready to be unleashed.

"Sean. A demon. Here. Now," she whispered, her lips darkening even more; her psychic power made her aware of things before they happened.

Elodie took Nicholas' arm to help him into the car, when he growled a deep, animal growl that stopped them all in their tracks. Right at that moment, the ravens took flight, their alarmed cawing cutting the sky.

"Winter, into the car," said Niall. Winter obeyed at once, blood draining from her face.

Elodie's lips were now black. Sarah's hands were burning. Niall was humming slowly, his song gearing up to hurt and destroy, while Sean's hand was curled around his *sgian-dubh*, ready to trace deadly runes. *We're in the open*, he kept thinking. *People all around. They want to destroy us so badly they don't even try to hide any more.*

Right at that moment, a terrible scream sounded from inside the petrol station. Sarah narrowed her eyes, peering through the window, trying to spot where the threat came from. The man with a moustache who'd been sitting at the till was now wearing a red handkerchief on his head. Sarah let out a small yelp as she realised that wasn't a red cloth covering him, it was half his scalp peeled back from his head.

All of a sudden the shop's door exploded in a million shards of glass – and something huge, white and hunched made its way out, unbelievably swiftly in spite of its mass, its flat, rubbery face sniffing the air, its long, clawed hands reaching out to grab and mangle. So that's what she'd seen in her dream, Sarah realised.

Out of the corner of her eye Sarah registered a couple ducking into their car, an elderly man cowering in fear behind one of the pumps, and a woman with a little girl running towards the forest. A child. *Oh God, please don't let them be hurt*, she pleaded, and raised her scorching hands, ready to use the Blackwater. Her eyes flared green with the Midnight gaze. The creature howled and jerked its head away, feeling the power of Sarah's gaze but not knowing quite where the threat came from ... until it sensed them.

"*Niryani!*" Elodie called out her family's battle cry and leapt towards the demon, dagger in hand. The creature howled in anger and pain as Elodie's dagger pierced its skin, black blood spewing from the wounds. Sarah stood, the Midnight gaze at its full power, her hands raised and burning. She was about to throw herself on the beast ...

"Sarah! This way!" Sean shouted. Sarah turned around just in time to see that a second demon had come out of the forest and was towering over the mother and child she'd spotted earlier. They had fallen on the grass in a trembling heap, the woman desperately trying to shelter the little girl with her body. Sean and Sarah stood frozen for an instant as the demon bent down and grabbed the girl from her mother's arms, lifting her up.

"Let her go!" Sarah commanded. Sean lifted his *sgian-dubh* and closed his eyes, tracing his runes with the blade, murmuring the Secret words. The creature shuddered with pain from the runes and Sarah's gaze, then it took a running jump and landed on Sean, flattening him on the grass. He tasted blood, and then consciousness trickled away from him until everything was black.

Elodie clung to the demon's body, her arms around its neck, trying to touch its lips with her own poisonous ones – and she nearly made it, gagging over the eyeless face and the cold, rubbery skin, when a clawed hand cut her skin open, running a trail of agony down her back. She fell.

Elodie's moan of pain resounded in the air and reached Nicholas. He was standing beside his car, the world whirling around him, his brain incapable of telling him what was up and what was down, his balance shot to pieces. He shook with fury and frustration. Leaning against the car door, trying to keep himself upright, he raised his arms. His fingers sparked blue. He was ready to strike, but he couldn't see where the demon was. To let himself be guided by noises only and start a fire in a petrol station was too risky. He let out a scream of rage. *Look what you've done to me, Father! I'm useless!*

He heard Elodie whimpering and his wrath rose again, mixed with terror. Instantly, the ravens heard his call and surrounded the white demon, trying to peck it – but the deadly, clawed reel of its arms prevented them from coming close. Nicholas felt a touch on his shoulder – he would have recognised that touch among millions – and Elodie's voice filled his ears. He turned around and wrapped his arms around her, taking care not to burn her. He couldn't fight, but he could protect her from the blows.

"Nicholas, I need to get into the car. I'll try to run the Surari over."

Nicholas helped Elodie inside, feeling his way inch by inch, his hands slippery with the blood that seeped from her torn back. Then he let himself slip in beside her. He felt the car starting, and the surge of the vehicle moving, and then a deafening noise exploded inside his skull and blood rushed to his head. There was banging, banging, and screaming.

"Elodie!" he tried to shout, but a raspy whisper was all that came out from the agony that was his throat, his face, his head. "Elodie!" he repeated, but there was nothing but silence.

Elodie . . . Elodie, he kept calling in his mind. She couldn't be dead. She couldn't be.

The strange bond between them, born of pain and suffering, had led him to save her life before, when his aim had been to kill them all except for his chosen bride, Sarah. Something tied him to Elodie, something he couldn't explain.

He couldn't lose her.

Once again he cursed his blindness as he felt around him with his hands.

And then he heard her breathing. She was alive. His hands met hers and held her tight.

"Elodie!"

"That thing sent us flying. We're upside down. We need to make it out of here!" she whispered. "Oh . . ."

"Are you okay? Elodie? Are you hurt?"

"I'm fine," she whispered, and banged on the window beside her. Nicholas started banging, too, his mind damning the safety glass, which was nearly impossible to break. His ravens were with him at once, pecking the glass on the other side until it cracked. Harder and harder he hammered the window, until his hands started bleeding too.

Sean opened his eyes just in time to see the demon standing over Sarah, its long white limbs poised to cut her throat, or take her head clean off her neck. He desperately tried to raise his hands and trace the runes, but blackness came over him in waves, and even if he kept willing his limbs to move, he couldn't. Confused, he heard Elodie and Nicholas screaming. From where he was lying he could see no sign of Niall and Winter, though he could hear Niall's song coming from somewhere far, far away.

The creature raised its clawed arms, ready to inflict the final blow. Sean knew then it was all over. Sarah would be dead any second, he realised, and a strangled sob escaped his throat.

What happened next made no sense to Sean.

The demon let its arms fall to its sides, and lifting its head up to the sky, it let out a long, eerie howl. Why was the demon not striking? Incredulous, Sean saw it stepping out of sight. With an enormous effort he scrambled to his knees, and then to his feet. The world went black once more, and he found himself on the ground, stars exploding behind his eyes. Again he tried to lift himself up; he was about to fall when a slender arm wrapped itself around his waist and sustained him.

Right at that moment he heard Niall's song starting to climb once more, like smoke, stronger and stronger. Sean managed to turn his head just enough to see that Niall and Winter were on either side of him.

The demon came back into view. It was convulsing on the ground, hit by the full force of Niall's song. It had something yellow in its hand – oh God, it was *someone*. Elodie? No, she was blonde, but smaller.

A child.

Behind the demon a woman was screaming and Sean held his breath, overcome by the horror of what he was seeing. The demon was shaking the child like a rag doll.

Sarah lay on the ground, stunned. She couldn't quite believe she was still alive. She regained composure and jumped to her feet. She heard Niall's song, and then screams. Where was the beast? She turned around and there it was, the white demon, crazy with the agony of Niall's song – and in its arms, the little girl Sarah had seen with her mother.

Sarah leapt towards the creature, her hands melting with the heat of her fury, her eyes blazing. A flailing leg nearly hit her, the white rubbery skin brushing her cheek, but she threw herself on the ground, and then stood behind the demon. She grabbed its back, burying her hands into its skin, and the demon screeched and arched itself in agony. It let the child fall to the ground. Sarah forbade herself from looking at the little girl – she couldn't let anything disrupt her concentration as her hands burnt and the creature's skin started weeping.

Through the haze of the Blackwater, Sarah saw Sean lift the child into his arms and limp away with her. Niall's song was dancing in the air, deadly and beautiful at the same time. The demon let out one last, terrible howl, and it exploded in a gush of Blackwater. Nothing was left of it but a puddle of foul-smelling liquid on the asphalt.

Sarah fell to her knees and took her head in her hands to try to regain control. Then the faintest noise caused her to look up. Her gaze darted frantically, and for the first time she realised that Nicholas' car was upside down, and somebody was trapped inside it. Somebody was banging on the windows. It was Elodie, and her face was covered in blood.

Sarah ran to the car and crouched in front of it, trying to ignore the ravens' feathered bodies twirling around her, pecking the glass. She rested her hands on the window where Elodie was hitting it with her fists.

"Hold on, Elodie!"

In despair, she tried to lift the car, but there was no way she could manage on her own. She realised that the sounds of Elodie's fists on glass had stopped. Silence had settled over the car. Only occasional cawing broke through the eerie calm.

Sarah tried once more to pick the car up, grunting. She knew that there was no way she could succeed, but she had to try. She had to do something to help Elodie.

A siren shattered the silence – the police. They had to go. They had to go now. But leaving Elodie ... and Nicholas, who was the only one who could lead them to the Shadow World ...

"Sean!" screamed Sarah. "Where are you?"

No reply.

"Sean!" she called again, a note of despair colouring her voice.

"I'm here!" he called back, and suddenly they were all at her side – Sean, Winter and Niall – and she wasn't alone any more. The noise of breaking glass filled her ears, and she looked at her hands, expecting them to be bloody and full of shards, but Elodie's window was intact. The noise had come from the other side of the car – and when she looked back, Elodie wasn't there. Nicholas had crawled out, his face and hands bleeding. In his grasp was Elodie. He was trying to pull her out.

"Be careful! There's glass everywhere!" Sean called. "Let me move her. You can't see!" Nicholas knew Sean was right, and reluctantly let him take charge, but his handsome features were twisted in frustration.

"We need to go!" whispered Niall. Two silver and blue police cars and an ambulance had appeared in the distance, their sirens flashing and blaring like angry spirits.

Sean got up, swaying a little. The blow to his head had messed with his balance. Niall took Elodie from him, her face covered in red, a long, bloody trail running down her back where the demon had clawed her. Sarah took Nicholas by the arm to guide him – just touching him revolted her – and they all ran towards Sean's car. They could already hear the police officers shouting in Polish. Nicholas tugged on Sarah's arm and stopped her.

"Where are the police cars? Take me to them," he whispered. Sarah's eyes widened, but then she understood. She grabbed his arms tighter and strode towards the police cars and the ambulance. People in uniform were already jumping down from the vehicles, med kits and guns at the ready.

Nicholas raised his hands, his fingers extended, and cold, blue flames sprang from his fingertips – the blue flames from her dream, Sarah thought. He guided them carefully in two parallel lines in front of him, over and over again, to build a wall between them and the cars. The policemen and paramedics were panicking, shouting something down their radios – possibly calling for reinforcements, thought Sarah. Dread knotted her stomach. *Soon there'll be more of them. Every escape route will be blocked.*

All of a sudden, Sarah heard a succession of short, sharp noises, like fireworks. They were shooting at them! A bout of pain travelled down her arm as something grazed her shoulder. Hurt mixed with horror filled her mind as she realised that innocent people would be burnt alive by those cold blue flames.

"Take me around in a circle!" Nicholas shouted, ignoring the shots. Sarah tried to ignore them too and block out the terrified screams of the people trapped inside the flames. The shots stopped and the screams intensified while she took Nicholas in a loop, until the police cars and the ambulance were surrounded by fiery blue walls.

There on the ground, not far from her, Sarah saw the

elderly couple she'd spotted earlier lying senseless near the store door. Her heart broke for them. The child and her mother were nowhere to be seen.

"Will the flames kill them?" she whispered, dreading Nicholas' reply.

No choice, no choice, no choice, she answered herself. *If we get arrested, we'll be easy prey.*

Nicholas didn't respond. His silence said it all. Sarah felt her legs give way.

"Come on," she said, and they raced back to Sean's car. Nicholas' Jeep was still upside down. They jumped in and Sean took off at once, the engine roaring, forced to its limits.

"Elodie?" called Nicholas, and Elodie turned towards him.

Sean's stomach lurched as she saw in his mirror the way Elodie looked at Nicholas. She couldn't possibly have forgotten that he was a half-demon, worse than an animal. A murderer. A monster. And the way he spoke to her, like he needed her, it revolted him. Sean feared that Nicholas was mind-moulding her. That he was trying to control Elodie like he'd tried to control Sarah. For now, he couldn't see any signs, but he'd watch over her. If he saw as much as a hint of Elodie's eyes glazing over, of her being dazed and unable to think clearly, Nicholas had it coming.

"I'm here. I'm okay. Just a few cuts." Elodie was bent forward, her head against Winter's shoulder. Her back was too painful to lean on. Winter's T-shirt was stained with Elodie's blood.

Sarah saw Nicholas close his eyes briefly, relief sweeping his face. It looked like he cared.

But he was a good liar, she reminded herself.

"Sarah, are you hurt?" Sean asked.

Sarah brought her hand to her shoulder, and felt blood between her fingers. It was just a graze, but it hurt like hell. "I'm all right. Sean, the little girl . . ." She felt her stomach tightening as she remembered. Maybe she didn't want to hear his answer.

"She was alive when I left her. She and her mother ran into the forest."

Sarah let out a sigh of relief. Then her thoughts went to the man in the petrol station shop: somebody's son, somebody's husband, somebody's father – and they'd brought destruction on him. She steeled herself, trying to get everything out of her mind except the only thing that mattered, why they were there: to kill the King of Shadows and stop this war with demons. There could never be another Time of Demons. If the Surari ruled the human world again, nobody's son, nobody's daughter, would ever be safe again.

They drove in silence for a while, anxiously watching behind them. But nobody followed. The police had lost them.

"Sarah," called Winter in a quiet voice. Her arms were wrapped around Elodie's waist, helping her to sit forward, the French girl's blonde hair strewn over her shoulder and chest. "The demon could have killed you."

"Yes."

"But it didn't."

A wave of unease swept over Sarah. She knew what Winter was trying to say. Sean looked for her eyes in the mirror, and unspoken words flew between them.

"Why?" Winter continued.

Sarah kept eyes locked onto Sean's. She shivered, her cuts and bruises hurting all of a sudden, her shoulder throbbing painfully where the bullet had grazed her.

"I don't know. How would I know?"

A voice resounded in Elodie's mind, strong and clear, the voice of her psychic power: *Because they need her.*

And then, the voice told her something else.

"Someone is following us," she said.

"Surari?" asked Sean.

Elodie closed her eyes. A pause. "I don't know. I can't tell."

"Is it close?" said Sarah.

"I think so."

"Let's just think of getting to the Gate," Nicholas intervened. He brought his hand to his forehead as if he were hurting. "There will be more attacks."

Elodie shot him a sideways glance.

Nicholas was in constant pain. Day and night, a life of endless agony. That was how his father had punished him.

Elodie could feel the heat of Nicholas' body beside her. She could feel the suffering seeping from his skin. Elodie dreamt of the day she'd meet the King of Shadows at last; she dreamt of every blow she'd strike, and after the first one – the one she owed to her husband and love of her life, Harry Midnight – the second one would be for Nicholas and what had been done to him.

4
Night Closes In

I keep my soul
Where I know you'll never find it

They wanted to drive on through the night, but none of them had slept for more than three hours in two days. They were all near delirious with exhaustion. One more stop only, Nicholas had promised, and then they would be there. They would leave in the small hours and be at the Gate before dawn. They saw to each other's wounds, ate a cold dinner of bread, ham, cheese and biscuits, and then they settled in for the night. Going against every human instinct, the primal urge to create light and warmth, they wouldn't light a fire, even in the freezing winter night in the forest. They couldn't afford to attract attention. Sarah couldn't remember the last time she hadn't felt cold.

She was curled up in the front seat of Sean's car, Niall and Winter entwined in the back. She had reluctantly agreed to sleep inside the car, cocooned in one of the sleeping bags they had taken from Midnight Hall, though the arrangement made her feel claustrophobic and squeezed the air out of her lungs. Sean would not allow her to sleep outside, and as much as she didn't take orders from him or anyone else, she had to admit he had a point.

She whimpered in her sleep and jerked suddenly, hitting her hand on the glove compartment and waking with a jolt. Her shoulder hurt. Once again her dreams had been meaningless, confused, a carousel of frightening images and swirling colours and lights – and then the deepest darkness, as if she'd turned blind like Nicholas. Reality seemed to mirror her dream, as everything was black around her.

She pulled the sleeping bag up to her throat, the silky waterfall of her hair tucked inside it to keep her warm. It was impossible to sleep. Not with all that was going on, not with the dreams tormenting her with their bloody, blurry pictures, not with the ache throbbing in her battered body.

She knew that if she opened the door and slipped outside she'd find Sean, sleepless like her. He was an insomniac at the best of times. Sarah couldn't remember any occasion when she'd seen him deeply asleep. Even when he'd first turned up at her house, pretending to be her cousin Harry Midnight but really bound by a promise to him to protect the last of the Midnights – Sarah. Even in those days, she could hear the soft sound of the radio coming from his room until the small hours.

Sarah blinked again as little flickers of red light danced in the darkness, briefly illuminating Sean's arms and hands as he composed his runes in the air. She sat upright. She'd never seen Sean's runes shining red before. What was going on?

Sarah let herself fall back, contemplating the total, utter

darkness that surrounded the car. The flickers of red light had gone. She closed her eyes, trying to imagine Sean's arms around her, her head on his chest and his hands caressing her hair . . . until her body, exhausted, forced her into an unquiet sleep.

The blink of an eye, a heartbeat, was as much as it took before the dream possessed her, like it couldn't wait, like the lack of sleep had stopped the visions from coming and made them even hungrier for her. She was in that place again, under a purple sky and standing in a sea of dancing grass, the colours heightened and unreal. She was alone, the wind blowing strong in her hair. All of a sudden, she realised that she was wearing the same clothes she'd worn during the last battle with the Scottish Valaya, the King of Shadows' worshippers who had hunted her parents down, and then her. A smell of smoke and burning demon flesh clung to those clothes.

Two things happened at once: she felt a terrible pain stab her in her ribs and fold her in two, and she saw swings, a roundabout, benches, a climbing cage – all the trappings of a playground – rise from the grass around her. She was home, back in Edinburgh, or a mirror dream image of it. She was where everything had begun. Where Nicholas had taken hold of her and stolen her trust, by saving her life; where Sean's lies had come to light and temporarily separated them.

Where she'd seen Cathy, her father's jilted first wife, pecked to death by Nicholas' ravens.

Do I have to go through it all again?

Is Nocturne going to come for me again?

What is this dream going to tell me?

Whatever it was, she was ready. *Let them come.* Her hands

were itching with the Blackwater, all her senses heightened and ready. She turned around in a circle, eyes narrowed, waiting, trying to ignore the bite from her cracked ribs. Every injury or pain she suffered in her dreams felt real. Death felt real, too, and she had died so many times . . .

She waited, listening to her breath and her pounding heart, surveying the swings and the benches and the roundabout that she knew so well, paint peeling from years of use and children's scuffing and scratching, incongruous and absurd in the sea of swaying grass. She waited, but no demons came.

She took a deep breath, her eyes shimmering with the Midnight gaze. "I am here! Come and get me!" she screamed, her voice frayed and weakened by the roaring wind. "Come and get me!" she repeated.

And they did.

A voice came from behind her. "Hi, Sarah. How are you, my dear?" Sarah's body whirled in the direction of her name, and there she was, Cathy, her blonde hair and her skin covered in blood from a thousand little wounds – ravens' pecks. And the most horrifying thing of all . . . where once her eyes had been, there were only bloody and empty sockets. The ravens had pecked her eyes out, too. Weeds hung from her hands, and her clothes were dripping. All of these were little reminders of when the ravens had attacked and thrown her corpse into the river. "Come and sit, let's have a chat. I can only stay a wee while. Then I'll leave you to Nocturne."

Sarah's blood ran cold. She remembered those words. They were exactly the same words that Cathy had said to her before breaking her bones.

A deadly heat spread across her shoulders, the smell of smoke intensified, together with the sickening scent of burnt flesh. And something with red eyes and gleaming teeth rose from the grass beside Cathy. Nocturne. Except his body was black and burnt, smoke rising from his blistered skin. They were dead, both Cathy and Nocturne. They were both dead and they had come back to haunt her.

A wave of rage overwhelmed her, drowned her. She ran to the dead woman and her demon and raised her scalding hands, but all of a sudden, they were cold. There was no Blackwater. Instead Sarah went white, and stood frozen, looking at her shaking hands. They weren't burning any more, they were icy cold. Empty. Her power was gone.

The Blackwater was gone.

It was exactly what had happened during the last battle. She'd lost the Blackwater back then. It couldn't be happening again. She was defenceless, her eyes opaque, the Midnight gaze gone, too. She was empty.

Cathy laughed. "There is no Sarah any more."

"What do you mean? Tell me! What do you mean?"

And then she saw it, something white and milky and opaque, a little sphere, twirling in front of her, a few inches from her forehead – a terrible pull originated from the sphere, as if it was stealing her energy, stealing herself.

She watched in dismay as the sphere flew into the sky.

"There is no Sarah. Your body is here, but you are gone," Cathy shrieked, and suddenly everything disappeared. Cathy, Nocturne, the play park. She was no more.

She woke up panting. A strangled sob took the place of the scream she'd felt rising in her throat. She forced herself to remain silent as she shivered violently on the car seat, covered in sweat, her wet skin freezing slowly.

What did it mean? What had they done to her?

The horror of Cathy's eyeless face and Nocturne's burnt, blistered skin kept dancing in front of her eyes. Silent tears rolled down her cheeks, the helpless tears of powerlessness; she'd faced something she simply couldn't fight. Something invisible, something that had turned her into nothing. An empty shell.

She turned around. Niall and Winter were asleep. Sarah felt for the handle with a trembling hand, and opened the door. The freezing night air hit her like a bucket of icy water.

I need to find Sean. I need Sean, was all she could think. There were no more red flickers in the air, and she didn't know where he was.

"Sean!" she whispered to the darkness. "Sean!"

He materialised out of the night and held her in his arms. She clung to him. For a moment, she allowed herself to let him sustain her. Sean's scent enveloped her once more – coffee, and something else, salty, manly, somewhere between the ocean and a unique Sean scent. He smelled of home and comfort. He smelled of strength. Being back in his arms was like being home. How could they keep denying themselves?

But soon, too soon, Sean disentangled himself from her embrace, leaving her bereft.

"Come here. Come on," he murmured, and led her away from the car to the oak tree he'd been sitting under. "You're freezing. There." He lifted his sleeping bag and covered her with it. He sat beside her, close but not too close.

"What happened?"

Sarah closed her eyes tightly. She took a deep breath and forced herself to find the words. "I dreamt. Cathy was there.

But she was dead. And Nocturne too, all burnt up. I was in the play park back home."

Sean frowned. He hated to remember when Cathy revealed the truth about him, the lie he'd been telling about his identity. That night Sarah rejected him and sent him away. That night Sean would have let her kill him, had she not lost the Blackwater suddenly.

She braced herself to tell the last part of the story. "I tried to use my powers against them, but they were all gone . . . I was gone. The whole of me. I can't explain it. It was like my body was there, but I didn't exist any more. There was something in front of me. A stone. A white stone. It was hovering in the air. It took everything away from me, and then it flew away. I kept asking myself: who am I? Who am I? I couldn't remember."

"A white stone?"

"Yes. White, with some bright-red edges," she recalled suddenly. "I have no idea what it meant."

"Whatever is coming, we'll face it together, Sarah. Try to sleep now, if you can."

Sarah knew that sleep wouldn't come, but she silently revelled in Sean's closeness. She allowed herself to believe that he would protect her, that he would save her from whatever was coming.

But she knew, deep down, that nobody could.

5
Awakening

Somewhere we can be
Just you and me and let the rest
Be memories

Sean

I try not to touch her, not to get too close. But I long to brush her fingers with mine, to hold her when nobody can see us. I call her name in my dreams. I dream of the day it will be only us: no demons, no mad suicidal missions, just us. To live our love, to even flaunt it, in that careless way Niall and Winter do. Their smiles, their whispers, the times they disappear and come back flushed and happy, all this can never be Sarah and me. How can we be together, knowing that children of a Lay man and a Secret woman won't carry Secret powers? How could we risk making the Midnight powers – so precious for this world, for all of us – disappear entirely? There are no other heirs to the Midnights. Sarah is the last one. If she marries me, it's all over.

And anyway, let's look at the facts here: what are the chances we'll survive our little trip into the Shadow World?

Probably zero.

Everyone is sleeping now, except for our very own Prince of Darkness, who's wandering around in little circles, leaning on whatever is at hand, like a drunken man, as always. He's worse than me when it comes to insomnia. I slip out of the car and sit with my back against a tree. I'll practise the runes a bit, to try to channel the thoughts gnawing at me tonight, like every night.

A while into tracing runes with my *sgian-dubh*, red sparks start to appear in front of me, and then they turn into red ribbons dancing and twirling in shapes and patterns. Suddenly, I can see the runes I'm tracing, burning bright red in the air. This only happened to me once before, when the soil demons attacked Elodie and me on the way to Sarah's house. I wondered why it hadn't happened today when I needed it, when the demon at the petrol station was on its rampage. But for whatever reason, it is happening now. The sparks are mesmerising, rivers of fire popping in the air around me like fireflies.

I stop at once, in case the lights attract unwanted attention. Something is awakening inside me, something that scares me and excites me at the same time. But it's still not fully awake. Not yet.

Not long ago, in the ancestral Midnight mansion on Islay, Sarah found a letter among her grandmother's things. A letter from my mother. Not my adoptive mother, but my birth one, Amelia Campbell, the one I was taken from. In the letter, my mother asked Stewart Midnight, Sarah's uncle, to look out for me, because I too have Secret blood. I thought

I was a Gamekeeper, someone trained by the Secret Families to guard and help them, someone with skills but no powers as such – and I was proud of it, it was all I knew and all I wanted – but it turned out that my mother was a Secret heir. Her love for my father, a Lay, was forbidden for the same reason that Sarah and I can't be together: children born from such a union don't inherit any powers.

My mother was banished from her family, the Campbells, and sent to New Zealand. She died young, but the letter she left for Stewart was her last wish. It was Stewart's son, Harry Midnight, who took up the task of fulfilling her request. Without telling me the truth about my birth, just like she'd instructed his father, Harry trained me as a Gamekeeper. For years I'd thought that our encounter late at night at my university campus had been a fluke of fate. Now I know better. Harry Midnight, the man who'd asked me as his dying wish to take his identity and watch over his cousin Sarah Midnight, had had me pegged from the beginning.

And I fell in love with the girl he'd wanted me to save.

So here I am, Sean Hannay of Campbell blood. As a child of a Secret woman and a Lay man, I'm not supposed to have inherited powers.

Then what about these red lights flowing from my runes, the surge of strength I've been feeling recently, as if there was something asleep inside me waiting to awaken and be unleashed? Can I dare hope? Because I'm not that good with hope. I'm not good at thinking things will work out for me the way I want them to. And what are the Campbell powers? The family seems to have been swept away by the Surari surge, like so many Secret Families. Sarah, Elodie and Niall don't seem to know what gifts the Campbells carried, and we left the Midnight mansion in such a hurry that I had no time to research in its library.

In a way, my blood is still a mystery. Yes, I can put a name to it now, but that's about it. If I had powers, would I kill people with a look like Sarah, or with a kiss like Elodie? Or maybe this seed of power inside me will just wither without ever sprouting. Barren, like I'd felt for a long time. Before meeting Sarah.

Before falling for her.

If it's so, if this little hope born inside me proves to be nothing, Sarah must marry a Secret man.

She must marry someone who's not me.

Just thinking about it makes me want to stick my *sgian-dubh* through my hand – it'd be less painful than contemplating the idea of Sarah with someone else, making love with someone else, another man running his hand through her hair . . .

Suddenly, I hear Sarah calling in the dark, calling my name. I lead her back to my sleeping place, beneath the oak tree. I wrap her in my sleeping bag. She's trembling. She's dreamt again, and this time it seems to be bearing a message. I would do anything to stop her pain and suffering and keep her safe. I can only dream of holding her through the night and stroking her hair slowly, cradling her like a child, just like I used to.

Since Sarah gave me my mother's letter, I don't know who I am. But I still live my life to the same rules. I'm still a Gamekeeper.

And I'm still in love with Sarah Midnight.

6
King of Pain

A mask on my face and another beneath
Ripping them off like I'd rip my own skin

Nicholas felt for the handle and opened the car door, shifting his feet on the grass. His head spun again as he lifted himself out and took a few uncertain steps, his arms extended in front of him. Elodie's slightly laboured breathing came from the back seat. Every night it was a little coarser, a little heavier.

Night or day made no difference to him. For him, it was always dark. He advanced until his hands felt something hard and rough – tree bark. He stepped towards the tree and leaned against it, his strong frame disappearing among the shadows. For a minute or so he stood still, listening hard to make sure he was alone. When he was satisfied, he took a deep breath. To his shame, his breath ended in a silent, terrified sob. He tried to calm his heart, but it was no use. The worst threat, the worst pain, was not outside of him: it was inside his head. There his father, the King of Shadows, could always reach him. No weapons, no magic, nothing could keep him out. Since he'd betrayed his father to save Sarah and her friends, Nicholas had been locked in his own personal hell.

He clasped his hands together to try to keep them from shaking. His body remembered what happened the last time he'd spoken to the King of Shadows, the burning pain of the brain fury that lasted for days and nights and broke him from the inside. And took his sight away.

His mind put up barriers, desperately. It wouldn't let himself go there. But he had to. He had to speak to him.

He whimpered softly in the dark, forcing his thoughts into shape, forcing his mind to destroy every wall leading to his father's consciousness. And finally, he succeeded. He was steady and calm as he heard the King of Shadows' voice resound in his mind.

"Father," he whispered in the darkness. "It's me. I'm sorry. I'm back. I've come back to you."

7
Untamed

Dead flowers and marsh waters
The endless sleep of dismay
The way your life stood still
And never moved again

Venice

A few months after they'd arrived, Ranieri was dead.
Tancredi had become so ill that he had run away on some
crazy mission, and Micol had found herself alone. So alone
that she'd taken to spending time with Lucrezia, as much
time as you could spend with a person who never held a
conversation with you.

She hated Lucrezia's room. The scent of flowers nause-
ated her, and the note of decay underneath made her feel
as though she was inside a tomb. Apart from her constant
whispering, it was as though Lucrezia was dead already and
in an open casket. And still Micol sat with her often – at first

because she was so desperately lonely, but recently because she didn't want Lucrezia to be alone either. For some reason, Micol had started feeling a bond with the sleeping girl. They were the same age, and they were two Secret heirs with the world crumbling around them. The only difference between them was that Micol's gifts were nowhere near as powerful, but they left room for her to live her life. Lucrezia's gifts were immense and unique, but condemned her to a living death.

And so Micol sat with her, curled up on the windowsill, the shutters open (against Vendramin's instructions) to let the Venetian winter sunlight seep in. Beyond the walled garden and its statues and fountains, the Grand Canal's water shimmered.

Micol tried her best to block out Lucrezia's constant, frenzied murmuring, and instead she told her little stories, about her life in Tuscany before it all happened, about her brothers, her parents, the horses and dogs they used to rear in the grounds of her villa in the hills. As she told Lucrezia about her old life, her recollection was so strong she could nearly feel the wind in her hair and smell the earthy scent of vineyards and pines and sunshine. Her favourite memory was riding Nero, her stallion – she'd refused a pony or a mare. Reliving those moments, Micol could once more feel the freedom of a life without boundaries, without fear. Lucrezia never paused to listen, of course. She continued her endless gibberish. But Micol spoke anyway, and sang little tunes she used to know, songs and lullabies her mother used to sing to her.

She sat there until it got too much, until she couldn't force herself to breathe that cloying air any more, then she ran out into the maze of gilded rooms that was Palazzo Vendramin and stepped into the garden, taking deep breaths of life. And still, it was the decaying smell of the canal that greeted her, not the pines, the lemons, the familiar scents of home.

Sometimes when she went to keep Lucrezia company, Alvise was already there, sitting on her bed, holding Lucrezia's hand. It was the only time when Alvise's expression seemed to soften and his flinty eyes harboured any emotion other than rage.

One day, as she perched on the windowsill in Lucrezia's room, she heard Alvise's voice down the corridor. He was shouting something or other to their long-suffering house-keeper. She could hear his voice and his footsteps getting closer. He was coming.

She tensed. Alvise didn't like finding her there with his sister. He was always suspicious of her somehow, as if she had some malicious plan. She thought the Vendramin were para-noid, and constantly scheming or fearing schemes. Usually she would have stood and stared him down in challenge, leaving the room in her own time, but the day before they'd had a terrible fight after she'd broken a few hexes around the palazzo and had wandered on the canals for hours, and he'd threatened her in a way she'd rather forget.

Alvise's powers had vanished when his mother had died, but this hadn't made him any less dangerous. There was a fury inside him, a rage that, even if she hated to admit it, frightened her. Sometimes she sensed that so much of Alvise's fury was directed towards himself – a self-hatred she didn't understand.

Instinctively, Micol jumped into Lucrezia's wardrobe, closing the door as much as she could from the inside. She stood, still and silent, watching the scene from the keyhole.

Alvise stepped in, a bouquet of white roses in his hands, and stood on the doorstep for a moment. His posture – coiled, as if ready to spring – and his slanted eyes reminded Micol of a cat. She remembered the balls and parties of her childhood, when the Secret Families used to get together in each other's villas and palaces, how her girlfriends had giggled and blushed whenever he was around and tried to steal a dance with him. Of all the young heirs, Alvise had been the most handsome, the most sought after.

But then the terrible news that Alvise had seen his mother's death at the hands of a demon, right there in the palazzo, and lost his powers swarmed. No Secret Family would now want to mix their blood with his, in case his children would be suddenly powerless too. In an instant, Alvise went from object of admiration and desire to a young man deserving only pity. Micol remembered Ranieri being dismissive of him. Her heart had gone out to him, thinking how it must have felt to lose his mother. She didn't have to wonder for long. Three years later, the same thing had happened to her. Her beautiful mother had died at the hands of a soil demon.

Now, however, Micol didn't have any sympathy left for Alvise, after having been at the receiving end of his white-hot anger too many times. But he didn't look angry now. He just seemed infinitely sad as he arranged the flowers in one of the many vases on Lucrezia's dressing table and sat on her bed. He placed a kiss on her white forehead. Lucrezia was murmuring as she always did.

All of a sudden, the grip on her brother's hand tightened, and her voice started rising.

It all happened too fast. Lucrezia's murmurs grew louder until Micol could make out the occasional words interjecting the nonsensical ones – and then she spoke perfectly intelligible sentences in the Ancient language. Micol's basic understanding picked out something about underwater demons. Alvise seemed to understand perfectly, and the two carried on what seemed to be a conversation, hushed and tense. After a time, Alvise called for his father.

It didn't take long for Guglielmo Vendramin to thunder into the room, a case of arrows and a great bow slung over one shoulder. He had his hunting robes on.

Then Lucrezia's arm twitched and began rising slowly. It was the first time Micol had seen anything but her mouth move. Was she awake? But her eyes were closed, her eyelids fluttering as they always did, day and night, and her lips kept forming words, some in the Ancient language, some in their native Italian. Micol caught a glimpse of something on Lucrezia's extended palm. A golden spiral burnt into the upturned skin. Suddenly, Micol felt a strange, hot breeze caress the side of her face and a swishing sound rose beside her. She dared opening the wardrobe door ever so slightly so that her gaze could reach the source of the noise. She tried not to gasp as she saw a golden ribbon forming in the air, and a sphere of molten gold forming within the spiral on Lucrezia's hand. The orb on her hand then took to the air, expanding before her eyes, away from Lucrezia to suspend itself before Alvise and Vendramin. Micol's heart started beating even faster as she heard Vendramin's voice echo in the high-ceilinged room.

"Good luck, my son," he said, and threw his bow and arrows to him. Alvise caught them and adjusted the pouch of arrows on his back. He extended his arm and took hold of his sister's raised hand, wincing for a second as they touched.

Then he stepped into the gold orb and disappeared, like he'd never been there.

Micol watched until the twirling golden ribbons faded and vanished, her hands shaking uncontrollably, trying to quieten her ragged breath. She heard Lucrezia's voice hushing until it was just a murmur again, and Vendramin's footsteps disappear in the distance. Alvise was gone.

As she tried to steady herself enough to slip out of the room, she heard the tapping of heels that signalled the housekeeper Cosima's presence. Micol knew she'd have to wait a little longer to retreat.

Her mind whirled. She couldn't believe what she'd just seen. Was it some kind of dream, or a vision brought on by the heavy, ill atmosphere in Lucrezia's room? Or by the onset of the Azasti? The thought made her tremble.

And then she remembered.

Sentences unfinished, innuendos she couldn't decipher, conversation interrupted by one recurrent word: *iris*. So that's what it was. The word she'd heard whispered, passed from one to the other as they discussed things she wasn't supposed to hear. She'd seen the iris, some kind of portal that had somehow . . . *disintegrated* Alvise the moment he stepped into it.

Where had it taken him? Wherever he'd vanished to, it was somewhere else.

A place that wasn't Palazzo Vendramin.

As she sat on the mosaic floor, waiting for Cosima to finish seeing to Lucrezia so that she could step out of the room, Micol Falco hatched a plan.

8
Children of the Sea

I am and I will be
Always where my love is

Finally, Sarah was asleep, tucked inside Sean's sleeping bag. The only two left awake, Niall allowed himself to kiss Winter's soft lips. It seemed so incongruous, so reckless, to be kissing when the world was crumbling around them. There was never time, never enough solitude, to do anything more than steal a few moments together and wrap their arms around each other, before they'd be interrupted.

What are the chances of meeting the love of your life when you're about to die? Niall wondered.

Winter was the most vulnerable in the group. As the daughter of a water Elemental and a human, her only real power was turning into a seal at will. She was not a fighter, and Niall was worried sick about her. He'd tried to convince her not to go with them on what seemed like a truly suicidal journey, but she'd refused. She couldn't bear to be away from him.

Niall Flynn was the heir of the Irish Flynn family. He was a shape-shifter and master of a powerful song that could control the weather and even kill living creatures. All Secret heirs were trained to fight – but he had never thought, growing up in a windy, wild place in the north-east of Ireland, that one day he'd be somewhere in the heart of Europe trying to save the world as they knew it from annihilation. His family were still in Ireland – his parents in the Flynn homeland of Donegal, and his sisters hiding somewhere in Dublin. Or so he hoped. He had no way of knowing whether they were alive or dead. The voices of his little sisters, Cara and Bridin, always filled his dreams.

It was too painful to think of them now. He had to concentrate on what was in front of him, the people he was with and the mission they'd vowed to complete. Because if they failed, there was no hope for anyone, including his family.

"We're like a bunch of superheroes. X-Men or Avengers," he whispered in the darkness with his Irish lilt. Niall always found a way to make light of things, even in the darkest of situations. Sean had found it bizarre at first, but he'd grown to rely on Niall's constant good humour.

Winter laughed. "Absolutely. Nicholas is Magneto. Sarah is Wonder Woman—"

"Can I be Thor? I like the hammer thing."

Winter placed another kiss on his lips. And then another, and another . . .

They both had a weird feeling like they were dancing at the edge of a cliff. Yes, that was exactly what they were doing. They were all about to fall.

"I wish you could go home," Niall murmured, suddenly

serious. He looked into her eyes, so like his own. They both had eyes grey like the sea in winter. Both of them were "of the water", like she'd said when they first met.

"Home is with you," she murmured, entwining her fingers with his – and in spite of the danger, in spite of the fear, a wave of happiness swept over them both.

9
Bialoweza

Don't hurt me again, she says
I'm sorry, he cries and throws her heart away

It was still dark when they took off again, driving as fast as the icy roads allowed, following the black cloud of ravens ahead of them. The night was waning, but there was no sign of dawn yet in the inky sky. They trailed the ravens into a side road that led them deep into the forest, immense snowy trees at either side of them, and not a light in sight. Sarah wondered what hid among those trees. She could feel eyes watching everywhere, waiting. Their car felt like a small fort in the middle of enemy territory. Should they stop, should they step into the forest, it might all be over.

But that was exactly what they were going to do, she thought.

The word "suicide" sprang to mind.

Nicholas stirred in the back seat. "We should be there already ... Sean, is there a building in front of us?" he asked, his chin slightly raised, as if he were trying to somehow sense what he couldn't see.

Sean found his black, blind eyes in the mirror. "Nothing. Just trees. Oh, wait ... yes. Yes, there it is. It's brown, and flat ..."

Nicholas nodded. "We're nearly there. Drive up to it."

Sean frowned as he gazed at the mysterious structure. The same questions he'd been asking himself since they left Islay whirled in his mind. If they had been fools to listen to Nicholas, and if they were just being led willingly to their deaths. He clasped the steering wheel harder.

The strange building seemed to have sprouted out of the ground itself, like an oversized mushroom. Brown paint peeled from the wooden sidings, and ivy climbed its walls, snaking inside the cracks of broken windows. Nicholas' ravens were already waiting for him, perched on the snow-covered roof like black music notes on a page. It was a weird sight – the remains of civilisation in a wild place, nature swallowing it bit by bit.

Sean stopped the car. There was a sign over the building's door, blackened and strewn with mould: *Bialoweza – Centrum dla Odwie* ... He gave up trying to make sense of the series of consonants. *Centre for something*, he thought.

"What is this place?" Sarah asked Nicholas quietly.

"A visitors' centre for tourists coming to see the forest. Don't worry, there's nobody around. It was abandoned years ago. Accidents happened here ... you know, wild animals. People died. They closed it."

Right. Wild animals, thought Sarah with disgust.

She wondered what had happened to the Secret Families there, so close to the opening of the Shadow World. The

Polish Secret Families had probably been the first to be exterminated. She didn't imagine that any of them would have survived the culling of the heirs. She didn't want to think of how the slaughter might have happened, of how many innocent people must have been killed alongside the ones the demons had come to kill. The many different ways people had died there – dragged underground by soil demons, drained of blood by a demon leech, strangled by demon snakes. In her dreams, Sarah had seen so many deaths, and she had experienced more than she wanted to remember. That was where they all crept in from, the Surari that her parents had hunted – there, where the Shadow World and the human world met, right on the seam between the two dimensions. She imagined it probably wasn't long before tourists had grown few and far between and then stopped altogether.

They got out of the car and took their backpacks out of the boot, full of the disparate equipment they grabbed from Midnight Hall before leaving in haste. It had occurred to Sarah many times that if the demons didn't kill them, cold and hunger might. Once inside the forest, they could only rely on their own skills, weapons and whatever they'd brought with them to keep them warm.

They got ready in silence, zipping up jackets, checking weapons, balancing backpacks. They were all wearing heavy coats – though some of them had been torn and slashed in the encounter with the white demon – and fur-lined boots to protect them from the bitter cold. Only Winter, whose seal skin made her nearly invulnerable to the cold, wore a zipped-up black sweatshirt.

Sarah looked around her as they prepared to step into the

Shadow World, however it could be done. Sean's handsome face was as tight as a fist, determined and fearless as if his whole life had taken him to this moment. Niall and Winter were standing beside each other, Winter's eyes full of a terror that she was trying to hide. Niall had a protective arm around her waist, and the frown lines on his forehead betrayed his worry. Elodie was holding Nicholas' arm. How could she bear to touch him, Sarah asked herself. She was still pale after the injuries the white demon had inflicted on her and which Sarah had bandaged the best she could. She looked tiny beside Nicholas' huge, strong frame, but it was she who was sustaining and guiding him.

"Nicholas," she called. Her voice was full of steel and ice. "How are we going to step through? What's going to happen now?"

"You follow me, and I'll open the Gate for you."

That was too cryptic for Sean's liking. "Is there a physical gate or something?" he enquired.

"You'll see."

Sarah's forehead creased in frustration. They were forced to trust the man. They were forced to trust the son of the King of Shadows. It was infuriating.

They began following him into the forest, untouched snow crunching beneath their feet. He seemed to be sure of the way, despite his lack of sight. Sarah looked overhead. Through the canopy of trees she could see a hint of a grey, gloomy dawn spreading in the sky. It was so cold that their breath condensed in white puffs. They'd be frozen to the bone, thought Sarah, and then she smiled a bitter smile to herself. She was worrying about being cold when they were about to step into a world where demons were the masters, where her death and that of her friends could come in a thousand different guises. *The irony of dying of hypothermia, after all this*, she said to herself, and laughed aloud. *Great. I'm hysterical.*

"What's so funny?" snapped Elodie, sweeping her blonde hair away from her face with one hand, the other resting on Nicholas' arm. In spite of the cold, a thin film of sweat was glistening on her forehead, Sarah noticed. Her skin looked clammy.

"Just worried about ending up frozen somewhere," said Sarah with a smirk. Elodie looked at her like she'd gone crazy.

"Nicholas. Will there be guards there, at the Gate?" Sean asked.

"No need for guards. Nothing can come in, unless I allow it."

"Will your father sense our presence? Will he know we've stepped into the Shadow World?"

"He always knows of my presence. He can feel it. And he'll know about you as soon as the forest tells him," said Nicholas. He was walking unsteadily, an arm in front of him to watch for obstacles in the darkness that surrounded him.

Sarah felt sick. Nothing, nothing could ever convince her that Nicholas was trustworthy. Not after he'd moulded her will and fogged up her mind to make her do what he wanted, for weeks. Not after he'd called that love.

Suddenly, Elodie stopped in her tracks. "Someone is here. Someone is waiting for us," she said, gazing around her. Sarah felt her hands flooding with heat at once – gone were the days when she had to struggle to call her power, when any distraction could suck the heat out of her hands. She had mastered the Blackwater now, just like her father had.

Sean's knuckles tightened around his dagger. "A demon?"

Elodie closed her eyes briefly, and shook her head. "Human."

"Maybe a hunter," Nicholas offered. "Not that they last long, around here."

Human or demon, Sean's grip around his *sgian-dubh* didn't slacken.

"We can't wait, anyway," Nicholas continued. "I can feel our presence being announced. We'll be sitting ducks if we stay here . . . We need to hurry."

The light of a muted dawn spread over their faces, through the branches and on the mantle of snow on the ground. Morning was breaking at last – the last morning they'd spend in the human world for a while, thought Sarah. Or forever.

They walked on, alert, until they reached a small clearing. Opaque sunlight funnelled inside it, the snow glimmering on the ground. Two mighty oak trees stood in the middle of the space, their ancient roots thick and gnarled like old hands clasped together, their branches reaching high into the sky. They reminded Sarah of the beautiful oaks in her garden, back home in Edinburgh.

"Ready?" asked Nicholas, and without further warning he lifted his right arm, his palm open for them to see. Sarah's eyes widened. Something was taking shape on Nicholas' palm, something glowing silver on his white skin – a pattern . . . a spiral, shimmering an opaque silver and grey, darkening as they watched in silence.

Winter gasped and pointed to the space between the oaks. There, the air was vibrating, rippling like water. Weak at first, then more and more visible, a silvery spiral took shape in between the tree trunks, whirling faster and faster.

"Put your palm on my palm and walk through," Nicholas commanded. Sean was the first, grimacing as he touched Nicholas' skin, as if it hurt him. Sarah hastened to do the same. Whatever was going to happen next, even if it was a trap, she wouldn't let Sean fall into it alone. They stepped into the spiral and disappeared among the silver ribbons tumbling and turning. Niall and Winter followed suit, Winter's silvery hair twirling for a moment like one of those otherworldly ribbons. Finally, Nicholas took Elodie's hand, burning the spiral pattern into her hand, and together they entered the Shadow World.

10
Deceptions

Rotten blood and still
We call this power

Tancredi Falco shivered uncontrollably as a feverish sweat drenched him and froze to his skin. He pulled his cape closer, fighting off the bitter wind. One minute he was so cold he thought his skin was turning to ice; the next he burnt with fever, and the leather mantle he wore to aid his flight and the headdress of feathers that helped camouflage him when he was high in the sky suffocated him. Nothing could save him now.

Not that he wanted to be saved. Everything he knew was gone. Nothing mattered any more but killing Sarah Midnight. And maybe then his sister, the last heir of the Falco Family, now sheltered by the Vendramins in Venice, would be given a chance to live. Micol's beloved face danced before his eyes. His *sorellina*, alone. Ranieri had been there with her, but he was dead now. He'd died soon after Tancredi had left for Scotland to look for Sarah Midnight. Tancredi had felt his brother's death one night, like a stab in his heart – and then emptiness. Another heir taken by the Azasti, instead of finding an honourable death in battle like they were meant to. Another piece of his family gone.

Tancredi staggered on, following the trail left by Sarah and her friends. He'd flown all the way to that point, using the last of his vital force, keeping track of his prey as they drove on the frozen roads. He'd witnessed the demon attacks, one after the other, and marvelled and seethed as Sarah survived every one of them. What were the chances of him killing her, when not even all those demons could? No point in even asking himself.

Long ago, he'd been more powerful than any of those demons; he could have cut them all in two with the Falco claws, forged of a metal unknown to anyone but his family, ambushing them from above. But that was before. Before the Azasti had taken every last ounce of strength from him. Now only despair kept him going. At Palazzo Vendramin, they'd believed he was delirious, that his search for Sarah was a consequence of the madness brought on by the Azasti. But he knew it wasn't. His dreams had told him to hunt her. They told him what was in store for her, and his dreams never lied.

He could not allow Sarah to survive. He had to destroy her, or make Sean Hannay and Niall Flynn see what he could see, tell them that Sarah would betray them all, that her destiny was written and there was no way to change it. Maybe then they would kill Sarah themselves. She could not be allowed to live after such betrayal. They couldn't allow a power like hers to join forces with the King of Shadows.

He made himself put one foot in front of the other, and one

more and one more, until he saw something black and shiny beyond the trees. One of the cars Sarah and her friends had been driving, abandoned. In front of him lay a condemned building, its windows broken and its paint peeling off the walls – a strange sight, right in the middle of this wild place. Tancredi examined the snowy ground and then followed the footprints in the snow.

Suddenly, alerted by something only he could feel, he crouched behind a fallen tree. A hundred yards away from him stood Sarah Midnight, slender and strong, her long black hair loose around her shoulders.

Tancredi's heart bled with regret as a painful thought travelled through his mind. Had she not been chosen as the bride of the Underworld, Sarah would have been a powerful asset for the Secret Families, maybe the most powerful. In other times she could have been their hope and their pride, a legend among the heirs. And now he was about to cut her throat.

A wave of fury hit Tancredi as he spotted Nicholas, tall and raven-haired, his skin otherworldly pale. He was the monster who, together with his father, had been the cause of the Secret Families' demise.

Tancredi tensed and held his breath as the French heir, Elodie, turned towards his hiding place for a moment. She could sense him, he knew that. The Bruns were known for their psychic abilities, among other things. He was about to take flight and pounce on Sarah from above when he spotted something flickering in front of them, something shimmering and twirling. They'd opened an *iris*! In his generation only Lucrezia Vendramin, as far as he knew, could do something like that. Tancredi watched Sean touch Nicholas' hand and then step into the rippling air, disappearing from view, out of his grasp. And then Sarah, the Flynn boy and the silver-haired Elemental followed through, and finally Elodie and the monster, the son of the King of Shadows. Without thinking, Tancredi ran blindly. He knew that he hadn't been marked, he hadn't touched the monster's hand. There was no way he could have followed them, but he was beyond rational thought. With a scream of despair he threw himself into the rippling air, expecting to bounce back, or burn up, or whatever happened to those who tried to step through unmarked. But none of that happened. He swayed and struggled for balance as he found himself in the Shadow World, barely registering a full moon shining cold in the black sky. And then he saw the spectre. He saw them all.

11
Heir to Silence

The day I saw you dying was the day
I died myself

Venice

A few hours earlier
Alvise threw the bow and arrow on the mosaic floor. The
sound echoed throughout the palace. Once again the Falco
girl had run away. Once again she'd put them all in danger.
Foolish, foolish girl. A child – fifteen years old, only three
less than him, but still a child. Alvise cursed the moment
his father decided to take the Falco children under his roof.
Ranieri died quickly – poor soul, eaten alive by the Azasti.
Tancredi had run away, in a delirium caused by his illness.
And Micol was left, hating every day she spent with the
Vendramin, convinced that they wished her ill, convinced
that they were torturing their own little Lucrezia, Alvise's
sister. Completely delusional.

If only he still had his powers, or their Gamekeepers were still alive. But they'd all been killed, in ways Alvise didn't want to remember.

He sat at the piano in anger and started hitting the keys. The music he played was full of sorrow and tension, and the face he saw was the face of a woman with long, nearly white hair, like his.

A dark-skinned woman with grey hair pinned back and a crucifix around her neck peeked through the door. Cosima.

"Signor Vendramin! Lucrezia is talking. Hurry!"

Alvise jumped up from the piano and ran down frescoed corridors towards Lucrezia's room. Immediately his sister's odd scent, a flowery fragrance so heavy it was nearly rotting, hit him like a wall. There were no flowers in her room that day. It was Lucrezia's chemistry, her skin and breath that produced the strange scent.

Lucrezia lay still in her bed, her eyelids flickering, her hands abandoned by her sides. Hair so light it was nearly white fanned over her pillow, loose strands at her waist. She was whispering, a jumble of words and sounds that made no sense – but they knew that soon her gibberish would condense into a message.

Alvise sat on her bed and held her hand. Micol could read in his face the pain that Lucrezia's terrible predicament brought to him. Forced into immobility, turned around like a doll to avoid bedsores, the endless, restless sleep and continuous dreaming. It was no life for his sister.

Alvise had spent many hours sitting by her bed, lulled by her murmuring. Occasionally he would stroke the loose hair away from her face or caress her hand. Whenever he touched her or spoke to her, Lucrezia's babbling seemed to soften, until just her lips moved and no sounds came out. At times she took a deeper breath, as if his touch brought her some relief, as if she were aware that she wasn't alone.

Sometimes silent tears rolled down her cheeks, and Alvise could feel his heart breaking. He sat there, eyes dry, wishing death would take his sister at last.

"You must go," Lucrezia's clear, young voice resounded in the high-ceilinged room. She had spoken in her native Italian, and not in the Ancient language. The cold light of dawn was seeping through the shutters, illuminating the girl's pale face and lips. Alvise leaned towards her, waiting for her to explain. A torrent of murmurs followed, something about a silvery winter and an incandescent stone, mixed with sounds in the Ancient language and some in a language that was only her own. And then, more Italian words, enunciated clearly, slowly, as if something else had taken possession of her vocal cords and mouth and was painstakingly forcing muscle and tissue into the right shapes.

"They are coming. You must go."

Alvise's mind raced. A new message meant a new task. More demons to destroy. He knew his father should hear this. "Father," he called, looking frantically at his sister. "Father!"

Within moments, Guglielmo Vendramin was at his side, sweeping into the room in traditional hunting garb.

"What is it?"

"Look at Lucrezia."

Slowly, slowly, Lucrezia began to raise her right hand and her thin white arm.

"You must go, Alvise," said his father.

"I know."

They had to be quick. Lucrezia's arm was rising, rising, revealing her palm. Burnt into her skin was a spiral, shining gold. A memory flashed before his eyes: his sister screaming as the spiral was carved into her hand under the eyes of the Sabha, and pure gold poured into the wound.

Between them the iris grew, gaining strength with every second.

"Good luck, my son," he heard his father whisper. He always did that before a journey through the iris, like a blessing. Alvise accepted his father's great bow and sling of arrows, then stepped toward his sister.

Already a golden ribbon was taking shape in the room, circling slowly to create an inward spiral. The scent of dying flowers was unbearable. Alvise stepped beside Lucrezia, lying immobile with her arm raised, a strange glow emanating from her palm. He took her hand so that their palms touched, and he felt a sudden pain – something that had never happened before. And then he stepped into the spiral.

He'd been through the iris many times and knew the sensations well, and still, this time there was something different, more intense, even violent. His body felt torn apart, fragmented into its molecules, whirling around like snowflakes in a storm, and then forced back together. It felt like all the bits of him were still unglued, kept together by some magnetic force, instead of bonding to each other, and the slightest force, the slightest shift in energy, would scatter them once again and he'd be no more.

Fear gripped his stomach and took his breath away, and for a moment he believed that Lucrezia had made a terrible mistake, that the iris wasn't functioning the way it was supposed to, that it would kill him. He twirled in gold for what seemed like a long time, every fibre of his being fighting to get a grip of itself, of the molten gold that danced before his eyes. And then, all of a sudden, it was over.

12
Shadows of the Moon

Indian or African skies
The southern hemisphere
Or the sky above the lochs of our home
You said you'd think of me
Every time you saw the moon

Sarah felt her hair standing on end, a soft buzz in her ears and a feeling like a painless electrical current running on her skin. A wave of nausea hit her as she realised she didn't know what was up and what was down any more. All she could see was a grey, opaque, cloudy light, as if she'd lost her sight.

She squeezed her eyes shut, and when she opened them again everything was black. She really was blind, she thought, and felt the sharp bite of panic. Then she realised that the blackness was dotted with twinkling silver lights – stars. She was looking at the night sky. It had been morning when they left the human world.

In an instant she was on her feet. Her elbow brushed

against something and she jumped, her hands flooding with heat already and her eyes burning green. But she saw that it was Sean. He was standing in a daze, looking ahead of him, slightly hunched on one side, as if unable to support his own weight. She took him by the arm and shook him.

"Sean! Sean!"

He blinked several times. Then his expression tightened as he steadied himself. Sarah felt someone behind her – movement, a cold current – and turned in alarm. Niall and Winter, followed by Nicholas and Elodie, stepped through. Relieved, Sarah turned around again and a spectral face, white like the moon, rose out of the darkness to meet hers. Two transparent arms followed, ready to grab her. She raised her hands instinctively. The Blackwater called her.

"A moon-demon! Don't touch it!" A voice came from behind. Niall. Sarah froze at once as the transparent face moved towards her. Niall's song began to rise into the air, deafening already.

Sarah stepped back, watching the spectre dance a fitful dance of pain. The white rays of the moon were everywhere, brilliant and pure and . . . moving, condensing into limbs and faces, horrendous faces with black holes for eyes. One, two, five more creatures took shape from the moonbeams and began marching towards them.

"Nobody touch them," shouted Nicholas above Niall's song. His hands were burning and crackling with blue flames. "They'll turn you into one of them."

Sarah's blood chilled. She remembered the demon shadow, immortal, forever unable to feel, unable to touch. A half-life worse than death.

She thanked Nicholas begrudgingly for having warned

her a split second before she'd tried to dissolve them, and narrowed her eyes. The Midnight gaze glinted green in the semi-darkness. She couldn't hit them all at once, so she chose one and concentrated on destroying it. Niall's song was now in full flow, a thing of power and fury, and soon two of the spectres were on the ground, jolting and shuddering like marionettes. Out of the corner of her eye Sarah could see Sean's hands tracing the invisible runes in the air, his *sgian-dubh* dancing so fast it was a blur – and then the sparks began, scarlet, like silent fireworks flowering all around them. Sarah blinked in wonder for a moment, and the moon-demon she was tormenting took its chance, jerking its way towards her at a terrifying speed – but something red and sharp hit its transparent body, lodging itself where the demon's guts should have been. One moment, just one moment, and the demon exploded without a sound, spilling moonbeams all around. Sean met her eye, and Sarah could see Sean's amazement at his own power.

Niall's song was arresting the moon-demons' advance. They were losing consistency, turning more and more transparent as he sang. Sarah shook herself and turned around to check on Winter, and she saw that the Elemental girl was standing still, a look of terror on her face, a useless blade in her hand.

And behind her, rising quietly, was a moon-demon.

"Winter!" Sarah screamed. She would not reach her in time. Winter didn't stand a chance.

And then blue flames burnt and crackled all around Winter, surrounding her in a wall of cold fire. She screamed in terror, falling to her knees. The spectre couldn't reach her through the flames. Elodie was holding Nicholas' arm and had her own arm around his waist. She'd shown him where to strike. Niall's song was slowly failing – the shock of starting it so suddenly had drained him.

A few straggly remains of Sean's red ribbons were still flickering in the air, glimmers of light among the black branches. Sarah was standing further away from the others, panting, eyes wide, unable to move. Winter and Elodie fell to the frosty ground, back to back. Nicholas crouched beside Elodie.

Niall leaned against an oak tree, trying to keep himself upright after the effort of the Song. His eyes were fixed on Winter. He'd nearly lost her. *What have I done*, he thought helplessly, *agreeing to bring her here?*

Sean studied his hands in disbelief. He couldn't believe what had just come out of them. He heard a soft noise above their heads.

It was then that something fell from the trees and jumped right on Sarah, dragging her to the ground with the inertia of its fall, and clawing at her back. She screamed as her knees hit the ground with a thump. She could already feel the thing's claws on her neck. She couldn't see what it was, but she could feel something soft against her skin, something feathery.

It's the demon-bird, she realised, and fury streaked through her. A searing pain made her scream as the thing began to dig its claws into her neck. Just as her friends were running to her rescue, Sarah turned around and overcame the demon with one fluid movement, throwing it to the ground and crouching over it, a knee on its chest.

Too easy, she said to herself, and her body tensed even further, expecting a nasty surprise. But none came. The

Surari just lay there, apparently having run out of energy.

Its face was black and thick like leather, and black feathers crowned its head. It looked like a hybrid between a bird and a human being, its eyes dark and almond-shaped, deeply encased in its skin. Sarah felt nauseous at its monstrous appearance, and pinned its clawed hands to the ground, without mercy. The demon seemed . . . weak.

Why is it so easy, she wondered as it offered nearly no resistance. *Why will it not fight back?*

Sean and Niall, as if of one mind, took Sarah's place in holding the creature's claws. Sarah placed her hands on its chest, ready to dissolve it into Blackwater – and then she remembered. Her powers, for some mysterious reason, didn't work on the demon-bird. She had learnt that the hard way the first time it attacked her, in Edinburgh. Sean lifted his arm, ready to plunge his *sgian-dubh* into the demon's heart.

"It's my kill," Sarah hissed. Sean's hand stopped in mid-air, but as Sarah was about to reach for her *sgian-dubh*, the creature spoke, its voice raspy and barely audible.

"Curse you, Sarah Midnight, bride of the King of Shadows. *Maledetta!*"

"It speaks!" Niall exclaimed.

"You are the shame of the Secret Families. Curse you to hell," it snarled. Sarah was still for a moment, as shock froze her thoughts and her hands. A trickle of blood seeped out of the creature's mouth, smearing its chin with red.

"Shut up," whispered Sarah coldly, and raised her dagger.

"Wait!" cried Elodie, and threw herself on the ground beside the demon.

Before Sarah could wonder what was up with Elodie, the creature raised its feathered head and spat in Sarah's face.

Without missing a beat, without hesitation and with a cry of fury, under the bewildered eyes of her friends, Sarah sank her *sgian-dubh* into its neck, as deep as it would go. A gurgle, a stream of blood on her hands. Her eyes widened as she saw red splatter her white skin – she was used to the Blackwater, the dark lymph of demons.

"I'll never be the bride of the King of Shadows," she hissed. "Never."

The demon gasped for breath, a steady stream of blood flowing out of its neck.

"He's not a demon!" Elodie cried out. She took hold of the feathers around the creature's head and pulled. The black halo came loose, together with the black skin of its face. But it wasn't its face. It was a mask. "He's human," Elodie said. "It must have been him I'd felt just before we entered the Shadow World."

Sarah recoiled.

She'd just cut a human being's throat.

We don't kill human beings, she remembered telling Sean when she'd been horrified by his ruthlessness.

And look at her now.

"But why . . . why . . ." Her voice trailed away as she looked at her bloodied hands. *Human blood is so red*, she thought confusedly.

Sean wrapped an arm around her waist. "It's okay, Sarah. It's okay," he whispered in her ear.

The demon–bird spoke. The colour was draining from his face as his life leaked out of him. His eyes were already opaque, losing focus. "Sean Hannay. Where are you? I have something to tell you."

"I'm here. What do you have to say to me?"

"You are a Gamekeeper. You are loyal to the Secret Families. You must kill Sarah Midnight. I'm begging you."

Sean's chest heaved in anger, and he had to stop himself from twisting the man's neck. They had to listen to what he had to say.

"She is cursed. It was my mission to destroy her."

"Who are you?" Sarah cried out.

"Tancredi Falco, of the Falco Family. We hail from Tuscany. We're the greatest family in—"

"Greatest? All you did was jump on me! It was like fighting a child!" snorted Sarah, and her laughter turned into a sob. She was watching a man slowly die by her hand. She was as white as snow, panting hard, unable to steady her heart.

"We'll all be dead soon. All of us but her. By a demon's hand, or by the Azasti. Have you spotted the signs already? Have you?"

Elodie's skin looked even paler all of a sudden. Once more Sean read fear in her eyes.

"How did you get into the Shadow World? Nobody can enter here with a body . . . unless they know how," said Sean, lifting his arm to show the burn mark.

Tancredi laughed, a bitter, gurgling sound that sounded like death. "The Shadow World? So this is where we are. I guess I entered because I'm as good as dead, my friend. I'm in between. And the shadows know that."

"We're here to kill the King of Shadows. Not to help him!" Sarah exclaimed, as if it were important for her that he understood. As if it were important that man knew she wasn't a traitor to her kind, like he believed.

"You fools . . . Kill the King of Shadows!" he sputtered. "That can never happen."

"What?" Sean cried out.

But Tancredi's eyes rolled and trickles of pinkish saliva dribbled from the corners of his mouth. His clawed hands curled in a final rictus.

"Sean Hannay, listen. Please. My little sister . . . the last of the Falcos . . . she's done nothing to you. If you are a true Gamekeeper, find her . . . protect her."

"What is her name?" asked Sarah. Maybe she had a chance for atonement.

Tancredi opened his mouth to speak, but no sound came out. He breathed in softly, a quick, imperceptible breath, and then his whole body relaxed in death.

Sarah closed her eyes, and felt empty, drained of all life. Pity ravaged her chest as she took in Tancredi's gaunt face, the signs of his long suffering ingrained in his features. But then she steeled herself. There was no time for pity, and certainly not for someone who'd desperately wanted her dead.

13
Like the Moon

The shadow of the wheel of fortune
Against the white sheet of our lives
Who ever said
That our books are unwritten?

Sean

I take Sarah aside for a moment. She's rigid with shock, eyes wide, like she can't believe what she has done. I hold her close, but she doesn't soften in my arms. She's trembling.

"He wanted to kill you," I whisper into her hair. "You had to do it."

"I could have let him explain. I could have given him more time."

"There was no time! The guy tried to kill you three times, Sarah. I don't know how he knew about you and Nicholas."

"He must have been a Dreamer."

"Whatever. It's finished now, finished. He's dead."

"Sean ..." She calls my name like I can try to help her

figure out what just happened, what made her kill the man. And I do know what happened inside her mind: her fighting instinct took over, generations of hunters before her told her what she had to do. I take her face in my hands and look into her eyes. She doesn't look like Sarah the huntress any more. Right now she looks like the Sarah she was when we met. Fragile, hurt. Unsure of herself.

When we first met, Sarah cried often. As her power grew, as she acknowledged how strong she really was, her tears grew few and far between. But now she's broken. I can see it, and I fear the consequences of this will be long lasting.

"I am a murderer. Like my grandmother," she whispers.

Morag Midnight, Sarah's fearsome grandmother, drowned her own daughter Mairead when she was just a child. Mairead wasn't strong enough to bear the power of Dreams, and Morag despised her for that. Morag had also planned to destroy Winter, and she had rejected my own mother when she needed Morag's help the most. Sarah's grandmother was a cruel, cruel woman.

"You are nothing like her."

"I am. I must be. It's in my blood."

"No, listen to me!" I fix my eyes on hers. *You're so beautiful*, I can't help thinking, even in this terrible moment. Her face is as white as the moon, her eyes the colour of new leaves, a shade of green I've never seen before. The shape of her forehead, the curve of her nose, the unique geometry of her face ...

"You are nothing like her. You are nothing like your gran. You are Sarah."

She buries her face in my chest and I feel her trembling.

I hold for a few moments, until she disentangles herself and raises her face to me.

"We need to go," she says, and she's guarded once more.

"Will you be okay?" I can't help asking.

"Yes," she replies simply. "Yes. I'll be fine."

I nod. I know she'll keep going, but I also know she's not fine. She's feeling her true self slip away with every kill, even if the victims are Surari. And this one – a human being. Something no heir should ever face. I know how that feels, to sense yourself changing into someone you struggle to recognise, losing what used to be your identity and becoming someone else. It happens when you take one too many lives. A bit of your soul departs and will never come back. You'll be forever grieving the person you used to be, the innocence you used to bear in your heart. Without it, even if your purpose is the complete opposite of theirs – to preserve, not to destroy – you are a step closer to them: the Surari.

"Sean."

"Yes?"

"You said I'm not like Morag. But she's in my blood, so how can I not be?"

"Your blood doesn't define who you are, Sarah!"

She looks at me more intensely, and suddenly I know where she's trying to lead me.

"If that's true, why does your blood matter to you so much?"

"Sarah, please. We can't change things, okay? We can't."

"But your runes. Did you see ..." I read hope in her eyes, and it hurts. So much rests on this. If I have powers, if I am somehow a Secret heir, then we can be together ... but to hope is to open yourself up to hurt and disappointment.

"My father was a Lay. I can't have powers," I say brusquely.

"I know. But you saw it yourself."

"It's just my runes being stronger than usual. I told you, it's a skill. Please let's not talk about this any more."

"Sean," she interrupts. "It doesn't matter if you have powers or not."

"It matters to me," I reply, and her face crumbles. We are so close we're nearly touching. I could hold her now, take her in my arms and kiss her. I wish the world could change for us. But it won't, I know that, and a sense of despair fills me until there's nothing else to feel or think. A world without Sarah. Having to let her go, having to disappear so that she's free to live her life with another Secret heir.

For a moment I'm frozen, studying her face, burning it into my mind, knowing that one day a memory is all I'll have left. All of a sudden, I see a strange reflection on her skin – bright pink and green. Her eyes are wide, but not with fear – with wonder. I follow her gaze and turn around. There's a gap between the trees just behind me and the starry sky is filled with dancing lights, pink and green and blue. I have seen many things in my life, but I've never seen anything like this before.

For a moment, we watch in silent awe. The beauty and power of the Shadow World have surprised us. None of us knew what to expect – maybe I was imagining volcanoes and burning pits and boiling seas, but this tree-laden world is in my genetic memory, because this is where my long-gone ancestors used to live. This is the way the world used to be thousands of years ago and more, pure and untouched and beyond the control of human beings.

"Sean! Sarah!" A voice breaks our spell. It's Nicholas.

Sarah walks away, and the sudden separation knocks the breath out of me for a moment, like when she's not around I can't breathe. She's all I need, all I want, but there is no time or place for us. We join the others. As she steps within the group, I see that Sarah's tears have dried up. She's ready to fight again.

14
Burning Lion

Look through the iris and you'll see
The life I left behind

The northern lights had faded and the sky was black once more, dusted with endless stars. The night had reached its peak and the first grey hints of dawn had started in the east.

"Shall we bury him?" Winter asked, gazing with pity toward Tancredi's lifeless body. He had attacked her, too, back on her native Islay. How helpless he looked now, his almond eyes closed forever, his face gaunt, his limbs tightening. She thought she could see blood staining his lips and feathers. Clearly, in life he'd been very ill. Compassion filled Winter's heart.

"No time," Sean answered.

Winter's throat constricted at the thought of leaving this dead man alone to decay, with no one to give him a burial. What if he'd been Mike? Or her? "We can't leave him like this. He'll be eaten by animals ... and demons." She shuddered. "We can't."

"We have no time," Nicholas intervened. "We need to keep moving. We're two days' walk away from my father."

Sarah closed her eyes briefly. Behind her controlled exterior she felt physically ill. She hated the thought of leaving the Falco heir like that, but she knew they were right. She knew that they couldn't waste any time digging a grave when they might be attacked any second, and then they'd join Tancredi in the hole they'd just dug for him. She steeled herself.

"Let's go," she whispered, feeling like she'd left yet another little piece of the old Sarah behind. The girl who'd been left helpless by her parents, who'd been sheltered from the knowledge and skills of the Secret Families – the child who'd been lying alone at night, terrified, listening for her parents' footsteps up the stairs, back from their nightly hunt – was now capable of things that would have horrified her old self.

"We can cover him with those stones," Winter insisted, pointing at some flat grey rocks that covered the ground like a natural pavement, ferns growing between them. "It really won't take long," she nearly begged.

"He's an heir. We can't leave him here," Niall said in his gentle way, speaking for the first time since Tancredi appeared. Sarah could read the abhorrence on his face, his shock at the suggestion of leaving Tancredi unburied, and trembled inside. Maybe he despised her because she'd killed an heir, and he'd be right to, she thought, drowning in a wave of self-hatred. Well, there was nothing she could do.

"Never mind being an heir! He's a human being!" whispered Winter, looking around her as if she couldn't believe what was happening. "His spirit might go wandering, like those lost at sea," she added.

At Winter's words, Sarah felt a sudden disquiet. "Fine then.

Let's cover him with stones." Sean gazed at her, surprised by her change of mind. Her eyes were haunted, and he understood. They'd take what little time they had to bury Tancredi. They'd run the risk.

"We can't—" Nicholas began.

"It's been decided," Sean interjected. "Elodie, keep watch," he said. He didn't want her to be lifting heavy stones; he'd spotted blood on her back during the fight with the moon-demons. The wounds she'd suffered at the petrol station were far from healed.

In perfect silence, Winter composed Tancredi's body, folding his arms in his lap and covering him with his cape, the feathery headdress resting on his face. She thought of the little sister he'd been talking about, and her heart went out to the unknown girl. Sarah looked on, eyes dry and no expression on her face. Only her pursed lips betrayed her inner turmoil. Together, she and Winter began to pile stones on top of him.

Sean threw a glance at Elodie. She was standing a few yards away, *sgian-dubh* in hand, lips black. There was something about her that ate away at him. She looked weak somehow. She *acted* weak, like everything was too heavy, too tiring – even breathing. Sean was afraid to think what the reason might be.

"Nicholas," he whispered while everyone was gathering stones. "What is this thing, this ... Azasti?"

"What? Do you not know? None of you knows what the Azasti is? The ailment, some call it. It's an illness of the Secret heirs. Rotten blood," he said. "It kills you slowly, painfully. That's how my father got the Sabha to work for him in the first place. He had his Valaya there offer a cure."

"That's how he corrupted the Sabha? They wanted a cure for this thing?"

"Yes. A cure he couldn't give. But the Secret Council were desperate. They collaborated."

"And Harry knew," Sean said. "He tried to stop it."

"Maybe. Maybe not. He certainly knew the Sabha were working with my father, otherwise he would have entrusted Sarah to them and not to you." Nicholas replied. "But I don't know if he was aware that my father had offered a cure for the Azasti."

"So Sarah is in danger too? Of getting ill, I mean?" Sean forced himself to ask.

"For some reason, there has been no trace of the Azasti in Scotland or Ireland. Maybe it's because they're on the edge of Europe, remote, by our standards. That's one of the reasons why Sarah was chosen as my bride."

Niall had overhead Nicholas' words. "I'm glad you didn't choose me," he joked. He was his usual self, ready to smile when things were far from funny, but his eyes were hard.

Sean felt sick to the pit of his stomach. "So that's what you meant when you said that Sarah's blood was strong." His hands were shaking. How he would have loved breaking his nose and a bone or two for good measure right now. He tried to steady his heart, beating too hard. His fury had nowhere to go for now. It would just consume him.

Sarah placed another moss-covered stone on Tancredi's body, the last one. It was done. She closed her eyes for a moment, still on her knees, recovering herself.

May your little sister be safe, she prayed silently. They were now a few yards from the makeshift grave, which they'd hidden among ferns and stones.

Suddenly, the whole world exploded in a golden light,

blinding them all. Sarah covered her face with her hands but peered between her fingers, squinting through the glare. A spiral had appeared in front of them, twirling and tearing a hole in reality. It looked like the Gate they'd used to step into the Shadow World, but golden, and more violent – like a gash in the air, one that hurt and bled, one that wasn't supposed to exist, but somehow had come to be.

15
Into the Gold

Rising out of golden light
The woman I will be

Venice

Micol forbade herself from thinking. Had she stopped and pondered what she was about to do, she would have never gone through with it. Where did the golden spiral lead? Where had Alvise gone?

Micol closed her mind and her instincts and opened her heart, her caged heart that only wanted one thing: freedom. She pushed open the heavy wardrobe doors and bolted in what felt like a single jump towards the iris, vaguely aware of someone shouting and Lucrezia's endless lament. She knew she had to touch Lucrezia's hand before she jumped, because that was what Alvise always did.

Out of the corner of her eye, Micol saw Vendramin re-enter the room and take a step forward, his arms outstretched, trying to stop her, but Lucrezia's bed was between them, and before he could go around it, Micol had already taken hold of the sleeping girl's hand. She felt something burn her palm, but the adrenaline coursing through her steeled her against the pain. She launched herself towards the spiral, and for a moment her body shivered. Half of Micol had disappeared into the iris already; it was too late for anyone to stop her. She was gone into the twirling gold and into darkness, towards what she hoped was freedom and not death.

Rising out of the golden light were a slim young man holding a bow and an almond-skinned girl with cropped hair and a long white dress. There was something shiny and crackling, like blue lightning, wrapped around the girl; the man tumbled for a moment and then jumped up, ready to shoot an arrow.

Sarah sprang to her feet, hands flushed with Blackwater, eyes narrowed and gleaming, ready to kill.

"Who are you?" shouted Sean, his *sgian-dubh* in hand.

"Who's asking?" the blond man replied. He spoke in heavily accented English. The girl with him stood, immovable, her hands raised and crackling blue, her gaze filled with what she hoped was menace, but looked a lot like fear.

Sean saw no reason to hide his identity. These strangers weren't demons, clearly, and if they were there to harm Sarah, he'd soon see to them. "My name is Sean Hannay, Gamekeeper of the Midnights."

"A Gamekeeper!" the stranger said, his voice dripping with relief. "I am Alvise Vendramin, of the Vendramin Family from Venice. And this is Micol," he replied, shooting the girl a murderous glance.

"Vendramin," whispered Niall, recognition spreading all over his face. Of course! He remembered the blond, slender boy and the gilded palace, and the light of the moon on the canals. Many years ago.

The girl called Micol took in the scene, her eyes wide. She studied them one by one as they talked. Micol could see auras; they told her the inner thoughts and history of people. Over the years, she had developed a kind of book of auras in her mind, instantly reading what they had to say about people – red for anger, white for loneliness, blue for sadness – and the happier colours, the yellow and orange of vitality, the green of hope, the pink of gentle love.

She saw a slender young woman, black hair about her shoulders like a waterfall, eyes glistening the greenest she'd ever seen. Her aura was white with a hint of red. *Purity, anger, and loneliness*, Micol thought.

The strong-looking man named Sean stood next to her, and his face said he could have killed her in an instant. His aura burnt scarlet with blue edges. A gentler-looking guy with grey eyes stared at Alvise, and at his side was a girl with hair as silver as moonlight. Their auras were very similar: blue and aqua and grey, the auras of people who might be reluctant to fight; but the man's was darker, suggesting a power that ran deeper than the eye could see. And then there was a slight woman, small as a bird, exquisitely beautiful. She reminded Micol of a porcelain doll. Her aura was blue, grey at its edges, as if it were losing strength slowly. Beside her, there was someone who made Micol's heart tremble. Someone tall, pale, eyes as black as coal. He was blind, she guessed by his posture and by the way his eyes seemed unfocused.

Someone whose aura was completely black.

She'd never seen anything like that. Terror streaked through her. Who was that man? Was he a man at all, or a demon about to tear them apart? Where was she? What had she done? What kind of trouble had she jumped into in her haste to escape Palazzo Vendramin? She took a shuddering breath. Whatever she was about to face, she'd show these people what Falco heirs were made of. She stood steady, her chest rising and falling in a crazy rhythm, green electrical charges shooting intermittently from her hands. She had to tell Alvise about the guy with the black aura.

"Are you a Secret heir?" Sean asked Alvise.

"Yes. Both of us are. I don't understand. Where are the demons?" He looked left and right, still not lowering his bow.

"I'm sure we won't have to wait long to see them. They're everywhere," said Sean, bemused. "We mean you no harm. Unless you're here to harm us," he added, his *sgian-dubh* still poised.

Alvise shook his head. "I'm a Secret heir. I kill demons, not human beings," he declared, and lowered his bow and arrow an inch and no more.

Micol shot a nervous glance towards Nicholas. They weren't all human.

"My sister sends me through the iris wherever there are demons to kill. But here we are."

"That's the iris?" asked Sean, nodding towards the twirling golden ribbons. They were still there, though fading slowly as they spoke.

Niall gasped, but nobody noticed. His hand took hold of Winter's. "What's beyond the iris?" he asked urgently.

Alvise met Niall's gaze. "Palazzo Vendramin. In Venice.

My home." Then he paused. "I . . . I think I know you. Yes, I remember you!"

"Our families knew each other. I'm Niall Flynn."

Alvise's face broke into a smile. "Yes! Niall! It is you!"

"Is your home safe?" Niall's voice was shaky.

Sean studied his friend's face. What was he thinking?

"My home is as safe as any place can be these days."

"Who lives there?"

"Niall, what does this have to do with—" Sean began, but Niall raised his hand to interrupt him. Something in his friend's expression quietened Sean at once.

"Who lives there?" Niall repeated.

"My father and my sister."

"And you said it's safe?" Niall enquired again, a strange, pleading note to his voice.

"Niall . . ." Sean questioned.

"My father does his best to keep it safe," answered Alvise.

Niall didn't let him finish. He grabbed Winter by the waist, whispered something in her ear, and pushed her through the fading iris as she called his name one last time. She disappeared at once, the golden ribbons fading and then finally disappearing. Winter was gone.

"What did you do!" shouted Sarah.

"I had to," whispered Niall, his arms limp at his sides and his eyes opaque, like he'd lost all reason to be. "I had to," he repeated, running a hand through his hair. "It was a mistake to let her come in the first place. I knew it when the moon-demons attacked. I knew she would die here."

"You don't know who those people are!" shouted Sean.

"Actually, I do. I told Winter what to say."

"And what would that be?"

"*Onoir, clan agus farraige.* They'll know," he said, the pleading tone in his voice once more. Looking at Alvise, he hoped he'd say that yes, Winter would be safe. That he hadn't made another terrible mistake.

Alvise nodded. "The Flynn motto. *Honour, family and the ocean.* Winter will be fine. The second she says the words, my father will look after her."

Their eyes met, Niall's full of tears he felt no need to hide. There was a moment of silence as they digested Winter's disappearance, when without warning the electrical charges around the girl who'd followed Alvise through the iris increased, crackling blue and green and red. She was holding her right hand in her left one, grimacing with pain.

"Are you hurt?" Sarah asked her.

"Just my hand." She looked at Sarah from under her eyelashes, still suspicious of them all, even if one of them had turned out to be an old friend of the Vendramins.

"If you stop that ... lightning," Sarah gestured to the multi-coloured sparks all over the girl's body, "I can have a look at it."

The girl shot Alvise a frightened glance, asking him a silent question. Alvise inclined his head. The charges crackled once more, shining brightly around the girl's body, and disappeared. She stepped towards Sarah, her hand extended.

"You are burnt," said Sarah taking her hand gently. "Something is burnt into your skin."

"Mine too," said Alvise calmly, looking at his palm. The symbol of a spiral was imprinted on his hand, the skin blackened and weeping. "I hadn't noticed ..."

"It's like the symbol Nicholas imprinted on our palms," said Sarah. "But we weren't burnt. It just hurt for a moment.

Does your sister burn you every time she sends you through? You'd have no hand left."

"No. It's never happened before."

"It's because they are not supposed to be here," Nicholas intervened. "That's why they were burnt. The iris was not supposed to take them into the Shadow World, and I have no idea how that Vendramin girl did it."

"The Shadow World?" Alvise whispered. All colour drained from his face. "As in . . . the world of the Surari? We actually are in the Shadow World?"

Micol took a sharp intake of breath, her eyes surveying the scene with more terror. The world of the Surari. The man with the black aura, was he one of them then? She'd never seen a demon's aura; she'd always thought they didn't have them. But human beings didn't have black auras . . . She took a deep breath, trying to stop panic from spreading in her chest.

Sarah nodded. "That's where we are. That's where your sister sent you this time, apparently."

Alvise frowned. "How did she . . . I mean, I didn't know this place existed in the first place. I thought it was a legend, one of those Secret history things we learn as children."

"Look, I hate to interrupt your chat, but we need to move," Nicholas interrupted. "Unless you want to sit here waiting for another attack."

"And you are . . ." Alvise threw his chin up in a gesture of challenge.

"Alvise," whispered Micol, a feeble warning. She had to tell him about the man's aura. She had to find a way to tell him.

"Long story," Niall intervened. "Come on, I'll fill you in," he said, taking Alvise's arm.

"We need a minute," said Sarah, gesturing to Micol. "She needs her burn seen to. Also, she can't walk dressed like this." She gestured to the girl's long white dress. Micol was shivering already, her bare arms covered in goosebumps. "I have a change of clothes with me. Come on," she said and led her behind a tight cluster of trees.

"Alvise," Elodie began as they waited for Sarah and Micol. "You are Italian. Do you know anything about the Frison family? They're Gamekeepers from Val d'Aosta, in the northwest. They hid me for a while. One of them died . . . Marina." She winced, remembering her black-haired friend, her warm smile, the prophecy she'd made about her, Elodie, loving again one day. "Frison, her father, ran to the mountains with a Japanese heir, a little girl called Aiko Ayanami."

"I know about the Frisons, but I haven't had news of anyone for a long time . . . anyone except a Sicilian family, the Montanera . . . but that was months ago. We are completely isolated, I'm sorry. As soon as my sister gets us back I'll try to find out."

"Your sister will get you back? How?" Sean intervened.

"She sends me through the iris to kill Surari, and then she knows when I'm done. Somehow. She opens an iris wherever I am and I can get back. I'm sorry about your friends," he added towards Elodie. She nodded, mute with disappointment.

Sarah crouched in the undergrowth, carefully took out packets of biscuits and tins of beans from her backpack, and unearthed a pair of jeans and a purple top. Both were perfectly folded, Sarah's way. Micol's dress, muddy already, went in their place back into Sarah's bag.

"My jeans are a bit long for you, but they'll do."

"Thank you," said Micol, zipping them. They were also loose around the waist. Sarah was slender, but Micol was tiny. "I don't know your name," she continued.

"My name is Sarah Midnight," Sarah replied and looked at the girl's face for a moment. She probably wasn't much younger than any of them, but she looked it – there was something childlike in her eyes, brown and deep like a doe's. Her cropped hair was dark brown, without the blue shades Sarah's hair had, and her skin was a golden amber. She reminded Sarah of a fawn, still not quite steady on her legs. Sarah felt instantly protective of her.

"Sarah . . . listen. That man . . . the blind one. With the . . . vampire skin. Who is he?"

"It's a long story. No time now. But don't worry about Nicholas. We have him under control. Get changed and Niall will fill you in. Hurry. And you can start that electric thingy again . . ." She wiggled her fingers. "We'll need it."

Micol resolved to ask Niall about the mysterious man. As long as he kept away from her. She zipped up the black fleece Sarah had found her, all the while contemplating the green-eyed girl's aura, its translucent white and its scarlet edges; and, she noticed only now, a core of blue. A core of sadness. Alvise's aura had a core of blue too, and she'd learnt long ago what his sorrow was – the loss of his mother. She wondered what was Sarah's story, because they all had a story of sadness, didn't they? All heirs had lost somebody, or everybody, since the culling had begun. Finally, she gratefully wrapped Sarah's scarf around her neck. It felt good. She'd been freezing.

"Ready?" Sarah asked.

"Ready."

What she could have never imagined was that all along, as she changed her clothes, Micol had stood a few yards away from her brother's mangled corpse, covered with mossy stones, waiting to be eaten by predators, animals or otherwise. And that he'd been killed by the green-eyed, striking girl who had been helping her, the girl with the white aura and its blue core of sadness.

16
What We Were Meant For

My story is in my dreams
Follow me there

"Winter will be fine. I'm sure," Alvise whispered to Niall as they walked. "My father is a good man. He won't harm her unless she's a threat, and when she tells him the Flynn motto he'll know for certain she's not."

"He'll know she was sent by the Flynns," Niall echoed Alvise's words, as if to convince himself. A flicker of doubt would always be in the back of his mind until he saw Winter again. If he ever saw her again, if he didn't die here in the Shadow World, on a suicide mission that was likely to destroy them all.

"So, fill me in."

"Do you have a few hours?" Niall smirked.

"Before something attacks? Probably not," Alvise replied. He was a whole foot taller than Niall, his cheekbones high as an elf's, slanted pale-blue eyes that betrayed his Slavic origins, like many people in the north-east of Italy. Niall had given him a heavy grey jumper to wear over his shirt, but he was still shivering, his breath condensing in white puffs.

"Alvise . . ." Micol began. She had joined him and Niall.

"What now?"

"Hey, no need to bite my head off!"

"You shouldn't be here. You'll get yourself killed." He'd had it with her. Her decision to follow him through the iris had been the last straw. She had complete disregard for her own life, her precious life as a Secret heir, putting herself in danger needlessly.

Micol saw that his aura was turning bright red. "Right, okay, following you probably wasn't a good idea. But listen. That man there, the blind one." Alvise's gaze rested on the tall, pale figure of Nicholas. "He's not a man. Not as such."

"How do you know?" Niall asked, curious.

"I can see his aura. It's black," she whispered, eyeing Nicholas with a mixture of fear and fascination.

"Black? *Mio Dio*," said Alvise, falling back into his native Italian. "Is he an Elemental? He reminds me of fire."

"Ah. He says that a lot. 'I am fire.'" Niall mocked Nicholas' deep voice. "He likes scaring people. Gets a kick out of it. He probably got it from his father. He's the son of the King of Shadows."

"He what?" Alvise stopped in his tracks, and Sean turned around briefly. He gave Niall a pointed look, having heard the last of his words.

"*Santo cielo!*" cried Micol, bringing her hands to her face. "I read stories about the King of Shadows. I thought he was just a legend . . ."

Niall placed a hand on Alvise's and Micol's shoulders,

gently pushing them along. "My grandfather told me stories about him, too. And he's real. Anyway, Nicholas is on our side. Or at least, we believe so."

Alvise ran a hand through his white-blond hair. "And you trust him?"

"No, I don't. None of us do. But we have no choice. I don't know how much you know about what's been happening ..."

"Not much. Only that we're getting slaughtered one by one and that all the lines of communication between us seem to be closed. We are very isolated. We know the Sabha are collaborating with the Surari, for some weird reason. And all of our Gamekeepers are dead."

"The Surari aren't acting of their own will. It's the King of Shadows who's behind them. He made us believe he didn't exist, that he was just a scary fairy tale to frighten the children. But here we are. Either we destroy the King of Shadows or it's all over."

"So that's why my sister sent me here. To help with this mission."

Niall shrugged. "It's always good to have an extra pair of hands."

"*Merda*," said Alvise, spitting on the ground in disgust.

Niall cleared his throat, unsure how to respond to that. "Anyway," he continued, "Nosferatu there. He turned against his father. He's taking us to him. That's how we entered the Shadow World ... he let us in. He repented."

"Repented, huh?"

"So we believe. So we have to believe. The King of Shadows punished him for his betrayal, and he lost his sight. You should have seen him ... I've never seen anyone suffer as much ... and I hope I never do again."

"So he hates his father. And he's leading you to him."

"Yes. Nobody knew where to find the King of Shadows. My friend Mike and I ..." He winced, like every time he spoke about Mike. He took a deep breath. Mike Prudhomme, the other Midnight Gamekeeper besides Sean, had been killed in the final battle with the Mermen that took place in Islay weeks ago. Niall would never forget how he died – saving Sarah from certain death. He knew why he'd done it – not only for Sarah, but as his final show of loyalty to the Secret Families and to the world. Mike was the most selfless person he'd ever met, and his best friend. Niall's heart throbbed. "Mike was a Gamekeeper. He got killed. Anyway, we sort of guessed the King of Shadows was somewhere in Eastern Europe, but we could never have found him had it not been for Nicholas. We could have never entered the Shadow World. I don't know how you made it ... Nicholas said nobody could, unless he allowed it."

A shadow of pain passed over Alvise's handsome face. "My sister's powers are a mystery. If only she didn't have to pay such a terrible price for them."

"I'd heard about Lucrezia's power. How old is she now?"

"Sixteen. My age," Micol replied for Alvise, frowning. Lucrezia's predicament made her angry, furious, really. She didn't know who to be angry with exactly, so she used the Vendramin family as her own personal whipping boy for everything that had happened.

"You are fifteen," Alvise said. "A child. A reckless child."

"I'll be sixteen in two days!"

Alvise ignored her. His face was dark. "Lucrezia is very unwell. She hasn't been awake for years. All she does is dream. Since the Sabha did what they did to her ..."

Micol's eyes studied Alvise closely. "What do you mean? How . . . What did the Sabha do? Did they hurt her?"

"It's my family's business."

"But . . ."

"Micol. I said it's my family's business."

"You keep her in the palace. You keep her asleep, a prisoner!" Micol hissed. "Just like you keep me prisoner!"

"You have no idea what you're talking about!" Alvise snapped. "My sister would die if she saw the light. As for you, we are just trying to save your bloody life!"

"Yes, right. You need her! You keep her inside because you need her to dream for you!"

"I'm not even going to reply to that, Micol," said Alvise. "You know nothing of me, nothing of us."

For once, Micol was quiet. The pain in Alvise's eyes was palpable. She knew she'd gone too far. "I'm sorry," she whispered, but he cut her short.

"Tell me, Niall. What about the others? Who are they?"

"That's Sarah Midnight, from the Midnight family. They're Scottish. They keep themselves to themselves . . ."

"I've heard of them."

"Have you? I thought hardly anybody on the continent knew of their existence."

Alvise studied Sarah as she walked ahead. She was striking, with that endless raven hair and her slender body, aloof and silent, like someone who has many secrets and a lot on her mind. "Somebody mentioned her to me once. What are her powers?"

"She's a Dreamer. She can dissolve demons with her hands . . . the Blackwater, she calls it. Also, her eyes are deadly, if she wants them to be."

"Better stay on her good side, then," Alvise jested, but there was an edge of truth in his joke. "The blonde girl?"

"That's Elodie Brun, heir to the Brun family. Her powers are pretty incredible," Niall said with genuine admiration. "She's psychic, she feels things before they happen, and kills demons with the poison in her breath. Once I was at the receiving end of her kiss, and it wasn't fun, I can tell you. I suppose you are an heir too," he continued, nodding towards Micol.

"Yes. I'm heir to the Falco family. My brother and I are the last of the Falcos."

Niall did his best to hide his surprise and horror in hearing Micol's second name. He kept walking, trying to keep his face expressionless. Sean and Sarah hadn't heard her, thankfully – they were striding on.

Maybe it was a coincidence. Maybe it was another branch of the same family. "What's your brother's name?"

"Tancredi Falco," she replied, and Niall felt queasy. No coincidence. No other branch of the same family. Micol's brother was the man they'd just killed. The man who wanted to murder Sarah.

"I had another brother, Ranieri, but he's dead now. The Azasti killed him. Tancredi wasn't in Venice with me when it happened. He'd left. He said he couldn't tell me where he was going, that he didn't want me to know. He didn't want me to follow him and get killed."

"He told me where he was going," said Alvise, his expression hard.

"What? He told you, and you never told me?" Micol looked pained. "He's my brother!"

"The Azasti had gone to his head. He was crazy. What he said made no sense."

"My brother isn't crazy!" Micol shouted, multi-coloured lights appearing on her fingertips and around her cropped head. Micol kept talking about her brother in the present tense, Niall noticed miserably. *Of course she would.*

"Whatever this is about, can you save it for later?" called Sean. "We need to keep moving. Niall, did you fill them in?"

"Yes. Sean, I need a word with you."

But it was too late. Alvise's voice resounded clear, for everyone to hear.

"Look, Tancredi said he had to find and kill Sarah Midnight. He's the one who mentioned her to me. She was going to destroy the world, or whatever. A lot of nonsense."

They all stopped in their tracks.

"My brother wanted to kill Sarah?" Micol exclaimed. "Why?"

Sarah felt her heart sinking. Now she'd have to face what she'd done. Her guilt. She'd have to look her remorse in the eye.

What were the odds?

"You are Tancredi's sister?" Sarah stood square in front of Micol.

"Yes. Where is he? Did you see him?"

"I killed him," said Sarah. It was surprisingly easy to say. And quickly met with a fantasy about taking a knife to her own skin, to punish herself for what she'd done.

A pause, a sharp intake of breath. "What?" whispered Micol.

"I killed him. I'm sorry."

Micol was in shock, eerily calm. "Tancredi is dead," she said, as if trying to wrap her head around that terrible truth. "Why did you kill my brother?"

Anger burnt inside Sarah again. "Because he wanted to cut my throat, Micol. And he tried and nearly succeeded. What would you have done?"

"Why? Why did he want to kill you?"

"He was convinced I would help the Surari. The King of Shadows."

And then the tears came, flowing hot out of Micol's eyes, her chest heaving. Suddenly, she looked like the abandoned child she was, and Sarah's heart bled.

All of a sudden, though, the girl's features twisted in anger. "He must have been right! My brother must have been right! He was a good man, a wise man," she protested, her voice interrupted by hiccupping sobs.

"Tancredi was right, in a way. That guy," Sarah pointed at Nicholas, "did try to lure me into marrying him. Because he's a sick bastard. But I was lucky. Nicholas saw the light," she added sarcastically. Nicholas was close, his blind eyes staring where the voices were coming from, his expression unmoved. "I told Tancredi, but he didn't believe me."

"This is crazy." Alvise touched his head briefly. "Tancredi was ill. He was mad."

"He was mad if he thought I was going to marry a demon," Sarah snarled. "Like I said, he tried to kill me three times. The last time, I cut his throat."

Silence.

"He was all I had left!" Micol cried out, and the sparks coming off her fingers increased in intensity until they wrapped around her like a cloak of lighting. Her cropped hair stood on end.

"Oh, here we go. Another Falco trying to kill me!" Sarah said, trying to hide her guilt, and failing. She'd killed that girl's brother, for God's sake. She had. Not a demon. Not Nicholas. She had. She could have given him one more chance, had she not given in to her fury, her fear.

But she'd killed him.

"Micol, listen to me. Sarah defended herself," Niall began.

"She did what she had to do. Get over it," Sean intervened, his cruel words shaking them all to the core. Sean wasn't heartless, but any threat to Sarah, in his eyes, was to be destroyed without second chances.

"You killed all that was left of my family!" Micol screamed again.

"Duck!" Alvise shouted.

All of a sudden there was a blinding flash and the forest exploded in a rainbow of colours, deadly lightning coming from Micol's hands. "There's nobody left," Micol sobbed. More charges left her as her body tensed and arched to release its power. The charges hit all around Micol like a deadly fan.

Sarah dived behind a tree, her body telling her what to do before her mind could register what was happening. A burnt smell hit her nostrils as she lay on the undergrowth, shaking with terror. She glimpsed from behind the tree, trying to gauge if she could get up or if she'd be hit again by Micol's lightning. Then she saw Alvise holding Micol in his arms. Micol was unconscious, and a bright-red flower of blood bloomed on her collarbone and soaked her scarf red. She'd lost her ballerina slippers, and her small feet looked like those of a child.

Please, let her be alive, Sarah prayed, and sprang to her feet, frenziedly checking to see if her friends were hurt. Nicholas and Elodie stood unharmed, but Sean was holding his arm, a gash on his black jacket. Niall's face was bleeding. Only then she spotted burnt tracks on the grass and in the trees around her.

"Is she breathing?" she asked Alvise. Her voice trembled.

"Yes. She'll come to in a little bit."

"I suppose I have you to thank."

"Don't thank me. I did it because I trust Niall, and Niall trusts you," Alvise replied. "Micol has to accept what happened. Her power is pretty strong, but she loses it quickly. You would have ended up killing her."

Micol whimpered.

"How did you stop her?" Sean asked, grimacing. Sarah was at his side at once, holding his arm. His wound was just a graze, but it looked sore.

Alvise gestured to an arrow, lying discarded and bloody on the ground. Only then they noticed that Micol's shoulder was bloodied. "I only nicked her," he said.

"Can you carry her?" said Sean, grimacing. "We need to—"

But he never finished the sentence.

"They are coming." Elodie's voice rose clear and strong.

"Surari?" Sean's *sgian-dubh* ready at once.

The French girl nodded.

"When?"

"Now."

"In a circle! Micol in the middle!" Sean managed to shout, and then they heard the roar.

17
On the Other Side

A new world and I pray
My old world will be there
When I wake up from this dream

Winter's world went black. One minute her eyes were on Niall, locked together like they were one. The next, she was spinning somewhere dark and viscous, not knowing up from down. Maybe they'd hit her over the head. Maybe the stranger with the bow and arrow who'd come out of that strange twirling golden spiral had killed her and this was heaven. But no, it had been Niall pushing her inside the golden door. She remembered. It had been Niall sending her away.

Why was everything black? Was she unconscious? Maybe she was asleep and inside a nightmare. She was turning and turning and turning inside a tunnel, her body carried by a force stronger than herself.

And then a golden light appeared from somewhere.

She heard a thud, but she didn't immediately realise that the noise she'd heard had been her skull hitting something hard. A terrible pain exploded on the side of her head, and she could feel her body again, stiff and throbbing. A wave of nausea hit her, and she squeezed her eyes shut, trying to regain some composure.

When she finally opened her eyes, the first thing she saw was her silver hair and a hand – her hand – covered in blood. A golden glow was reflected on her fingers, and her face felt cold and sore, leaning on something tough and slightly uneven. A confusion of voices made its way into her ears, in her mind – words she didn't understand, the voice of a woman, then a man, and footsteps – and arms around her shoulders, around her body.

She was too sore, too confused to do anything but whimper. And then she saw the blades pointed at her face, and she froze.

"*Chi sei? Da dove vieni?*" said a voice. To Winter it was gibberish. She had no idea what language it was. She had no idea where she was. She had no idea who was at the other end of the blades pointing at her face, her chest. She raised her gaze and saw two dark-skinned men. The expression on their faces said that they would not hesitate to pierce her there and then.

"Where am I?" she managed to whisper, her instinct telling her that it was best if she spoke, if she at least told them that she was human and not demon.

"*Parla inglese,*" one of the men said.

"Who are you?" said another voice, in English. It was neither of the two men. Winter moved upwards an inch, hoping that the blades would move and let her sit up – and they did, but the daggers remained unsheathed and pointed as she replied.

She looked around her. The question in English had come from an older man with grey hair and a white beard, immaculately dressed in what looked like a black fighting suit. His eyes were fearsome, and Winter's heart skipped a beat. "My name is Winter Shaw. I'm from Scotland."

"Surari?"

Winter shook her head. It was probably too early in their acquaintance to tell them about her real nature, half human and half water Elemental. After her experience with the Midnights and their horror of what they called half-breeds, she was not keen to reveal her origins.

"Secret heir?" the man asked again. She shook her head once more.

"Human."

"You came out of the iris. Nothing like this has happened before. Only Alvise comes back to us from the iris."

Winter shifted uncomfortably on the hard floor. Her head hurt. A sudden noise, like a wave of the sea, rose behind her. She turned backwards to see that the golden iris twirling behind her had gone. She was alone and she had no way to get back. Niall had pushed her in without a word of explanation. He'd sent her away.

To her dismay, tears prickled behind her eyes. She didn't want to appear weak to these strangers, but she couldn't help it. Frightened tears began rolling down her cheeks as the realisation that she and Niall were apart rose inside her.

"Are you hurt?" asked the older man.

Winter was too choked to speak. She shook her head again, miserably.

The silver-haired man raised a hand, and the blades pointed towards her receded, but they were not put away.

"Can you stand? And please don't just shake your head," the man continued. His English was surprisingly good, though heavily accented. He rolled his "r" like a Scotsman. Who was this man?

"Yes. I can stand," Winter replied, and climbed to her feet. As she did so, she swayed a little. One of the men came to sustain her, and she saw the admiration in his gaze as he took in her long, silvery hair and the pure grey of her eyes.

"Where am I?"

"You are in Venice. In Palazzo Vendramin. My name is Guglielmo Vendramin. I am the head of this family. Do you know how you got here? And why?"

"I was in the Shadow World . . ."

Vendramin gasped, a deep gasp that seemed to steal all the air in the room. "You were in the world of the Surari?" His eyes were suddenly menacing. Winter froze in fear, and then she remembered what Niall had told her to say. "*Onoir, clan agus farraige*." She struggled with the words in the unknown language, and hoped with all her heart she'd made herself understood.

"The Flynn motto. Did the Flynns send you? From the Shadow World? It makes no sense!"

"Niall Flynn sent me here to keep me safe. He told me to say that to you, so you would know I'm not an enemy."

At that moment, a stream of whispers and sounds and nonsensical words filled the air, coming from somewhere behind her. Winter turned towards the source of the noise, and for the first time since she'd landed on the mosaic floor she took in her surroundings. She was in a huge room, half empty of furniture, with gilded ceilings and long, silky gold and green drapes at the windows. And in the middle of the room, lying on an immaculate bed, was a girl, still, her eyes closed, but whispering, her lips moving incessantly. All of a sudden, the flow of whispers turned into words, in English.

"She belongs to a place of sea and wind and she was in the Shadow World with Alvise," the girl said, and then started whispering again.

Vendramin staggered. His face lost all colour. "Lucrezia . . . You sent your brother to the Shadow World?" he exclaimed.

The whispering stopped and the girl in the bed spoke, again in English. "I sent him there to fight alongside Sarah Midnight and the brave ones. The seal will help us here."

"The seal? Who is the seal?" Vendramin asked, but Lucrezia did not answer.

Instead, Winter looked at the old man with her sea-grey eyes. "I am the seal," she said.

18
My Brother

Only you know what it was like
Back there, back then
When we were safe

As she looked at the stony mound before her, Micol remembered the men she'd once called her brothers.

Micol, the girl who climbed trees and roamed the countryside, the girl who had jumped fences and ridden horses since the age of eight, was scared of water. The sun shone on her hair as she sat on the shore, watching her brothers dive and swim. Ranieri swam like a fish. His tanned, strong body glistened in the sunshine, his black hair wet and swept back. He was in his early twenties, tall and strong and her sister's idol. Micol was desperate to impress him.

"Micol! *Vieni, dai!*" he said once again. "It's beautiful!" Ranieri couldn't believe his fearless sister had such a phobia, not when all of them had been swimming in the lake since they were babies. She knew that later he'd tease her around the dinner table. And it hurt.

But she couldn't help it. She jumped up, determined, and took wobbly steps on the pebbles towards the water. She wet her toes and forced herself inside the lake up to her knees. And then the wet feeling of weeds and slimy floating things around her legs began, and she grimaced, panic twisting her stomach, her resolution waning.

And then, one day, when she was ten years old, Tancredi simply convinced her. She still had no idea how he'd done it.

"Take my hand. I won't let you go," he'd said, and something in his voice made her really, really want to do as he said, made her believe that she could do as he said. She was frozen with fear and all her limbs were rigid. Her heart was beating in a crazy rhythm, but she still took his hand.

They jumped together, and like he promised, he never let go.

She emerged spluttering and scared, but triumphant.

That was her brother, Tancredi Falco. Sweet and kind and brave.

And now he was cold and alone, dead in another world, never to see his home again. A memory of him, sunshine and water and a strong, sweet hand holding hers, was all that Micol had left.

19
Tigers of the North

If only I could go back
To our home in the sun
Weave again the threads
Of life the way it was

Sarah had heard that roar once before, in her garden in Edinburgh. That night her cat Shadow had been mangled, left as a little bundle of bones and bloodied black fur. That night her friend Bryony had also learned the truth of the mystery that surrounded Sarah, and both their lives had changed forever.

Now, once again, Sarah took her place in the circle, facing out. In the middle of the circle this time was not Bryony but Micol, still unconscious. Another roar came from the trees. A trickle of sweat ran down Sarah's back as the branches of the oaks above their heads danced and swayed, and they all instinctively jerked their heads towards the sound.

But the first demon-tiger came from the opposite

direction, making its way from behind a fern bush, slowly, leisurely, like it could take its time to kill. They gazed on the monstrous creature. Sarah remembered it well – something between a tiger and a hyena, muscles rippling under its fur, a mouth full of row after row of pointed teeth. This one was white, and two enormous fangs sat at either side of its mouth. It reminded Sarah of a sabre-toothed tiger. Another growl came from the back of its throat, its eyes narrowing into two black slits. Its instinct told it to kill and devour.

"Don't break the circle! There might be more around us!" whispered Sarah. Beside her, Sean was already tracing the runes, little red sparks dancing around his *sgian-dubh*.

Sarah, Sean and Niall faced the demon, while Elodie, Nicholas and Alvise had their backs to it. It took them all their willpower not to turn around, but they listened to Sarah. The Surari advanced slowly, and its white fur started turning brown and green against the grass and leaves scattered on the ground.

Camouflage, Sarah remembered.

All of a sudden, without a sound, the demon-tiger pounced on Niall with bone-shattering force, digging its claws into his chest. As soon as it touched Niall's jacket the beast turned blue. It raised its head, rows of yellow teeth glistening with drool, ready to bite Niall's face, but Sean's runes hit the Surari, scarlet ribbons taking shape in the air. The creature stood paralysed, its teeth touching Niall's cheek, its saliva dribbling on its face.

Sarah could see the terror in Niall's eyes. Her hands were ready to strike with the Blackwater, but she didn't dare move in case she disturbed Sean's concentration – a second would have been enough for the beast to snap its jaws shut. Wounds appeared on the creature's throat as the scarlet ribbons from Sean's runes began cutting its skin, black blood pouring over Niall's face and chest.

"Sarah! Now!" Sean called, interrupting the flow of Ancient words. Sarah threw herself on the Surari and dug her hands into its fur with a scream of fury. The beast growled and fell on Niall, burying him under its huge weight, its eyes open and staring. It started shuddering, growling in pain, Blackwater sprouting from its mouth, its ears and its black nostrils, mixing with black blood.

Sarah kept digging her hands into its fur without pity, growling like a Surari herself. She threw her weight sideways, carrying the beast with her so that Niall would be free. As it touched the ground, the Surari went from red to dark green again.

Niall lifted himself up, one bleeding hand supporting him, the other feeling the ground, looking for his *sgian-dubh*. Then he fell again, agony contorting his face. He clasped both hands on his chest. The Surari was contorting itself in torment, black blood and the black liquid from its weeping skin mixing and soaking the ground. A seizure tightened its muscles in painful spasms until it dissolved with a final gush of Blackwater.

Sarah took a series of breaths until she could finally speak. "Niall, are you okay?"

"Yes. Nothing a little time won't heal."

"Watch out!" shouted Sean. Sarah and Niall turned around to see Alvise, Elodie and Nicholas standing in front of another two demon-tigers, camouflaged black against the dark backdrop of the bushes. Nicholas' hands sparked blue and a wall of flames rose between them and the demon-tigers. But the bolder of the two Surari jumped through, narrowly missing Elodie, thin smoke rising from its singed fur.

"*Niryani!*" Elodie shouted, and threw herself at the creature's side, stabbing it repeatedly, drawing black blood. The beast shuddered, throwing Elodie off and nearly crushing her with its weight, when suddenly it fell. An arrow jutted out of the Surari's mouth.

"Alvise," a small voice said. Micol had come to. Alvise dragged her to her feet, trying to lead her away from the wall of fire, but the second demon-tiger pounced on him, its fur rippling green as it left the shadows, then blue while through the flames, then black again, and he had to let go of Micol. She stood in a daze, still too weak to call on her power.

Elodie was on the demon at once, her poison seeping inside it. The beast tried to snarl, but its snarl turned into a yelp. As the poison worked its way into the Surari's veins, the demon-tiger pounced once more, blindly trying to destroy everything in its path – and in front of him was Micol, still stunned, defenceless. It happened in a moment: the beast opened its jaws, its fangs ready to sink into Micol's throat, when Sarah jumped on the creature, rolling over with it and away from Micol. She sank her hands into its fur. Already weakened by Elodie's poison, with one last shiver and a deep, painful howl, the demon-tiger was still. For a second, Sarah's eyes met Micol's.

Atonement, she thought. She'd saved Micol's life.

Sarah let herself fall back on her heels, but before she could take a breath the demon that had been hiding among the branches of the tree above them – the one who'd made the first warning noise – finally struck. It let itself fall on the ground and clawed the first thing it saw – Sarah. She fell on her back, the Surari upon her. She felt her breastbone breaking, and cried in pain. The Surari growled and poised itself to bite, its jaws pouring black saliva over her face ...

And then it stopped.

It stepped off Sarah, surveying the scene with its malicious eyes, and growled once more. Nicholas followed the noise. He growled, too, like a demon would, and grabbed the Surari by its fur. He lifted it off him as if it'd been nothing more than a big cat, hurling it against the ground as hard as he could. They heard a crack, and the beast was still. Nicholas had no power over those Surari; his father was in control now. They would not kill him, not while Nicholas was doing his father's bidding, but they would hurt him, and his father would take pleasure from it.

Sarah clung to her bloodied chest, her heart and soul filled with terror. The demon-tiger had been about to bite her head off, but it had spared her. Just like the demon at the petrol station had done.

Twice her life had been spared.

And then she came to the natural conclusion, and the realisation chilled her to the bone: *They need me. They have a purpose for me.*

Her eyes met Sean's across the mauled carcass of the demon-tiger, and they spoke without words. She dragged herself upright – and that's when she saw Elodie's gaze upon her, her expression unreadable. Quickly, Elodie looked away.

"Thank you, Alvise," the French girl said instead, looking to the newcomer. "The Surari would have killed me had it not been for you."

"Is that all you can do? Shoot arrows?" Nicholas said. "Like a Gamekeeper?"

"He lost his powers," Micol cried out. She was afraid of the son of the King of Shadows, but she was also furious. For her brothers, for her parents, for all those who'd died. For herself. "They killed his mother in front of him, and it was demons like you who did it! So don't dare speak to him like that!"

Alvise looked at Micol, surprised. Was she not supposed to hate him? "It's okay, Micol. It doesn't matter," he whispered, but his eyes told a different story.

"And in case you didn't notice, he can hit a bull's eye with an arrow from a mile away!" Micol's Italian accent was now stronger than ever, and her cheeks burned red, her hands crackled.

"Stop it! You'll get yourself killed!" Alvise snapped.

"Ignore him, Alvise. Is that what happened to you?" Sean intervened. "You lost your powers?"

Alvise nodded. "Yes. Overnight."

"And what was it? Your power?"

"Does it matter?"

Sean stroked the back of his head, as if he were making casual conversation. "So people can lose their powers . . . and maybe gain them too?"

Sarah tensed. She understood Sean's deep, deep need to find out about his family of origin, but it disquieted her.

Sarah's heart filled with tenderness for him. In his mind, so much depended on him having inherited powers or not. To her, Sean was just Sean, with or without Secret blood, with or without powers.

"I'm sorry . . . I have no idea. Why?" Alvise replied, tightening his quiver across his chest once more.

Sean shook his head, disappointment filling him. "Never mind."

Sarah looked for Micol's eyes. A part of her was hoping that saving the Italian girl's life would have granted her forgiveness. Finally, Micol approached.

"You saved me," she said.

"Yes."

"Thank you," Micol replied, looking down. Maybe, in time, she could forgive, but she would never forget.

"Micol," said Sean, "your brother asked me to look after you. I'll do my best, I promise."

Micol bit her lip and didn't reply.

"Let's go," Seen commanded, lifting his backpack.

Sarah didn't usually like open displays of affection – her feelings ran too deep to be paraded for everyone to see – but she came to his side as they walked, and her fingers brushed his for a moment.

"I love you," she murmured, so low that nobody but Sean could hear her.

20

Another Nail in
Our Cross

I believe that's the thing with guardian angels
You can't see them,
But they're there

Sean

Sarah's eyes are haunted. I know she's trying to block out
what happened with Tancredi. I wish I could hold her in my
arms forever, take all that's cruel and painful out of her life.
Shelter her from everything. Let her play her music and do
what she loves to do in her home in Edinburgh, live a sweet,
happy life without anger, without violence, without constant
danger.

But I can't.

It used to be me guiding her, keeping her strong,
comforting her. Then it was Nicholas, during that terrible

time when he exercised the mind-moulding on her and made her dependent on him. Now it's her, it's Sarah who looks after herself. She shoulders her dreams, and these horrific days, and the kills and the fear and the pain. She still looks for me, though, for my hand to hold. She still needs me, but she's not helpless any more. She's never been. It's just that she didn't know how strong she was.

There was a time when she knew nothing of all this, when the truth about the Midnights and the Secret Families hit her like a kick in the face, so hard she fell; but a core of strength was always there.

I remember the first time we met. I remember the first thing I thought when I saw her green eyes, the proud way she tilted her chin, like Harry Midnight. At that moment I thought she was strong, and I was right.

We walk side by side, and I long to take her hand. We don't need to talk. We know what the other person is thinking. We're drained, and hungry, and the sun, though high in the sky, offers no heat at all and hardly any light. I want to stop and light a fire for Sarah, wrap her in a sleeping bag and give her hot tea and food. I want to take the pallor away from her face and put some colour back on her cheeks. I want us to be alone, and I want to kiss her and hold her until dawn. But none of this is possible.

I catch a glimpse of Micol Falco. Her eyes are swollen from crying. I feel sorry for her, but that doesn't mean I won't hurt her if ever she shows a hint of wanting to harm Sarah. Her dying brother entrusted her to me, and I'll do my best to do what he asked – he was, after all, a Secret Heir and I'm a Gamekeeper. I have a loyalty to all of the Families. But my first loyalty is and always will be to Sarah. There's a lot more at stake than Micol's life, as cruel as this sounds. There's a lot more at stake than Tancredi's dying wish, the man who stalked us throughout and tried to kill Sarah three times. The second time he tried, on Islay, it was a miracle she survived. He'd had it coming.

I slow my steps to walk beside Nicholas. There's something I need to know. He's marching on, his arm through Elodie's, his steps so much steadier than they used to be. He's slowly getting used to his blindness, which is good for us. The steadier he is, the faster we walk.

"Is there a cure?" I say without ceremony.

He knows at once what I'm talking about. "There's only one way to cure the Azasti, but there are reasons not to use this remedy. There are ... side effects," he grumbles, his unseeing eyes closed and his face tilted up, as if smelling the wind. Once again I notice the sheer size of him – he's a fearsome enemy in every way. And part of me believes he's still an enemy, and he always will be.

"What is it?"

"This I can't tell you."

"What is it, Nicholas?" It's Elodie. My heart skips a beat as I catch a glimpse of her hand resting on Nicholas' arm as she leads him. Her fingernails are blue. A terrible thought hits me again, but I can't quite formulate it in my mind. It's too cruel. I just can't look it in the face. Maybe if I deny with all my might, it'll go away.

"I can't say. And anyway, it's impossible to use. Like I said, there are side effects. Consequences."

"What is worse? To face these consequences ... or to die from the Azasti?" Elodie whispers, her French accent strong. I throw a glance at her out of the corner of my eye. She sees me looking, and controls herself – but it's too late. I've seen the terror in her eyes.

She knows what's happening to her. We all know, I suspect, but nobody comes out and says it.

Another nail in our cross.

21
Mine Is This Path

My mother and my father
And all those before me
Their story was written
In the blood that is mine

When they thought it was safe, they stopped in a sheltered thicket to rest. The others settled down gladly though cautiously, and let their backpacks fall to the ground. A water bottle and a packet of biscuits soon passed from person to person. Further from the group, Sean sat purposefully in front of Nicholas, and Sarah joined them.

"Right. Time to answer some questions, Nicholas." Sean always said his name like it was a curse, or an insult.

"What questions?" He crossed his long legs in front of him. His face was still scarred from when his skin had ripped open during the brain fury, the torture his father inflicted on those he wished to punish, the fire in the brain that caused terrible pain and even death, but the marks were fading, now light pink on white. Once again he was only wearing a T-shirt, his tolerance threshold against the cold a lot higher than any of them. Sean noticed Nicholas had lost a lot of weight, but the muscles in his arms still flexed at every move. His strength was beyond natural.

"Well, I have quite a few, I suppose. Mainly about your father."

"Sure. I'll tell you all there is to know." It was a lie, of course, but Nicholas was a good liar.

"Can he hear you while you talk to us? Will he know what you're saying?"

"Not if I shut him out."

Sean paused for a moment, still studying his face. His eyes were perfectly black, like a raven's wing. They would not reveal his secrets.

"Nicholas. If you're lying to us I'll rip you apart. I swear," Sarah said in a low, menacing voice. She'd been quiet until then, listening intently. Sean gazed at her. Once again he considered how much she had changed. Ruthless, was the way he could have described her sometimes, but it frightened him. When they'd first met he'd thought that what she was going through was like taking a rose and dipping it in steel, and he now saw that he'd been right.

A rose made of steel, and tempered in tears.

"What does your father look like?" Sean asked. "How will we know it's him?"

"It's difficult to explain if you've never seen him." Nicholas paused, as if gathering his thoughts.

"Try us," said Sarah.

"My father's form is not always fixed. It changes. He can take different shapes, and sometimes all of them at once."

Sean frowned. "How can we hurt something as powerful as that? There must be a way. You must know of his weaknesses."

"There is only one way to kill him. One weak spot. Everybody has one, don't they?"

Sean said nothing, but his eyes went instinctively to Nicholas' throat, where the blood was pulsing beneath the skin. *Yes, everybody has a weak spot.*

"My father is a spirit, his life force permanently confined in one place, this place. But he can will his spirit to become different shapes."

"As in, real shapes? Physical shapes?" Sarah asked.

"Yes. His power is such that he can make these shapes tangible, becoming a physical body, more or less. Say he decides to be a bull. Then his horns can gut a bear in an instant."

Sarah's eyes widened at the mention of horns. What monster awaited them? She met Sean's gaze and for a moment, they shared the same fear.

"When he takes the form of lava, he burns. He does have a physical presence. And in the middle of it sits his essence. His soul, whatever you want to call it. That's where we can hurt him. And only when he stops changing form, when his shape is definite, even just for a few moments, that's when he's weakest and it's best to strike."

"Are you talking blades or Secret powers, or what? Can you stab the King of Shadows?" Sean sniggered. "Just like that?"

"Yes. You can stab him or pierce him with an arrow, and you can use Secret powers on him. If these are enough to actually kill him, I don't know, but they can certainly hurt him. His weakest point is between the eyes. Strike there.

But first we need to get through the Guardians around his dwelling. They are part of his Valaya in the Shadow World, and they are more frightening and fiercer than any demon you've seen yet. Some will attack our bodies, some our minds."

"Our minds?" Sean asked.

"Psychic attacks. Ever experienced one?"

Sean's heart skipped a beat. He had. In Japan. And he didn't want to recall it. He said nothing. "We need to try our utmost to stay together and face the King of Shadows together. It might be that a blade or an arrow or our own individual powers . . . and skills," he corrected himself quickly, "are not enough."

Sarah nodded. "All of us together will have more of a chance than any of us individually," she repeated, trying to sound matter-of-fact, but a terrible memory ran through her mind: the battle of the Mermen on Islay. Back then, it had been impossible to stay together. What were the chances of them being able to now? The vision of one of them – maybe herself, or Sean, or Niall, or Elodie – standing alone in front of the King of Shadows cut her mind, and she was afraid.

22
The Memory of the Sea

When all that's left between us
Is silence and longing

Winter was brushing Lucrezia's hair, softly following the long, fair strands with a silver brush. It was her third day there, and already she was fond of the ailing girl, so much so that the housekeeper had allowed her to see to Lucrezia's needs, under her watchful gaze, of course.

Since Winter had arrived, Lucrezia had made no mention of talking to her friends in the Shadow World, and her hopes to somehow contact Niall were crumbling.

A few days before, Vendramin had taken her into his study, where she'd sat surrounded by hanging tapestries and swords and various weapons, as if she'd entered another era. The two had chatted before the topic quickly descended to thoughts of her friends and Guglielmo Vendramin's son.

"And your friends are there to kill the King of Shadows and end all this?" Vendramin asked.

"Yes."

"Can we help them?"

"If Lucrezia opens another iris, yes, I suppose. Can we ask her?"

"Lucrezia's ways are mysterious. She decides when she is ready to help us, to speak to us. She sends my son Alvise hunting wherever she thinks he's needed. We cannot rush her."

"Alvise? The blond boy with the bow and arrow?"

"Yes," Vendramin replied, and looked down, suddenly reserved, as if his feelings for his son were too deep, too raw for her to see.

"You must be very proud of him," Winter said gently.

His eyes gleamed as he leaned forward in his chair. The two were seated on leather armchairs as soft as butter before a log fire. "I certainly am," Vendramin responded. "And your parents must be proud of you."

"My mother is dead. My father is in the sea somewhere," said Winter without sadness. She had a calm sense of acceptance for the way life unfolded.

"Lucrezia said you'd help us speak to my son and the others in the Shadow World."

"I'm not sure what she meant, Lord Vendramin. If there's anything I can do to help you I will, but I don't know how."

"Conte Vendramin, actually. My family are fond of grand titles. Some good they'll do us when every one of us are dead, the victims of a demon's bite."

"Don't say that. It's not going to happen."

Vendramin stood in front of the window, looking over the Grand Canal. "Only last year we never dreamed this would happen." He opened his arms. "We never thought the Secret

Families would have been decimated, entire generations dead, but here we are."

Winter lowered her head. She wasn't sure what to say. Her heart and soul screamed at her to hope. They pulled her towards the light; it was her nature. But this man who'd seen so much, lost so much, was draining the last of her strength.

Winter cleared her throat. "I'd like to spend some more time with Lucrezia, if it's okay with you. Maybe she'll speak to me. Maybe I can find out what she meant." She paused. "Maybe together we can contact Alvise . . . and Niall in the Shadow World." Winter's heart skipped a beat at saying his name.

Vendramin nodded. "Yes. Please do. I'll tell Cosima you are allowed at her side even without her supervision."

"Thank you," Winter said. Hesitantly, she walked to the elderly man and placed a hand on his shoulder. He didn't pull away.

23

A Feast of Souls

You feed off me and I let you
It's a slow death and yet
We call this love

Sean sat upright, his back against a tree and his eyes burning
from lack of sleep. The light was cold and livid, and the sky
wintry white. He wondered why the Bialoweza forest was
under snow in the human world, but not this one – and
why there seemed to be a few hours' difference between
human time and shadow time. Or so they thought. But who
knew? Maybe time here ran faster, or slower. Maybe it'd be
like in one of those fairy tales in Harry's book, where a man
went to a fairy feast and when he returned to his home
three hundred years had passed. He wondered how many
other little differences there were between the two worlds
that they might not notice now but that would later come
to haunt them.

A thought hit him: they were all being given the chance to

experience how human beings used to live before the Secret Families rose, when there was only one world and the Surari ruled it. Before the Secret children, the human tribes were constantly besieged, their lives so full of danger that they had no time left for anything but survival. It must have been like this – cold and dark and frightening. No shelter and never feeling quite safe enough for sleep.

Which sounded a lot like his life as a Gamekeeper, really.

Sean closed his eyes for a moment and took a deep breath. His body was battered and bruised, aching in ways he never thought possible, and the lack of sleep was slowly wearing him out. He feared he'd become so weary that he would not be able to think clearly, and would end up making the wrong decisions. But he had to keep going.

Absent-mindedly, he scratched his neck. Something wriggled against his skin. He scratched again. Suddenly, he let out a small groan and jumped to his feet, ripping his own jacket off in a frenzy.

"Demon-leeches!" he shouted. "Wake up!"

"Sean!" Sarah screamed, on her feet at once, her hands already scalding. She saw he was bare-chested, his clothes in a heap on the grass. She followed his gaze to the nest of clothes. Something was struggling beneath them, something tiny and black and writhing.

"Stay away!" Sean shouted, opening his arms to stop his friends from getting too close to the creature. He took a step back but it was too late. The demon had appeared from beneath the heap of clothes and bounded towards him with deadly speed, attaching itself to his skin. He ripped it off just one instant before it managed to sink its teeth into him, and kept tearing at his collarbone, scratching his skin. He took hold of his *sgian-dubh* and began murmuring words, gazing around to spot more demon-leeches. Not far away, Niall had started singing his deadly song, his eyes half-closed, arms outstretched. As he sang, a strange, unnatural wind made the trees shiver. Sean turned to face Sarah and saw something writhing in her hair, black against black. He leapt, but Elodie was faster. She ripped the Surari off Sarah's hair, taking a lock of her hair with it. They watched in horror as the creature squirmed on the ground, black hairs — Sarah's — trailing from its body.

Niall's song was slowly killing it as it gasped like a fish out of water, with its round mouth full of minuscule suckers open and ready to attach itself. Sarah threw herself at the creature, ready to finish it off and melt it into Blackwater — but two things happened at once: another leech fell from a branch and bit Niall's neck, interrupting his song, and the Surari on the ground, free from the torture of the song, righted itself before Sarah could touch it — towards Elodie's face. On impulse, Sarah threw herself in front of Elodie, and the demon landed on Sarah's neck, sinking into her skin with a horrible squelch.

Niall tore the leech away before it could properly attach itself, but his song had been interrupted so abruptly that he stood in a daze, panting, trying to summon his power once more.

On the ground, Sarah clawed at her neck as the Surari's black body swelled with her blood. Elodie kneeled beside her at once. She knew she couldn't place her lips on the creature as it would simply attach itself to her mouth, but she went to stab it with her dagger. She was about to lower the blade when another demon-leech fell on her head, and she missed. She jumped up, horrified. The Surari fell to the earth but pounced as soon as it landed, attaching itself to her thigh ... and then the creature fell off her and onto the ground.

It didn't want her blood.

Then, the realisation hit her. Everything slowed down around Elodie, as if the world was suddenly in slow motion. The Surari knew. It knew that her blood was tainted, ruined. She didn't need any more proof now.

As Niall's song rose higher and grew more lethal, Elodie winced and covered her ears. A few seconds later and the leech was still.

Exhausted, Sarah had fainted, her eyes rolling back as more and more blood drained from her. Sean's hands were moving faster and faster, sweat rolling off his forehead and into his eyes, the terrible knowledge that Sarah was being bled dry intensifying the power of the runes. Scarlet ribbons began appearing in the air, and one of them wrapped itself around the demon on Sarah's neck, strangling it slowly, growing tighter and tighter. Finally its suckers began to lose their grip ... when suddenly Sean felt something bite his bare back. He screamed and his *sgian-dubh* fell, the runes interrupted. The demon-leech bit Sarah's unconscious body with renewed hunger.

"They're falling off the trees! Get away from the trees!" Sean yelled, throwing himself against some rocks jutting out of the mossy undergrowth. He banged his back against the rocks, ignoring the pain in his ribs, until he felt the demon-leech being squashed and broken, a gush of blood – some of which was his – soaking his back.

"Come away!" Alvise echoed Sean's words, and led Niall

and Micol to a small clearing removed from the danger. But it was a mistake. Niall's song came to a halt as he was dragged out of his trance, and a leech crept under his jacket. Niall screamed as the Surari sank its suckers into his back and began draining him at once.

Without hesitation, Alvise went to Niall, helping him remove his jacket and fleece. He shuddered when the leech appeared. The demon attacking Niall was fat with Niall's blood, already as big as a rat. It looked different from the others, bigger, its skin thick and leathery. Niall doubled over in pain, while Alvise grabbed an arrow from his quiver and started stabbing the demon-leech with it. His arrow could not pierce the creature's skin, and the Surari didn't move an inch. It was as if the steel arrowhead wasn't even causing it pain. Niall whimpered and fell face down on the undergrowth, the creature sucking his life away.

Alvise growled in frustration. He unsheathed his *pugnale* – his dagger – and tried piercing it again, to no avail. He tried prising it off, pulling it with all his strength ... but nothing worked. Its skin seemed thicker and stronger than any other leech, a leathery hide that protected it from blades and arrowheads, and its suckers' grip seemed unbreakable.

"Sean! Sarah! Help!" he called, but there was no reply.

"Sarah is on the ground!" Micol cried, intermittent charges of a million colours buzzing off her in her fear and distress; no demon-leech could attach itself to her without ending up burnt to a crisp.

"Micol! Help him!" Alvise pleaded.

"I can't! I'd kill Niall along with the demon!"

"We have no choice but to try," Alvise yelled back. "He doesn't have long. Micol, you have to!"

"Alvise," Niall coughed with bloodless lips, his grey eyes closing, shadowed by long black lashes. And Alvise's heart broke in two.

A memory appeared in his mind – a long, warm summer evening in Venice a few years before. The Flynns had come to visit their family. Their parents had Secret business to attend to and a ball had been organised in their honour. They were all gathered in the gilded, frescoed ballroom of Palazzo Vendramin, the men in white ties or the ancestral attire of their families; the women in evening dresses, bright and colourful like spring flowers. And then Niall appeared down the grand stairs, in between with his parents, his auburn hair down to his shoulders, his eyes a colour Alvise had never seen – dark grey, like soft steel. He was wearing jeans and a white shirt – he'd refused evening dress. Alvise remembered the ripple in his heart as he saw Niall stepping down those stairs, a half smile dancing on his lips . . .

Now Micol was shaking. "I can't do this, Alvise . . . please don't make me . . ."

"Micol, listen to me," Alvise said, looking her straight in the eye. He went to take her by the shoulders, but her electrical armour prevented anyone from touching her, and Alvise's hands hung empty. "It's his last chance," he begged once again. "Look." Micol followed his gaze. The demon-leech was swollen and tight with Niall's blood, but its body kept expanding to accommodate more. It wouldn't stop until there was nothing left.

A small sob left the girl's lips. He was right. There was no other way.

She placed her sparkling hands on Niall's back, closed her eyes, and let go of an electrical charge with a soft buzz and a flash of orange. Niall's body tensed and jumped, and Micol removed her hands, horrified. What was she doing? His heart would stop, and it'd be all her fault.

But his heart would stop anyway if they couldn't remove the creature.

Steeling herself, she hit him once more, twice, until the demon-leech shrivelled up and fell off. An overwhelming stench of burning flesh filled the air, smoke coming off its black, swollen body. Micol let herself fall alongside Niall, without daring to touch him again. Alvise was on him at once, turning him around gently, placing his fingers on Niall's throat.

"Wake up. Please wake up," Micol whispered, tears drying up on her scalding skin as soon as they trickled out of her eyes.

Elodie recovered herself. The creature didn't want her blood? Then she could use her power. Sean was lying prone, the demon-leech drinking his blood in pulsing gulps. Elodie placed her poisonous lips on its skin, gagging in revulsion at the feeling of the slick, wet hide against her mouth. It was strong. It didn't stop guzzling down Sean's blood, even as it was being slowly poisoned by Elodie.

Elodie gasped for air, but she didn't lift her lips from the demon sucking away Sean's life. *Where is Nicholas*, she asked herself in despair while her life force ebbed slowly into the venomous kiss. She felt weaker and weaker, her head spinning as she closed her eyes and a small prayer left her heart. *Don't let Sean die.*

Finally, just as she thought she couldn't take any more, she felt the Surari move slightly, loosening its grip. With a noise that was half growl, half sob, Elodie prised it off, and it detached itself from Sean with a wet, sloshing sound.

She dried the black slush from her lips with her sleeve and watched in disgust while the leech pulsed like a ripped-out heart, opening and closing its round mouth, until it was immobile. Only then did she let herself fall forward, her head on Sean's chest, listening to his faintly beating heart. She was so tired. She was always so tired . . .

"Elodie," whispered Sean, but she couldn't move. He wrapped his arms around her and they lay together for a moment. Until a whimper made Elodie lift her head and roll herself away from Sean.

She gasped as a terrible scene appeared in front of her: Nicholas lay on the ground, covered in demon-leeches. On his neck, his arms, his legs. He lay open like in a crucifixion, his eyes closed and his face to the ruthless sky. Mustering the last of her strength, Elodie dragged herself on her hands and knees towards Nicholas and started placing her deadly kiss onto the creatures.

Sean pulled himself toward Nicholas too, dizzy from the loss of blood. He'd lost his *sgian-dubh*, he realised with dismay. He was lost without it. He began scrambling around when finally he saw a glint of silver in a branch. He lifted himself on his toes to reach his blade, and he saw them. The tree was full of leeches, dozing on the branches. His breaths coming out in ragged pants, expecting to be hit at any moment, Sean retrieved his *sgian-dubh* and began tracing his runes.

Sarah's consciousness was ebbing and flowing, until finally she came to her senses. It took her a moment to realise what she was seeing – Nicholas on the ground, leeches all over him; Elodie poisoning them; and Sean, looking up at the tree, his hands weaving slow runes.

"Sean," she slurred, dragging herself to her knees.

"Sarah. Listen. Elodie, you too," he whispered urgently. "Get away from here. Take Nicholas with you. Try not to make a noise. The tree is full of *them*."

All of a sudden a shower of leeches began falling on them, but right at the same time Sean's red ribbons appeared and began cutting them, slashing the air underneath the trees, cutting up the leeches before they could hit the ground.

Sarah and Elodie dragged Nicholas' unconscious body away from the death-laden trees, inch by inch, leaving a bloodied trail on the grass. Sarah looked over to Sean, who was walking backwards, whispering words in the Ancient language, his hands dancing faster than the eye could see. Little black bodies were being torn to pieces by whirling ribbons of light.

Elodie kissed the last demon off Nicholas' chest and then, with a whimper, she let herself fall beside him, her hair soaked in black and red blood.

"Elodie!" Sarah whispered, and took the French girl in her arms. She didn't see one of the Surari they'd prised off Nicholas' skin leap up with its suckers ready. It blindly attached itself to Sarah's neck and began sucking her blood, doubling its size in seconds.

Everything slowed down at once. She was on her back, gazing at the sky. She could hear voices shouting, calling, but they were coming from far away. Her life was flowing out of her and into the creature in a stream that could not be stopped. A sweet, heady scent filled her nostrils – blood – her blood. It was a sweet demise, to bleed out. It was peaceful. The sky was very white and very still, like death.

She heard a whisper in her ear. It was Sean's voice, calling her name. *Let me go*, she wanted to say, but she couldn't. *It's so peaceful. Let me go.*

Something covered the sky – a girl's face, surrounded by multi-coloured lightning. Micol.

The Falco girl had seized her moment to kill her then, Sarah thought. She saw sparkling hands rise to her throat, and a soft buzz started in her ears. *She found a way. She found a way to kill me ... What's the point in trying to stop her? I'm dying anyway.*

The pain was horrendous as the first charge hit her in an explosion of red and orange. She could smell burning, and she was sure it was her flesh. In a second, she was jolted out of her blood-loss-induced trance.

"No," she begged. That was not the way she wanted to die. That was not oblivion. It was just more pain. "No!" she pleaded once more, her voice coming out weak and ragged. "Sean, help me ..."

But Sean didn't help her, and Micol didn't stop. Again she hit Sarah, and again, this time with a blue charge that made her body convulse and her eyes roll into the back of her head. After that, she couldn't feel any more.

Sarah blinked. Once. Twice. Slowly, the world came into focus.

There were trees above her. *Trees are danger*, she thought, and tried to move, but her body would not comply. Her arms and legs felt infinitely heavy, way too heavy to be lifted. A face appeared over her. Sean. She realised her head was resting on Sean's lap, and relaxed slightly. "I'm alive?"

"Yes. Thank God, yes. You're alive," said Sean, caressing her face. She saw tears in his eyes and felt guilty – she never wanted to cause him pain. "You were out of it for a long time."

"Was I?" And then she remembered. Micol, her hands sparkling . . . the pain. "She burnt me. Am I burnt?"

"Just a little. Your eyebrows."

"My eyebrows? I'm going to kill her." Sarah scrambled to get up, but couldn't. Her head spun and her chest hurt.

"Hey, take it easy. Just lie down for a bit. Micol saved your life," said Sean.

"She what? That stupid little girl electrocuted me!"

"She didn't electrocute you. She fried the leech. She saved you," Sean repeated.

"You should thank me, Sarah!" Micol came into focus, her arms folded, her expression dark. "I have saved you. And I'm not a little girl. I turned sixteen today. I think . . . Or maybe tomorrow. I lost track of time."

"Happy birthday," said an Irish voice. Niall – and he wasn't even being sarcastic.

Sarah sat up, Sean's arm around her shoulders. She saw Niall leaning against a tree, his clothes bloodied and torn. His skin had a blue tinge, and there were deep shadows under his eyes. He must have been bled half to death too. He had Alvise's jacket around his shoulders, Sarah noticed, and felt another pang of guilt for not having been there to help them. Being in two places at the same time – now that would be a good power to have . . .

"Are we all alive?" she whispered.

"For now," Sean replied tersely.

"Elodie?"

"I'm fine," she said. Sarah gazed at her, sitting beside Nicholas with her back to a tree. Elodie's breathing was shallow and her fingernails blue, and her exquisite, porce-lain-like face was whiter than ever. Nicholas looked pretty shaken up, every visible part of his body bearing the marks of suckers. Sarah remembered him lying on the grass, covered in leeches. Nobody human could have survived such a thing. Could he walk?

"We need to go," Nicholas said, as if he'd heard her thoughts.

Beyond the trees, in the west, the sun was setting. Night was falling on the Shadow World, and on them all.

24
Fireflies

I remember
The scent of sunshine and of pines
The coral and the sand
And the girl I left behind

They resumed their march, but not for long. Soon they had to stop again. Niall, Sarah and Elodie were too weak, and even Nicholas was staggering, his hands and face covered in little round wounds.

They found their resting place a few hours from where the demon-leeches attacked. It was a little round copse of trees, shaped so that if anything targeted them they would see it at once. Nowhere was safe in the Shadow World; this was as sheltered as it would ever get. The least affected members of the party – Sean, Alvise and Micol – had to keep watch and wait until the others felt better.

Twilight had turned into night. As usual, they didn't dare light a fire or use their torches; they huddled together in the dark and cold. Sarah, Elodie and Niall ate some biscuits and chocolate and drank a little, then they lay nestled in sleeping bags, waiting for their strength to return. Animal calls and noises came from the trees, and every fern blowing in the breeze, every branch creaking made their bodies tense up and their hearts gallop. Everything around them felt threatening anyway, in spite of Sean's reassurances that they had perfect visibility, that if any Surari attacked they would see it in plenty of time. They were on edge, and this could never change until they returned from the Shadow World. If they ever would.

Sarah was furious with herself for letting the demon-leech hurt her to the extent that she couldn't march any more. How long would this forced stop last? How long would they need to remain here, open to attacks, like sitting ducks?

She closed her eyes and willed her body to recover. Suddenly, little yellow lights started dancing in front of her closed eyelids. Her eyes snapped open, fearing an attack, but all she saw was a small cloud of fireflies twinkling in the darkness in front of her.

"Sean, look," she whispered. She didn't need to look to know he was awake.

"I see them. They're beautiful," Sean replied. Out of the corner of her eye, Sarah saw a gleam coming from his hand – the light of a firefly reflected on his *sgian-dubh*.

"Are they really just fireflies?" she asked. She couldn't believe that any creature of the Shadow World could be harmless.

Sean half-smiled in the darkness. "I'm sure. Just fireflies. Rest, now ..."

Sarah closed her eyes, praying that no dreams would come. She was so tired . . . Sean's presence beside her made her feel a little safer, a little warmer. Reluctantly, she let herself fall into a shallow sleep.

Sean could never allow himself to rest. He looked over to Nicholas, sitting slightly apart from the group, as ever. His eyes were closed and his expression intense, as if he were thinking very hard. He'd been nearly killed, Sean considered. He'd been covered in those demon-leeches. Maybe that was the ultimate proof of his loyalty? But they could never be sure. Beside him, curled up in his sleeping bag, Niall stirred. Sean saw that his eyes were open.

"Try to get some sleep, Niall," he murmured.

"Aye. I love fireflies," Niall whispered in reply. Even lying down, the world was spinning around him. He'd never lost so much blood in his life, though he'd been wounded many times before. "There were so many of them in Louisiana . . ."

Memories of the time he and Mike had hidden in Louisiana flooded him. They'd spent weeks there, in a shack on the beach, until the corrupted Sabha found them. They were attacked by sea demons and survived by the skin of their teeth. Technically, Niall had been killed, but had come back to life, because Flynns can't die from drowning. He'd never forget Mike's expression as he'd sat up and spoken, just as Mike was mourning his death, drunk on bourbon. He'd never forget the night they'd spent listening to Cajun music, when Niall had played his fiddle to a rapt audience, the sweet Celtic sounds filling the night.

"I wish we could have brought Mike home to Louisiana,"

Niall said. "When all this is finished, we're going back to Islay, all of us. We're going to give him a proper send-off. Make music all night. For him."

"It's a plan," Sean replied softly. *If we are still alive*, he added in his heart but didn't say anything.

Niall was quiet after that, gazing at the fireflies blinking in the darkness like tiny stars. His heart was heavy. He longed for Winter, for his family, for the sea, and for music. But he'd never talk about his burdens, he'd keep smiling and making little jokes and gliding through life like he always seemed to do.

He wouldn't let anyone know that when Mike got killed, the old Niall had died too, and now the new one didn't know nearly as much joy as the old one had. The new Niall was wiser, and darker. He shut his eyes tight and imagined himself back home in Donegal, with music and whiskey and his family and friends, and Winter, her silver hair down to her shoulders and her eyes shining in the light of the peat fire.

She was in his mind constantly. Not an hour went by without him wondering if she'd found shelter, if the Vendramins had welcomed her, if once there, she'd been really safe and not caught up in more Surari attacks. One thing was sure: he had not made a mistake in sending her through the iris, whatever had happened to her next. The demon-leech attack had once again proved that to him. Had she stayed with him, Winter would have been dead by now. The mistake had been in agreeing for her to come with him, instead of putting her in hiding somewhere. They'd been unable to go their separate ways – and he had not been strong enough to convince her to stay.

I just want to see you again, Winter, he prayed, and drifted off in an unquiet sleep.

Alvise and Micol sat side by side, huddled underneath Sean's sleeping bag. In the soft light of dusk, before night had fallen, Alvise had seen Micol's eyes red-rimmed and shiny. At some point, without anyone noticing, she must have cried – for her brother, Alvise was sure. And still, in spite of her rage and pain at what Sarah had done, she'd saved her life. Alvise was beginning to see new sides of Micol, and he had to admit that what he saw was pretty impressive. She was brave. She was strong.

"Fireflies," he whispered.

"Yes. There are a lot of them back home, but they only come out on summer nights. These must be some weird species resistant to the cold. Demon-fireflies . . ."

"God, don't make me think about it."

"Sorry."

"By the way . . . you were amazing today," he said simply.

Micol looked at him, astonished. "What?"

"I mean, that electric thing you do. I've never seen you like . . . like that."

She was bewildered by his praise, and for a second she was at a loss for words. This guy whose anger she could feel in the air in every room of Palazzo Vendramin, who had seemed to dislike her so much, was actually commending her?

"You thought I was just a helpless little girl," she murmured, a hint of resentment in her voice.

"I did actually, yes. Well, not helpless. But spoiled."

"Anything else?" she asked.

"Selfish?"

"Right, thanks. Because I was trying to get away from Palazzo Vendramin? Or fortress Vendramin, more like. You would have done the same."

"No. I would have helped keep the hexes in place, instead of breaking them." They were silent for a moment, watching the fireflies dance as guilt spread in Micol's chest. She could see his point of view now that she wasn't incarcerated, breaking her wings against the bars of her cage like a little bird.

"And you think I'm a monster," Alvise continued. He sounded upset somehow. Alvise actually cared about her opinion of him? This conversation was proving to be quite surprising.

She chose her words carefully. "I thought you kept Lucrezia prisoner. And you seemed to hate me. But I don't think that any more."

"I never hated you."

"You certainly put on a good show, then."

"I was just cross that you kept running away! Putting us all in danger!" he blurted out.

"I'm sorry. I know it was a stupid thing to do. That place ... suffocates me! And anyway, I might have changed my mind about you too."

"Why?"

Micol shrugged, tightening Sean's sleeping bag around her. She'd never been so cold in her life. "I don't know. You just seem ... different out here. Not a monster any more."

"Right. I suppose that's a compliment."

"Not really," she said, and he couldn't help but burst into soft laughter. Then his face turned serious.

"Micol. I must tell you this. Whatever you might think of us ... my father and I were so fond of your brothers. I'm so sorry about them both. We tried to convince Tancredi not to go ..."

"He wasn't crazy. He was right. Sarah Midnight had been chosen as Nicholas' wife, we know it now."

"Shhhhh ... keep it down." Alvise shuffled closer to Micol. He didn't want her overheard, in case it created more problems for her. "You heard Sarah," he whispered, looking around him. Nobody seemed to be listening. "She's not under Nicholas' control any more."

"So she says."

"If you doubt her, why did you save her life?"

"Because I might be wrong, and you might be right."

"Fair enough." A short pause. "For what it's worth, I believe her," Alvise said in a low voice.

"You don't even know her. Nobody does. Nobody even knew the Midnights existed."

"True. Then put it this way: I believe Niall Flynn and Elodie Brun ... they come from two ancient, honourable families, and they trust her. And think about it logically ..."

Micol snorted. Her heart was broken, her family had been exterminated, and he asked her to use logic?

"No, listen," he insisted. "Lucrezia sent me here. Sent us here. I was furious you snuck into the iris, but then it occurred to me: Lucrezia marked you too. She wouldn't have if you weren't supposed to come with me."

"I hadn't thought about it that way. I thought I'd just got away with it ... but I couldn't have gone through had she not marked me?" Micol ran her fingers over the burnt scar on her palm. It still hurt.

He shook his head. "She chooses who goes through and who stays. But why did she mark you? Why did she send us both to this place? Not to save Tancredi. He was already dead when we arrived."

Micol breathed in sharply.

"Not to kill Sarah, or my sister would have given us some indication. There's only one explanation. Lucrezia sent us here to help them."

Micol lowered her head and said nothing. She suspected Alvise was right, but her brother's death at the hands of a fellow heir hurt so much. Absent-mindedly, she brought a hand to the shoulder that Alvise's arrow had grazed. Niall had disinfected it and bandaged it lightly – it was just a cut and it would heal soon. Alvise saw her rub her shoulder. "I'm sorry I had to do that."

"Well, you saved Sarah."

"That wasn't my first thought, Micol. You were so lost in your power you didn't see what was about to happen."

Micol raised her eyebrows. "You should know by now that the Falco heirs are immune to other heirs' powers. That's why my brother thought he could have the best of Sarah, even if he was so sick, because her powers wouldn't have worked on him."

"Sean was about to throw that dagger of his at you. Did you know that? Did you see?"

Micol was silent.

"I suppose you never noticed how sharp it is. It could cut air. I really, really didn't want to see that thing piercing your heart," Alvise continued. "Unless the Falcos are immune to steel too . . ."

"I didn't know," she whispered, her voice shaking a little,

and then she snorted. "Sean said my brother had asked him to look after me. Some fine job he's doing. "

"He's in love with Sarah. Anything that threatens her, he won't hesitate to kill. And I couldn't let him kill you. I couldn't let that happen."

"Why?" Micol asked.

"Why? How can you ask me that?"

"You threatened to hurt me yourself many times."

Alvise looked down. "I would have never hurt you. We did our best to look after Ranieri as he was dying and stop Tancredi from going on his mad quest, but we couldn't save either of them. I seem to have a habit of letting people down," he said, a hint of self-loathing shining through. "I won't lose you too."

Micol gazed at the blond man's face, incredulous, trying to make out his features in the gloom. For the first time Micol noticed how delicate his face was, with his high cheekbones and full lips. *He looks a bit like an elf from a storybook*, she thought.

Was this the same person she used to loathe? Okay, they had established that he didn't hate her, but was he actually actively protecting her?

"*Grazie*," she murmured, and Alvise gazed at her. Their faces were very close, and suddenly in Alvise's eyes she looked very young and very vulnerable. Like a dark-haired, olive-skinned version of his own sister.

Something stirred in the darkness not far from them, a tall, wide-shouldered shape silhouetted against the starry sky: Nicholas. They watched him trail off and disappear into the night. Even in the darkness Micol could feel his black aura. She shivered.

"What is he up to?" she whispered.

"God knows. Micol . . ." Alvise began, and then he buried his hands underneath his jacket. He fumbled around a bit, took something from one of the pockets, and slipped it into her hand. "This is for you."

She opened her palm. At first she couldn't make out what it was, but then she realised it was the golden brooch he wore as a symbol of his family. It was shaped like a lion crowned with flames.

"Why?" she breathed.

"I know you hate the Vendramin, but *you have nobody left*. So this is my offer. To be one of us."

You have nobody left. Alvise's words stung, but they were true.

She was alone in the world.

"Thank you, but I can't be one of you. I can never be anything but a Falco." Alvise bowed his head. "But I'd love to be a protetta of the Vendramin." *Protetta* was the Italian word that signified a charge, a foster child entrusted to a Secret Family. The Secret equivalent of an adoption.

"You'll be our protetta. You might not be our blood, but you're like our own, Micol Falco," he said solemnly. Back home there would have been a ceremony – but here in Shadow World, words whispered in the night had to do.

"I am like your own, Alvise Vendramin," she responded.

Alvise nodded and fastened the brooch to her coat.

Maybe she wasn't completely alone after all, Micol allowed herself to think.

"And by the way, I heard it's your birthday. It's a good age, to be sixteen," said Alvise with a smile.

"Oh, yes. My life is just great."

"Mmmm. I take it back. I suppose when I was sixteen my mother died. Not the happiest of times either. You don't look sixteen, anyway. Thirteen at most," he added, and spoiled the moment.

"You're a pain, Alvise."

Alvise laughed. "Happy birthday, Micol."

25
The Message

We found so many ways to speak
and still
We cannot touch

Winter spent most of her days in Lucrezia's room. Often Conte Vendramin sat with her, and they had long conversations about the Secret Families. They were learning much from each other and developing an unlikely friendship, strengthened by a common bond: both had someone whom they loved dearly lost in the Shadow World. Often they discussed whether to ask Lucrezia to try to contact Alvise and Niall, or wait until Lucrezia decided it was time.

"She decides what to tell us and when," Conte Vendramin explained again. "It's like she can speak to us, or something speaks through her, but she doesn't really take in what we say unless it's information important to her task: the hunt or otherwise. It's hard to explain unless you've observed her behaviour for as long as we have."

"I think I understand. But we can always try. The worst that can happen is that she ignores us," Winter replied. "We wouldn't be forcing her or upsetting her, surely?"

"No, of course not. *E va bene*. Let's try." Conte Vendramin's eyes were anxious. Winter could see he was beside himself with worry for Alvise, the heir of the Vendramin Family, and for what Lucrezia might reveal to them if she decided it was time. With Lucrezia in such a state, Alvise was Conte Vendramin's only hope to keep the family going. Without Alvise, Vendramin would have no one left.

"They'll be okay," she reassured him.

Vendramin smiled faintly. "*Si*. He'll be fine."

Now there they were, in the gilded room, breathing in lilies and decay. Lucrezia was whispering nonsense, words they couldn't understand. Because of the incredible acoustics of the palazzo, sometimes Winter could hear her whispering at night, and it broke her heart to know that the poor girl had no rest. As horrible as it was to listen to, Winter had become used to Lucrezia's babble. It had transformed into a strange lullaby for her.

She sat on Lucrezia's bed softly, carefully. She brushed Lucrezia's hair away from her forehead, and then clasped her own hands on the sleeping girl's.

Leaning close, she whispered, "Lucrezia. Please. Tell us if Alvise and Niall are alive. If you can speak to them, let Niall know I'm okay." Winter squeezed the girl's hand, cold against her warm seal skin.

Lucrezia showed no signs of hearing what Winter had said; she continued her constant whispering.

"Tell him ... tell him I'll see him soon," Winter continued. She didn't know if she believed those words herself – Niall was in so much danger – but she had to hope.

Yes, she had to hope.

"Please tell him that we'll be in the sea together soon," she whispered, embarrassed that Conte Vendramin should hear such private words, but if there was a way to communicate this to him, she wanted Niall to know what was on her mind . . . and be comforted by that.

"Tell Alvise we think of him all the time. That we are so proud of him," Conte Vendramin interjected. "That we—"

Suddenly, he was interrupted by a strangled sound coming from Lucrezia's throat. Lucrezia squeezed Winter's hand so tight it hurt. Her whispering became a torrent of words in a language Winter didn't recognise. Then, she began to speak in English.

"Winter is here. She is safe," Lucrezia said clearly, then paused. "Palazzo Vendramin. She's safe and well. I have a message for Alvise. I tried to reach him but you are the only Dreamer among them strong enough to hear me. Tell him his father is proud of him. Tell him his sister is proud of him too," she said, speaking of herself in the third person. She paused for a moment, then: "Winter wants you to give a message to Niall. She says she'll be seeing him soon. That they'll be swimming in the sea soon."

A soft sob escaped Winter's lips.

Lucrezia was silent for a moment, and then she spoke again. "Listen to me, Sarah. I saw your path. Your destiny is preparing. You must be ready . . . Oh . . ."

Winter jerked her head towards Conte Vendramin. He was listening intently.

Suddenly, Lucrezia seemed upset. "No! *Lasciami andare!*"

She began to toss her head back and forth across the pillow, as if she were in pain. "He wants you. He needs you, Sarah. Don't let him take you!" She yelped, and then grew still.

"Lucrezia! *Figlia mia!*" Vendramin kneeled at her side and took her by the shoulders.

Lucrezia was screaming, shouting, begging. "Sarah! Listen for me! I'll return—" She took a sharp, ragged breath and stopped breathing altogether. Her face began to turn blue.

"What's happening?" Winter asked the count.

"I don't know!" came his reply. "This has never happened before. Lucrezia!" Conte Vendramin called again. The sharp clicking of heels on the floor announced Cosima's arrival. She barged into the room.

"Lucrezia! *Stella mia!*" she cried, joining Winter and the count at Lucrezia's bed. She wasn't breathing – she was purple – and then, slowly, she returned to breathing normally. Her hands were twitching and her whispering frantic.

"Is she right? *Mio Dio.* You right, *stella mia?*" Cosima's English was very broken. Lucrezia was still, whiter than before, but breathing. Conte Vendramin rested his head on her chest to check her heartbeat. It was feeble, but it was there.

"She spoke to Sarah Midnight. She was trying to tell her something, but something happened. She was interrupted," he murmured.

"She gave her our messages, though," said Winter. "Does that mean that both Niall and Alvise are alive?"

"I don't know. We won't know until she tells us herself." He pressed his daughter's shoulder. "Is Alvise all right? And Niall? Are they alive?" Vendramin asked in vain.

But Lucrezia's eyes were closed. She was drained, and said no more.

26
Voice of the Seal

I call you every night
In my dreams

Little yellow lights danced before Sarah's eyes, her cheek resting on soft moss; the lights' cheerful dance was surreal in the night of the Shadow World, tight and tense with danger. Sarah felt a small ripple of joy, and it was weird, like that feeling could not possibly belong to her. It couldn't be her, smiling in the darkness, the ghost of a smile that danced on her lips for a few seconds only, but still it happened. A strange sense of peace filled her, coming from somewhere inside her, a place she had forgotten. Images of Sean danced before her closed eyes, the scent of him, the feeling of his arms around her, his lips on hers, as she drifted into sleep.

A voice resounded in her mind at once, a voice she didn't know. Words in a foreign tongue, and then in the Ancient language. The voice began calling her, and Sarah's heart sank even in her sleep – she had wanted that moment of peace to last forever, and not turn into another brutal dream. She whimpered in the darkness.

"Sarah Midnight," called the voice, and Sarah found herself standing in a room flooded with golden light, white silk curtains floating around a window open to reveal a sun-kissed sea. It was warm, so warm, and she enjoyed the feeling – she'd been cold for what seemed like forever. There was a familiar scent in the air – the same scent as Islay.

Seaweed, that's what it was. Water and seaweed and the sea. And sunshine, sunshine filling her eyes and her mind and her soul.

A shape took form in front of her – long hair, a floating dress – the shape of a girl. Her heart beat faster for a moment. She'd had a vision of her mother after her death, and in the vision Anne had her long black hair loose around her shoulders and was wearing a long nightdress. Was it her? Was her mother back to help her once more?

"Mum?" she whispered.

"No, I'm sorry," said the figure, in English. She had a young voice, almost childlike. "I'm not your mother. I miss my mother too." As soon as she finished the sentence the girl started whispering again, a stream of words in the Ancient language.

As Sarah's eyes adjusted to the golden light, she could make out the girl's face, her body. Straw-coloured hair, nearly white, hung down past her shoulders, and pale-blue eyes bore into her. She wore a long, pale-blue dress in shimmering silk. Her arms were thin and white. Was she human? A ghost? She certainly wasn't a Surari. And then her scent hit Sarah's nostrils, stronger than the smell of the sea. Lilies, sweet and with a hint of decay, like a bunch of flowers left in the heat for too long.

"Winter is here. She is safe," the girl said. Her words had a strange echo, as if they were coming from far away.

"Winter!" Sarah repeated. "What do you mean by 'here'? Where is 'here'?"

"Palazzo Vendramin. She's safe and well."

Sarah couldn't stop herself from smiling with relief.

"I have a message for Alvise," the girl continued. "I tried to reach him but you are the only Dreamer among them strong enough to hear me. Tell him his father is proud of him. Tell him his sister is proud of him too."

"I'll tell him."

"Winter wants you to give a message to Niall. She says she'll be seeing him soon. That they'll be swimming in the sea soon."

"I'll tell him." The apparition nodded.

"Listen to me, Sarah. I saw your path. Your destiny is preparing. You must be ready . . . Oh . . ."

"What's happening? Are you okay?" Sarah took a step towards the girl and reached out to her.

"No! *Lasciami andare!*" she exclaimed, her tone pleading, and she brought her long, thin fingers to her temples. Sarah had no idea what those words meant, but she could see the girl was in distress. She extended her hands to hold the girl's, but instead of meeting solid, warm flesh, she felt nothing. Sarah's hands went through the girl's body, as if she were a ghost. As if she weren't really there.

"He wants you. He needs you, Sarah. Don't let him take you!" Her words were lost in a golden glare that blinded Sarah and silenced all noise.

She woke with a jolt, opening her eyes in the night of the Shadow World, and someone was calling her name.

"Sarah!"

"Sean?" She blinked for a few seconds, finding herself again, and then she remembered the message she was to give. "Niall! Where is he? Niall!"

"What ... wait," said Sean, and rummaged in his sleeping bag. He found his torch and switched it on, illuminating his friends' sleeping forms until the beam of light enveloped Niall. Sarah followed the beam on her hands and knees until she was close enough to him to whisper in his ear.

"Niall ..."

"Yes! Surari?" He sat upright, his dagger unsheathed at once.

"Shhhhh! No, no attacks. I had a dream. I had to tell you! Winter is fine," she said.

"Winter?" he whispered.

"A girl told me that Winter was with her in a place called ...Vendramin? That's Alvise's home, isn't it?"

"Vendramin?" A sleepy voice beside them. Alvise. "What's all this about?"

"Sarah dreamt of Winter," Niall began.

"Not exactly. I dreamt of a girl ..."

Alvise stared at her in the light of the torches. "A girl? What did she look like?"

"She had long blonde hair, like yours. She was very thin and she was whispering."

"Lucrezia. That's my sister Lucrezia," Alvise replied, his voice full of emotion. "Was she well?"

"It seemed so to me. She told me that Winter was safe with them, that she wanted you to know," she told Niall. Niall breathed in sharply. Sarah could see the emotions on his face, like the changing colours of a kaleidoscope – hope, relief, fear, and longing, a longing Sarah could only imagine. She and Sean were separated by a wall of belief and loyalty, but at least they were physically together.

"She said Winter is fine?" Niall repeated slowly.

"Yes. She wanted you to know. Lucrezia tried to reach you but she couldn't, so she told me."

"Thank God!" Niall covered his face with his hands and sank back against a tree. "Thank God," he repeated, and a muffled sob rising from between his fingers told Sarah that he was crying. Not long ago she would have been paralysed by his show of emotion and unsure what to do, but they'd been through so much together, she and Niall, and she cared about him more deeply than she could ever say, she couldn't help throwing her arms around him, without embarrassment.

"It's all fine. She's alive and well. You'll see her soon," she reassured him.

Niall couldn't speak. Alvise placed a hand on Sarah's back. "Did she say anything else? Lucrezia?"

Sarah freed Niall from her embrace. "Yes, actually," she replied, and her eyes looked for Sean's. "She said she saw my path, that my destiny is preparing and I must be ready … but she was … dragged away somehow. Yes, it felt like her mind was dragged out of mine. She couldn't tell me anything more, but she said she'll be back."

Sean's face was tight, his forehead creased in worry. "Do you have any idea what she might have meant?"

"No. Alvise?"

"All I know is that my sister's mind … travels. She knows a lot, she tells us a lot. She must be aware of something you need to know, Sarah. I can't imagine what might have forced her to leave your mind. I don't know of anyone that could do this to her. Did she say anything else? Maybe in Italian, or in the Ancient language?"

"She whispered in the Ancient language, but the words were all jumbled up. She also spoke in Italian . . . something like lasha-me andaray? Something like that?"

"*Lasciami andare*," Alvise said.

"What does it mean?"

"It means 'let me go'," a small voice piped from behind him. Micol, rubbing her eyes. "Someone stopped her from talking to you."

"She said she'll be back," Sarah whispered in the semi-darkness, the beam of the torch shining on the grass at her feet.

Micol sighed in the darkness. "If whoever took her away today will let her."

27
A Soul of Stone

When you said you'd keep my soul safe
You meant it would not be mine any more

Unsteady and disoriented, the weakest he'd felt since his father used the brain fury on him, Nicholas walked a few steps away from the group, into the heart of the night. Not that it made any difference to him, as darkness was his constant companion. He used his other senses to guide him, walking with his arms extended to detect any obstacles, feeling the rough bark of the oak trees and the branches zigzagging ahead of him. He could smell the night, he could smell the frost and the trees, and the wind in the huge open sky, which he remembered covered in millions of stars – so many of them that they looked like silver dust. There were no other lights here in the Shadow World to obscure their light.

He would never see a starry sky again. He would never see the moon again, he thought, and the realisation hit him so hard he felt like doubling over. There had been no time to grieve the loss of his sight, not with the rest of his life crumbling around him – and he was pretty sure he would not live long anyway – but every time he thought about what he'd lost, his heart bled. His father had chosen the most terrible of punishments.

Finally he felt he was far enough from the group. He could speak with his father in his mind, but he always preferred to be alone when he did, in case something – a whisper, a grimace – gave him away. He stopped and listened for a moment. No twigs breaking, no branches swept by touch, no sound of footsteps, just the low song of the wind in the trees and the calling of night birds having a conversation on the branches above his head.

It was time.

Trying to ignore the deep, deep terror that gripped him every time he had to speak to his father, the instinct to scream and run and fight the intrusion inside his head, inside his thoughts, Nicholas called him. He felt a drop of sweat trickle down his temple, immediately freezing on his skin.

"Father. I'm here."

Nicholas.

At the sound of the King of Shadows' voice, rage filled Nicholas' mind. The dozens of wounds from the demon-leeches' mouths still throbbed all over his body. "Why did you let them do that to me? I was nearly sucked dry. If I die, how are you going to get her to you in one piece?"

We have to make them believe you're still on their side.

Nicholas shook his head. He didn't believe him for a moment. That wasn't the reason why his father had allowed the demon-leeches to cover his body and suck his blood. He had done it because he enjoyed seeing his son suffer.

He enjoyed pushing Nicholas to his limits and beyond, to inflict pain onto his body and onto his soul – and Nicholas knew why: because the King of Shadows wanted complete, unlimited power over everyone around him. He wanted to dominate Nicholas just as he'd dominated his mother, and ultimately broken her.

His mother's face appeared behind his blind eyes – a mane of black hair, sweet black eyes, a voice that soothed him like no other. Her name was Ekaterina Krol, and she'd been young and innocent when his father had preyed on her. He mind-moulded her like Nicholas had done to Sarah, and convinced her to marry him and carry his child – Nicholas. By the time her baby was born, the King of Shadows had showed his true self and his true nature, and Ekaterina feared him and hated him with all her might. When Nicholas was just a few days old his father took him away from her and back into the Shadow World – what choice did she have but to follow? She couldn't have borne to be away from her son. As the years went by, Ekaterina was forced to shed her body – to take on the form of rulers of the underworld. Her spirit was allowed to leave the King of Shadows' lair every summer, and she'd wander the human world, but being unable to touch and feel and being forced to ultimately return to the darkness, Ekaterina slowly lost the will to live.

And then came the last blow. Nicholas had met Martyna, the love of his life. Ekaterina begged him not to listen to his father, not to use mind-moulding on Martyna, to let her be, but Nicholas could not challenge his father's will. In order to have her in their complete power, they burnt her family alive in the space of one night, and Martyna drowned herself. That day, Nicholas broke inside, and Ekaterina let her spirit dissolve – the ultimate decision to cease to exist – and be no more. Mother and son had been destroyed.

Nicholas often thought that had he refused to help his father, maybe both his mother and Martyna would still be alive. He was responsible for their deaths. He'd killed the two people he'd loved the most.

A new wave of anger swept over him, but he suffocated it quickly. He couldn't let his father hear his thoughts.

If you do as you're meant to, my son, you'll be allowed to come back. As if nothing had happened. You'll be spared.

Nicholas squeezed his eyes shut in an effort to annihilate his own mind, to shut his father out of his consciousness.

"I'll be grateful for that, Father," he forced himself to say.

"Nicholas?" A voice behind him. He jumped. It was Elodie. Her hand rested gently on his arm, like cool cloth on feverish skin.

"Sorry. I didn't mean to scare you. What are you doing out here?"

Nicholas raked his mind for an excuse. "Well, you know I don't sleep. Hours of sitting in one place drive me crazy. How are you feeling?"

She seemed to accept his explanation. Elodie's psychic powers weren't strong enough to overcome the walls around his thoughts. "Better," she lied. "There's something I need to tell you. Something I've wanted to show you for a while."

"What is it?"

"This," she replied, and took a small opal out of her pocket. She'd found it inside his backpack back at Midnight Hall, on the day his father first hit him with the brain fury. Now she slipped it into Nicholas' hand. Nicholas felt the stone with his fingers – smooth, cold. A flash of white appeared in his mind, though he couldn't see colours any more, and he knew at once what he was holding.

"There's something about this stone," Elodie continued. "I don't know. I sense something inside it. But it's ... shut. It's difficult to explain."

Nicholas' eyes widened, remembering what that stone contained, but he controlled himself and nodded. "It's just a stone I use in spells. Thank you," he said, and slipped it into his own pocket. *This will make things so much easier*, he thought, *when the time comes*.

At that moment, the sound of distant thunder filled the sky. Elodie looked up, and saw columns of light break up the darkness, beyond the trees.

"Nicholas, I think I'm ill," she whispered suddenly, her soft French accent thicker, like it always was when she was upset. A pause. Nicholas' heart was bleeding silently, in a way he didn't think possible any more.

"I've known for a while, but I didn't want to believe it. The blue nails ... the fatigue ... and when I bleed, it doesn't stop." Nicholas could see the wounds deeply scarred into her flesh, some still weeping blood. When she spoke again, Elodie's voice was a whisper. "It's the Azasti."

"I know."

Suddenly, she began to weep, silent tears streaming down her face. There in the darkness, with fireflies flying all around her, her thoughts drifted between their insect dance and death. *How long do fireflies live*, she asked herself confusedly. *One night, and then their lights just go out forever?*

It was all so hard. So much harder to really leave your life behind, compared to just feeling you wanted to. When Harry died she was sure she wanted to end life too, but now that the end was near, Elodie longed for another chance. The hardest part was knowing the choice was out of her hands – she had no power over the decaying of her blood, and no way to stop it.

"Nicholas. I'm scared," she murmured.

"I know that too," he replied.

When limbs freeze, they don't hurt. It's when they thaw that the pain begins. Nicholas' heart had felt like that, when he met Sarah and began to believe he could rebel against his father. He'd felt like coming alive again, and it hurt like hell. He placed his hands on Elodie's hips and drew her closer. She smelled sweet, too sweet, like flowers wilting. Again, distant thunder resounded in their ears, and a flash of lightning illuminated the scene. In the sudden light, Elodie took in Nicholas' face, his perfect features – his eyes so black that iris and pupil were one, the perfect whiteness of his skin. A hard, powerful face, like a god from an ancient civilisation. She barely came up to his chest, she was so small. He took a step towards her and wrapped his arms around her. Elodie tensed for a moment. This was the man-demon who'd deceived them all, who'd killed so many heirs, including her husband. He was evil.

But he'd been blinded for having rejected that evil, and he was the only one who could understand the depth of her sorrow, of her loneliness. Nobody else could. Not Niall, not Sarah. Not even Sean, tied to her by a deep friendship she had briefly, wrongly, mistaken for love – not even he could follow her where she was going.

Nicholas brought a hand to her face, the other still holding her by her waist. She closed her eyes, raising her chin like a sunflower towards the light. "I wish I could see you," he whispered, feeling every inch of her features – her forehead, her cheeks, her lips. His hands were hot on her skin, nearly scalding. How long had it been since somebody had touched her that way? She took a step forward too, until her face was on his chest, and in one liquid movement they were entwined.

Elodie remembered when in a moment of absolute, black despair, she'd asked Nicholas to unleash his ravens on her, to help her forget. She shivered as she remembered how close she'd come to getting killed. That had been the first time she'd felt a weird, dark bond with Nicholas.

"Elodie," he murmured in her ear, and she felt his lips grazing her skin.

"I'm here. I'm here with you," she heard herself saying.

Suddenly, he pressed her harder. He could have crushed her, he could have taken her breath away, put an end to it all, without any more suffering. Elodie was suddenly horrified. She disentangled herself and hurried away, leaving Nicholas alone with the thunder and lightning.

28
In the Mirror

Abandoned things and abandoned hearts
Your hair still in the silver brush
Your story in a jewel
Your tears in a silver box

Blue lightning kept cutting the sky, and thunder resounded from far away, but there was no rain and the sky seemed too clear for storms. There was something not quite natural in the lightning – its blue hue too vivid, too strong, something that could have never existed in the human world. Once more, Sarah considered how the Shadow World had this archaic, powerful way of presenting itself, as if the explosive energy that produced the universe itself was still running just beneath the surface. What in the human world seemed faded, domesticated, in the Shadow World was vivid and wild.

The storm felt like a warning. Like a message.

"Time to go," Nicholas called.

Easy for him to say, thought Niall, ill with tiredness, dragging himself up. *He doesn't need to sleep.* The loss of blood from the leeches' attack had taken a toll on him. Every time he moved his head the whole world danced in front of his eyes. Images and thoughts of Winter had come to him while he slept, half torturing, half comforting him.

"Are you okay?" Alvise asked, offering him a hand and helping him up.

"Aye, never been better!" he replied, but his voice sounded weary. "And how are you on this fine morning, Micol?" he asked the dark-eyed girl.

Micol shrugged, running a hand through her hair. "Freezing. But this is better than being stuck in Palazzo Vendramin, anyway."

"Fair enough. Good to see someone who thinks the glass is half full, I always say!" Niall replied. "God, I wish we had some whiskey . . ."

"For breakfast?" Sarah couldn't help smiling. If anyone ever brought a smile to her face, it was Niall.

The Irishman shrugged apologetically. "It's good for warmth."

"I'm afraid this is all we have," said Sean, and threw him a packet of dry biscuits. Their provisions were thinning at a worrying rate; thankfully there were many wells and little ponds in the forest they could draw water from, though Sean constantly worried about what hid in them. And what they might be drinking with the water.

They began packing up their sleeping bags, the pink light of a dawn that promised to be spectacular bleeding through the jigsaw of branches.

"In a few hours we should reach a stream," Nicholas interrupted. "Just beyond it, there's my castle."

"Your castle?" Sean enquired. "How can that be? You have a castle in the Shadow World?"

"This is the first we've heard of this place," Sarah added, crossing her arms.

"I lived there a long time ago. Not any more," he said, and there was a bitter, pained note to his voice. She wondered if Nicholas had built the castle for Martyna, or if he'd lived there with her – and she did so with no emotion. She had no sympathy for Nicholas, in spite of all that he'd been through. Nothing was left in her heart for him except anger.

"I built two castles, one in each world, so it exists in both," Nicholas explained. "The castle in the human world and the one in the Shadow World are mirror images of each other. The one in the human world was destroyed a few centuries ago, but the one here has lasted. I haven't been there since . . . In a long time. We can find shelter there for a few hours."

He turned his face towards Elodie, who was standing beside him, a light hand on his arm as ever. She was always at his side, always guiding him, protecting him from obstacles and threats he couldn't see in his blindness. Sarah's gaze rested on Elodie's white, slender fingers touching Nicholas's arm, and a thought made its way in her head, a thought too uncomfortable to be borne.

No. Elodie was a Secret heir, and she was on a mission – to destroy the King of Shadows, the man who murdered Harry. Nicholas was a tool in her mission; Elodie was doing what she had to do. Was he really looking for somewhere Elodie could have some respite, Sarah wondered. Was there any room in his black soul for thinking of others?

Sean's eyes met Sarah's, and she saw that his thoughts were

going along the same lines. "Have you heard of this place before, Elodie?" he asked. He was shocked at how worn the French girl looked after the leeches' attack. Her skin was almost translucent, and her soft chocolate eyes were lined with blue. Her willpower was the only thing that kept her going, as her body was failing. No one could ignore that fact any more.

"Not until now," she replied.

"What do you think?"

Elodie shot a glance at Nicholas. A few times before Sean had noticed how she looked at him. Yes, there was still hatred in her eyes sometimes − but something else also. A weird bond that made Sean afraid for her once more.

"I think if Nicholas had wanted to lead us into a trap he would have done so by now," she said simply.

"Fine. But who knows what has taken residence in your castle, Nicholas. The place must be swarming with Surari," Sean observed.

"It's sealed shut. Magically. Nothing can get inside. There are spells all over the place. Everything was left like the last time I was there, before I left for Scotland."

To look for me, thought Sarah, feeling sick to her bones. *To come to Scotland to try to snatch me away from everything and everybody I knew, and make me yours. I hate you*, she thought with an intensity that frightened her.

"If this is a trap, Nicholas, I swear I'll gouge your eyes out," said Sarah coldly. He believed her.

They took off, the darkness around them thinning slowly, like ink mixed with water.

"Alvise. Look," Micol whispered, turning her face up. The

sky was on fire, burning with the rising sun, bright-pink rays drenching the canopy of trees. "Have you ever seen anything so beautiful?"

Alvise shook his head. "It's amazing," he said. "Shame we don't get much chance to see the sights," he smirked.

"This place exists alongside our world, and we never knew."

"I wonder who else knows," Alvise replied. "The Sabha do, for sure."

"They must do. My nonna used to tell us a story ... to me and my brothers. It was about a Secret heir, long ago, who rebelled against his family. His father had no heart to kill him, but he sent him away to the Other World. I used to wonder what this 'other world' was ..."

"I suppose all the Secret heirs used to know about the Shadow World and the King of Shadows, but the memory got lost in time."

"The King of Shadows wanted us to forget," Micol murmured, gazing at the tall, white-skinned half-man half-demon who walked in front of them, his black aura swirling around him like a curse. She tried to keep going with her eyes turned upwards, drunk with beauty. Everything in the Shadow World seemed heightened, sharper, more vivid – it was a world untamed, ancestral, raw, as enchanting as it was frightening.

"You'll end up banging your face on a tree," said Alvise, smiling. "Come on," he said, and took her by the arm.

Their boots were making barely any noise on the soft, mossy undergrowth. The calls of birds and beasts waking up were the only sound. Some of those calls were Surari's, Sean thought, tightening his hand around his *sgian-dubh*. He never let it go, day or night. The dagger that had belonged to James Midnight, Sarah's father, had become an extension of his body.

He surveyed his small company of friends: Alvise looked strong, unafraid, walking ahead with a single-mindedness that amazed Sean, considering the Italian man had been thrown into the Shadow World with no warning or indication of what was about to happen. Micol looked so young, walking with her face towards the pink rays of the sun like a bewitched little girl. He couldn't believe she was really sixteen, with her small, slender body and childish face. And still, he'd seen the power hidden inside her. Silently, Sean thanked his lucky stars that they'd been sent to help, even if Micol's arrival had been so fraught.

Sean's eyes moved to Niall. He seemed to have recovered a little from the demon-leeches' attack, as there was some colour in his cheeks and he was walking steadily. Sean suspected that the idea of having to cross a stream had put a spring in his step.

And beside him, silent, determined, her hair in a long braid and her face alight with the dawn, was Sarah.

Sarah.

Why does love always have to go hand in hand with terror? In his life, at least, it seemed that way. Every time he looked at Sarah, Sean felt sick with fear.

I love her too much.

It's not good to love someone – anyone – as much as I love her, he couldn't help thinking, as if his feelings for her were a jinx. Because everyone he'd loved before, he'd lost.

Sarah caught him looking at her. "You okay?"

"Yes. Yes, fine," he replied. It was time to snap out of his thoughts. "The stream we're going to. Is it deep?" he asked Nicholas abruptly. "Can we walk around it?"

"Yes, it's deep, and no, we can't walk. Can everybody swim?"

"A bit," said Niall cheerily. The idea of being anywhere near water again made his heart soar.

"I don't like to swim, but I can walk on water," said Micol matter-of-factly.

"Good for you, lassie!" Niall exclaimed, and Micol frowned, thinking he was making fun of her. Would anyone ever take her seriously? But Niall was being sincere in his admiration. As a child of the sea, he felt a bond with anyone who had a power relating to water.

"We'll be freezing afterwards," Elodie said.

"We can light fires at the castle," Nicholas replied gently. "You can get some rest."

"I'm fine." Elodie cut him short. She didn't want to call attention to herself. She didn't want to be a burden on their mission. She steeled herself – she'd just ignore the wounds that kept bleeding, and the dreams that tormented her. She might be a flame about to go out, but she would burn the King of Shadows before it was all over.

The sun had risen; and as the last pink rays burnt themselves out the strange lightning started again, its blue flashes intermittent, the clap of thunder breaking up the sky.

A warning, Sarah thought again. And maybe a sign that they were getting closer. She walked beside Sean and touched his arm briefly, to show him she needed to talk to him. "What do you think about this castle thing he sprang on us?" she said in a low voice.

Sean frowned. "I don't trust him, and never will. But I

want Elodie to have some proper rest, and if she can get warm and sleep on a bed for one night at least ..."

Sarah nodded. She took a breath and braced herself for the conversation that was to follow. It wasn't easy to broach the subject with Sean.

"Sean ... I'm worried about Elodie. I mean, apart from her health. I'm worried that Nicholas is mind-moulding her like he did to me. That this is all an act, that he's still looking for a wife and he's moved on from me to Elodie."

Sean felt cold. "It can't be. Remember what he said, about the way he chose you because your blood is strong? Elodie's blood is ... tainted." He struggled to find the word, his chest tightening as he thought of his friend, so ill, so vulnerable.

"So if he's mind-moulding her, he must have another purpose. Some other plan."

"When he was doing it to you, you were in haze. Every time he was around, your eyes glazed over as if you were drunk."

"How do you know? You weren't there. I'd sent you away," she said. She'd been furious about his lie. But how could she have ever lived a life without Sean?

Like a life without light, forever.

Sean smiled. "I never left you, Sarah. I was watching you day and night. You just didn't see me."

I love you, she thought, and once again, she wished they'd be alone, that those words could be spoken aloud. That they could find each other's bodies and be close. For a moment they were silent.

"I'm going to ask Niall to take over," Sean said finally. "I mean, to guide Nicholas instead of Elodie. They'll do as I say."

Sarah raised an eyebrow. "Niall, maybe. But Elodie will do as you say? She's her own person, you know that."

"You do as I say all the time," he said, a mischievous smile in his eyes. "You wouldn't dream of disobeying me."

Sarah laughed. "Sure. In your dreams. Nobody tells me what to do, Sean."

"I noticed."

"But if you say 'please', I'll do whatever you want," she said and walked forward, with a backward glance that made Sean's heart double its rhythm.

Soon they heard the sound of running water. The stream began where the trees ended, with barely a ribbon of pebbles between the forest and the water. There were no forests left in the human world as strong, as thick as this ancient one in the Shadow World. It was beautiful, and dangerous. And not made for human beings.

Sarah crouched and felt the water. It was cold but not freezing, running white and foamy. Just over a hundred yards from them there was a little dam made of fallen branches and reeds, which slowed the water slightly.

"Sean. Everything is going to get soaked," she said in dismay. They'd have no food left except for a few cans. They had no time to hunt or forage. They would starve.

"No, it isn't. I'll carry your stuff," Micol intervened. Under everybody's astonished gaze she took her shoes off, grabbed Sarah's backpack and stepped into the water – onto the water.

"Be careful. There are things in there," Nicholas admonished her.

Micol's body lit up with electrical charges, and the stream turned multi-coloured, running in blue, green, yellow, red, and orange waves. They watched in awe as Micol walked on confidently, one foot in front of the other, her face focused, as if staying afloat was an effort. She was a little figure wrapped in deadly rainbows against the backdrop of the running stream. The water magnified the power of Micol's charges, electrifying the stream all around her. Nothing will have survived that, thought Sarah. No fish, no little water creatures – no water demons. One by one, she took all their backpacks through and stood on the opposite shore.

"I've fried everything!" she called over the sound of the water, and pointed at a few dead fish that had floated to the surface, entangled in a barrier of reeds.

"Shit. Look at that," said Niall. They followed his gaze towards the little dam. Something else had come to the surface, besides fish. Two strange bodies lay belly up, thick brownish skin and clawed paws, mouths semi-open to show pointed, deadly teeth. Like crocodiles, but smaller, longer, thinner – and it seemed to Sarah as she considered the length of their fangs, even more lethal. For a few moments the Surari's corpses lay entangled in brambles and branches, hidden in the water, their edges bobbing on the surface, and then the power of the water propelled them downstream.

"I've cooked them. Surari barbecue," Micol smiled triumphantly.

Alvise gazed at her with a half-smile. *This young girl holds her own*, he thought with admiration.

"What?" she said, a challenge in her eyes.

"Nothing. Just ... you're pretty incredible," he said. And he meant it. They were so different, and still Micol reminded him of his own sister somehow. The same courage in the face of challenge. Micol looked away, pretending she didn't care – but she did.

"Half of us go in the water, half of us keep watch. Nicholas, Elodie, Alvise. You're first. Quick!" Sean commanded. The first cohort stepped into the water, one after the other, swimming as fast as they could as more corpses of those horrific demon-crocodiles drifted downstream.

As she dived, Elodie felt a shiver run down her back. She didn't like the water. The memory of what happened on Islay – the demon jellyfish that had dragged her in the water with its sticky tentacles and nearly drowned her – was too close for comfort. Winter had saved her life, dragging her onto the stones where Sean found her, cradled by this silver-haired naked girl who looked as if she'd been born of a wave.

Nicholas swam on blindly, clutching Elodie's hand. Somehow he seemed to know exactly where to go, as if the senses he had left were guiding him while underwater. Alvise was used to the warm Mediterranean waters, and hated every stroke. He emerged with blue lips and shivering so violently his teeth were chattering.

"Ready?" Sean asked Niall and Sarah as soon as he was sure that the first group had got to the other side safely. They nodded and jumped in without hesitation. Sarah wasn't an exceptional swimmer, but she was good enough, and having swum in the chilly waters of Islay, she wasn't too affected by the cold.

Niall had been waiting for this moment for weeks. His heart soared as the water enveloped him. He was in his element at last. He crossed through easily, as if stepping across a sunny meadow, and he couldn't help trying to steal one minute more in the water. But it could only be one minute – he knew that. He could breathe underwater and he couldn't drown, but not even his Flynn powers could protect him from the demon-crocodiles and whatever else lurked in there and was waiting to take the place of those that Micol had exterminated. He too joined Sarah and the others onshore, and while they were still on the ground catching their breath, he jumped straight to his feet. He had never stopped breathing and the cold had no effect on him.

In a split second, they realised that not all of them were on the other shore.

Someone was missing.

"Sean!" Sarah screamed, just as Elodie scrambled to the waterline on her hands and feet, peering into the running water. Sarah was about to dive back in when Elodie grasped her forearm. "Don't!" she cried out. "Let Niall go. He stands the best chance!"

Sarah dragged herself onto her knees, panting in terror and frustration. Niall was nowhere to be seen; he'd already vanished back into the water.

29
If I Die Here

If I die here –
Your name will be the last word I say

Niall swam against the current in frantic strokes, looking for Sean. He remembered the bodies of the demon-crocodiles trapped in the dam-like reeds not far from where they crossed – maybe Sean was trapped there too? It was worth a try.

It didn't take long for him to manoeuvre his body towards the dam. Niall was of the water, born to navigate it, and his powers were strong. The murky water made it difficult to see, but as Niall approached, he could make out the faintest flash of colour, the same colour as Sean's clothes. And there he was, among the debris and brambles and floating branches – Sean, trapped inside the dam, his limbs secured to it with interwoven reeds. He was twitching, desperately trying to free himself, his cheeks puffed out in his attempt to store oxygen. Suddenly, Niall saw something out the corner of his eye – a dark-green arm ridged with minuscule tassels that flowed like seaweed – and then it was gone. Something was there, a Surari – but Niall couldn't do anything about it. Sean had to be taken above water soon or he would drown.

Niall threw himself on the dam, trying to free Sean's limbs. He gathered at once that the dam couldn't be a natural barrier. It had been woven, made by hands. It was a nest. Or a trap. The realisation filled him with dread. He'd seen the hand that had made the barrier, and that hand belonged to something that was still swimming around him, something that would not let go of its prey so easily.

"Sean!" called Niall, breathing water like air.

Sean's limbs were flailing as he desperately tried to free himself, his face purple. He felt like his lungs were bursting. He needed to breathe. He needed air . . .

Niall was nearly there. He could nearly touch Sean's hand . . . but powerful fingers wrapped themselves around his ankles, pulling and pulling, trying to drag him away from Sean. Niall bent his body backwards – he was as agile as a seal – and his eyes met the creature's. Finally he could see it. It looked very similar to a Merman, but its scaly skin was dark green and not blue, its gills faintly throbbing at the sides of its face. Its eyes were yellow with slit pupils, and there were too many teeth to fit in its mouth – pointed, thin, needle-like. Weeds were dangling from its arms and legs like ripped clothes, and little black creatures had made a home on its chest, attached to it like leeches or growing larvae. All of a sudden, he realised that a sickening smell had spread in the water around them, and he felt himself gag. Niall took a deep watery breath and kicked his legs towards the creature as hard as he could – the demon had to let go.

He did a somersault in the water, and his eyes met Sean, who was still trying to free himself. Only then did he notice that a trickle of blood was leaking off his friend and colouring the water around them. Niall knew that there was no point in trying to free Sean there and then, the mer-creature would have stopped him again. He had to destroy it first. He took hold of his dagger and lunged at it, stabbing its arms and hands and chest, green blood leaking from the wounds.

The demon howled, an eerie sound that travelled underwater to the ears of those on shore, and threw itself at Niall, grabbing blindly with its bleeding arms extended and trying to claw at his face. Niall tasted his own blood but felt no pain. It had been all too quick. Rage burnt inside him, and terror. *How long can a man survive without air? How long will Sean last before his heart gives in?*

Sean wanted to call out, but he couldn't. His lungs were exploding, stars dancing at the edge of his vision. The reeds were like chains, and he couldn't free himself. He was suffocating. He desperately tried to keep his mouth closed until his instinct got the best of him, and finally he gasped for air. But there was no air, only water that filled his mouth and his throat and his lungs. He jerked for a few seconds – darkness was all around him, every bit of his body and mind screaming in panic. *I'm dying. Who's going to look after Sarah?* was his last conscious thought. And then his body was still.

The demon, bleeding and weakened but animated by its survival instinct, grabbed Niall's arm and shook it violently. Niall's dagger went floating away with the current. The mer-creature wrapped its slippery hands around Niall's neck. With enormous effort, and the Surari's grip tightening around his throat, Niall pulled upwards, upwards, carrying the demon with him.

On his way up Niall grabbed Sean's hand and held on to him, trying to take him to the surface. At first, Sean didn't budge, and Niall's upwards arc was interrupted with a jerk – but he wouldn't let go. The Surari's hands were unyielding around his neck, and he was slowly suffocating. He couldn't take any more. He sank a knee into its chest, and propelled it away in a cloud of green blood.

He hadn't let go of Sean. He tugged harder, now with both hands, but it wasn't enough. He pulled and ripped reeds, ignoring the cuts in his hands and how the water was coloured red around him, until finally Sean's body shifted slightly, and then some more. Niall swam towards the surface, his left hand tight around Sean's wrist, his right hand propelling them – and this time Sean's body followed.

As they emerged from the water Niall managed to scream, "Take him onshore!" before strong, cruel arms pulled him down again. Niall caught a glimpse of a pair of male arms clad in a white shirt – Alvise? – drag Sean away.

He'd done it. Sean would survive.

Niall prepared himself to fight. *Winter*, he called silently.

It all happened very fast. The mer-creature was now in front of him, hands poised to strangle, teeth ready to bite. And then it stopped, and shuddered, and its eyes went wide in shock and horror. Its unconscious body began to float upwards.

Niall stared, not quite believing what had just happened, and then he felt something brush his leg. The dark, toothy shape of a demon-crocodile swam around him. He was filled with blind terror, and his instinct kicked in, leading him upwards and towards the shore faster than he'd ever swum, where friendly arms waited to pull him to safety. As he was pulled onshore, he felt a red-hot pain coming from his legs. The skin on his shins had been shredded, but it was too late for the demon-crocodiles. Niall would not be their next meal.

"Sean," was the first thing he said as he breathed air again.

30
Breathe

Your words to me
Are oxygen

Sean

This time, I really think I am dead. And then my eyes open of their own accord, and I cough and splutter and vomit water until, at last, air comes into my lungs. Above me the sky is on fire – dawn, sunset? I don't know – and Sarah's face appears. Water keeps trickling from my mouth and another coughing fit splits my sides.

"Sean ..." She's calling my name, like a prayer. Her hair brushes my face as she leans above me. Her closeness is like oxygen. "It's okay. You're safe. You're safe ..."

A few ragged breaths – painful, but so blissful – the feeling of Sarah's hands on my face. Elodie's anguished face above me now.

"Ça va? Sean, ça va?" she keeps saying.

Sarah helps me up and I can't quite believe I'm alive. My

192

lungs are hurting more than I can say, my heart beats furiously, as if trying to make up for all the time it was still underwater, when I was trapped in the Surari's nest.

"Niall?" I manage to rasp and gurgle before taking another deep, painful breath. His voice comes from somewhere behind me. I turn around and I see him, his hands clasped in his lap, bleeding profusely.

"I'm fine. I was in the mood for a long swim anyway ..."

"Your hands!"

"Just a graze. We owe Alvise our lives." He points at the water and I follow her gaze to the Surari's body, tangled, face-down in the same dam where it'd trapped me. Two arrows are sticking from its back, green water flowing over its body.

I'm about to thank Alvise, when somebody screams, and I turn back to the water in time to see another Surari jump out of the stream with a leap that would be impossible for a human being. It attacks the first thing it sees – Micol – and flattens her on the grass.

I fumble, looking for my *sgian-dubh*, my reflexes slow and sluggish – but there's no need. Sarah has thrown herself on the creature already, freeing Micol, and they roll on the ground together. Sarah's hands sink into its skin. The Surari raises its head to the sky and howls, a howl of pain that has something unsettlingly human about it. The creature does resemble a human being, one that evolution has programmed to live underwater. The eerie sound stops quickly, and the mer-creature lies still, Blackwater seeping off its body, until it dissolves in one last gush. So there was a pair of them. Probably male and female. Sarah must be thinking the same, because she's looking at the dead Surari with something resembling pity. I'll leave compassion to her. There is no room in my heart for it now.

"Are you okay?" she asks Micol. The Italian girl looks ashen, but she's unharmed.

"Yes. Thank you," she says, and looks down. I can feel she still resents Sarah – and no wonder.

"Let's get away from here," I say, and take Alvise's hand as he helps me up. The world spins around me, but I soon find my feet. I want away from this place; there might be more mer-demons, and who knows what else hides in those waters.

"Not far now," says Nicholas, his stride more confident than ever. He can almost walk as he used to before he was blinded. Maybe it has something to do with getting closer to his home. "Soon we can rest."

Yes, of course. We can all comfortably rest in your house, I think to myself. *I'll sleep like a baby for sure.*

We're all soaking, and the cold wind is biting us. Freezing white mist rises from the ground. Alvise is carrying my backpack, as I'm still weak. I still stumble a bit, but I'm recovering fast. Sarah walks shoulder to shoulder with me. I catch a glimpse of her profile – her face is hard, set. Determined. But there's a strange look in her eyes.

"Hey. I'm okay. I'm here," I whisper.

"If something should happen to you . . ." She doesn't finish the sentence.

"Then you'll keep going. You'll finish this."

She takes a breath, and nods. "Yes. You must promise the same."

"I promise." I'd keep going long enough to do what I must do. And then give up. A life without Sarah is not worth living.

Weird, how I knew that already soon after we met. Like whatever binds me to Sarah is the same thing that binds me to life. I hold her hand harder, tighter, and I don't want to let go. I don't care if everyone can see us, though neither of us likes making a show of our feelings. I won't let her go.

The sun is setting behind us in an explosion of pink, red and orange, and we cast long shadows on the ground. Intermittent buzzing sounds accompany us, as Micol's hands shine with multi-coloured charges. Strange sounds come from the trees, calls and animal growls and deep, bird-like squeaks. What's hiding in those trees? More leeches? Surari whose existence we have no idea about? What will come next, to try to destroy us?

In my time in Japan, when the culling of the heirs began, I saw things that I'd rather forget – but I can't. I can never forget the creatures that slithered out of the Tokyo metro, and the things they could do to human bodies. I hold Sarah's hand tighter as memories of old horrors crept into my mind.

I think of Mary Ann. A Gamekeeper like me, and my former girlfriend. I never loved her, not like I love Sarah, but I cared about her. I care about her still. For a while, Harry Midnight, Elodie, Mary Ann and I were a team, fighting together in Japan. Harry is dead, Elodie is sick, and Mary Ann . . . I'm afraid to find out what happened to her.

Shadows are falling all around us, the patches of sky we see between the oak branches getting darker by the minute. Twilight, the hour that always struck fear in our ancestors' minds, as predators sharpen their senses and ready themselves for the hunt. Night is falling fast, the air turning from lilac to purple in a heartbeat. Everything is wilder in this world, bigger, more vivid. An ancient wind-swept sky extends above us, the shadow of the moon getting stronger as darkness falls ... In the Shadow World, even moonbeams can be deadly. I shudder, remembering the moon-demons.

"Eyes open for the moonbeams, everyone," I remind them.

"What does he mean?" I hear Alvise asking Niall.

"Moon-demons," Niall explains. "Sort of ghosts, really. Like animated moonbeams. If you touch them, you'll turn into them. They attacked us the moment we arrived."

"I always wonder if there's an end to demons' variety. New ones seem to spring out all the time," Alvise says.

"In the Midnight library I saw a Surari Compendium," Niall replied. "I swear, it freaked the hell out of me. And I'm a Dreamer, I've seen my share of Surari."

"I wonder what's worse, another night outside or one inside Nicholas' castle," I whisper to Sarah.

"Why did he not tell us about it before? Did he think it was an unimportant detail?" she replies.

I catch a glimpse of his imposing silhouette moving between the trees. "Who knows what goes through that dark mind of his?"

I long for some warmth, my body still frozen from the long immersion in the water. I feel like my bones will never dry up. We're all so cold. We've been cold for days and nights without ever warming up fully. A fire would be a godsend.

All of a sudden we emerge from under the roof of trees, and find ourselves under a black sky full of stars. I can see the Great Bear just above us, and the Big Dipper, and more. The constellations are so clear it's like watching every star in the universe being born. Only in the wildest, most remote places on earth could you see as many stars as this – a whole sea of them. Sarah is looking up in awe, the light of the moon reflected in her eyes.

We make our way along the curve of a steep, stony hill, barren of trees. I'm nervous, aware of what might lurk above us, or among the rocks of its ragged ridges. Past the hill there's yet another ridge, black and steep and completely smooth, making the climb impossible, and against it, a stone building that seems to have sprouted from the rim, its windows dark like empty sockets, its walls covered in vines. Nicholas' castle.

"Welcome home," I whisper under my breath.

31
Shouts and Whispers

Memories screaming
They will be never silenced
But the day will come
When our children will forget

"Are we sure this is a good idea?" Alvise murmured.

They stood in front of the wooden portal, daggers at the ready. The door was double their height, decorated with abstract carvings. In the middle there was a heavy iron ring shaped like a serpent biting its tail.

Sean's voice was low and lethal. "Nicholas. If this is a trap I swear I'm going to rip the flesh from your bones."

"It's not a trap, Sean. There are fires to be lit inside and beds and water. Unless you want to keep going through the night."

Sean ignored him. "Everybody ready?"

"There's nothing inside," said Nicholas impatiently. "The place is covered in spells, sealed all over. Nothing can get in here while I'm away."

"I'll believe it when I see it. Open that door," Sean replied, his *sgian-dubh* moving already, readying itself to trace the runes.

Nicholas rested a hand flat on the door – suddenly, the nightly calls and growls in the woods behind them and the stony hills above them seemed to rise in intensity, like a weird greeting for Nicholas' return. He whispered a few words in the Ancient language and the door opened under his touch, noiselessly, as if the heavy wood had been as light as a feather and its hinges oiled that same morning. Nicholas and Elodie entered first, followed by the others. It wasn't completely dark. Dusky light was seeping from the windows carved in the stone – but it was hard to make out shapes in such a muted light. Sean, Sarah and Niall retrieved and switched on their torches, their beams illuminating a stone floor, high ceilings, and a cavernous hall.

As she stepped inside, Sarah felt her head spin. She was entering a place between two worlds, present in both dimensions and still suspended between the two. The air inside smelled damp, mould grew on the high ceilings, and in every hidden corner invisible spores flew through the air. It was cold, colder than outside. The place felt heavy with memories, heavy with history – unhappy history. A strange weight settled on Sarah's chest, and once again she sensed ghostly fingers touching her face, her arms, travelling down her back. She breathed in softly.

"Are you okay?" asked Sean at once. His torch was darting around, and all his senses were alert for possible attacks.

"Yes," she replied and gazed at the cold stone walls and the ancient weavings hanging from them, greyed with time, the scenes they depicted now impossible to decipher.

"You're a dab hand at interior design, aren't you, Nicholas?" Niall said, his light Irish voice sounding absurd, out of place, in the gloomy atmosphere. "This is lovely," he continued, eyes resting on the weapons and trophies hanging on the walls, severed heads of enormous, prehistoric stags and weird buffalo-like creatures. "Airy and bright and . . . just very you."

"There's someone here," Elodie interrupted, her lips darkening. The sound of thunder accompanied her words, and blue lightning flashed outside the windows, striking black stones on the hills.

"Surari?" asked Sean.

"It can't be," Nicholas said, adamant.

"I . . . I don't know. I . . . Wait. I can't feel anything any more," said Elodie, uncertainty creeping in her voice. "I'm not sure what I felt. Sorry." Flashes of blue light illuminated her delicate face and her blue, poisonous lips.

"There is no one in here but us," Nicholas repeated. "Nothing can come in. I made sure of that. Let's light the fires and get some rest. We're safe for a few hours."

Sean studied his face at the light of the torch. "Elodie sensed something," he said. "She's always right."

"Whatever it was, I think it's gone," Elodie whispered, eyes closed to sharpen her psychic sense.

"Or it's hiding," Sarah intervened.

"Fine. Feel free to explore the place," Nicholas said, his anger now out in the open. "I've been blinded and half killed, I've saved your lives, and you still can't trust me. You won't find anything. The whole place has been sealed shut by hundreds of spells, and they were all unbroken when we arrived. I checked. You don't need eyes to sense them. We're the first living creatures to step inside since the last time I was here, and that was hundreds of years ago."

"You haven't been back here for as long as that?" asked Elodie.

Nicholas shook his head. "Too many memories," he said, too softly for anyone to hear but Elodie, who was standing the closest to him.

Sean would not be convinced. "Niall, Alvise, Micol, check upstairs," he said. "We'll have a look down here. Nicholas, you stick with us, and stay where I can see you. Elodie, keep an eye on him."

"You don't need to tell me," she replied testily.

"Safe, sorry, and all that!" Niall quipped in Nicholas' direction and began humming softly, making his way up the steps.

Sarah followed Sean inside the castle's depths, her eyes glowing green. The place, as spooky and as eerie as it felt, looked lived in, like its inhabitants should all be asleep, waiting to come downstairs and start the day. Apart from the freezing cold and the ever-present thick grey dust, you would have thought people still lived here, or had abandoned the place a few hours before and not hundreds of years ago.

Sarah, Sean, Nicholas and Elodie entered what looked like several sitting rooms, every wall covered in tapestries, the dusty curtains open, untouched. Unmoving, Sarah noticed. For such an ancient place, there were no draughts at all, unlike in her Islay mansion. She remembered Nicholas' words: the place had been sealed shut. Maybe he wasn't lying when he'd said that nobody could have come in.

And nobody could have gone out, she couldn't help thinking. Her hair stood on end as a picture of long-dead people piled up somewhere in the castle entered her mind.

Next they stepped inside a dining hall. In the centre sat an enormous table dotted with candelabra, and more sinister trophies hung from the walls. Sarah stopped for a moment to retrieve matches from her backpack and lit the candles. They glowed orange and golden in the gloom, casting long flickering shadows throughout the room.

"Logs on the fire," she pointed out to Sean as they passed an ornate fireplace, a note of longing in her voice. Oh, to light a fire and finally get warm!

Then came what looked like a grand hall, with its floor worn and uneven after years of being stepped on. Silence hung as heavy as the stones the place was made of. No sounds, no movements. It was as if not even the mice and flies and earwigs, and all the other little creatures that crawl in abandoned places, had been allowed in. No spider webs embroidering the ceilings like lace. There was no sign of life in any form. But it was the kitchens that spooked Sarah the most: pots and pans and crockery on the big wooden tables, cloths covered in dust that seemed to have been left there mid-cleaning ... Sarah was reminded of the *Mary Celeste*, the ship found with nobody on board, and everything untouched, everything ready for use – like it had been left in a heartbeat, or everybody there had vanished.

Sarah's heart leapt as they stepped into what looked like a laundry room, with stone basins and an iron-carved pump. "Tell me there's running water," she said to Nicholas.

"Well, the pump should still work. We can light the fires and warm the water that way. There are tin baths in the bathrooms ..."

"Bathrooms?" Sarah exclaimed. She couldn't help herself. The idea of washing off the grime and sweat and bruises was too good.

"Yes. Upstairs."

Sarah closed her eyes briefly. She could not wait for a proper wash at last – the unexpected luxury felt like a blessing. She tried the pump. It was rusty and heavy, and the water wasn't exactly clear, but it was passable.

"All okay, I suppose. Elodie?" said Sean.

"I can't feel anything," the French girl replied, looking around her.

"Let's get the others." Sean would not let his guard down, not while they were on Nicholas' territory.

32

Winter Shaw

Bloodlines forever
Stretching through the land
And those of us
Who were made to leave

Venice

Since her conversation with Sarah, they had heard no more
from Lucrezia. Winter had sat with the girl every waking
minute, waiting, hoping. She'd even asked Conte Vendramin
if she could sleep in the room too, in case Lucrezia had a
message for them in the middle of the night. The count had
agreed and ordered a wrought-iron bed to be brought in for
Winter.

Now she lay awake, listening to Lucrezia's frantic whispering and watching the grey Adriatic Sea from the window.
She couldn't stop thinking of Niall. Never before in all fifty
years of her life – Elementals age very slowly – had she felt

that way for anyone. Since the Midnights had tried to take her life, horrified by her hybrid nature, her trust in human beings had been shaken to the point that she'd preferred the company of seals. During her long exile from Islay, she'd been content with the seals for companions, and the occasional conversation with islanders, who were curious about her but reserved enough not to pry. She had a passionate nature, and a few young men had drifted in and out of her life. But, her desire for freedom had always been stronger than her need for love. She'd seen her mother lose her heart to Winter's Elemental father, but then settle down with Hugh Shaw in a loving, loyal marriage that had healed her after the loss of Winter's father. Winter could not accept anything less.

That was why when she returned to Islay and settled in the whitewashed cottage that had been her parents', she had no plans to let anyone in her life. She was happy managing her time on land and her time in the sea with the seals.

And then Sarah Midnight had arrived, and with her Niall Flynn, and everything had changed. She thought the Irish boy would have been a joyous interlude in her solitary life, that she would let him love her but not get too close, but she had fallen for him.

After fifty years, life had surprised Winter, given her so much happiness and then taken it away. But it was not in her nature to despair. She was always drawn to the light, to joy, just like she could see that Sarah was drawn to sorrow. Lying in her bed in Venice beside the sleeping girl, awake and listening to Lucrezia's whispering, Winter's heart was full of hope. She would not cry, she would not despair, until she was sure she had reason for it.

Winter freed her arm from the sheets, and extended it

towards Lucrezia. She felt for the girl's hand until she found her cold, thin fingers, and held it. It might have been her imagination, but she had the distinct impression that Lucrezia squeezed her hand ever so slightly back.

She closed her eyes and let herself drift to sleep.

33
Locked

I keep you in a box
Inside my heart
And nobody needs to know

"Let's stay together," Alvise whispered to Micol as they prowled the first floor at the light of the torches, his pugnale in hand. Micol's fingers were shimmering and crackling more and more as they advanced.

"I'm not going anywhere on my own. This place gives me the creeps – even more than Palazzo Vendramin!" Micol exclaimed, and a brighter spark left her hands. A strong smell of cloistered air, like air trapped in an airplane, spread around them.

"My hair just stood up, Micol. Can you turn it down a notch?" asked Niall kindly.

"Okay. Sorry. It's so weird that the beds are all made," said Micol, running a sparking hand along a dusty silk duvet, decorated with green and yellow patterns. "Like they all left so suddenly. Didn't even carry their stuff somewhere else . . ."

Every room was the same. Four-poster beds, dark wooden furniture, heavy hangings and rugs. In every room there was no noise, no sign of life, the air perfectly still.

"Nicholas didn't live here on his own, that's for sure," Alvise observed as they reached the end of the corridor. "I wonder if he had a family. Do half-demons have families?"

"I know I had one. Before him and his father decided to kill us all," said Micol bitterly.

There was one room left to check. It had a double door, different from the others – the wood was lighter and carved in gentle patterns, leaves and flowers. Niall stepped in first. The room was panelled in light wood, the same shade as its door. Yet another four-poster bed stood in the middle, perfectly made in white linen sheets and white draping, though dust had turned them grey. Against the small window there was a dressing table with a vase of long-dead, blackened roses. They checked every nook and cranny – and when they turned to go, Micol threw one last look inside. And there it was, a small orange light, flickering beside the dressing table, and then floating past them out of the room. Micol gasped.

"Something wrong?" asked Alvise.

"No . . . No. Everything fine." She didn't know how to explain what she'd just seen. "I just saw a . . . light."

"Niall's torch, maybe?"

"Yes, it must have been."

"Are you sure?" said Niall, studying her face.

"I don't know. It didn't look like a Surari, at least. Just a light. That's all."

The last two rooms looked completely different. They

were both covered in what seemed to be glass tiles, deep amber in colour, and in the middle of them stood two copper baths, dull with time and neglect but still a beautiful, deep-red colour. There were piles of linen towels folded on the dark wood cupboards, left ready for use like everything else, but covered in dust. One room was grander than the other, probably used by the master and mistress of the castle, while the other was a bit smaller.

"I suppose this must have been quite luxurious, at the time," said Alvise.

"I wonder when he lived here last. A hundred years ago? Two? There's no electricity, obviously," Micol mused.

"I don't intend to ask him," said Alvise.

Micol frowned. "No. I'd rather stay away from him. As far as I can."

"Nobody around, it seems. Let's go," said Niall, treading out into the corridor again. "All clear up here!" he called on his way down.

"Same here," Sean cried out as they strode back into the entrance hall. Night had fallen outside, the darkness occasionally broken by flashes of blue lightning from the rainless storm. He didn't like the place. It felt dead. He hated to be on Nicholas' territory. Like being in the Shadow World wasn't enough, they had to be guests in his bloody haunted castle.

"I told you," Nicholas shrugged. Sarah threw him a dirty look: The king of liars, asking to be trusted. *How ironic*, she thought darkly.

"There's wood and kindling in the fireplaces. We can light a few fires, warm the water, have a wash in the tin baths ..." Sarah had to stop herself from running back into the kitchen to get some water.

"Tin baths ... Height of comfort," whispered Micol to Alvise.

"A lot better than nothing. We smell," Alvise replied.

"Speak for yourself," she said, and gave a soft laugh.

Nicholas turned towards the sound, and fixed his unseeing eyes on Micol's. Once again, Micol saw his black aura around him like a stormy cloud, but there was something else. There. A warm, orange light, like a little sun, hovering beside him. It was the light she'd seen upstairs. An aura without a body?

"Let's go," said Alvise nervously, taking her by the elbow, and she followed gladly upstairs.

Sarah looked around on the first floor. There were rows of heavy wooden doors, dark and carved with intimidating animals' heads, all open after their reconnoitre; and at the end of the gloomy corridor, she saw a double door carved with roses and leaf motifs. It looked nearly ... pretty. Different from the other doors.

"What's in there?" she whispered to Niall, gesturing to the carved doors.

Niall shrugged. "Just another room. Very grand."

"That was my bedroom," answered Nicholas, his tone flat, like it didn't matter, like there were no memories tied to it. "Nobody will sleep there. Not me either," he added.

"He'll sleep in a coffin full of soil," Alvise whispered to Micol. She felt the corners of her mouth curling up, but stopped herself. She was too scared of Nicholas, even if she couldn't have seen her smirking.

"Nicholas, who lived here with you?" Elodie asked him in a whisper, so nobody else could hear.

"People from long ago. They are all gone now," he replied curtly. But Elodie was not to be deterred.

"Did your father live here? Your mother?" Nicholas flinched. He frowned, and Elodie thought he'd cut the conversation short. She was surprised when he replied.

"My father would not live between four walls. My mother ... she was in the shadows with him, but I saw her often. It was my fiancée who lived here with me."

"The shadows?" Elodie had much to learn about Nicholas and the workings of this place.

"Where my father lives."

"I see." She didn't press further. "You were engaged?"

Nicholas had mentioned the girl once, in one of those strange moments in which Elodie had felt so close to him, so close to her worst enemy and Harry's killer. They had just stepped onto dry land after leaving Islay, and he was still ill after his father's punishment. He had been burning with fever, struggling to stay upright, and he'd called a woman's name in his delirium. When he'd come to his senses, Elodie had asked him about her. She had wanted to know as much about him as possible, anything that would help them bring down the King of Shadows.

"For a short while. She died," he said now, coldly, like it didn't matter, but Elodie could see the pain etched in every line of his face. "Her name was Martyna."

Yes, that'd been the name. *Martyna*. "Was she to be ... the bride of Shadows? Like you wanted Sarah to be?"

He nodded. "Our line needs to keep going. The King of Shadows needs a wife to join him in the darkness where he lives, and an heir. A son or a daughter."

"What happened to your mother?"

Nicholas took a deep breath and turned his face away. Elodie cursed herself for having asked, for having cared. She should not speak to him unless it was to gather information. She prepared to go, pulling his arm just a bit, enough for him to know she was ready to end the conversation. But to her surprise, he spoke.

"She let herself dissolve. She couldn't stand life in the shadows any more. You see, my mother didn't know who my father was when she fell for him. He deceived her."

"Like you deceived Sarah," Elodie couldn't help saying.

Nicholas nodded. "It's the way of things. What human girl would choose that life otherwise? My father took me away from her when I was just a baby. She couldn't bear to be away from me, so she followed. She shed her body – something that all rulers of the Underworld do. It's like … adopting a different body while keeping your soul. It's hard to explain unless you see it. Once she was here, my mother then became the bride of Shadows. But she hated the darkness, she hated being a spirit when she wanted so badly to be human, and touch and feel and live." Nicholas' voice trailed off for a moment.

"What was her name?" murmured Elodie. She didn't even know why she'd asked. Somehow, it felt important to her.

"Ekaterina Krol. Her family called her Kati. She was beautiful."

"And your father never remarried?"

"He has his heir. There is no need."

"What happened to your fiancée? Did she let herself … dissolve too?"

"She was never a spirit, she never shed her body. She was still human when she … When she decided to end it. We destroyed her, my father and I. I can never forgive myself."

"And still you planned the same for Sarah."

"I thought I had no choice, but I was wrong. I'll never force another woman to go through what Martyna went through. I'll never be the King of Shadows. It ends with my father."

Elodie felt him shaking. His unseeing eyes burned with anguish, and regret. Guilt. And that was exactly what he should feel, for all the evil he and his father did. *Even if he thought he had no choice*, Elodie said to herself. And still, a spark of compassion had been kindled in her heart, and her hand squeezed Nicholas' arm lightly as they joined the group once more.

They chose their rooms and lit the fires – real, warm flames, not Nicholas' cold ones – and tried their best to clean up the sheets, but they were so dusty and mouldy that they gave up. They stripped the beds and spread the sleeping bags on them instead. They wrapped their jackets around the pillows. It felt like a luxury hotel, after days of sleeping in a cramped car or on the hard ground in the cold. The heat and light couldn't fully dispel the gloom, but they made everything less spooky.

They were nearly cheerful as they carried basins of water upstairs to the bathrooms. The girls went into the main one, and the men into the smaller one. They relished the first chance of washing they'd had in days, the water draining away tiredness and dried blood from the wounds they all had.

Sarah couldn't believe she could finally feel water coursing over her skin again, and she relished every moment. She thought of her own bathroom back home, of how safe and comfortable it was . . . well, it had been, before it all went wrong. The head of the Scottish Valaya, Cathy – her astral drop, really – had materialised in her bathroom once. So much for safe.

213

For a moment, she wondered if she'd ever see her home again – her room with the silver walls and the floating white curtains, and her purple cello leaning against the wall; her garden, wide and beautifully kept ...

The water was getting cold as she dreamt of home, and a long shiver travelled down her spine. She shook herself. "Want some help?" she asked Elodie. The French girl had removed the bandages around her middle, and the wounds were still bleeding even though they were days old.

"Thank you," she said, and Sarah began washing her carefully. She had scars all over – her forearms in particular were covered with little ones, from where Nicholas' Elemental ravens had pecked her. Sarah shivered once more, remembering how the ravens had attacked Elodie and nearly killed her when they still didn't know about Nicholas' true identity. But then her own body had many scars, Sarah thought. It was not unblemished like it used to be. It now told the story of many battles, just like Elodie's. Sarah was shocked at how fragile her friend looked and felt under her touch, like a little bird.

Elodie saw the pity in Sarah's eyes, and she wanted to hide herself, but the feeling of warm water on her skin was so blissful, she wanted it to last forever. She wanted to feel fresh and sweet-smelling again and lie in a clean bed, and sleep for a long time.

She wanted to wake up and find Harry beside her.

She wanted to be healthy and strong again.

But none of that would happen, she thought as she let Sarah pour warm water over her shoulders.

"Like a princess in a fairy tale," Micol whispered. Elodie looked up and saw the Italian girl gazing at her from under her eyelashes.

"What did you say?" Elodie asked.

Micol blushed. "Nothing . . . that you look like a princess from a fairy tale."

Elodie smiled wanly. She carried the book of Polish fairy tales in her bag, the one Harry had left to her before he died, having hidden a message inside it. On the cover there was a grim illustration, a girl in a long dress, wandering in a wood at night. The girl held a stick with a skull perched on top of it, blue rays of light coming out of the skull's eyes. A bit like the blue lightning that had been following them, Elodie thought. The words hidden in the book, Harry's secret message, came back to her. *Watch over Sarah, she's the key.*

How? How is she the key? Elodie asked herself. Because of her unblemished blood? And now that Nicholas had relinquished her, now that he had refused his own destiny as the future King of Shadows, with Sarah as his bride, was she not the key any more?

Then why are the demons not touching her, she wondered. *They hurt her – but refrained from killing her. Twice. What do they need her for?*

"There you are. Get dressed now. You'll catch a cold," said Sarah, smoothing her friend's wet hair one last time.

Sarah could be hard, cold, unreachable – and then she surprised you with a kindness you could have never imagined. At first, Elodie had been resentful of Sarah's closeness to Sean, and irritated by her aloofness. But with time they'd grown to know each other better, and now Elodie couldn't bear the thought of something happening to that brave girl who was fighting so hard for the Secret Families. Elodie would always watch out for her, whatever or whoever wanted to hurt her. Surari or humans.

Or Nicholas.

She felt so close to him, unexpectedly, maddeningly, she thought as she slipped her T-shirt over her head. It was like they were cut from the same sorrowful cloth. But her eyes were open. She would not let Nicholas stray; she would not let him betray them. Sean was worried they were getting too close, Nicholas and her, but Sean didn't really know her any more. He didn't know the hard core that she'd developed since Harry had died. The realisation that in that new world they'd all found themselves in, a world of continuous danger, she could never, never let her guard down. And she never would. For all the time she had left. Which wasn't much, she was sure now.

The Falco girl had said she looked like a fairy-tale princess. One with blue nails and wounds that don't stop bleeding ... And then she remembered the Polish fairy tale she'd read in Harry's book, the one about a princess prisoner in a white tower, and a prince saving her and taking her to freedom on the wings of a raven.

I don't believe in happy endings any more, she said to herself.

34

The Blood that Runs in My Veins

The day of you and me
A butterfly's life

Sean

I had a shower, if you can call a shower dumping water from a basin over you with a ladle. I swear to God, washing never felt so good. Even if I were sharing the washing room with the bloody Prince of Darkness, and Niall didn't stop singing Irish songs. It's a miracle I didn't hit him over the head with my ladle.

Thankfully everybody is in their rooms now, and I'm alone. But the loneliness gets to me after a while, and I don't give myself time to think as I obey an irresistible impulse.

I step out of my room and down the corridor, and knock on Sarah's door. I fear she will not answer. She doesn't want me there, not with the way things are between us, but she invites me in with a quiet, "Sean."

She quickly sits by the fire, studying me. All I can think about is how amazing she looks, drying her hair, her cheeks flushed with the heat. Her hair seems so soft, softer than silk. She has wrapped a fleece around herself, her long legs folded underneath her. I think I might go crazy just looking at her. I feel in my bones something is going to happen that should not happen. I try to distract myself and begin to unwrap energy bars for her, our makeshift dinner. It's all we have left. She shakes her head. "Please. Just one. You must eat."

She sighs and takes it. "We're running out of food. We'll need to hunt."

"Nicholas said we're not far away now. We'll be okay."

"As right as rain, like Niall says. Sean?"

"Mmmm?" I reply. I dream of running my fingers through her wet hair, spreading it out like a silky curtain so that the fire dries it quicker.

"Have you thought of the journey back?"

Cold spreads through my bones as I realise that no, I haven't. I just don't seem to be able to picture it, like what's ahead of us is so terrifying that I can't think past it.

"Yes. Of course. Once we've killed the King of Shadows all we need to do is find the way back to the Gate . . ."

"Do you really think we can kill the King of Shadows and survive?" She looks at me with those clear green eyes, and it's impossible to lie.

"We can't give up hope. And my hope is that you, at least, will survive."

"I'm not going anywhere without you. I don't want a life without you." She clings to me, her arms tight around my neck.

"Oh, Sarah. Look. There's no point in thinking about all this. Let's just do what we need to do."

She takes my face in her hands. "What you asked Alvise . . . about the Campbell powers . . ."

My heart sinks. Discussing my blood is always painful. But she has the right to know what's going through my mind. "I can't stop asking myself if I have powers. I know I'm not supposed to."

"You're not supposed to have powers, or you're not supposed to ask yourself?" She attempts a joke, but her eyes aren't smiling.

"Sarah . . ."

"Sean, this means nothing to me, do you understand? Your blood, I mean. It means nothing at all. Powers or not, it doesn't change my feelings."

"But I need to know. I need to know who I am."

"You won't have your answer, Sean. You just won't. We'll never be sure if your runes are so powerful because of your Campbell blood. And even if you have some kind of power because of a genetic fluke . . . how do we know it'd be passed on to our children? It might end with you! But none of that matters to me. Why does it matter to you?"

I rub my forehead. Sarah is furious with frustration. Stubborn and stuck in the past, that's what she probably thinks of me, and she has to pay the price for my blind, senseless loyalty.

"Look what generations of inbreeding did to the Families!" she whispers in a way that makes it sound like a scream. "We're all dying! We don't need the Surari to kill us, Sean. My blood might be strong now, but what if I marry another Secret heir from some ancient family? What are the chances of my children developing the Azasti? Look at Elodie! She is dying too. Her wounds are still bleeding – I mean, the ones she got from the white demon. I saw them as we were washing."

I stare at her. Even if I knew it already, to hear Elodie's death sentence spoken aloud cuts me inside. My friend is dying. My brother's wife. My dear, strong, loyal, infinitely sweet Elodie. And there's nothing I can do. I can't defend her. I can't save her. I can't stop her blood from decaying.

A memory comes back to me: back in Edinburgh, when Sarah wasn't letting me near her and I was living in a crumbling cottage in the middle of nowhere. Elodie's voice lullabying me to sleep at last, after days of insomnia, and then waking up and finding her sitting there, watching over me.

And now she's dying.

Sarah sweeps her wet hair away from her face. A single tear rolls down her cheek and breaks my heart. "This is what inbreeding has done to us, Sean! This ailment thing . . . it's because we married among each other for generations. Only men are allowed to look outside the gene pool, and that's why my blood is clean. My family had only sons for four generations – except for Mairead. They all married Lays and our blood was kept strong, or so they thought. Strong with powers, but vulnerable to the Azasti. Secret women marry Secret men, and have children who are condemned already. Is this what you want to happen to my children? Do you want me to marry Alvise, and have heirs who can't stop bleeding and whose nails turn blue and who go crazy, like Tancredi? And then die in their twenties? Is this what you want for me? Keep my powers going through the blood-line, until the Azasti affects us all?" Tears are running freely down her cheeks now. I can't reply. I don't know what to say. Everything is so confused now.

"If we don't destroy the King of Shadows, there isn't even a point in asking this question because there will be no future. Come here," I say, and gather her in my arms. I bury my face in her hair, inhaling the soft, sweet scent of Sarah.

"I can't lose you, Sean. If we die, then whatever. But if we live . . ."

"You won't lose me. Love finds a way," I whisper. I don't know if it's true, but I can't break her by saying anything else.

I can break myself, but not her. Her fingers stroke my throat and my collarbone until she finds the protective pouch she made for me. I have no idea what's inside – one of her mother's spells, probably – but I never part from it.

Despair mixes with desire as I take her face in my hands and I kiss her, slowly this time, not quickly and secretly like we always had to do. I slip off her fleece and marvel at her beauty, and marvel at her being mine – after all we've been through. After all the lies and danger and mistrust and obstacles, here we are, skin against skin, nothing between us.

We lie together, Sarah asleep and me awake, as usual. I have my arm around her waist and my face in her hair, and I feel the sweet, soft rhythm of her breathing. Suddenly I feel her tensing up, and a whimper escapes her lips.

I close my eyes briefly and curse under my breath. I was hoping tonight the dreams would leave us alone. I resist the instinct to wake her: we need to know what the vision has to tell us. I hold her throughout, bleeding inside as I feel her tremble and shudder and cry out as the dream unfolds. It doesn't last long, thankfully. Her eyes jolt open, her breathing ragged, and she calls my name.

"It's okay. I'm here. What did you see?"

She blinks a few times, taking in her surroundings. The transition between the dream and reality is never straightforward for Sarah, the remnants of terror and distress colouring her awakening. She takes a deep breath, her voice shaking but controlled.

"I was in the place of dreams. There was grass, and wind, and a huge sky ... I used to dream of different places, depending on where the demons appeared, but since all this happened it's nearly always been there, in that one place. This time, there was a tree, tall and strong, like one of these oaks. Something scurried close to me, in the high grass ... and then another ... A few of them. I couldn't see what they were. And then I saw that something was dangling from the tree. I walked closer, and ..." Sarah's voice trails off as she forces herself to remember the horror. "It was some kind of cocoon, wrapped in a white web. I touched it, and my hand stuck to it ... it was all sticky and slimy. I couldn't get the web off my hand ... The cocoon turned towards me, dangling from the branch ... and I realised that there was a human being inside."

"Did you see what had done that? And who was inside the cocoon?"

"No. Whatever was in the cocoon had a face, though. It was black and dried up." The horror chokes her. "Like it'd been mummified, sucked up from the inside. But I'm sure of one thing ..." I raise my eyebrow in a silent question. "It was a woman."

The light of dawn shines through the window, bright and

vivid like a scream. It's time to get up, to continue on our journey.

It's physically painful to disentwine our bodies – when will I feel her skin against mine again, if ever? I catch glimpses of her body as she dresses, pink rays dancing in her hair, and my breath is taken away once more. I can't help thanking God, or whoever is up there, for having made us meet, for our stolen time together. In Japan, they have a belief: two people who are meant to meet are tied by an invisible red thread that sooner or later will bring them together. It's like that for Sarah and me. We were always meant to meet. I wonder what Morag Midnight would think if she knew that her precious granddaughter and the bastard son of the friend she abandoned are in love. But it doesn't matter, does it? Her spiteful ghost can't hurt us now.

35
A Torture of Gold

Watch out for those who say
They'll take care of you
Look out for the dagger
Hidden in the velvet sleeve

"Alvise! It's me ..." Micol's voice carried through the door. Alvise jumped up, alarmed. He grabbed his bow and arrow in one fluid movement and yanked the door open.

Micol tensed, and her hands sparked red and blue. She let go of Sean's sleeping bag, and it fell in a blue heap on the floor. "Put that thing down! Nothing dangerous going on! It's just me."

Alvise breathed a sigh of relief and lowered his bow and arrow. "Come in," he gestured and stepped aside, letting Micol in. The only light in the gloomy room were the embers glowing in the fireplace, red and orange in the semi-darkness. "What's wrong?"

"Can I sleep here? My room is ..." She shrugged. "Scary."

"Every room in this place is scary. Sure," he said and sat on the four-poster bed once more. He patted the space beside him.

Micol gaped. "In the same bed?"

"You don't want me to sleep on the stone floor, do you?"

"But ..."

"I wouldn't touch you, Micol, if that's what you're worried about. Believe me."

Micol blushed and crossed her arms, stung. "Right. Clearly, I'm completely revolting!"

Alvise laughed. "You're very pretty. You're just not my type."

Micol studied his face. He arched an eyebrow.

A light bulb went off in her head.

Alvise, the boy all her friends used to be mad about, the boy who always had a cluster of girls fawning over him at every social event. But he never really gave much attention to any of them. He just didn't seem to be interested ...

She blushed even deeper. Of course.

"Oh!"

"Penny dropped?"

"It did. You're lucky. It would have been the floor for you!"

"I'm lucky indeed. Also because all I have to keep me warm is my jacket and this dusty old thing," he said, lifting a corner of an ancient blanket he'd found in the room. "But now I can share your sleeping bag. Maybe you'll make me change my mind ..." he said in mock-seductive tone. Micol rolled her eyes and lay beside him on the bed, spreading the unzipped sleeping bag over both of them.

"Your feet are freezing!" he complained.

"Sorry, I forgot to pack socks before I jumped into the iris!"

He smirked in the gloom. The way they used to fight constantly at Palazzo Vendramin was so far away. It seemed impossible that only a few days ago they could barely be in the same room without wanting to gouge each other's eyes out.

"Alvise ..." Micol whispered.

"Yes?"

"We don't really know what we're doing, do we?"

Alvise shrugged. "Thing is, I never really know what I'm doing. I go where Lucrezia tells me, do what I need to do, come back when she opens the iris for me. I never looked beyond slaying what I had to slay. It was hard enough having lost my powers ..." He pursed his lips. "With all this happening to the heirs all over Europe – all over the world, probably – we had to try our best to survive, that was all. Keep doing our job and survive. I thought there was nothing else we could do. And then we were sent here."

"To help this bunch of weirdoes."

Alvise laughed. "Well, Niall is not a weirdo."

"Niall is spoken for. Get him out of your head."

He laughed again. "Seriously, though. All we can do is keep going."

"They say they're going to kill the King of Shadows."

"I think it's likely the King of Shadows will kill us," Alvise replied sombrely.

"Probably. I just hope we can inflict as much damage as possible ... maybe we won't save the day, but perhaps we'll start a little hope ... You know, like those primroses in your garden? All around the fountains. It's January, and they're starting already. I can see them pushing through the soil. Maybe we can be a bit like that ... and someone will take it from where we left."

Alvise was quiet for a moment. A sixteen-year-old girl talking so fearlessly, so generously, about her own death. Her brothers would have been proud.

"Maybe you're right. I don't know what's going to happen. I know where my duty lies, anyway," he said.

"You're so brave. To do all this with no powers. I can't imagine . . ."

Alvise shrugged his shoulders again. "I'm not brave. I just do what I need to do. Lucrezia . . . now, Lucrezia is brave. She's my heroine, Micol. She's . . . she's the best among us all."

Micol didn't say anything. She could sense that Alvise was about to talk about his sister, and she didn't want to break the spell.

"Lucrezia wasn't always like that, the way you see her now. She was a happy, cheerful little girl. She loved to dance. She loved our mother . . ." He paused for a moment. "When she turned thirteen and her dreams started, she was so frightened . . . but she took it in her stride. It was the year after our mum was killed. I had lost my gift, and we were in pieces . . ."

"Alvise . . . what was your gift? If you don't mind me asking?"

Alvise smiled a bitter smile. "I don't mind you asking, but what's the point in telling you? Whatever I used to be able to do, I can't do it any more."

Micol was quiet. She sensed that Alvise didn't want to talk about that.

"Lucrezia felt it was her duty to keep going, to help the family. My mum had been the Vendramin dreamer. Now it was up to Lucrezia . . . But then she started showing signs of something else, something that had never been seen in the family before. She could start these spirals, these golden things in the

227

air ... I had no idea what they were, but my father knew. And he made a mistake. He told the Sabha." Alvise's voice broke, and he hesitated, like recalling all this pained him greatly. Micol held her breath, and finally, he began talking again.

"The Sabha sent two elders from Germany. They came and examined my sister and saw what she could do, and then summoned my father and me.

"They told us they had a way to open up Lucrezia's power, to let it develop fully. They said that it was like a river whose course was interrupted by boulders: they had a way to remove the boulders. It was a ceremony, and it would hurt a little, but it held no danger. Liars. They were all liars," Alvise spat. He took a shaky breath. "My father was torn, but my sister wanted to do it. She said she wanted her power to help the family. Sometimes I think had I not lost my powers, she wouldn't have felt obliged—"

"It wasn't your fault!"

"No. It wasn't my fault, but I can't help wondering what would have happened had I been ... myself. Lucrezia said she wanted to help us catch the Surari that killed our mother ..."

"I would have done the same," said Micol with total conviction. She wasn't boasting; she meant it. "I'd do anything to catch my parents' killers."

"What happened to them?" Alvise's voice had lost its edge and was replaced with sympathy.

"They weren't young any more. They had me late in life ... but they went out hunting again because so many things were seeping through. We did our best to convince them not to, but they wouldn't listen. Our Gamekeepers had just been killed, and they wanted to track down the ones responsible. Of course it was Surari. They decided to hunt separately.

My mother and Tancredi went in one direction, while my father went in another alone. I stayed with Raineri, since he couldn't be left with no one to watch him. My father . . . when he hadn't been seen for hours, we went searching for him. I . . . I found him."

Alvise put a hand on her arm. "*Mio Dio*, I am so sorry."

She sighed. "My mother was never the same after that day. Eventually she went off to hunt, alone, and was caught by one of the soil demons. I don't even think she fought for her life . . ." She shook her head. "The funny thing is, I think it's my fault, too. She was out for a long time and I didn't go to check on her. I was home with Ranieri again. He was showing more signs of the ailment. I was scared to leave him alone . . ."

"Sorry. I didn't mean to make you remember. Just like you said to me, it wasn't your fault."

"It feels that way. But tell me what happened to Lucrezia."

Alvise began slowly. "She had no idea what they had in store for her. What happened was so horrible none of us could have imagined."

Micol held her breath once more. She thought of Lucrezia lying in her bed, her white-blonde hair on the pillow, forever prisoner, forever trapped in a nightmare. She thought of her screams of terror, of her constant whispering, her bloodless lips moving day and night, somewhere between sleep and wakefulness. She was in hell, her body growing into a woman's, but her mind forever the one of a terrified thirteen-year-old.

"I never thought the Sabha could do something like that. I was so naïve. I thought they were infallible. I thought they were good. That they would never harm a Secret heir."

Micol nodded. "So did I," she whispered. "What you're telling me ... it goes against all I know."

"They all came to Venice, the whole Sabha. All except one – you know the way it works. They're never all in one room at once, in case they get attacked. Lucrezia was wearing her long blue dress, the one embroidered in gold. She loved that dress."

"Cosima often puts it on her," Micol murmured, remembering.

"She felt she had to dress up for the ceremony," he smiled bitterly and tenderly at the same time. "I remember she had pearls in her hair ..."

Micol squeezed his hand in the darkness.

"They had her lie down on silk cushions on the floor. I could see her chest rising and falling fast. She was scared, but at that point, we had no idea. Then one of the elders pinned her legs down, and another her left arm. She called for my father. She didn't understand why she had to be restrained. My father was horrified – I could see it – and he tried to go to her, but they stopped him. One of the elders held her right arm out, and straightened her hand. Another took a knife out of his robes and traced a spiral onto my sister's skin. She screamed, her blood dripping on the floor ... there was blood on her new dress ... and then she passed out because of the pain. But it wasn't over. Somebody took out a vial ... and they poured liquid gold onto my sister's hand. She screamed again. The pain was so strong she'd come to. And she didn't stop screaming for hours. It was like she was possessed. And maybe she was. Even the elders didn't know what to do. We brought her to her room, and we had to tie her to the bed. She would've hurt herself if we hadn't. She kept going until dawn ... and then she stopped screaming and started whispering. An iris opened in her room.

"The elders explained to us what the iris was for. They said that the ceremony had been successful, and they left. We waited for Lucrezia to wake up. She never did."

Micol dried her tears with her hand. "I'm sorry."

"I know. I know you are. I'm sorry for having chased you away from her room. I'm always scared for her, scared someone will hurt her again."

"That won't be me. Ever," Micol said fervently. She felt something wet on her arm, Alvise's tears. With the protection of darkness, he'd let himself cry for his sister, at last.

"There's something I don't understand. You said daylight would kill her ..."

"Yes. Not daylight as such, but being taken out of the Palazzo. We tried to take her to Switzerland, to the Jardin des Iles, you know, the famous clinic. Secret doctors work there. We thought they could help her. We took her to the canal and into our boat, started on our way to the airport, and it was fine, she was okay for a bit. Then motorboats started darting around us, and the gondoliers were singing and tourists were calling to each other ... it was all too much. She had some sort of seizure. She nearly stopped breathing. We had to rush back. When we were inside her room again, in the silence, she started breathing normally again, and she stopped convulsing. It was terrifying."

"Maybe the doctors of the Jardin des Iles could come to her?"

"They did. Three times, once a year. My father paid them well even though they didn't want to come after the first time. They didn't have a clue. They said that they had no idea what had happened to her or how to help her. They told us something terrible, Micol ... That they had seen the gold ceremony, as they called it, performed before on bearers of the same powers, and this was what happened. To all of them. Nobody ever recovers."

"Oh, *Mio Dio*! So they knew. The elders knew."

"Yes. They knew what was going to happen to Lucrezia, that thing about being a bit painful and that was all a lie. They couldn't tell us, of course, or we wouldn't have let them."

"But why? Why did they do this to her?"

"Because they wanted her power. They wanted her to be able to open an iris. That's all they think about, our powers. We're not human beings to them. We don't matter. All that matters to them is what we do for the fight."

"The bastards ... I'm going to find them. I'm going to fry them all!"

"They're probably all dead by now, Micol. And anyway, I should have protected her. I hate myself for having let it happen."

To her intense shame, Micol burst into proper, sobbing tears. "I can't bear it," she said, her soft heart aching like never before, not even for her family – her parents had been killed in an honourable fight, her brothers by illness. But Lucrezia had been torn to pieces by the very people who were supposed to protect the heirs. "They destroyed her!"

"Yes. They did," Alvise whispered, and hugged her. "But I haven't lost hope, you know. I can't lose hope that one day she'll wake up and it'll be all over."

"She speaks, though. Does that mean that some part of her is awake?"

"She does, but I don't think she's even aware of doing

it. It's like her power speaks through her. She has kind of conversations with me, when she has something related to demon hunting to communicate, but that's not really her talking." Alvise drew a deep breath.

"If we survive this, Alvise, we must find a way to help her. There must be a way."

"Sleep now. You need all your energy to ... electrocute things," said Alvise, helping her lie down and tucking her in.

Micol smiled in the darkness, her face still wet with tears. She held on to Alvise's hand like a frightened child.

36
This Painful Love

You took me to the edge and showed me
What would happen if we stepped into the light
And I recoiled and dreamt
Of our destruction

Elodie opened her eyes in the darkness, her lips flooded with poison, her hand curled around the dagger she kept under her pillow. She'd heard a voice calling her name.

She blinked in the gloom, the glowing embers in the fireplace the only light. She lay perfectly still, and listened for noise. The silence was unbroken. There was nobody in her room. And still, she felt a presence... the same she'd felt briefly when they'd come in. It was stronger now. Mournful, infinitely sad.

Hungry.

Again, Elodie heard her name being called, this time from beyond her room, beyond the closed door. She got up slowly, shivering in the chilly night air. The stone floor felt cold under her feet. She lit a candle, its warm light flickering in front of her face, then walked out in silence. She stood in the corridor for a moment, looking left and right. And then, all of a sudden, she felt her body moving of its own accord. She hadn't commanded it to, but it did – one step in front of the other, as if a foreign will had possessed her. She tried to resist, she tried to call for help, but it was no use. She couldn't stop herself, and she couldn't force out anything more than a whisper. She called for Sean, but nobody could have heard. Her muscles were tight with the effort to stop, and a trickle of sweat fell down her temple, freezing in the cold air.

Elodie shuffled all the way down the corridor, each step a struggle between her will and the strange force that had possessed her, until she stood in front of the rosewood doors. Her hand rested on it, pushing it open effortlessly, and her body forced her to step inside. A deep, musky scent hit her. It was like a perfume, a heady mixture of flowers and fruit and spices, and something stronger, heavy, something she couldn't identify. Once again she tried to call Sean's name, but no sound came out of her lips; her throat was frozen. She whimpered once more as her body took her in front of the wooden wardrobe, heavily carved and decorated. She was forced to open the mirrored doors – the glass was rusty and speckled, and a strong smell of mould and dust and times past enveloped her. Rows and rows of dresses were hanging in the wardrobe on wooden hangers. They looked like they'd only been left there yesterday, though the pungent smell gave their age away.

And then, she heard the first whisper. A voice in her

mind, a voice saying something she couldn't quite make out. Someone had taken possession of her body, someone who was talking inside her head. Somehow her thoughts were still there, her consciousness remained, but she held no power over her body or her voice. Elodie felt her heart pounding even faster as she contemplated the terrible possibilities – a demon, a malevolent presence that would make her harm her friends ...

Elodie panted in fear, her forehead covered in sweat, as those arms that weren't hers any more began taking off her jeans and her top – she'd slept dressed, as the room was so cold, even with the fire on. She stood in her underwear, shivering, her body hurting with the effort to resist – and another whisper resounded in her mind, one single word that once again she couldn't make out.

Her hand swept the rows of dresses and skirts before tightening on a white one. She slipped it off the hanger and contemplated it: it was a simple cotton dress with short sleeves and colourful embroideries around the neckline and the hem. Elodie watched helplessly as her body forced her to slip on the dress, and then take out what looked like a corset from another hanger. She tied it around her waist, struggling to make it fit – it was too big for her, and the hem of the dress touched the floor.

She tried to close her eyes. She didn't want to see what she was turning into, who she was turning into. But the spirit forced her to keep her eyes open, and she examined herself in the mirror – her face, her hair, her hands – she was herself, she was Elodie ... And then, just for a second, she saw her, a black-haired woman, sweet-eyed and red-lipped, taller than Elodie, her hair falling in soft waves around her shoulders, kept back by a gold band. She looked young and sorrowful.

In the blink of an eye, she was gone and Elodie's own reflection stared back at her. Her hands travelled through her blonde hair and down her waist and hips, and then felt her face, her arms, her thighs as if she were rejoicing in her own body. A wave of panic swept Elodie as she felt the other woman's emotions invading hers, and her own receding further. She felt full of a strange sense of joy as her hands travelled up and down her own body – the sheer joy of being alive, of having a body at all.

The third whisper came: and this time she understood.

"Martyna," said the voice inside her head. Elodie gasped. *Martyna ... Is she back to take her revenge on Nicholas? Using my body?*

Elodie tried to stop herself from stepping out of the room, but she couldn't. The film of sweat froze on her forehead, and all her muscles tensed once more against Elodie's will – but Martyna's spirit was too strong. Martyna took Elodie's body out of the room, and into the corridor. The candle had been abandoned. She knew her way in the darkness. Martyna knew where she wanted to go.

"Nicholas," said the voice in her head, and then some words in a language she didn't know. The words she couldn't understand, but the tone was clear: tenderness and longing and need. So she didn't want to exact revenge. She didn't want to kill him? Unwillingly, desperately trying to stop herself, Elodie opened Nicholas' door.

Nicholas was standing in the middle of the room, a pained,

incredulous expression on his face. "I felt you returning," he whispered.

"Nicholas," Martyna said through Elodie's mouth.

"Martyna . . . how . . . how?"

Elodie's voice replied, "I never left this place. You sealed our home. You sealed me inside. I couldn't leave, I couldn't look for you. I knew you'd come back."

"I'm sorry. I'm so sorry for what my father did. I didn't stop him."

"You couldn't have stopped him. Loving you destroyed me. And still I would do it all over again . . ."

It wasn't Elodie who placed a kiss on Nicholas' lips, as soft as a feather, tasting him like the sweetest liquor. It wasn't her who cried silent tears of relief at feeling his presence again. It wasn't her who wrapped her arms around Nicholas' waist and moaned softly. What was left of Elodie was prisoner in a body that wasn't hers any more. She was in Nicholas' arms, the son of the King of Shadows, the man responsible for Harry's death, and so many others'. The confusion she felt made her shiver uncontrollably as all her muscles struggled to move, but Martyna's spirit was stronger.

Elodie's lips opened and spoke words that didn't come from her, words in a foreign language, of love and longing and pain for the long, long separation. She realised that Nicholas' face was wet with tears, maybe his, maybe hers, and a small ripple of pity travelled through her. Suddenly, she didn't know if it was Martyna or her who took his face in his hands, who studied his coal-black eyes and felt the bones and flesh of his features as if it were she who was blind. Horror and confusion made room for something else as he touched her with infinite love and a hunger for her that melted her heart.

He loves her, she thought, *but it's me he's holding.* Desire swept through her as she didn't know where she ended and Martyna began. She was powerless under Nicholas' touch. And she realised that she didn't want to stop him any more.

37

I'm Coming to You

The missing piece of my soul
That piece you took with you

Nicholas didn't want to move. He knew everything was about to crumble around him, and he wanted that stolen moment to last forever. His time with Martyna, grabbed away from death's hands. She wasn't angry with him. She loved him still, even after death. The realisation made him cry tears of relief and regret.

He had no idea it was going to happen. He hadn't planned any of this. He didn't know that Martyna's spirit was there, trapped inside the house they used to share; that his spells, designed to keep every living being out, had trapped her inside. He didn't know she'd come to him one last time.

If only he could stay there. Forget about the world outside, shed his body, live with Martyna's spirit in eternal twilight. How could this have happened? Her spirit was here all along, and he never knew. He'd never been back in the home they shared, and she couldn't leave. He'd always longed for life, real, human life – but now that he'd discovered that Martyna's spirit had survived, that she didn't hate him, that she longed for him, everything had changed.

But at the same time, nothing had changed. There was still no tomorrow for him. His father would not leave him alone, whether he was a warm body or a wandering spirit.

He folded Elodie's body against his. Was it still hosting Martyna's spirit? "Martyna," he whispered. She was soft and warm, and he placed a kiss on her forehead and stroked her face, her hair. A wave of guilt overcame him. They'd used Elodie, him and Martyna. And still, it was Elodie's body he'd held.

Nicholas.

A sudden bout of pain made him double over, and Elodie sighed softly in his arms. *Nicholas,* his father insisted. *You'll speak to me now.*

Sick with the pain throbbing in his mind, Nicholas released Elodie. She stirred, then turned over and took another deep sigh. He got up slowly. It took a moment for him to steady himself. He felt for his clothes and slipped them on, and then he stepped out of the room. He knew the house like the back of his hand, and had no problems walking down the corridor, one hand against the wall, and down the stony steps.

Nicholas. It is nearly time.

"I know. I know."

There will be blood now.

Nicholas felt his legs give way.

"There is no need . . ."

Do you want to spare them? Do you want me to find a place for them in the new order, when we take over the human world?

Nicholas forced himself to steady his voice. He knew it was a trap. His father had never showed mercy. He was testing him.

"No. I want them all dead."

Good. You are making me proud once more, Nicholas.

"That's all I want, Father …"

Right at that moment, something pierced his mind, a silent scream resounding in his head only. A call for help.

"Elodie," he breathed.

His father was a man of his word.

38
Webs

Every time I can't stop looking for you
The ropes get tighter around my wrists

When she opened her eyes the next morning, she was free. Martyna was gone. And Nicholas was gone, too, she realised with a mixture of relief and disappointment. Elodie lay in an empty bed, bathed in the light of dawn, her body sated and her soul starving, bracing herself for a wave of shame and guilt to drown her. And they did, but with them was something else. A feeling she could not bring herself to name, or to acknowledge. On her skin, the scent of ash and fire, the scent of Nicholas.

Memories of the night before flooded her. His touch, his body against hers, his lips on hers ... All those images and visions that had flooded her while their bodies were one. For a psychic such as Elodie, intimacy of the body meant intimacy of the mind, too. And to wander inside Nicholas' mind, with all his dark memories and fear, had been terrifying. Some of the doors in Nicholas' mind had been shut, even to her – and she was grateful for that. She didn't want to know what was behind them.

Maybe it hadn't really happened. Maybe it was all in her imagination, somewhere between a nightmare and an impossibly sweet dream. Sweet and terrible at the same time. Yes, it must have been a dream. It didn't feel real.

Elodie closed her eyes for a moment, probing her mind, but to her immense relief, there really was no trace left of Martyna. Her body was her own again. She concentrated for a moment, scanning the room with her inner eye – but she couldn't feel anybody there.

Nobody. She was alone. She felt beside her. Nicholas' place was still warm, so he hadn't been gone long. Where was he? She sat upright, covering herself with the sheets. She felt a wave of panic freeze her muscles and stop her from breathing. She placed a hand on her chest, desperately trying to breathe, but she couldn't. Silent tears fell down her cheeks. It had all been too much, it was all too much . . .

She slipped out of bed and got dressed. All she could find was Martyna's dress and her shoes, but the panic didn't seem to fade. She knew she would not suffocate, that it was all in her head, but she couldn't help being terrified. The scent of Nicholas, ash and fire and salt, choked her. And so did that other scent, the one she now recognised as Martyna's. On impulse, she strode across the room, grabbed the heavy iron handle and pushed the glass out, opening the window as wide as it could go. She closed her eyes and breathed in the morning air – one, two breaths – as her skin puckered up in goosebumps. At last. She could breathe.

It hit her psychic sense at once – a presence, and not

Martyna's spirit, not a spirit at all. A Surari. She took a step back instinctively, then she fumbled with the iron handle once more, trying to close the window. Her lips were darkening.

But it was too late. A black limb – leathery skin with black, coarse hair – had slipped inside and was now stopping Elodie from closing the window. A moan escaped her lips as a terrible realisation hit her. She'd broken the spells that Nicholas had put on the place. She had allowed the Surari in.

Elodie opened her mouth to call for help, but before she could make a sound a black body had squeezed itself through the window and had propelled itself onto her face, blinding her, suffocating her. She fell backwards and felt something sticky, something that was at the same time light as a feather and as hard as metal, binding her mouth, her eyes, her whole face. The Surari moved onto her chest, building its cocoon around her body so fast that she couldn't move. Her arms were bound to her sides, and then her legs were sewn together, as tight as an Egyptian mummy. Elodie tried to scream, but only muffled sounds came from her mouth, gagged and silenced with silk. From between the white, sticky threads, Elodie could see a little. She moaned and shuddered as the Surari's grisly face appeared above her – that of a spider, its pincers rattling, ready to pierce.

In horror, Elodie remembered something she'd read long ago: that spiders feed on their victims while they're still alive.

39
The Price to Pay

Once you look into the abyss
There is no going back
You will forever carry
The abyss with you

"Sean! Sarah! It's Elodie! Niall! Help!" Nicholas ran back upstairs, as fast as he could go with no eyesight, tripping and falling and hitting his face on the stones.

"In my old room!" he screamed, ignoring the blood coming from his lip, where he'd hit it. He ran down the corridor, bursting through the rosewood doors and feeling his way across, calling Elodie's name. He felt something jump on his face and attach itself to him. Instinctively, he fell backwards, falling heavily to the stone floor.

Sean had found Elodie's room empty. He'd gone to see how she was feeling, if she had got any sleep.

Stepping into the hall, he saw Nicholas barge into the

room with the double doors, and followed. He nearly tripped over Nicholas, who was lying on the ground with a demon-spider on top of him. It was already weaving its deadly web. And on the stone floor there was something else, a white cocoon, as big as human being – a slight, thin form – blonde hair escaping from the silky threads . . .

"Elodie!" Sean threw himself on the ground beside her, clawing at the threads until he freed her face. "Elodie . . ." He took her head in his lap. "Please wake up."

Close behind were Sarah and Niall.

Sarah knelt beside Nicholas and buried her hands deep into the Surari's skin. She saw Nicholas' fingers sparkling with blue fire.

"Don't! You'll set me on fire!" she warned him. At that moment, Sarah's hands began to prickle – it was as if she'd touched a nettle – and then they were hurting, a searing pain. She howled as a liquid as corrosive as acid seeped from the Surari's skin together with the Blackwater and burnt her skin.

Nicholas couldn't breathe any more; the demon-spider was covering his nose and mouth. Dreadful sounds were coming from his chest as he desperately tried to draw oxygen into his lungs. Sarah didn't move; she kept dissolving the creature, even though her hands were so sore she feared they were going to melt away.

Niall's song rose into the air, but all of a sudden he noticed the open window, banging in the wind. He leapt towards the glass, but it was too late. A black leg covered in thick, coarse hairs had slipped in. He stabbed it with his dagger, trying to keep the window closed, but it was no use. The blade couldn't penetrate its thick hide. The demon-spider crawled inside and crept down the wall with a horrible scuttling sound. Niall's song rose again as he watched the creature climb onto one of the columns of the four-poster bed and perch itself on top of the canopy, waiting to pounce. But before it could attack, an arrow broke through the air and embedded itself between its pincers. Niall turned back towards the window, just in time to see that another demon was on the windowsill, trembling with the pain of his song – but it wasn't stunned enough. It leapt on Niall and silenced him, making him fall backwards.

Alvise growled with rage. He, too, tried to stab the demon-spider over and over again, but the blade couldn't find a way in through its armour-like shell. He had to hit the creature between its pincers, to try to make it turn around, to expose its soft spot . . .

Sean saw the creature attaching itself to Niall's face and Nicholas trying in vain to breathe. Still on the ground with Elodie's head in his lap, he started tracing the runes, red lights condensing into ribbons in the air. The ribbons tightened on the Surari clinging to Niall's face, dragging it away from him, strands of a silky web hanging from its pincers. They threw it on the ground, and Alvise was on it at once, piercing its soft spot with his pugnale, black blood spraying from the wound. Some of the liquid sprayed Alvise's face, and he screamed. It burnt like acid. Right at that moment, Sean realised that Sarah was moaning softly. He turned to see her on the ground beside a puddle of Blackwater, holding her red, raw, blistered hands in her lap. Nicholas was free.

"Sarah!" he called, horrified. "Are you hurt?"

She dragged herself up and kneeled beside Sean and Elodie.

"It's okay. I'm alive, anyway. Elodie?" she whispered, gazing at her friend's grey face, the remains of silky webs still all over her body.

"I feel a pulse, but she's so weak. It's like there's no blood left in her!" Sean took her bloodless hands in his. After all they'd been through, to die like this, in this alien world, from a wound they couldn't even see.

Nicholas felt his way towards Elodie, white threads still hanging from his face, sticking to his skin. *Yes, my father is a man of his word*, he thought bitterly. "The demon-spider couldn't have had enough time to feed on her," he said, his voice shaking. "It's the Azasti, making every little wound deadly. She's bleeding inside."

To die of rotten blood. "No. Not Elodie," Sean begged without shame. "Nicholas. Nicholas, please. Is there anything you can do for her? The cure your father promised . . ."

"There's nothing I can do. He didn't have a cure," Nicholas said.

Sarah's eyes widened as she heard the pain in his voice, saw it etched all over his face. He wasn't lying. He cared for her, she realised.

Nicholas felt for Elodie's hands and took them from Sean, and surprisingly, Sean let him.

A million thoughts were racing through Nicholas' mind. He couldn't possibly do it. He couldn't possibly inflict that on Elodie. It was better for her to die . . .

"Nicholas, if there was even a grain of truth in your father's promise . . . If there's anything you can do . . ." Sarah pleaded.

"He. Was. Lying!" he stated. Nicholas was telling the truth. There was no way he could have given them the cure.

Because the cure was him: Nicholas. And the side effects were too horrible for words.

He couldn't do it.

And then Elodie opened her eyes slightly, and she saw Nicholas above her.

"Don't let me die," she whispered.

It was a moment. A split-second decision. For once, he wouldn't let someone who loved him die – like his mother, like Martyna. "Sean. Your dagger," he commanded.

Sean looked at him for a moment. He'd never thought he would give Nicholas his *sgian-dubh*, but something in his voice made him obey. Nicholas grabbed Sean's *sgian-dubh*, took off his jacket and rolled up his sleeve. He cut his own arm, digging a deep, bloody trail from his elbow to his wrist. Blood began dripping from it in a scarlet stream. For a moment there was perfect silence, except for Elodie's ragged breathing.

Nicholas took Elodie from Sean and sat her up, one arm around her shoulders, the other – the bleeding one – against her face . . . He let his blood drip into her open lips, smearing her face and chin. Sarah gasped, while Sean and Niall were frozen in silent horror. Alvise stood aside, memories of his sister's marking stronger than ever. Micol clasped her hands over her mouth – Elodie's aura was turning from grey to black as she drank.

"Sean . . ." Sarah whispered. Sean shook his head, revulsion and dread painted all over his face. He would not stop him. He couldn't stop him, or Elodie would die.

They all watched Elodie drink Nicholas' blood, her chin and lips smeared with it as if she'd been butchered herself. She fell into what looked like a deep sleep in his arms, the back of her head resting on his chest. Her breathing wasn't ragged any more, but deep and slow.

Nicholas carried her onto his bed, laying her down gently.

"Is she cured from the Azasti?" Sean's gaze wasn't leaving Elodie.

"Look at her nails," Nicholas replied. Elodie's fingernails weren't blue any more.

Sean's legs gave way with relief. "She'll live, then," he said, stroking Elodie's bloodied face. Only then did he notice that she wasn't wearing her own clothes, but a long, embroidered dress.

"I don't know," said Nicholas. "My blood has ... consequences. But she's strong."

"What consequences?" whispered Sarah, and couldn't keep the rage and suspicion out of her voice. "Is she going to obey your orders now? Have you turned her into a minion?"

"Elodie is alive and breathing. It's all we can ask for now," Niall said in his gentle way. A thud interrupted him – it was coming from downstairs.

"So much for your powerful spells!" spat Sarah. "There are Surari all over the place!"

"Elodie opened the window," Nicholas explained simply. "The spells were broken. I'm sorry. I should have warned you ..."

"Too late now!" she replied, and her eyes glowed green.

"Niall, get Elodie up," Sean commanded. "You can still sing while holding her, but I need my hands to trace the runes. Alvise, you'll lead Nicholas—" Another thud interrupted him, and this time it was closer. It came from the corridor ... and then another bang against the door, and scraping, and scuttling. Niall's song was rising already as he held Elodie's unconscious body in his arms.

"Micol, open the door and jump aside," whispered Sean. Micol hesitated for a moment, but she steeled herself. She jerked the door open and immediately a fan of electrical charges spread from her fingers as she jumped back. A landslide of spiders, some as big as a human head, some as small as rats, rolled into the room. The battle was a frenzy. Everything was so fast that only instinct kept them going, directing their blows, telling them where to hit next. There was just one thought in all their minds: don't let them jump on your face and weave their webs . . .

"Out! Everybody out!" Sean bellowed over the din.

"Our stuff!" shouted Sarah. They needed their jackets and blankets and food. They couldn't survive in the forest without them.

"No time!" Sean replied as they ran, the demon-spiders after them, impossibly fast on their thick black legs.

They made their way down the corridor – and then there was a thump.

Micol had fallen, but just as a spider leapt on her she raised her electrical hands, enveloping the creature in blue charges. The Surari fell on the ground, but another one was on her at once, and another. She screamed. Would Sean and the others not stop? Would they not stop to help her? And then she heard Sean's whispered words in her ears, and Alvise's grunting as he stabbed the spiders with deadly precision. And she was free.

A strong hand held her up – Sean's – and she kept running blindly, throwing herself down the stairs, through the open door and into the night.

The Surari would not be deterred, scuttling behind them and camouflaging their black hides among the trees and in the undergrowth. Alvise kept turning around to shoot arrows into the Surari pack. Every arrow he shot was one less in his quiver, and these ones he would never retrieve. Sean and the others had stumbled ahead, but Micol was running beside him — until suddenly, she stopped and turned to face the spiders.

"Micol!" he called. Did she have a death wish?

"I have an idea!" she shouted, and raised her arms, throwing her head back. The night lit up in a rainbow of colours, as lightning shot from her hands, her mouth, her eyes, lifting her up off the ground in an electrical storm. A lethal web of lighting spread in the air around her, hanging in between the trees and among the branches as if it, too, were a spider web.

Micol folded her body in half like a coiled spring, the edges of the electrical web trailing from her fingers, moving with her as she stepped aside and crouched among the trees. She'd created a kind of electrical fence, and her body was the generator.

Alvise watched in disbelief as one, two Surari threw themselves against the barrier and were immediately electrocuted, caught in the multi-coloured rays, their hairs smoking and flesh burning with a nauseous smell. The other spiders stopped and cowered, flat on the ground. Alvise took his chance, hitting the rest of the demon-spiders through the electrical web with a shower of arrows, leaving his bow one after the other as fast as the eye could see. They were both immobile, Micol crouching among the trees, shaking with the effort to continue the charges, and Alvise ready to shoot. There was no sign of the others, and the night was still.

"I can't keep going for much longer," Micol whispered, panting as if she were running, her hands, spread out with rainbow rays trailing from them, trembling. Suddenly the charges disappeared, and with a soft whimper, Micol let herself fall to the ground.

"Let's go." Alvise took her by the hand and helped her up.

A voice came from the darkness. "Alvise! Are you okay? Micol?" It was Sean, emerging from the shadows, his *sgian-dubh* glinting in the moonlight.

"She killed the lot," Alvise told him proudly.

Sean was speechless for a moment. "I wish I'd seen that," he said finally. "I left the others further on. Let's go. Quickly."

They ran towards the others – only then did Micol notice how cold she was. Her teeth were chattering so hard she could hear the noise inside her head. Creating the electrical barrier had taken everything out of her.

They were sitting in a circle facing outwards, Elodie in the middle, lying on the grass.

"This girl fried the spiders up," Sean announced.

"All of them?" Niall asked.

"There's no way to know. Let's move. I want to get as far away as I can from that place. Elodie?"

"Still asleep." Niall's arms were aching, but he went to pick her up again, holding her against him. *She's as small as a bird*, Niall thought with tenderness. He remembered when they first met. She mistook him for an enemy, and stunned him with her poisonous kiss. The deadly princess, he'd called her.

"I'll take a turn," said Sean, stepping towards him. "Stand by if I need to use the runes," he added, and Niall nodded. He took Elodie in his arms, and was shocked at how hot she was. It felt as if she were burning with a fever, but when Sean placed his ear against her chest he felt that her pulse was slow and regular, and her breathing deep. "Will she sleep for long, Nicholas?"

"I don't know." His face was tight, his forehead creased in a frown. Sean's heart sank – there were things Nicholas wasn't saying, about what would happen to someone who'd drunk his blood. Sean didn't want to ask.

"We're left with this, and nothing else," said Sarah patting her backpack as they marched on in the muted light of early dawn. They'd had to leave everything. They had no sleeping bags to keep them warm through the nights, no jackets, no food, no water.

"How did you manage to bring it with you?" Sean asked.

"I grabbed it as we ran. It was near the door. I hadn't finished packing, though, it's half empty."

"So what's in there, Sarah?" asked Sean, the strain of carrying Elodie evident in his voice.

"A water bottle, half empty, two packets of biscuits. Matches. A bar of chocolate. That's all. The rest was still unpacked."

"At least we were dressed," Niall pointed out, forever the optimist. "Had this happened in the middle of the night we'd all be in our underwear now."

"And we have our boots on," Alvise added.

"Speak for yourself. My shoes are falling apart," Micol said miserably. She could feel the ground at every step, with her feather-light ballerinas shredded from walking and running.

"Have we finished complaining? We're alive!" Sean scolded them.

"For now," Niall said in his 'this-is-great-fun' way that defied even the most tragic of circumstances. "After a night in the forest with no jackets and no sleeping bags demons will just lick us to death, like ice lollies," he said.

"It's not long to my father's lair," Nicholas intervened. "We'll be there tonight."

Micol shivered and wrapped her arms around her small frame. And then she saw it again, a warm orange light, hovering at the edges of her vision. Before she could turn around, the light was gone.

It was then that Elodie started screaming again.

40
A Life in Shadows

When we lay together at the lakeside
I kissed your hand and then
I realised it was mine

Sean

Elodie is twitching so violently I fear she might fall. I lay her on the ground as quickly as I can. She keeps screaming at the top of her voice, screams that go through me and make me want to cover my ears and block them out.

"You've killed them all!" she cries. "And now she's dead too!"

"Who is dead, Elodie? What's happening? What do you see?" I plead with her. "Sarah ... could this be a vision?"

"I don't know. I've never dreamt like this. It must be what Nicholas did to her," Sarah replies, her voice icy, her face composed, but she's trembling.

"You killed her like you killed my mother!" Elodie screams again; this time her voice breaks on the last word, fading into a rasp. Her eyes are open, but they don't focus on anything. They seem to be looking beyond us, beyond now.

A sob escapes Nicholas' lips. "I'm sorry. It was the only way."

Elodie takes her head in her hands and curls up like a child. "It hurts. Please don't do this to me," she whimpers, and I echo her cry.

"What are you doing to her!" I shout, moving towards Nicholas and taking him by the collar.

"Nothing. I'm doing nothing. It's not happening. It's a memory," he says. His skin is grey, his eyes as unfocused as Elodie's. My hatred for him knows no bounds. In one quick movement, I'm behind him with my arm wrapped around his neck. He's strong, but it would take me only a moment to break his neck.

I hear Sarah's voice from somewhere far away. "Don't kill him! We still need him! Let him go."

"Make it stop," I hiss in his ear.

"I can't."

"Sean. Let him go," Sarah repeats, her hands up, palms out, as if to calm me and contain me – and I know she's right. I release him, but as Elodie whimpers again red mist descends on me and I hit him. I feel something crunch under my knuckles, and my hand is wet. He doesn't retaliate. He falls on his knees, towering over Elodie's shuddering form, and I'm ready to hit him again. Niall and Alvise grab me and hold me back.

"Sean, stop!" cries someone – Niall, Sarah – and strong arms restrain me.

"Stop! Please stop!" Elodie echoes their words in her delirium.

"What's happening to her?" I growl. "The truth!"

"I told you the truth. She's processing my memories. Now she's remembering the brain fury," Nicholas says, blood streaming from his nose.

He must be lying. He must be. "This makes no sense ... How ..."

"Through my blood. This is the only cure to the Azasti, the blood of a half man, half Surari. And only one exists: me. But this is the price to pay."

"I can't take this any more! Sean, please kill me!" Elodie whispers, curled up on the ground. She looks at me, and I see her eyes are focused. Suddenly, she's lucid.

"Elodie, what's happening? Who's doing this to you? Is it Nicholas?"

Elodie clasps her hands on her forehead and sobs some more. "It's not Nicholas. It's the King of Shadows. Just kill me!" she screams, and her eyes lose focus again as her body doubles over.

"There must be a way to help her. Please, Nicholas!" Sarah pleads with him.

"There isn't. Do you think if there was I wouldn't try? We can only wait. If she survives ..."

"If?" I shout, lunging for him, and again Alvise and Niall restrain me. "You knew! You knew this would happen!"

"I did, yes. What choice did I have?" he whispers. "It was this or immediate death. And you know it, Sean."

Elodie is murmuring under her breath, still delirious. "Stop ... Father, please no ..."

"You always wanted us dead," Sarah hisses. "You're getting what you want, aren't you? One by one, we'll all go. You found this way with Elodie. A knife in the heart would have been kinder."

"I never wanted Elodie dead," Nicholas says, and his voice is so pained I don't know what to believe.

Elodie is moaning and shuddering, her head still in her hands. If Nicholas is telling the truth, this is a memory. The memory of a terrible pain. Will it kill her? Or, like Nicholas, will it blind her? I look around me. Sarah, Micol and Niall are near tears. Alvise is leaning his forehead against a tree. None of us can do anything.

"Elodie," I call helplessly. For a moment I want to take out my *sgian-dubh* and run its blade over my own arm, to share her pain.

Elodie screams once more, a long piercing scream that breaks my heart in two. I let myself fall on the ground beside her, on the other side from Nicholas, and call her name several times. She opens her eyes, gazing up at something only she can see. Her lips part. "Nicholas," she whispers, and I can't quite believe she's called his name.

"I'm here. I'm here," he says, and feels for her hands. He clasps them in his.

"Nicholas," she calls once more, and then her body collapses. I think she's dead.

"No!" someone sobs, and that someone is me. My hands are on her face, on her shoulders, on her arms, and I shake her, I call her name. But she's dead. She can't hear us.

All of a sudden, there's a slight movement under my hands. A breath.

"She's breathing! She's alive!" Nicholas says suddenly, taking hold of her wrist. "Her heart is beating!" He lifts Elodie onto his knees, her head lolling against his chest. They're like the Tao, white and black, folded together.

"Elodie? Can you hear me?" I call.

She blinks a couple of times, and then she opens her eyes. Gone are their warm, chocolate brown. They're black, like obsidian. I try to take her from Nicholas, but she moans, and holds on to him. She calls his name once again, and wraps her arms around his neck like she never wants to be apart from him, never again.

I know at once that we have lost her.

41
Together

I wish I didn't have to
Drag you down with me
Follow me
Follow me down

Nicholas
I know I must close my mind before my father discovers that
I don't want Elodie to die – but it's too late. As I cradle her
in my arms, he knows. I feel the disapproval in his thoughts
before he speaks.

Another one, Nicholas? I see that Martyna was easily forgotten,
as was Sarah. Are we on to another love of your life?

My heart burns with rage. *It's not like that. I care for her.*

And my father laughs, like it's all really funny, to play with me
like a cat with a mouse, to deliberately destroy everything I love.

Stop torturing her, Father. Please.

But I'm not. Like you said, it's just a memory. It's your memory.
I couldn't stop it, not even if I wanted to.

I'm doing what you said! Leave me alone!

Just having a bit of fun.

My rage spills over. *I'll kill her, the one you need. I'll set her on fire, and your plans will go up in smoke with her. Is that what you want?* The brain fury hits me at once, but I'm too angry to care or react. *Keep doing this to me, and I won't take her to you. You're too weak now to come this far. It'll be all over. We'll all die.*

And suddenly, after one last, piercing beam of pain right between my eyes, he's gone. I seem to have won this one. Which means he'll make me pay.

Right at that moment, Elodie quietens. The recollection is over. For a moment I fear she's dead. She's so still and so cold ... but she's breathing. Her heart is beating, her blood – mixed with mine – running beneath the soft skin of her wrist. She's alive. Sean tries to take her away from me, but we hold on to each other. "Nicholas," she calls.

"I'm here. I'm here."

And then she speaks inside my mind, like only my father and mother could ever do, because we share the same blood. Nobody – not even Martyna – could do that.

I can hear your thoughts, she says. *How can this be?* She's frightened. I can feel it. My head is a scary place to be.

You drank my blood. You're part of me, I explain.

I feel ... strange. Like I used to be. Like I'm strong again.

The Azasti is gone. You're cured. A wave of happiness floods my thoughts – Elodie's happiness – and I smile a little. But then, a cold bout of fear, like icy water in my veins, pierces me. She's cured, but she's one with me. And that means she shares my pain, my father's torture. There's no going back for her. She'll never be the same again.

And now she'll know of my plans. Will she give me away? Will she stop me?

I picture her, those lips I kissed, that body I held – even if when I did that Elodie was controlled by another woman – and I feel a rush of desire. I want to be alone with her. Right now. I want our bodies to fuse together again, like our thoughts. I shouldn't feel this way, not with Martyna's spirit still alive. But it's not love, it's something different.

Possession. The word flashes through my mind. My face is close to hers and I can feel her features, though I can't see them. I want to kiss her more than ever. "We need to go," I say instead, getting to my feet. I help Elodie up, and she sways for a moment and leans against me. It's the other way round now. It used to be me leaning on her, in my blindness. I feel something wet on my face, trickling down my lips and chin. My nose must still be bleeding after Sean's pounding. *Before all this is over, I'll twist his neck, I swear.*

Elodie and I cling to each other. I can't see, and she's weak and dizzy, but we remain close. Her words resound in my mind once more.

I know what you're doing, she says. *I know what your plan is.*

It's the only way.

I know it is. I'll help you.

Relief fills me whole. She won't give me away.

You must keep quiet, even in your thoughts.

I will. It will be done.

She squeezes my hand, and we walk on like one.

42
Faces

My heart hardens
Every day a little more

They were all shivering, their breaths condensing in little white clouds. The forest kept getting thicker and darker, and very little light seeped from above as more and more branches weaved a tighter canopy. It was the middle of the day, but it felt like twilight, and Sarah kept seeing shadows out the corner of her eye, hiding behind the trees, moving swiftly before she could look straight at them. She was on edge, her hands flooding with heat at every noise. It hurt because of the wounds inflicted on her by the spider's acid, and over-using her power like this would wear her out in the long run, she knew that — but she couldn't stop.

"How are your hands?" asked Sean, gently taking her fingers in his, and letting them go at once as the Blackwater burnt him. "Ow!"

"Sorry. I don't seem to be able to turn it off."

"Is it painful?"

Sarah shrugged. Her hands should have been dressed, covered in burns and blisters as they were. "It doesn't matter. How are you?"

"I don't know how I'm still standing. It doesn't matter either, I suppose," Sean replied, and stood closer to her, their arms touching for a moment since their hands couldn't. Sarah revelled in his closeness, her jagged nerves relaxing slightly.

"How far, Nicholas?" Sean asked.

"We'll be there tonight." The blind man's face was illuminated by the lightning, blue shadows dancing on his features. As the electrical storm continued above them, Sarah kept thinking of the illustration on the cover of the fairy-tale book Harry had left for Elodie – the rays emanating from the skull were blue, just like the lightning. Strange. It must have been a coincidence ... or did the old folk tales know about the Shadow World?

New storms kept coming, one after the other. They were all stemming from the same place, somewhere ahead of them. The King of Shadows' lair, Sarah suspected, but didn't want to ask. Her stomach lurched. She knew it was likely that these were the last hours of her life, and she was ready – but a part of her couldn't help being scared. She couldn't help looking around her, at the trees and the purple sky above, and feeling the cold air all over her body. To consider that soon all this would be no more ... Would there really be a time when she would not know anything, not feel anything? Where would Sean be? If they died together, would they remain together, wherever they were going? It didn't really matter, not to anyone but them. If the whole human world was hanging in the balance, their love had to be an afterthought. Her shoulder brushed Sean's arm again, and she wished she could wrap her arms around his waist and lean her head on his chest, to rest and let him rest, and forget about the world . . .

Suddenly everything spun around her, too fast for her to acknowledge what was happening. The sky and the ground swapped places; she felt herself fall, and her bones ached with the impact. She saw Sean's knees and hands, and dancing blades of grass. Everything blurred, like through a rainy window – and then she saw nothing. Everything disappeared. It was as if a black curtain had been pulled over her vision.

When she opened her eyes, she was somewhere else. On a beach, open and windy and free, without the tapestry of branches above her to hide the sky. A vision, she realised – one of the rare times in which dreams came to her when she was awake.

Sarah smelled salt in the air, and felt a cold wind move through her hair and over her face – was it Islay? She couldn't tell. In front of her was the vast expanse of sea. If she took a step, she would walk into the water.

Suddenly, she felt she wasn't alone. She looked around her, searching, but there were no Surari. Instead, Sean was at her side – and Niall, Elodie, Nicholas, Alvise, and Micol – all of them were there, standing along the water's edge, gentle ripples lapping at their feet. They all had a strange look in their eyes, as if they were asleep with their eyes open.

The air darkened all of a sudden, and Sarah looked up. She saw black clouds galloping on the horizon towards them, surging faster than any cloud could move in real life. The storm was getting closer and closer at an unnatural speed, taking over the sky. The sea turned grey and foamy in the space of a second, and Sarah gaped as a huge wave rose in front of them from nowhere, ready to swallow them. Sarah thought she'd seen a shape in the water – a face. An enormous face with its eyes closed and mouth open . . .

"Sean!" she screamed, but he didn't reply. She took a deep breath and caught one last glimpse of Sean's profile as he stood frozen and silent in front of the rising wave. Then the wave descended.

As the roar of the water deafened her, Sarah braced herself for the wave's impact, digging her feet firmly in the sand beneath her, expecting the force of the water to sweep her away like a broom sweeps dust. But the wave passed over her somehow, and left her standing, and completely dry. The roaring too had stopped.

She looked around her, desperate to know what happened to her friends. Her knees nearly buckled in relief as she saw Sean still beside her. But she barely had time to take a breath when she realised that not everyone was still standing. Some had been swallowed by the sea. Elodie . . . And Niall . . .

She tried to dive into the water, but she realised she couldn't move. Her feet were planted in the sand, tied by invisible ropes. To her horror, she saw that in the distance the water was rising again.

She tried to keep calm. "Sean. We need to go. Another wave is coming." She shook his arm, but her feet would not move. Sean didn't even turn towards her. He continued standing mute, gazing ahead of him. Sarah could only look helplessly on as another wave rose from the sea and landed on them, taking Alvise and Micol away. Now only she and Sean stood together on the waterline.

"Sean. Sean, please look at me. Talk to me!" she pleaded, but there was no reply. He stood immobile and without expression, looking ahead of him at the stormy water.

Another wave came. Sarah closed her eyes. All of a sudden she felt peaceful, even happy, that the sea had decided to take them together. When the water fell on her once more, she let herself go. It was time.

But the third wave was gone too, and Sarah stood dry and unmoved on the shore. Sean was gone. She was still on the waterline, alone, tears mixed with seawater falling from her eyes and an empty heart beating in her chest.

"Sarah? Sarah?"

Sarah blinked over and over. There was a strange taste in her mouth – soil, she realised, and brought her arm to her mouth, cleaning her lips. The darkening sky came into focus, and then so did Sean's face. Sean. He was there. He was alive.

"Was it a vision?" he asked, helping her sit up. She saw that the others were standing in a circle around her, facing out, watching for danger. She nodded.

"Yes. It just came over me . . ."

"Can you tell me what you saw?"

"All of us were standing on a beach somewhere. On the waterline. Three waves came, and with each wave more of us were gone. Until everyone was dead. Except me."

Sean frowned. He couldn't say what he thought, that if that was going to be the end result – they'd all die and Sarah survived – he was too relieved that Sarah would be alive to entirely mourn the loss of his own life, and the others'.

He held her hands and helped her stand. "Can you walk?"

"Yes. I'm okay," she said. But she wasn't.

In the dream everyone had died except for her. Another sign that she had to be kept alive. Why? What did they want from her? And who were "they"? Nicholas? The King of Shadows? Both? Something else?

Elodie stepped beside Sarah and Sean. "In the book Harry gave me," she began, "one of the tales talked about two children on a quest to free their parents' soul from a witch. In order to free them, the children had to face three waves of evil. I read that book twice, but there were so many stories . . . I can't remember exactly what the waves were. And then there was this spirit who held a mirror to the children's faces and made them see horrible things."

Sarah gazed at her. Those black, black eyes, in place of Elodie's warm chocolate ones, unnerved her. "What happened to the children?"

"They died. Their souls turned into flowers. Bluebells."

"Great," said Niall. "It's a good sign, for sure."

As soon as the others were out of earshot, Sarah took Sean's arm. "Sean. In the dream, only I survived. They have a plan for me. That's why I'm not dead yet."

Sean felt cold. He wished he could dismiss Sarah's fears, but he couldn't. "Do you think Nicholas is betraying us? That he still wants you as his wife?"

"I don't know. But I want you to promise something."

"What is it?"

"If this is still what he's planning . . . don't let him drag my soul away. Kill me before he can take me."

Sean took hold of her wrist, gently. "I won't let him take you," he whispered in her ear. When he looked up once more, his eyes met Elodie's. She'd turned around and was looking at Sarah with those new, obsidian eyes. Looking straight at her with an expression neither of them could decipher.

They walked on for another while, the freezing air cutting their skin. All of a sudden dazzling light flooded their eyes – there were no more trees. They stepped into a clearing, the white, frozen sky hanging heavy over them, high grass swaying in the wind. A circle of grey stones – double Sarah's height – rose from the grass, and three enormous boulders stood in the middle. They were roughly sculpted to resemble crouching figures. Two were beasts, one that looked like a monkey, one a kind of lizard, and another was an etched human being with a small body and an enormous face. They were like statues in a long-abandoned temple, moss half covering them, the elements having rounded their corners and smoothed the carvings.

Sarah looked around her. She knew that place. It was her place of dreams, the one she'd gone to in nearly every vision since her parents had been killed. She remembered the first time she'd been there, how she'd been trapped under those stones, and then she'd crawled out to stand under the twilight sky, the wind on her face, every colour heightened, vivid, the way it was in the Shadow World. She recalled the demon attack, and then Nicholas, the pale, black-haired boy she used to call Leaf because he gifted her autumn leaves, saving her life.

Everything was meant to bring me here, Sarah realised suddenly. Since it all started, this was ultimately where she was supposed to be – in the Shadow World. She stared into the white sky, the lilac light of dusk spreading from the west, and then around her at the swaying grass, the visions that had taken place there going through her mind one by one.

"Sean . . ." she called. Sean came to stand beside her, gazing at her profile as she kept looking around her, astonished and still somehow accepting, as if some part of her had always known. "This is my place of dreams," she whispered.

"The place you see in your visions? Are you sure?"

Sarah nodded. "I am sure."

At that moment, a deafening noise exploded in their ears, and blue light swallowed them. Lightning had struck right in the clearing, and then another, and another, hitting the three boulders and disappearing into the ground.

"The King of Shadows is here," Sarah said, and everyone stood still.

"Is that right, Nicholas? Is this the place?" asked Sean.

Nicholas nodded and remained silent, his chin slightly raised as if listening for something. At that moment a long, deep, growling filled the air, and it wasn't thunder – it came from the ground beneath them. The earth shook, the boulders trembled as they all lost their footing and fell in the long grass.

Nicholas called to his father. *She's here. I brought her to you.*

43
Figlia Mia

The me I see in you
Is the part of you I hate

Venice

They heard her screams resound throughout the Palazzo.
Winter, who was helping Cosima bake bread, ran as fast as
she could through the frescoed halls. Reaching Lucrezia, she
kneeled beside her. The Italian girl's screaming stopped and
she was as still as a doll.

"Lucrezia? What did you see?" she whispered urgently,
drying sweat on the girl's face with a lacy handkerchief
Cosima kept on her bedside table.

At that moment, Conte Vendramin barged into the room.
"What did she say? Something about Alvise?" he enquired
hopefully.

"Nothing yet."

"Lucrezia. *Figlia mia*," he began, but then his daughter
interrupted him.

"I must remind her," she said in English.

"What, Lucrezia? What? Remind who?"

"I must remind her she is Sarah Midnight."

Conte Vendramin's and Winter's eyes locked. They had no idea what Lucrezia meant, but they both could sense a change in the atmosphere, a shift of fate. The day of reckoning was here. The destiny of the Secret Families was being played out in the Shadow World, and somehow, Sarah was the key.

"Is Niall alive?" Winter murmured, but she knew Lucrezia would not answer. Her nonsensical whispering had resumed already.

44
Every End is a Beginning

Every step I took had a reason
Every decision I made had a pattern
Every breath I took had the purpose
To take me home to you

The earth stopped shaking, and Sarah got back on her feet. She gazed at each of her friends, standing around her in the wind under the purple sky, and her heart bled as she realised with sudden intensity that not all of them – maybe none of them – would make it home.

Elodie, with her obsidian eyes, the memory of Harry weighing on her shoulders and her soul poisoned by Nicholas' blood. Niall, brave and cheerful and forever the optimist, Winter in his heart with every step he took. Alvise, with his lost powers and ailing sister, who had given them his loyalty without question, embracing the mission and its dangers. Micol, younger than Sarah was when it all started – alone in the world, just like she was. And Mike, gone but with them always.

And then her thoughts went to the people back home:Aunt Juliet, who would wait for her for a long time, until finally she'd accept that Sarah was never coming back. Bryony, who would grow up and get married and live the life Sarah would never have. Or if the Time of Demons happened again, what would happen to them? She'd never know.

And above all this, above the people in her company and the memories of home, was Sean. Memories of their time together – of those stolen moments when they were in each other's arms – flowed in her mind like a cool, fresh stream ... something pure and beautiful among all that death, all that strife.

Sarah smelled them before she could see them, a foul stench of wet beast and rot, and then high-pitched screeches, somewhere between the calls of monkeys and the screams of birds.

The first wave of evil, thought Nicholas. *The Guardians.* "Demon-apes. Be ready," he commanded.

And then, the voice in his head: *Protect her. I need her.*

Yes, Father, he replied at once. Elodie looked at him. She'd heard the voice too and she knew what she would do when the time came.

Sarah's eyes narrowed and shone deadly green, her hands smouldering with the Blackwater. Sean had his *sgian-dubh* in his hand, and was already whispering his deadly runes. Niall started humming softly, eyes semi-closed. Elodie's lips were taking on a deadly shade of blue. Alvise's bow and arrow were ready to shoot, though only four arrows remained in his quiver. Micol's hands were shimmering and crackling with electrical charges. Only Nicholas was standing completely still. Deadly energy was building inside him, ready to burst.

The night was still and dark and silent for a moment – and then it all happened. The foul smell intensified, and the trees at the edges of the clearing shattered in a shower of broken leaves and twigs. White, hairy limbs appeared, and monkey-like faces with enormous yellow teeth, mixed with branches and ferns, running in the grass, climbing over the boulders, banging their chests and baring their teeth. They were as big as humans, too many to be counted, long arms out to grab and teeth bared to devour. The creatures of nightmares, creatures that should have never seen the light, that should have never been born – creatures that, in the human world, nature had decided to obliterate.

Screeching ape-like calls that chilled the blood, the Surari pounced on Sarah and her friends, clawing and biting and shrieking so loud it hurt their ears. Soon they realised that the demon-apes didn't just want to bite; they wanted to eat. They threw their heads backwards and smelled the air, savouring the scent of human flesh, tasting it already.

In a haze of fury and terror, Sarah heard Elodie calling, "Niryani!" and Niall's song rising into the air, thick and powerful and singing of death. Sean's mouth was moving incessantly, pronouncing Secret words she couldn't hear, while his *sgian-dubh* traced deadly scarlet ribbons in the air, flying around like shards of glass, cutting and stabbing and lodging themselves inside the demon-apes' foul white fur. And then her powers flew through her so intensely that they swept her away to a place where only the battle mattered. She focused on the beast closest to her and glared at it with bright-green eyes, the Midnight gaze cutting it between the eyes. The creature shuddered and shrieked and then it bent double, unable to move, trembling. Sarah was on it at once, sinking her hands into its fur and holding on to it with all her might, giving it no chance to recover enough to bite her. And then she was everywhere, stabbing and paralysing and dissolving the demon-apes with silent, deadly efficiency. One after the other the demon-apes began falling, cut and burnt and dissolved. Blackwater was soaking the ground and the stones and the grass, turning them black. The forest itself had turned on them; the whole place had become polluted, poisonous, a place where no human being was ever meant to set foot.

Soon Niall's song was at its peak, high-pitched, painful and deadly. Quickly, it began to affect them all, hurting their ears and their heads. Sean touched his ear and saw blood trickling from between his fingers. The only one who was unaffected by Niall's deadly sound was Micol.

Sarah surveyed the scene. Demon-apes' corpses were all around, and only a few were still standing, shrieking in fury at their own demise. She allowed herself to breathe for a moment. She dared to hope that they'd overcome the demon-apes and were closer to the King of Shadows ... And then she heard a strange sound coming from the trees that crowned the clearing, somewhere between crickets and scurrying rats. In horror, Sarah realised it was the sound of rattling teeth.

They crawled down from the trees, falling like deadly rain, scurrying through the long grass. They were black, thick-skinned, furry and fat like rats, but their faces and tails were reptile-like, and had a fan of leathery skin around their heads that reminded Sarah of a small dinosaur. Another abomination, another creature that evolution had concocted to be as deadly as it could be. Micol shivered, reminded of the fat black rats swimming in the canals in Venice.

The second wave, Nicholas thought. "Demon-lizards!" he shouted. "Don't let them bite you. They are poisonous!"

"Too late for me," said a voice, strangely cheerful, as if beyond despair.

They all turned around to see Niall clutching his chest, his clothes so ripped and slayed that his skin was bare to see; right in the middle of his breastbone was the imprint of two sharp animal teeth.

45
Sacrifice

I always knew it would be you
I would call on my deathbed

An abominable stream of demon-lizards was on them, but Alvise stepped backwards, his pugnale in front of him. He had to try to help Niall.

"Micol! Cover me!" he called, and Micol stood in front of him, a deadly shield of light around her body. A demon-ape crouched in front of her, growling and gnashing its teeth together. Suddenly it pounced, and Micol exploded in a storm of multi-coloured lightning. The trees around them were illuminated red, green, yellow, blue, as she hit the Surari over and over again with her deadly charges. Sean gaped as he saw the outline of her skull through her skin, her bones through her arms, as her hair stood on end and her eyes sparked and glimmered.

The demon-apes kept trying to get close to her, but time and time again they were hit with her electrical current and thrown back, their fur smoking. Soon they didn't try any more, and Micol began looking for them, sending sparks to ignite and singe.

"Niall!" Alvise shouted above the demon-apes' shrieks and the demon-lizards' scurrying towards him. Niall was still standing, trying to get the song going again. But no sound could come out of his mouth any more – the poison was spreading through his body.

"Alvise . . ." Niall had time to say before his legs gave way and he fell to the grass. Alvise saw a demon-ape rising as if from nowhere and lolling in front of the Irishman, as if it were enjoying the spectacle. It pounced on Niall, ready to bite into his flesh – but Alvise threw himself onto the Surari and stabbed it over and over again with his pugnale. The beast shrieked and released Niall, turning around with its arms open, ready to tear off Alvise's head.

Alvise was faster. He sank his pugnale just between the demon-ape's eyes, and the Surari started screaming and pawing at the blade, trying to dislodge it. But it had sunk too deep, and the beast fell backwards and didn't move again.

"Alvise! Watch out!" It was Micol. Alvise didn't manage to turn around fast enough when two demon-apes leapt on him from behind. One sank its teeth into Alvise's back and took a bite of his flesh, while another grabbed his legs and threw him onto the grass. Micol was on them at once, one hand on each beast, frying them with bright-red charges. Smoke was coming out of their ears and nostrils, and they were juddering and trembling as the fire consumed them from the inside.

Alvise lay stunned for a moment, then crawled on his hands and knees towards Niall. The Irishman lay pale and lifeless, his throat and chest bloodied, strange purple bruises surfacing all over his skin. He was still breathing, but his heartbeat was as soft as a butterfly's touch.

Alvise sobbed, a sob full of all the sorrow of the world – and then his cry was interrupted by a swarm of demon-lizards that ran towards him, their bodies tight together like black molten rock, their pointed teeth making a rattling sound. For a moment, Alvise stared death in the face – and then he saw a shroud of blue flames envelop the whole horde of Surari, a terrible smell of singed fur and burning flesh hitting his nostrils and making him gag. The flames were so close they brought tears to his eyes; through his tears he saw Nicholas holding his head in his hands and crumpling on the grass, blue sparks still emanating from his fingers.

Elodie watched in horror as Nicholas wailed. His father had struck him again.

"No! Please, no!" he was pleading, his words confused and jumbled, as the pain was too strong for him to concentrate on making sense. Soon he could only scream.

"Nicholas! Nicholas!" Elodie kept calling, as if her voice could somehow guide him back from the world of pain he was lost to. And then she started feeling it too.

Acid began burning her from the inside, her brain, her forehead, her eyes, her ears, her neck. She screamed, and then curled into a ball, hot tears rolling down her cheeks. Even in her agony, she felt around for Nicholas' hand, and they held each other, their souls one in the searing pain.

Sean heard Elodie screaming and called her name. While she was whimpering on the ground, another swarm of demon-lizards emerged from the trees and began their descent towards them. Sean's runes exploded scarlet, like shards of glass, impaling the lizards against the trees before they could reach Elodie.

"Elodie!" he called again, trying to reach her, but a demon-ape rose from the high grass and threw itself on him. Sean fell supine, the dead weight of the Surari falling on his chest and crushing his ribs, so heavy that he couldn't breathe. Everything around him went black.

Leave Elodie. Please leave her alone! Nicholas kept begging, but it was no use. Through the haze of his own agony, he listened to Elodie's desperate screams until he couldn't take it any more. Blue flames burst from his fingers once more. He could accept being tortured – in a way he deserved it, with all the horrible things he'd done – but not Elodie. He wouldn't let his father hurt her.

Soon the flames were everywhere, thick smoke blinding him, suffocating him. He couldn't hear his father's voice and he couldn't hear Elodie any more. Everything was silent; everywhere he turned there was only smoke. He closed his eyes, tears of pain and despair flowing down his cheeks. He wished the flames would eat him, too, but the cold blue fire would never kill its creator.

And then he realised that grey and blue and white were dancing in front of his eyes. The darkness was gone. He blinked and blinked. There was no more black. He walked on and he emerged from the flames. He saw the green of swaying grass and the black and silver of a starry sky.

The screams had stopped. Elodie dragged herself to her feet, agonising pain still behind her eyes but slowly dulling.

She took Nicholas' face in her hands, sweeping the ash away. Nicholas looked back at her. He saw her face, her eyes black like his.

He couldn't rip his gaze away from her – the lips he'd kissed and the body he'd made his and the golden hair he'd sunk his fingers into – and a wave of sudden, absurd happiness swept through him. A blessed moment of pure joy in the middle of hell.

"Elodie," he whispered.

"You can see me?"

"Yes. I can see you. I can see again."

But the moment was short-lived. Something moved behind Elodie, something rising from the stones – a cloud, a shadow, a shapeless figure.

The three waves of evil, and the third is coming, Nicholas thought, and he wished he still had no sight, as he saw the face of the third Guardian take shape in front of him, opening his mouth and letting its deadly fog hit them and swallow them all.

46
Spirit

Raise a mirror to my face and see
What I really am and what I'm scared to be

Alvise cradled Niall's head in his lap. They'd moved him, as gently and urgently as they could, far from the fighting, at the edge of the clearing. Alvise remembered the last time he'd sat with a loved one dying in his arms, and how he couldn't save her. A sob escaped his lips as a face he once knew and loved dearly took shape in his mind's eye – his mother's. She too, had lain with a flower of blood on her chest, breathing slowly, too slowly, her white-blonde hair sticky with blood and sweat, her hands clutching her heart as if to stop it from failing. He could have saved her. Why hadn't he? Why had his powers stopped right at that moment, never to return?

"Please, don't die. Please," Alvise kept murmuring now, and cursed himself once more. History repeating itself – and again, at the centre of all the failure and loss and pain was him, Alvise. What good was he to anyone? All the self-hatred he had felt through the years since he lost his powers overcame him. It would have been better if it were he lying there instead of Niall. Maybe it would have been better for everyone if he ...

He didn't have time to finish that terrible thought. Through his tears, he saw something hovering over the carved stones – a sort of fog, or steam, like a low-lying cloud. Alvise blinked once, twice, as he realised that something was taking shape within the cloud – a face, its eyes closed, its mouth too big for the rest of its features, the furls of vapour fluid and dancing and ever-changing. Its mouth was a gaping hole full of darkness. His hands tightened around his bow, but he knew very well that there was no point in shooting – the thing had no body, nothing of substance to hit. As he watched it, the feeling of uselessness he'd felt as he watched Niall lying in pain crept deeper and deeper into his mind and soul. It was as if by gazing at that creature, he was gazing at the darkest part of him.

The face opened its mouth further and further, like in a yawn, and a strange, unnatural smoke rose out of it, silent and creeping and spreading through the clearing too fast to be outrun, too insidious to be avoided. It filled the air and the sky and it sank into the ground.

"Don't breathe the smoke," Alvise told Micol, who'd remained close to him all along, and the Italian girl crouched, covering her head with her arms. Alvise curled tightly around Niall, trying to shelter him. He tried holding his breath, but there was no point. The fog swallowed them, and soon Alvise's lungs hurt so much, he had to open his mouth.

It tasted of nothing, smelled of nothing, like anaesthetic,

but something was happening. Alvise prepared himself for what he hoped would be a quick death and feared would be a slow, painful poisoning. He threw a glance at Micol and saw that she was lying on the ground, unconscious. He tried to call her name, but all of a sudden, like a switch going, everything went black.

A moment later, Alvise opened his eyes and looked around him. He saw golden ceilings and mosaic floors, and from the window, the water of the Grand Canal shimmering in the sunshine. Palazzo Vendramin. He was home. How had that happened, he thought, confused. They were all trapped in the Shadow World. How had he made it back to Venice? Had he stepped into the iris without knowing? Or maybe he was dead. Maybe this was the chance of a final goodbye.

"Alvise," said a voice, a voice he knew well.

Lucrezia. She hadn't said a conscious word in years, nothing that wasn't the oracle-like talk she did while in her coma ... For a moment, the sense of despair that possessed him shifted to a ray of hope.

Lucrezia was on her bed, her eyes closed, her body still and floppy, her hands dangling from her sides instead of being in her lap, or beside her body, like he and Cosima always made sure they were. And then she opened her eyes, and before Alvise's incredulous gaze, she lifted her head. Lucrezia was awake.

All breath left him. "Lucrezia," Alvise managed, and went to kneel beside her. He lifted her hands and laid them gently on her chest, lacing her fingers together in a gesture of forgiveness. He then gave her hands a squeeze, and stroked her white face. "You're awake."

"If you hadn't lost your powers, I wouldn't be like this now," the blonde girl said, her eyes watching but her body immobile. A talking doll, spewing hatred instead of the love he was expecting. Her words were like blades in Alvise's heart. It was true, then. The terrible dread that had tormented him since Lucrezia had fallen into her coma – the thought he had never spoken aloud to anyone but Micol – that it was all his fault, that if he'd saved his mother, if he'd still had his powers, Lucrezia wouldn't have felt forced to undertake the ceremony. It was true.

"I'm sorry," he whispered, pain stinging behind his eyes, his heart. Guilt clung to his throat and made it hard to speak.

"You must make amends," Lucrezia continued, still unmoving, her eyelids fluttering. Her eyelashes cast dark shadows on her skin.

"How? Tell me how, and I will!"

"Look on the ground beside you, brother."

Alvise obeyed. His quiver was there, brimming with arrows. Sunbeams seeped from the window and shone on the metal arrowheads, making them glimmer. He lifted the quiver and secured it to his back, but he couldn't see his bow. "I'll slay whatever you want me to slay. Just tell me . . ."

"Yourself," she said, her tone cruel, cold.

Alvise felt a terrible chill invade him. "What?"

"It won't take long. And it'll be less painful than what I've had to go through every day and every night since I was thirteen."

"I . . ."

"Do it!" she screamed, her voice suddenly loud and high-pitched. Her hands were little fists, her eyes blazing with an emotion he never thought her capable of feeling for him: hatred. "Do it!" she screamed again. "You let them kill me and take away my childhood. You let them trap me in these nightmares, allowed to do nothing but dream and open portals into the unknown for *you*! My own brother, who doesn't have any powers! Rather than hunt and kill the demons myself, I had to watch in silence as you did it, a job I should have been doing, but one I couldn't because of you! Now it's your turn to die!"

"I didn't know what they would do! We didn't know ..."

"You know now. You know now what happened to me. It's time to pay your debt," she hissed.

It made sense. Her horrible, horrible words actually made sense.

Trembling, Alvise slipped an arrow out of the quiver and felt the smooth wood he'd watched his father whittle and its steel tip, unflinching under his touch. To pierce his skin with such a thing, to let it bleed his life out of him ... He couldn't do it. He didn't want to.

"I can't," he said, almost pleadingly.

Lucrezia shrieked again. "It's your fault! It's your fault I'm like this! Kill yourself! There is no other way to make amends!"

"Please, Lucrezia, don't make me do it," he begged. And still, his hand curled around the arrow.

All of a sudden, Lucrezia hissed, her eyes locking on his. They were white inside.

"You must die," she said, as if it was an unquestionable truth, a fact that nobody could deny.

Alvise gazed into her white eyes, and all hope, all joy he had ever felt in his life, drained out of him. Of course he had to die. She was right. He deserved to. He hadn't saved their mother. Instead he'd lost his powers, let the Sabha break his sister, and now he had watched Niall die. All that had gone wrong in his life was his fault: suddenly it was clear. It was foolish to resist.

He opened his shirt and positioned the arrowhead against his heart, his hands trembling so much that the arrow nearly fell. He wouldn't push it in. He was worried his resolve would waver, and his strength would fail as the steel pierced his flesh. He had to let himself sink on it, let gravity do its duty. The arrowhead felt cold on his skin. He held it with both hands, bracing himself for the fall . . .

"Alvise." Another voice resounded in the room. The first voice he'd ever heard in his life, the sweetest. His mother's.

He looked up slowly. Ludovica Vendramin was standing beside Lucrezia's bed, dressed in combat gear similar to what he was wearing: a long tunic tied to the waist, laced boots on her feet, her bow and arrows strapped to her back. Her white-blonde hair was loose about her shoulders, and her pale-blue eyes shone in the light of the sun.

"Alvise. Listen to me. This is not Lucrezia. It's a Guardian, the sentinel of the stones. It's deceiving you. What happened to me, what happened to your sister . . . it wasn't your fault."

"It was! She wouldn't have done it had it not been for me having lost my powers!" Alvise sobbed. "You'd still be here . . . and Lucrezia would be the way she used to be . . . our family would be together . . . but I failed you all!"

"Yes, you failed us all!" Lucrezia screeched from her perch, her voice hungry, deeper, like it didn't entirely belong to her, as if another being was coming to the surface within her. "You must kill yourself! Do it!"

"No. That's not true," his mother said. "You did well by your family, Alvise." Her blue-green eyes stared into his soul. "Always. Put down that arrow."

Alvise took in his mother's beloved face, her kind eyes, the power in those hands that could kill Surari, but could also heal. "I lost my powers. Lucrezia and Father are all the family I have left. She was our last chance for dreaming. That's why she accepted undertaking the ceremony. She wouldn't have done it otherwise."

"You don't know that. Lucrezia made her own decision. And you didn't lose your powers," she said, and at that moment, Lucrezia started screaming again, convulsing on the bed.

"I . . ."

"You didn't lose your powers," his mother repeated above Lucrezia's screams. "They are still in you, my son. You just have to call them back to you."

Alvise took a breath. His powers were still with him? They weren't gone?

"I can't . . . I can't call them back," he whispered. His voice was lost under Lucrezia's screams, but somehow his mother heard him.

"You can, Alvise. My son, you can, I promise you. Put down that arrow. You must live, not die. You must live and call your powers back. There are lives that depend on you."

His sister kept howling – but as he glimpsed her, he saw that she wasn't herself any more; she'd lost her shape. And was slowly dissolving into fog.

Alvise let the arrow fall on the mosaic floor. He opened his mouth to speak, but once again, everything went black in a heartbeat. Palazzo Vendramin was gone, and so was Lucrezia's foggy shape. And his mother – his mother was gone too. The loss of her twisted his insides . . . He wanted to stay wherever he was and see her again, speak to her once more.

But suddenly, he was conscious again. His eyes opened on the Shadow World around him. The purple sky, the swaying grass. There was an arrow in his hand and a sharp, nipping pain in the skin over his heart. He touched it, and he saw his fingers were red. But it was just a graze; he was alive, he wasn't even injured badly.

His mother's words came back to him: *You must live and call your powers back.*

His gaze fell on Niall's unconscious face, poison raging through his body, his chest rising and falling too slowly to sustain life. *You didn't lose your powers. They are still in you, my son.*

Micol braided her fingers over her head – the smoke was coming. She desperately tried to hide her face in Niall's chest, to hold her breath, but she was panting so hard she couldn't stop breathing, not even for a second. As the smoke reached her, she became unconscious at once, her head resting on Niall, her arms around his waist, folded in two like a rag doll.

She awoke with the sun in her eyes, and the scent of lemons and Mediterranean pines all around her. She recognised the place at once – how could she not? As a child, she'd spent more time there than anywhere else. She was in her family's lemon grove, at the edge of the pinewoods, back home. She could see her tanned arms and legs in her short cotton dress. Beside her was a basket full of bread and fruit. She and her brothers spent whole days outside, so Elsa, the housekeeper, always gave them a hamper of food to take with them.

But Elsa was dead, and so were her parents.

Micol took a short, sharp breath. It couldn't be. She couldn't really be here. She was in the Shadow World, and she was dying, poisoned by that weird smoke. Nothing else was real, nothing else was true.

And then she heard her father's voice. "Micol! *Aiuto!* Micol!"

She jumped. Her father was calling for help. How could that be? He was dead. He'd been mauled by a demon-dog only a few months before, when Ranieri had started showing signs of the Azasti. They were both dead. And Tancredi too. All of them, the family, the Gamekeepers, every single soul who lived in the house with them was gone. Except her, Micol, left to keep living, alone and bereft.

And still her father's voice calling felt so real. "Micol! *Aiuto!*" Somehow, her father was back, and he was calling her. He needed her. She had to listen.

She ran on among the lemon trees and into the pine-woods, the warm light of the sun on her face and her arms.

"Micol!" Her father kept calling.

"I'm coming! Papà, I'm coming!"

She ran, following her father's voice, until she reached a small slope paved with strong-smelling brown pine needles. Lapo Falco was at the bottom of the slope, his chest and arms covered in bright-red wounds. He was bleeding out slowly – all over again. Except before, Micol hadn't found him.

Instead she'd stayed with Ranieri that day. The memory flashed before her eyes: his delirium had begun not long before, and Micol was terrified to leave him on his own. The two Falco Gamekeepers had just been killed, and her mother and Tancredi had gone hunting for the killers together. That day had been one of the rare times when her parents had gone hunting separately. Micol could recall such a thing happening three, maybe four times in her whole life. This time, their luck hadn't held. Her father wasn't found until he'd lost too much blood, and it was too late to do anything for him.

She remembered her mother's face when she was told her husband had died. Her eyes were empty all of a sudden, as if she'd lost the will to live. Not long after, she'd been dragged underground by a soil demon. Their hounds had found her buried in the pinewoods. Since then, Micol had been haunted by regret. If only she'd gone hunting with her father. If only she'd gone looking for him when he'd been absent for one hour rather than after a few hours. But Ranieri had been banging his head against the wall, screaming curses and nonsensical words, all that day. She'd been too terrified to leave him until it was too late. She'd been put in front of a choice, and she'd made the wrong decision.

Maybe now she was being given a second chance, to change fate. Maybe this was her chance to put things right.

"Micol, jump in, *figlia mia*!" Lapo begged, extending his bleeding arm. Micol threw herself on her knees, peering into the ditch. Multi-coloured charges were buzzing around her body, brought on by her distress. Lapo's face, once handsome with the amber skin and almond eyes all his children had inherited, was a mask of pain, caked with blood and soil.

Micol's mind whirled. Maybe she could save him this time. And then her mother wouldn't go on a suicidal mission alone, leaving Ranieri, Tancredi and her behind in her quest for death, and they'd both survive, and she wouldn't be alone.

"Papà! I'm here! Give me your hand!" she called, her arms stretching as far as they could. The walls of the ditch were so steep that she feared if she jumped in she would not be able to drag herself and her father out, and they'd both be stuck there, easy prey for any demons on the prowl.

"I can't reach. Jump down here. Please help me ..."

"If I jump in too neither of us will make it out!"

"Don't leave me here ... Please don't leave me here, Micol." His chest was bright red. Pine needles stuck to the wet wounds in his skin, causing him pain Micol didn't want to think about. She watched her father's face lose its colour, becoming ashen. Through his pain, he struggled to speak. "You abandoned me once, Micol. Don't do it again," her father pleaded.

His words cut deep, and Micol felt sick. She shut her eyes briefly, trying to think, trying to decide. Her best judgement was to go against her father's desperate calls, but this was the man who had raised her, who had taught her to be fierce, to never give up, especially not on your family.

She turned around, preparing herself to let her legs dangle off the ditch wall and throw herself down.

"Don't!" A voice had come from behind her. Micol's heart skipped a beat as she looked up. It was her brother Tancredi, standing under the canopy of a pine tree – the shadows cast by the tree were such that she couldn't fully make out his face. He was wearing the leather cape he used when he flew.

"Tancredi! Is it really you?" She peered, not daring to step any closer.

"It's me, yes. My *spirit*. But that is not our father. Come away," he said, taking a step towards her, his hand extended. As he walked out of the shadows so she could see his beloved face, she cried softly. It was really him, Tancredi. Her brother was back.

Or was he? Who was telling the truth? Her brother or her father?

"That thing is not our father. He's a Guardian. He's the

sentinel of the stones, the third wave of evil. Micol, please. Step away from him, come with me."

Micol jerked her face left and right. Tancredi was on one side of her, his slender arm extended, her father on the other side, broken and bleeding at the bottom of a ditch, torn apart by Surari claws and fangs. "I must help him! He'll die! Papà!" Micol called. She wanted it to be her father. She didn't want him to be an illusion, or even worse, evil, this Guardian her brother (was it really her brother?) talked about.

"Don't listen to him, *figlia mia*. That's not Tancredi. Come down here. Help me!"

Tancredi echoed Lapo's words. "He's not our father. Please, Micol, you must believe me."

Micol took her face in her hands for a moment. "If he's not our father, how do I know you are you?" she said in desperation.

"Remember when you were so scared of the water? And I said to take my hand, that we'd jump together?"

How could she ever forget?

"Remember, Micol?"

She nodded. "*Sì,*" she said softly.

"You trusted me then. Trust me now. Take my hand."

Slowly, Micol entwined her brother's fingers with hers. They felt cold, icy to the touch. Together they stepped away from the slope.

Just then a terrible growl came from inside the ditch. She looked at who she thought was her father, and immediately she wished she hadn't. A red mass of muscles and fangs and claws, growling and snarling, blood and gore dripping down then taking shape again, had taken her father's place. From an opening that looked like a misshapen mouth came one last call: "Micol ..."

But Tancredi was holding her by the shoulders. "It can't hurt you, now that you know it's lying. *Sorellina*, listen. I must go ..."

"Please don't go!"

"I can't stay. I'm sorry. Don't worry about me. I'm at peace. Don't forget me."

"Never!" Micol said among her tears, taking in her brother's face one last time, and then she couldn't see any more.

When she woke up, the first thing she saw was soft grass – and someone lying beside her, someone she couldn't recognise at first. And then it all came back to her. The figure lying on the ground was Niall Flynn, the Irishman. She was in the Shadow World. And there was Alvise, sitting on the grass beside them, blood on his chest – whose blood?

"Micol!" he called. "Thank God, you are awake!"

"I ... I think so. Are you hurt?" she asked, gesturing to his chest.

"No, I'm fine. The smoke is gone. Did you see ... things?"

Micol nodded. "I took his hand," she said, her thoughts hazy. "Tancredi's. He saved me." Moving to Alvise, she wrapped her arms around his neck. The Venetian man held her tightly as she trembled in his arms. "Something was pretending to be my father. But it wasn't. I had to make a choice. I still can't believe I made the right one ..." Suddenly, from over Alvise's shoulder, she saw it again: the orange light, dancing beside the stones.

The smoke enveloped Sean, and he fell like a dead weight. For a few seconds he saw dancing grass in front of him, swaying in the cold wind. A tiny spider crawled up a blade of grass, over a particle of soil and onwards, until it stood at the edge of it – and then nothing.

When he opened his eyes, a familiar face was above him. Fair skin and a mop of blonde hair, and green eyes, just like Sarah's.

"Harry?" he murmured.

"Come on, mate. Time to get up. That was a good party last night!"

Sean sat up and tried to get his bearings. The wooden sliding doors, soft light seeping from behind the paper that covered them; the thin square cushions on the floor; the *kotatsu*, the little table traditionally heated with hot coals, used to keep warm and have tea or sake on. He remembered many winter nights spent sipping tea at the *kotatsu* with his friends. The smile of a red-haired girl, the stories of hunting, the togetherness they'd experienced. All of the sights, sounds, experiences flooded back to him.

Beyond a semi-open sliding door, Sean could see a sliver of the garden he used to know so well, with its koi fish pond and the little stone bridge.

He was back in Kyoto, in the house the Ayanami family had given him to share with Harry, Elodie and Mary Ann. Sean's head spun so violently he thought he'd throw up.

"You are alive," he whispered to Harry.

"Barely, after last night! I don't want to see a glass of sake for . . . until tonight." He laughed. "How are you feeling?"

"I . . . I'm fine."

"Good, because there's something you need to do. Come on," Harry said, and led him next door. In a room empty of everything but *tatami*, a black-haired girl stood with her back to the door, dressed in the black kimono of temple workers, a wide grey sash wrapped around her waist. With hair that dark and straight, you could have mistaken her for a Japanese girl, but Sean knew the shape of that body, the curve of those hips.

"Sarah," Sean breathed. It made no sense. It had to be a dream, a vision of some sort. It couldn't be happening. He couldn't really be back in Kyoto: Harry wasn't alive, and Sarah had never been in Japan with them. It would be a long time before they met. No. None of this was true.

Sarah turned around. She was very pale, her green eyes uncannily similar to Harry's. "Sean. I'm so glad you are here."

"Sarah," Sean repeated, as if that was the only word he could say. His thoughts were a mass of questions and memories and doubts and skewed perceptions. He couldn't even begin to unpick them.

Harry crossed his arms. "Yup. Just the one. Sarah Midnight. I need you to kill her."

"You what?"

"Sean, she's just like our grandmother, Morag Midnight. She's cruel and heartless, and she'll end up killing us all. Tancredi was right. She needs to die."

Sarah was in the corner, doubled over, saying nothing. She wasn't pleading, not even with her eyes. Sean saw that Sarah's arms and hands were shackled.

"No, it's not like that," Sean reassured his friend. "You are wrong, Harry. She's good, and kind, and ... She's a Secret heir, Harry! Take those chains off!"

"She'll be the end of us all. She's been chosen. In your heart of hearts, you know as well as I do. She is cursed."

"What are you talking about? Sarah." He tried to kneel beside her, but Harry stopped him.

"She'll tell you herself, if you don't believe me."

Sarah raised her head and for the first time, she looked him in the eye. He expected to see anger, or terror, or defiance. But he saw acceptance – even desire. "He's right," Sarah agreed. "I'm just like Morag Midnight. Nicholas saw the black blood in me, that is why he chose me. I can kill anyone, anything. I am the strongest Dreamer. But I need to die. No one but the King of Shadows can have that much power. You must kill me before it's too late."

Harry lifted a katana off the floor, its blade glinting in the sunlight that flooded in from the windows. "Sean."

Sean put his hands up in front of the blade. "You are delirious! Both of you!" Or were they? That was Harry, for heaven's sake. He always knew the right thing to do, he always had a plan. Sean had always trusted what he said. But this? Underneath all of this, he knew that as a Gamekeeper he had to obey.

"You know what to do," Harry said, offering him the katana.

"No! You are crazy!"

"You must do it. There is no other way," Sarah said. "If you don't kill me, I'll destroy the world."

Sean ran a hand through his hair. "This can't be happening!"

"I must die," she repeated. "If you don't kill me now, millions of lives will be lost. Please listen to me."

"I can't."

"You have to! Kill her! Sean, kill her now! If you are a true Gamekeeper, this is what you must do!" Harry's green eyes were glinting, his face contorted in fury.

"Kill me, Sean."

Sean raised the katana. It hovered over Sarah for a moment, then he lowered it with a sharp thrust, sinking it into his own side.

Sarah clasped her hands over her mouth, trying not to breathe in the fog. But it was no use. She had to breathe. She inhaled the white, creeping mist, and she waited – waited for her lungs to burst, or burn.

The next thing she knew, her grandmother, Morag, was standing in front of her. Sarah blinked. What was her grandmother doing there? Was it a vision? Was it a dream, or something induced by that evil fog? Her eyes were hard blue nails. "You killed them," Morag said.

"I didn't mean to. I didn't want to . . ."

"You are just like me."

"I'm not!"

"It's your turn now," Morag said, handing her Mairead's *sgian-dubh*, engraved with Celtic patterns, her name burnt into the blade.

"No. I won't!"

"You must. You deserve it. Remember Leigh? And Angela? They are dead because of you. You are a monster." Sarah's heart tightened at the mention of her school friends, both killed by a demon belonging to the Scottish Valaya. "Your Aunt Juliet, scarred for life. Tancredi, not even decently buried. Because of you."

"No," she said, more feebly this time. She took the *sgian-dubh* from her grandmother's hands . . .

And then something strange began happening to her grandmother's face. Its left side started melting, losing its shape, and then its right side. Horrified, Sarah watched as a white, thick fog started seeping from her grandmother's body, until it all dissolved in mist.

A deep, growling voice came from somewhere beneath her feet. It instilled terror in her heart, a terror so strong she thought her heart would stop there and then. At once she realised that her day of reckoning had come.

"Sarah Midnight," it said. "You shall not die."

All of a sudden, death seemed desirable.

47
The Abyss

You knew all along
That we were bound to lose

Sarah's eyes snapped open. She jumped to her feet and lost her balance just as quickly. On her knees, she dragged herself up again. There was nobody around, not that she could see. All her friends were gone.

And then she spotted something blue in the high grass, a crumpled mound of clothes – a body with golden hair, a shape she knew like the back of her hand. A silver-handled *sgian-dubh* was buried deep in the body's side.

Sean.

Sarah stood silent and unmoving, contemplating Sean's senseless body, a red flower slowly blooming on the right side of his stomach, its petals flowing down his arm and into the grass in a black puddle.

She didn't need to see his face to know that Sean was dead.

Her heart stopped, all air leaving her lungs in an icy chill. Her body trembled at the loss of Sean. How could this be real? Sean? She wanted to scream, to fall to the ground and never get back up. She tried to calm herself, to will her eyes to open to reality, to the real world where Sean was alive. But anything she tried was no use. She had to compose herself and silence the only thought running through her mind: *Sean is dead. Sean is dead.*

Suddenly she felt nothing. It was as if she'd flown away, far away, and she was now looking down on a desperate girl whose whole world had crumbled. She was somewhere else, somewhere cold and dark where nothing moved, nothing stirred, where nobody could ever follow. She was dead too. There was nothing to live for, nothing left to lose.

She was free.

"Come and get me!" she shouted all of a sudden, just like she'd done before the last battle with Cathy's Valaya. She would not wait for the King of Shadows like a harmless, powerless creature. She had no hope left. She had no fear left.

The voice she'd heard in her vision resounded again, and it seemed as if it filled both the air and the inside of her mind.

I am here, Sarah Midnight.

Another seismic shock shook everything around Sarah, throwing her down again, and with an ear-splitting roar the ground opened right in front of her feet, stone crumbling like chalk. A chasm appeared, and from it came smoke, and a terrible heat.

Sarah rose up once more, her hands scalding, the *sgian-dubh* in her hand, her eyes gleaming with the Midnight gaze, and an unquenchable rage. She knew she had no chance, but after all they had been through she couldn't let Sean and her friends die in vain. Maybe there had been no chance all along. Maybe they had all been fooling themselves. It didn't matter anyway. All that mattered was destroying the King of Shadows before she died.

"Where are you? Show yourself!" she shouted, her voice resounding above the buzzing of the lightning and the roars of splitting rock around her. And then the King of Shadows rose, as big as a hill, his shape fluid, forever changing. He was an elemental force made of earth and fire, blue flames and liquid soil boiling and whirling, a huge mass of material that seemed to be about to pour itself on Sarah, bury her alive and seal her in rock.

Sarah flinched for a moment, but she stood firm in front of the whirling mass, trying to make out its shape. She saw that the creature was a chimera of a thousand Surari welded together, a knot of limbs and heads and claws and fangs and tentacles that somehow made one being. As she watched, the mass condensed and took its final shape – an ancestral beast, somewhere between a bull, a wolf and a bear, still changing and whirling, shifting shapes like a kaleidoscope switches colours. The bull and the wolf and the bear following each other, then melting, then turning into something else, something that had no name in the human world. Never changing and steady were his eyes, red like dancing flames, fixed on her with something that looked like hunger. Sarah was reminded of Nicholas' claim – *I am fire* – and there it was, the fire he had come from, that had shaped him.

Sarah looked up at the King of Shadows with the courage of despair. She knew she was about to die, but she would destroy that thing first. For Mike, for Harry, for Angela, for Leigh, for all those who'd been devoured and clawed to death and burnt and suffocated since the culling of the heirs began, for all those human beings who had died because their path had crossed a Surari's. Most of all, for her parents.

For Sean.

She braced herself to fight, a tiny figure, her hair blowing behind her in the scalding wind, her face illuminated by the blue lightning. She remembered what Nicholas had told them, that as soon as his shape stopped changing, as soon as he took one form, they could strike. And it had to be right between his eyes, the only vulnerable point, the only small area of flesh and blood susceptible to a physical wound.

Was it true, or had Nicholas been lying all along? She was about to find out.

A thought wormed its way into the back of her mind: why had it not poured its mass of magma and melting soil on her? Why had it not hit her with blue lightning, burning her from the inside? Was that not a quick, efficient way to get rid of her?

Why was it not killing her already?

You will not die, Sarah Midnight.

"What do you want from me?" she shouted. The King of Shadows' changing shape froze for a moment, a deep growl rising from him – and finally, it stopped changing.

Sarah Midnight and the King of Shadows stood facing each other. She wanted to run, but she knew she had to fight. She would face this monster if it was the last thing she did.

Sarah took in the deer antlers, the bull's face, and the human torso perching on a wolf's hind legs, and the bear's claws, and her heart trembled. But she would not waver. With a scream that came from the bottom of her soul, she threw herself on the King of Shadows, *sgian-dubh* in one hand, the

Blackwater burning in the other, her eyes gleaming with the Midnight gaze. She was pouring out her whole essence, the whole of herself, into one final stroke. From the night of her first hunt, when she felt the Blackwater and her powers as something terrifying and alien and somehow not belonging to her, to the duel with Cathy and Nocturne, to the battle with the Mermen on Islay, every challenge had hardened her a little more, tempered her a little more. Preparing her for this moment.

The King of Shadows didn't move as Sarah leapt, his red eyes steady and fixed on her. He made no attempt to defend himself, Sarah noticed, sinking her blade deep between his eyes, and in a moment, Sarah knew for sure that it had all been too easy.

It didn't hurt, at the beginning. It didn't hurt at all. What was happening to Sarah was such a weird feeling, so unnatural, that her body and soul didn't know how to register it. Her hand was welded to the *sgian-dubh* stuck between the King of Shadows' eyes, her body extended to reach his forehead. She stood frozen on her toes. Her green eyes were fixed on the King of Shadows' red ones, beast and Dreamer locked together.

And then it hurt like hell. Something black and nasty and painful, something ancient and merciless, had made its way inside her eyes, and down her neck, along her spine and into her heart. It filled her body and soul and stretched them to the point of ripping her apart, and it did rip her and then put her back together.

Now she knew what the plan had been for her, what they'd wanted all along.

She fell backwards, the *sgian-dubh* still stuck in the King of Shadows' forehead. She lay immobile for a moment, her consciousness screaming to keep hold of her body. She looked up at the sky, grey clouds galloping in a sea of purple. Then there was no more noise, no more pain.

Tears ran down her cheeks as she felt herself being replaced by something other. An evil she couldn't escape. She felt his spirit, his otherness, invade her body. Violate her in a way nothing human could.

Now the King of Shadows looked out from inside her body, that much she realised.

So that's what her dream meant, the one where Cathy said to her she would be lost forever. There would be no more Sarah Midnight. She would not be the bride of Shadows.

She would be the King of Shadows himself.

48
Burning Sky

When I let go of myself
The sky opens and we fly

Night fell with a burning sunset so bright that people all over the city were alarmed. They had never seen anything like it. Was the sun dying, they wondered. Was this the last sunset they'd see? The fiery sky disquieted the inhabitants of Venice.

Winter stood at Lucrezia's window, the scarlet clouds instilling fear in her heart. She'd never seen a sunset like this, not even in the north, where skies could be so spectacular that they took your breath away. But this? This was unnatural.

"Winter?" Conte Vendramin had walked in, back from one of his hunts.

"Conte Vendramin! You are home. Thank goodness."

"You saw the sky, I take it." He gestured towards the arched window near Winter's bed.

"Something is about to happen," Winter replied, wrapping her arms around her. She was afraid.

"I'll sit with Lucrezia. Why don't you go and get something to eat? Some rest?" the count offered.

Winter shook her head. "I'd rather stay."

"Very well," said the man. "We will sit together."

They sat near Lucrezia's bed, the sky casting strange lights over their faces and on the sleeping girl. Twilight was supposed to be seeping in, but there was no sign of the sky fading.

The longer she sat, the harder it was to resist falling asleep. She hadn't slept at all the night before, and Lucrezia's low whispering was now lulling Winter to sleep. Her thoughts drifted to Niall, to her seal companions, the years spent in the water, her mother. She had neared the edge of sleep when suddenly, the sleeping girl began to twitch. Winter looked to Lucrezia's father. His eyes were brooding, brow furrowed with worry.

Under their frightened gaze Lucrezia sat up, her eyes closed, and she spoke. Her childlike voice was strong, determined. "Sarah Midnight. You are Sarah Midnight. Don't lose yourself. Remember. Remember," she said in English, and then she fell against the pillows, as if the effort of speaking those words had drained all the energy from her. Her constant murmuring began again.

"I think the time has come," Winter whispered. "The moment she said she'd look for Sarah again."

Conte Vendramin nodded. He looked exhausted, Winter noticed, like he'd been burdened by a huge weight for so long. She didn't know how much longer he would be able to bear it.

Lucrezia's murmuring turned into moans of pain. She tossed and turned, as though fighting a cruel battle somewhere far away. They watched in horror as her inner strife intensified until she was foaming at the mouth, her eyes rolling back into her head.

"They're hurting her! They're killing her!" the count cried out. He didn't know who was doing this to his daughter, and he was going crazy with frustration.

"Sarah!" Lucrezia called again, and then she raised her arms, her hands reaching for someone they couldn't see. "Sarah!"

A final, anguished moan, and then Lucrezia fell back and was still once more. Her chest rose and fell frantically, and a thin film of sweat shimmered on her forehead. Instinctively, Conte Vendramin's and Winter's hands entwined, seeking mutual comfort. Lucrezia was whispering again, and every once in a while they could make out Sarah's name.

"Help me, seal!" Lucrezia said all of a sudden. "Help me reach her!" Winter let go of the count's hand and held Lucrezia's.

"How? How can I help you?" She stared into Lucrezia's sleeping face, eyes searching for a sign to guide her.

"Help me find her," the Italian girl said. For a moment, Winter's heart sank. She had no idea what Lucrezia was asking her to do, or how to help her find Sarah. She looked to Lucrezia again, but all she saw was her stony face.

Instinctively, Winter closed her eyes, and to her wonder, thousands of images began to twirl before her eyes. People. Places. Among them, somewhere, was Sarah.

Winter took a deep breath and looked for a memory of the girl. She had never seen Sarah as a small child, because of the years spent in exile, but she'd seen pictures inside Midnight Hall. One in particular, of Sarah and Morag on the beach when Sarah was about ten. Sarah's long black hair flew in the wind, her neck snuggled into a scarf. Her jeans were wet at the hems, like she'd been in the sea. She had a serious, thoughtful look in her startlingly green eyes.

As Winter pictured the photograph in her mind, the twirling images stopped and settled on the girl. All she could see was Sarah as a child, standing on the beach with her grandmother. All of a sudden, Winter heard Lucrezia's voice calling Sarah's name – and she joined her. They called together, until a terrible scene filled Winter's mind. It was Sarah, and yet it wasn't. Her body had changed and took on terrible shapes. And then she heard Lucrezia talk: *Sarah Midnight. This is who you are. Remember!*

Fire burnt Winter's mind. She gasped in pain, but she couldn't let herself stop. *Don't let go, Sarah. Remember who you are. Remember!* Lucrezia kept saying.

A new burst of pain made Winter cry out, and broke the silver thread that kept them tethered to Sarah. She saw black, and then she opened her eyes.

To her horror, she saw that Lucrezia's face was covered in blood, streaming in two red rivulets from her nose. She felt her face was wet, and when she touched it and looked at her fingers, she realised that she, too, was covered in blood.

Her eyes met Conte Vendramin, who'd been watching in horror.

"I think we lost Sarah," Winter said desolately.

"Remember," Lucrezia said once more, her bloodied face leaving scarlet marks on the pillow as she curled up, all energy gone.

49
Power

All the grief in the world lodged behind Sarah's eyes. Her body wasn't hers any more. She was alive, but she was dead. A hot, tight mass resided in her heart now − and as the new consciousness settled in her, a rush of memories and knowledge and power flooded into her like a river of magma. She saw the Time of Demons, and the wandering human tribes and the tribute of blood they paid every day. She saw the rising of the Secret children and the way the two worlds were split, a wedge of nothing inserted between them so that they could never meet again. She felt the lives of King after King flow through her, until it came to the one who had possessed her. She felt his power, stronger than any King of Shadows' before him, and she felt his rage, the all-consuming fury at his exile, his desire to claim back the earth.

She saw Nicholas' birth. She saw the death of his mother, the King's wife, and the destruction of Martyna, and felt the King of Shadows' absence of emotion as he observed every event. Horribly, unexpectedly, she felt a wave of wild, cruel joy as the gates were opened and the culling of the heirs began. She rejoiced as the blood of the Secret heirs cascaded over her. She felt every bite, every cut, every kill. Every Secret life extinguished made her cry in anguish and sing in ecstasy.

She felt the King of Shadows' iron will, his cold soul, the dried well of his heart. He didn't love; therefore, he could not be hurt. His power was such that nobody could oppose him.

Sarah felt his power.

And she liked it.

With him controlling her, she rose to her feet, her body stronger than she could ever imagine, her muscles tense with vigour. She could hear everything that happened in the Shadow World, from the slow-falling leaf to the flowing of the rivers, to the crunching of bones of a deer falling prey to a demon-tiger. She could see the snowy peaks and the roaring oceans thousands of miles away, the packs of white demons running between the trees, the moon-demons touching little creatures and turning them translucent, the fire Elementals dancing in the lava underneath the ground. She *was* the Shadow World.

Sarah raised her head and roared, a roar so deep it shook the mountains and filled the skies. The King of Shadows felt the last of her consciousness opening; in a moment he would possess her entirely. His consciousness would replace hers. What was left of Sarah would give way, and Sarah herself would disintegrate into the nothingness of humans.

He would not be weak for much longer. This fragile human body would be tempered and forged ... His plan would succeed.

And then, just as she was about to lose herself, a small voice resounded in Sarah's mind, calling her name, reminding her of who she was.

Sarah Midnight. You are Sarah Midnight. Don't lose yourself. Remember. Remember, said the voice.

Just then, Sarah and the King of Shadows felt something strong and heavy land on their body, taking their breath away. It was Nicholas.

He stared into Sarah's eyes and said, "Time to die, Father."

What was left of Sarah trembled.

50

The Emperor of the North

And so comes the last time
You'll ever hurt me

Elodie opened her eyes, and the first things she saw was swaying grass, the three carved stones, and above them, a red–black sky. It couldn't be. Was the forest on fire? Was the sky on fire? Was she in hell?

And then Nicholas' thoughts resounded in her mind, and she realised that the melting mass blackening the sky was the King of Shadows rising from the depths. In front of him was the slight figure of Sarah Midnight, silhouetted black against the sea of embers. Elodie watched in awe and terror as the writhing mass turned into a knot of Surari's limbs and head, and then condensed into a creature that looked like a jigsaw of animals. She saw Sarah throwing herself against the King of Shadows and sticking her *sgian-dubh* between his eyes, like Nicholas had told her to do.

Elodie's heart tightened. She knew what was going to

happen next. She knew what was in store for Sarah. She shook herself. This was it. This was where she'd help Nicholas take his plan to fruition. She felt Nicholas' voice in her mind, and saw that he was standing behind Sarah, waiting.

Elodie ran on, her lips black, watching as the King of Shadows' spirit left his body and entered Sarah's. She saw Sarah fall backwards, her eyes open towards the sky, her skin as white as the dead. That was their moment, when the King of Shadows' consciousness took hold of Sarah's body, but hadn't fully poured his power into her. The moment when the King of Shadows resided inside a fragile, vulnerable human body. She ran as Nicholas jumped on top of Sarah and landed on her, crushing her. A memory crossed Elodie's mind – the vision she'd seen reflected in the plane window on her way from Italy to Scotland. Sarah's death at the hands of a stranger. She hadn't seen Sarah's killer's face. Now she knew who it was.

Elodie struggled onto her feet, her body shivering with adrenaline and excitement. Reaching Nicholas and Sarah, she threw herself on the ground beside them.

"Time to die, Father," she heard Nicholas saying.

"I . . . I am Sarah Midnight," Sarah whispered slowly, as if trying to cling onto a memory from long ago. "Please, Nicholas. Don't let him do this to me. Don't let him take me. Kill me."

Nicholas nodded. His hands were raised already to twist her neck, when she laughed. The laughter stopped him in his tracks, and made Elodie's skin pucker up into goosebumps. At once, they knew that Sarah was gone, and the King of Shadows had taken over.

"Kill me," she laughed again. "Go ahead, kill me!" But it wasn't Sarah's voice.

Nicholas bore down on Sarah's body, feeling her ribs under his knees, so weak, so tender. If he leaned a bit harder, her ribs would crack and would puncture her lungs, and that would be the end of the King of Shadows. Not even a spirit as powerful as his could survive if its host body was killed. But something in his father's laughter made Nicholas stop. Something that spoke of deceit.

"If you kill me," Sarah warned, "there is no King of Shadows. No King of Shadows, no barrier between the worlds. The Shadow World and the human world fuse together and your precious humanity is gone."

Elodie saw Nicholas' features freeze. It was as if he'd been struck by a bolt of blue lightning. A knot of terror settled in her throat as her mind ran through the consequences of what Nicholas' father had just said.

"You are lying," Nicholas whispered.

To see the Surari speak with Sarah's lips, to hear his voice come out of Sarah's throat, was horrifying. Elodie wanted everything to be over. She leaned down to administer her deadly kiss, but before she could, the King of Shadows spoke again.

"Kiss me, Elodie, and I'll be gone. Or you, Nicholas, break my bones. I'll be out of the way, and your precious Dreamer will be dead. Sorry, not much I can do about that. But you know what will happen if I'm gone. Chaos will ravage this place. They will come for you, Nicholas. All of the demons. You can try to hold the portal, but you can't hold them off for long. A million Surari against you. The human world will be invaded, too fast for anyone to do anything about it. Unless . . ."

With sheer hatred in his eyes, Nicholas looked at the girl who his father had possessed. "Unless?"

"Unless you claim this land as your own. Become the

King of Shadows, Nicholas. You take a wife and have a son or a daughter, like I did. If you do that, you can kill me, and have it all. Your precious human world will be intact, and I'll be dead. Except for one detail: you'll be me."

Nicholas crumbled inside. He was unable to speak, buried under his father's revelation.

"So if you kill me now, you must become the King of Shadows. But I don't think you want that, do you? You want to continue pretending you're a real human with *feelings*." Sarah screamed with laughter. "The shadows aren't where you want to be. You'd rather live in light, with the people you've tried so hard to protect." Sarah's eyes crawled over Elodie and she smirked. Elodie shivered.

"I'm the only one who can be the King of Shadows until I'm ready," said Sarah with that terrible voice. "Until I decide. You can't kill me. I just got here. I want to see what the Dreamer can do, how much panic this little girl can wreak on the humans she wanted to protect. You can't stop me."

A moment of silence, and then, "You knew all along, didn't you?" Nicholas murmured finally. "You knew that I hadn't really come back to you, that I wasn't really going along with your plan to bring you Sarah."

"Of course I did," said his father, and Elodie spotted a hint of burning red, like embers, deep inside Sarah's green eyes. "But it wasn't important. Your betrayal means nothing because, you see, you never had any choice, not really. You planned to bring Sarah to me, let me possess her, and kill her and me with her before her body was transformed. And then you'd all be free." Sarah laughed a cruel laugh. Nicholas' hands tightened around her white, slender neck. One quick move and it would break.

"So, what do you choose?" the King of Shadows said finally, and jumped up with unexpected, violent strength. Sarah stood with her head thrown back, her hair blowing in a sudden, unnatural wind. Blue lightning shone all around them, casting strange shadows over Sarah's face. "Oh, this is a good, strong body. I can go back into the world now! The humans won't suspect a thing." He laughed and wailed in joy and Sarah's hands flew out, Blackwater flooding from them in black gushes. The body was transforming. Soon the choice would be made for them.

Elodie watched, frozen, unsure of what to do.

Nicholas' heart was bleeding. If he took his father's place, he could stop the culling. He could stop the Surari from seeping through. He couldn't save Sarah, but the world would be safe once more. And his father, the object of all his fury and hatred and revulsion, would finally be dead. But he couldn't, he couldn't. It was too cruel. He couldn't step into the abyss, the chasm that separated the shadows from the Shadow World. He couldn't kill Sarah. He'd thought he would be free in death, and now he was being offered a life that was a thousand times worse than the one he had had before, and more permanent than death. His mother had begged him not to take his father's place – and he'd tried to do as she'd asked. He'd tried so hard ... But the King of Shadows knew all along that there would be no escape for him, not ever. That was why he hadn't destroyed Nicholas with the brain fury. He'd had something even worse in store for him.

Nicholas met Elodie's eyes. Tears were flowing down her cheeks.

It must be done.

I know.

It must be done, he repeated, but he was scared. He was so scared. *Please, don't let me go.*

I'm sorry, said Elodie, a soft sob escaping her lips.

Nicholas bowed his head.

With his eyes fixed on Nicholas, the King of Shadows didn't see it coming. Elodie leapt up and kissed Sarah's lips, throwing her on the ground. For a moment, Sarah was overwhelmed, her eyes and consciousness rising to the surface again, but just as quickly as she'd reappeared, the King of Shadows' power took over once more, and it was Elodie's turn to be on the ground, screaming in pain, filled with the brain fury.

Sarah Midnight. This is who you are. Remember! It was Lucrezia's voice again, breaking through the King of Shadows' consciousness and reaching Sarah.

With a huge effort, overcoming the demon's will, Sarah bent over Elodie and kissed her. Sarah's consciousness and the King of Shadows' battled for a few long moments, one wanting to continue the kiss, the other struggling to be set free. Sarah's heart and skin and veins and brain and muscles were still human, and vulnerable to the Brun poison. It was already beginning to act on her, slowly turning her face blue.

Don't let go, Sarah. Remember who you are, remember! Lucrezia's voice kept saying from somewhere far away, keeping Sarah tethered to her own identity.

A scream of rage thundered over the land, from the hills to the caves in the forest. Blue lightning rose from the ground to meet the bolts falling from the sky. The Shadow World shuddered and trembled, but Sarah forced her body to cover Elodie's, their lips joined, as the poison filled her. With a cry of pain, she fell to the ground and was finally still.

Elodie gazed at Sarah's face. There was a purple contusion on her forehead, her lips cut where Elodie had bitten her to try to make the process quicker. Her silky black hair was matted with blood and soil. Was the King of Shadows really gone? Nicholas, too, stared at Sarah's lifeless body, as if in wait.

Finally, a reddish smoke rose out of Sarah's mouth and danced in front of their eyes, frantically, in fury and disbelief. The mist changed shape from bull to wolf to bear to burning blue flames, until it fell on the grass with a hideous thump of shattered bones and squashed tissue.

51
Fate (part one)

All the times I thought
I lost myself
It was you who found me

Elodie found Nicholas' hand. "Is he dead?"

"I think so. And Sarah too."

Elodie looked at him. His black eyes were so full of fear, so lost. He was like a frightened little boy, destined to live in shadows forever. Her heart broke. "What's going to happen now?" she asked helplessly.

"I don't know. I don't know," Nicholas whispered. "All I know is that now it's me. I am the King of Shadows."

He looked at his hands, his arms, his legs. He didn't feel any different. He thought that maybe his body would start to transform into something like his father, a chimera. But nothing was happening. All around them there was only silence and the rustling of grass. Sarah and the King of

Shadows lay immobile, the chasm that had opened in front of them still spewing smoke and heat.

Suddenly, an immense burst of blue lightning fell from the sky, and struck the monstrous body that had been the King of Shadows'. Under Nicholas' and Elodie's horrified gaze, the body began to twitch.

It's not so easy, my son.

The voice resounded in Nicholas' mind and echoed into Elodie's just as the brain fury hit them both, burning them like acid.

I can't kill you, Nicholas. You know that now, because I need you to take my place one day. But I can torture you. I can do this for as long as I like, and still keep you alive . . .

In the throes of terrible pain they watched as the chimera rose from the ground, bull and wolf and deer and buffalo and creatures they couldn't name, racing, fluid and deadly and infinitely powerful. Another wave of the brain fury hit them both with its full force and they fell to their knees, blood seeping from their eyes and nostrils and ears, and only one wish left for them to make: for death to come. In his agony, Nicholas realised the full meaning of what his father had said, and what it meant for Elodie.

He won't kill me. But he'll kill her.

He screamed and screamed, watching Elodie thrash in agony on the ground as her blonde hair turned scarlet.

52
The Reason

I touched their world
Like a comet

Sean

Pain flashes through me, and again I see black. I'm so sore everywhere that I can't tell where this new agony comes from. I realise that something is stuck inside me – close to my hip. I look for it with my fingers, and there it is. I feel sick as I realise I've done this to myself. In a flash, I remember. Harry wanted me to kill Sarah. No, not Harry. One of the Guardians.

Sarah. Where is Sarah?

Screams and howls hit my ears. I don't know who's screaming. I've lost so much blood, I feel dizzy, but I drag myself up and kneel on the long grass. My side is killing me with every movement. I curl my fingers around the handle of my *sgian-dubh* and pull. Somebody screams again, and I realise it's me. I see black for a moment, blood gushing from the wound along my leg – and then, I'm not sure how, but I rise on my feet. Everything around me is shining blue. Lightning keeps hurtling from the sky. I take a few steps in the electric light, and the first thing I see is Nicholas and Elodie, holding their heads and screaming, blood flowing out of them. The brain fury. That monster is taking Elodie to hell with him!

And then I see her. My Sarah. She's lying on the ground, her face up. Her hair falls around her in waves, her face as white as alabaster, lips black. I take another few agonising steps until I reach her. I let myself fall on the grass beside her and touch her face, kiss her black lips, stroke her hair.

It's over. It's all over for me.

But if Nicholas and Elodie are being punished with the brain fury, it means that the King of Shadows is alive. So there's something left for me to do. I drag myself up and raise my *sgian-dubh*, dripping with my own blood.

"Where are you? Where are you!" I scream, my *sgian-dubh* beginning its deadly dance.

Who's looking for me? Oh, it's the little Gamekeeper, says a disembodied voice. I turn around. Where is he? I don't even know what he looks like.

The soil itself rises in front of me, and within the mass of earth I can make out a burning heart of embers. The rippling mass takes different shapes. I can see different animals, horns and claws and muzzles, but no shape is held for more than a few seconds. I blink many times, squeezing my eyes shut. The fluctuating shape is confusing my sight to the point that the whole world seems to sway.

There must be a mouth in there somewhere, because a growling voice speaks to me. *Here you are. The one who thinks he has powers.*

I try to steady my gaze. His only vulnerable point is right between his eyes: that is what Nicholas had told us. Was it the truth, or was he deceiving us all along, inventing a weakness that doesn't exist? It doesn't even matter at the moment, as I can't make out a forehead, or a head at all. My hands trace slow runes.

Let me tell you the truth, Sean Hannay. You have no powers. Your blood is as common as dirty water. Your runes are a joke. You are a joke. It's pathetic how you want to be a Secret heir, when you never can be and never will be.

Does he think this is going to hurt me? Sarah is dead. What do I care whether I have Secret powers or not?

Deadly ribbons appear in the air. The King of Shadows laughs again. *Dirty water! That's what you are! Blood as common as muck.*

But his words can't touch me. I don't care about dying, not with Sarah gone, but I'll do my duty as a Gamekeeper as long as I draw breath. In spite of what this devil is saying, without Gamekeepers there would be no Secret heirs left alive. I'll do what I was trained to do, what I swore I'd do.

One of my red ribbons ties itself around the King of Shadows' swirling mass, wrapping itself around it, slowly caging it. All of a sudden, the mass shudders and shakes and solidifies into a weird shape: a bull's head over a human body – a minotaur. Its horns shake and dance as he tries to get rid of the scarlet ribbon, to no avail. I feel sweat roll down my forehead and fall into my eyes, and I'm suddenly aware of the blood trickling down my side. My life force flowing out of me.

The King of Shadows growls in fury. I am hurting him. It's my runes doing this to him, the runes he said were a joke.

I trace another ribbon, murmuring the secret Ancient words, and it ties itself around the King of Shadows' body. As I try to sustain both ribbons it feels like my body is going to snap in two with the effort, all my muscles hurting and stretching. The ribbons expand and flow until they join, tying his arms together. The King growls, and more blue lightning falls from the sky, all around me. I don't stop. I don't move. I don't waver. I pray I don't die before I can kill him – that's all I want. After that, I hope I go up in blue flames until there's nothing left of me but ashes, and my spirit joins Sarah's.

The scarlet ribbons tighten around his wrists and cut into them. With one last effort that makes me roar in pain, I tighten the runes even more. We both fall to our knees. The minotaur's body lands on the ground with a thud that resounds in the sky and echoes in the earth. I create one more ribbon, and tie it around his throat this time, but the King of Shadows throws back his face and opens his mouth. It all happens very fast: blue lightning comes rolling out of his eyes and mouth and envelops me, blinding me. I can't see and I can't hear anything. A burning smell fills my nostrils. It's my own flesh, I realise. Everything sways, and I feel the soft grass under my cheek.

It's the end.

The blue light fades, leaving dots dancing in front of my eyes, and I can make out the King of Shadows towering over me, the red ribbons still tied around his wrists, black blood seeping from his wounds. He raises a fist, and I close my eyes . . .

But the blow I was expecting never happens. Something holds him back. Something stops him from hitting me and smashing my skull, but I can't see what. I can make out a pair of white hands on the King's shoulders, as if someone has jumped on his back – black liquid seeps from where the hands are touching. The King of Shadows collapses face down, and finally I can see what is hanging onto his back.

It's Sarah. Sarah is alive. Her lips are still black, her face so white it glows, her hands sunk deep inside the King of Shadows' skin, dissolving him as he yells; echoing screams and yelps fill everything around us. And then there's someone else there – Nicholas. My heart sinks as he raises his hands, flaming blue. He's going to set Sarah alight, and I can't move. I can't save her . . . The pain in my side is so bad it's started affecting my eyes. Black dots shiver through my vision.

Nicholas cries out, something I can't decipher. In response, Sarah leaps away from the King of Shadows.

She stands and watches as Nicholas sets his father on fire.

53
Fate (part two)

And all that sorrow
Was meant to take me here

"Sarah," Sean murmured, gazing into Sarah's face as if he'd seen the very first dawn on Earth. She was beside him at once and they held each other, rejoicing in each other, not quite believing they were both alive.

The King of Shadows was burning, burning, still and rigid, his limbs twisted and tight as he leaked Blackwater into the soil. He was silent through it all.

Neither of them asked themselves what was going to happen next – if the sky would fall, if the Shadow World would collapse on itself as its King died. They were alive, they were together; they wanted this instant to last an eternity.

"How are you alive?" Sarah asked. "I saw you on the ground, dead. You were bleeding."

"I . . . I don't know, but I am. And I should ask you the same question! How are you here?" His heart raced. His fingers traced her skin, refusing to believe she was so close. "Elodie. Was it her ... she poisoned you!" Sean said in her ear, not wanting to release her from his embrace.

"She had to! The King of Shadows took my body. I was him, Sean! The power ... it was incredible. And terrible at the same time. I was lost, I was dead. Nicholas and Elodie thought it was the only way to kill him ... to kill me when he was inside me. He had begun to transform my body ... into something stronger. But he wasn't quite done. That's why Elodie kissed me."

"Elodie knew about Nicholas' plan?"

Sarah nodded. "She knew everything. And then the King of Shadows took over, he was about to kill Elodie ... but Lucrezia Vendramin made me remember. She told me who I was."

Sean took Sarah by her shoulders and looked into her eyes. "Lucrezia?"

"She spoke to me. Twice. I don't know how, but it was her. The first time the King of Shadows was too strong, I couldn't resist ... but the second time I held on to myself. Lucrezia's words saved me. And Elodie too, in a way. She poisoned me to the extent that I was knocked out, but she didn't kill me."

"Thank God. Thank God," Sean whispered and held her tighter. Then he released her again and looked deeply into her eyes. Her lips weren't black any more, but they were still dark; the poison still swam through her blood.

"What about the others? Elodie? Niall? Alvise and Mi—"

Her words were obliterated by a low, roaring sound coming from the sky. They looked up, expecting to see more Surari, or the King of Shadows resurrecting for a second time, but it was a plane. A plane flying in the ancient sky of the Shadow World.

Sean and Sarah watched in astonishment as shapes and shadows began to appear around them, flickering and dissolving and then reappearing – pavements, and cars and houses.

"It's beginning," Nicholas said. He had been standing still and silent throughout his father's agony and Sean's and Sarah's embrace.

"What's beginning?" Sarah whispered, looking from left and right. The ground she was standing on was shifting between grass and a wooden floor. Beside her, the shadow of a table. A few yards away, a lamp post and a shop window materialised . . .

"Do you not remember, Sarah?" Nicholas answered. "My father told me when he was inside your body that the King of Shadows exists to keep the worlds apart. Niall and Winter's discovery in your grandmother's library was true. Since the splitting of the worlds, any King of Shadows is bound to the Shadow World, keeping all in it at bay. Since he was a chimera, he was used to changing shapes, but the only way to truly exit the Shadow World was if he could take on a powerful human's body. That's why he needed you. The only way he could get out was by inhabiting your body, the most powerful Dreamer's body. He wanted to take over the world, both worlds. But without a King of Shadows bound to the shadows, the worlds will fuse. And it's happening now."

Silhouettes of men, women and children were appearing all around them, and they were looking up, falling on the ground, raising their arms over their heads in alarm.

"What are they doing?" Sarah asked.

"I think they can see the worlds melding together. They can see . . . things. Surari."

"How do we stop this, Nicholas? How?" Sean shouted, and then clutched his side, the effort making him double over in pain. Sarah shivered. In the human world, were they seeing trees sprout from the streets, and streams flow out of doors and windows? What creatures were seeping through already? How many people were losing their lives as the Surari materialised?

"There is a way to stop it," Sarah said, her eyes never leaving Nicholas' face.

Sean's eyes darted between Sarah and Nicholas. "How? How, Sarah? Nicholas? How do you stop this?"

"It's up to me," Nicholas said. In his voice, there was despair so deep that even Sean's heart tightened. "I need take my father's place. It's up to me to be the King of Shadows now." Then he gazed at Sarah, his black eyes never leaving hers. He buried his hand into his pocket and took out a white, opaque stone. Something scarlet was whirling inside.

Suspicion wormed its way into Sean's mind. He didn't trust Nicholas; he never would. "What is that?" he said, putting a protective arm around Sarah.

And then he saw the way Nicholas was gazing into Sarah's eyes, and his heart began to pound.

Sarah's gaze left Nicholas'. It locked onto the stone and could not leave. "The King of Shadows needs a bride," she whispered.

"Sarah," Sean called, but Sarah didn't reply or look at him.

She extended her hand and took Nicholas', and then they rose together. The open chasm lay before them, black smoke rising from it, heat rippling the air like a mirage.

"No!" Sean cried and leapt towards them, the wound on his side spurting scarlet once more – but Sarah's eyes sparked green. The Midnight gaze paralysed him, and he fell on his knees, the green blade cutting between his eyes. "Don't do it, Sarah! No!" he screamed, trying to get up, but Sarah's gaze kept him pinned to the ground.

"Sean. Together, Nicholas and I can stop all this. And I can make amends for my family ... You saw what I was becoming, didn't you? The way I killed Tancredi. The King of Shadows. Now it's my chance to make everything all right. I'm sorry ..."

"Sarah, please." Sean was now sobbing without restraint, like an abandoned child. "Don't go. Don't go into the shadows. Don't go."

"Listen to me, and remember my words." Her eyes softened, fingers reaching out for him. "I'll love you forever."

Another burst of the Midnight gaze, and Sean's muscles gave up. He lay on the ground, his head turned to helplessly watch Sarah and Nicholas walk towards the abyss.

Sarah gazed into the black ravine. It was so dark, mist and smoke seeping off it like serpents scurrying in for a kill. She could hear Sean screaming, but he was so far away, like another life, like he was calling somebody else. She took a step, holding on to Nicholas' hand. The blackness was open in front of her. A memory hit her – dancing leaves, a black-eyed boy about to kiss her – the first dream she'd ever had of Nicholas. The sweetness he had evoked in her, and then the revulsion, and finally, acceptance of what she felt was her destiny. All that happened had led her here, to the final sacrifice. She'd be the bride of Shadows – not through

Nicholas' deceit or through his mind–moulding, but by her own choice.

Sarah caught a glimpse of Nicholas' face as they stood before the chasm. His eyes were full of despair, and at the same time, determination. There was no way back.

They stepped forward, clinging to each other's hands.

"No! Sarah!" Sean's screams were further and further away as she left her old life behind.

Sarah closed her eyes as she took a step forward, and readied herself to fall . . .

But she didn't. Something light and fast sent her tumbling backwards, her back hitting the ground painfully. The fall knocked the breath out of her lungs, and the pain in her bones made her see stars. When she recovered herself and managed to sit up, she saw that someone else was standing with Nicholas.

Someone dark–haired and amber–skinned, an orange light all around her.

Martyna.

54
The Day I Knew

The day I knew was meant to be
The day I saw my life-to-be
But never could I have realised or seen
What was in store for me

Elodie thought she would die of pain. She couldn't possibly go through such agony and survive. It was even worse than when she'd drunk Nicholas' blood and remembered his agony – then she'd begged to be killed. This time there was no need to beg for it. The brain fury would kill her all by itself.

At first she could hear Nicholas' screams, she could feel his hands holding hers, and the blood streaming out of her nose and mouth and ears, but after a while – an eternity – she could hear nothing, see nothing, feel nothing but pain. She was pain herself. No consciousness, no memories remained. She wasn't screaming any more. She wasn't moving. She lay with her eyes open but blind, burning inside.

And then it stopped. As suddenly as it had started, it

stopped. The blackness began to blur and lighten as shapes and colours came into focus – and noises, a voice, Sean's voice, calling Sarah's name.

Sarah. Was she dead? Or had she managed to keep an ounce of life in her, as planned – so that the King of Shadows would die and Sarah would survive?

Elodie squeezed her eyes closed and opened them again. She dragged herself up and immediately she retched, bringing up bile and acid that burnt her throat and her mouth. Sean kept screaming. Where was he? She looked around, but turning her head was so painful she saw black again.

Eventually she managed. She saw him lying flat on the ground, trembling, still calling for Sarah. His face was turned towards the ravine, his eyes fixed on something ... Elodie's heart stopped as she followed Sean's gaze. Nicholas and Sarah were walking on, hand in hand. Sarah was alive. She had succeeded. But what was she doing? Suddenly, Elodie sensed Nicholas' thoughts in her mind, and she knew. Sarah was to be the bride of Shadows.

All of a sudden, Elodie saw an orange light dancing in front of them. Something seemed to take hold of her throat and tighten around it. A black-haired woman, with skin like dark honey and full red lips, materialised in front of them.

Martyna, she heard Nicholas whisper in her mind. And then she saw him throw something towards her, something small and white that landed on the grass beside her. She wanted to hold it, but her throat became too tight to breathe. Stars danced before her eyes, and then everything went black again.

Sarah was barely conscious as she saw Nicholas and Martyna hover on the edge of the chasm and then step in, holding hands. They were suspended over nothing for a few seconds, and then they fell, heads thrown upwards and arms distended, jerked apart and then thrown down by a terrible force.

A stream of blue lightning rose from the chasm – and then a cloud of earth and blue fire and melting soil. A new chimera, somewhere between a bull, a wolf and a bear, its shape changing in front of their eyes, appeared at last – until finally it took shape: Nicholas, bare-chested, black eyes shining like two pools of darkness, stag antlers rising from his head. And the woman beside him, raven's-wing hair, her eyes as black as Nicholas', dressed in what looked like a dark mist, a crown of scarlet flowers on her head. And then every noise was silenced, the earth stood still and the lightning ceased. The silhouettes of the people and cars and buildings seeping through from the human world vanished, and peace filled the land at last.

55
The Silenced Song

Some destroy
And some heal

Sean and Sarah clung on to each other in silence. Sarah was in a haze. She couldn't be joyful or happy or even relieved yet. She was in *disbelief.* The feeling of Sean's skin against hers, his breath, his body, strong and solid, after so much fear, so much pain. Was it real? Was it really happening?

She folded herself into him. There wasn't a part of her body that wasn't hurting; she needed a moment of respite. She needed a moment with nothing in her eyes and ears and soul, nothing that wasn't Sean. She held him tight and felt the wetness on his cheeks. Her own eyes were dry, but Sean was crying, coming loose and undone with her in his arms. Suddenly he moaned softly. Alarmed, Sarah slipped a hand onto his side and looked at her fingers. They were red with blood.

"Sean . . ."

"It looks worse than it is," he said, but Sarah didn't believe him. She took off her fleece and made a makeshift bandage, tying it as tight as she could around his waist, and then she helped him up.

Elodie was standing a few yards from them, looking towards the place where the abyss had been. The earth was closed again now, the three mossy boulders standing immobile as before. The only signs of what had happened were the scorched trees and the freshly turned earth, the grass mangled and muddy. Sarah sustained Sean as they limped towards Elodie. They both wrapped her in their arms and held her tight, and she, listless, dazed with shock, her face bruised and empty, let them.

"We were one. And now he's gone," she whispered, and Sarah didn't know if she was talking about Nicholas or about her primal, deepest loss, the one that had triggered the change in her, the darkness spreading inside her soul — the loss of her husband, Harry Midnight. "It was Martyna who went with him," she explained. "She came with us. I thought I'd felt her presence but I wasn't sure. She was in Nicholas' castle, trapped there ... We freed her spirit and she's gone with him."

"You are here with us. You won't be trapped in darkness with Nicholas," said Sarah uncertainly. Did she have to comfort Elodie for not having followed Nicholas into the shadows? Was that what Elodie had actually wanted?

"We were one," Elodie said again.

"I'm sorry. I'm sorry," Sarah said, holding Elodie tight.

She owed Elodie her life. She couldn't believe what the French girl had had to shoulder all alone for all that time, knowing about Nicholas' plan and not being able to say anything. And still, Elodie had gone behind their backs, keeping them in the dark about what the King of Shadows had in store for Sarah. She had taken it upon herself to decide the course of action.

For a moment, Sarah wondered what she would have done had she known about the King of Shadows' design for her. Would she have accepted being his vessel so that Nicholas could kill her while the King of all Surari possessed her? Would she have risked such a terrible fate, to have her body belong to him forever?

With a shiver, she remembered how she'd felt when the King of Shadows had possessed her – the horror, the despair. The *power.* The sense of being omnipotent, omniscient, the whole of the Shadow World flowing through her veins, beating in her heart. For a moment, she had *wanted* it.

And that was the most horrifying thought of all: that without Lucrezia's voice calling her back, reminding her of who she was, she might have lost herself forever. She might have really killed Sean and her friends and lived eternal days as the King of Shadows.

Sarah held Elodie tighter. Whatever darkness was inside Elodie, Sarah wasn't immune to it either. She was a Midnight, after all. How could she judge anyone when her family had been guilty of so much evil?

"I *knew* Nicholas was going to kill you, Sarah," Elodie whispered in her ear. "I helped him. It was the only way," she confessed.

"I know. I know. But you saved me, too."

"I was almost sure it wasn't going to work. It's so hard to gauge how much poison to use to knock somebody out but not kill them. I just can't believe you are alive."

"I can't believe I'm alive either," Sarah said truthfully. One second more of Elodie keeping her lips on Sarah's, a little more poison seeping into her system, and she might never have woken up. She released Elodie, and their eyes met. Sarah tried to find the words to express that mixture of emotions she felt, but she couldn't.

Suddenly, Elodie remembered the stone. She picked the opal up from where Nicholas had tossed it, right in front of her. It felt hot, hotter than it would be just from her body heat. A streak of scarlet played inside it, like blood in milk. "This stone contains a bit of your soul," Elodie explained. "Nicholas took it. He stole it away from you and gave it to me right before he ..." She couldn't finish her thought.

Sarah's eyes widened. Nicholas' hold on her had been stronger than she thought. A shiver travelled down her spine. "How ... how did he do it?"

"I don't know how or when he did it, but I had a vision on the plane, coming to Scotland all those months ago. I saw someone using this stone to kill you. I didn't know who – I didn't see their face. I know now." Her eyes met Sean's, and there was a prayer inside them, the hope for forgiveness.

Sean took Elodie by the shoulders and locked his eyes on hers, those black eyes that didn't belong to her, somehow. Would they turn back to their natural colour now that Nicholas was gone, Sean wondered. Would she still feel his thoughts now that he was the King of Shadows himself? Would their souls still be linked? He tried to look beyond those obsidian eyes and speak to his friend, the girl he'd known forever, the girl he'd shared so much with. The voice that had lulled him to sleep back at Gorse Cottage after all those weeks of insomnia ...

"Elodie, it's over. We made it. We stopped the King of Shadows. You are not ill any more. You don't have the Azasti any more. You are going to live. It's all ahead of you now."

"Sean," she whispered in reply, like a question, or a prayer.

"I'm here. We're here. You're not alone. Do you hear me?"

Elodie covered her face with her hands, and Sean took her by the shoulders again. It was as if she kept drifting away from them into despair, and Sean and Sarah were trying to hold her back, to not let her go.

"It was supposed to be me, the one who went with him. We were one . . ."

Sean studied her face. He saw the devastation, but this time, mixed with the loss and despair, there was a light of relief. The part of her that wanted to live, however small, was rejoicing. And another part of her, the part that was one with Nicholas, was grieving. But there was something that Sean needed to know, something that didn't make sense to him. "The whole Martyna thing . . . I don't understand. How did you know about her? Did you read it in his thoughts?"

Elodie shook her head. "I . . . I knew her spirit. I felt it in the castle. She *possessed* me."

Sean stared at his friend, shocked. How many secrets had Elodie kept from them?

Elodie continued, "He didn't know her spirit lived. It was trapped in there, and then I freed her by mistake. She followed us. She wanted to protect Nicholas. She loved him still."

Sarah winced. How could anyone love Nicholas, and all the darkness inside him?

But then, somehow, it was he who'd saved them all.

"Can you still feel Nicholas?" Sarah asked. She wanted to know he was gone, gone for good.

"I . . ." Elodie began.

"Sean! Sarah!" A young voice interrupted Elodie. It was Micol, standing at the edge of the clearing, silhouetted against the pine trees.

"Oh my God. Micol is alive!" Sarah whispered. The relief was immense, all encompassing. A soft sob escaped Sarah's lips as Micol ran to them, and they fell into each other's arms. Sarah held on to the younger girl, feeling her sparrow-like body and inhaling the scent of her skin, a mixture of lemon and ozone, like the air before and after the lightning strikes.

"Niall? Alvise?" Sean and Sarah asked, their anxious words overlapping.

"They both survived. Come!"

They half walked, half ran, Sean holding his side, leaning on Sarah. Soon they reached the edge of the clearing, where the trees were thickest and provided the most cover. Two figures crouched there, one kneeling, the other in great pain. Niall was lying on the ground, his eyes closed, head resting on Alvise's lap.

Sarah knelt beside them and caressed Niall's white face, sweeping his auburn hair away from his forehead. "Are you sure he's okay?" she murmured. *Please let him be okay, for Winter, for his family back in Ireland. For us, his friends.*

"I am sure. I healed him," Alvise replied. Only then did Sarah notice that Niall's face looked peaceful, glowing, like a huge load had been taken off his shoulders.

All of a sudden Sean let himself fall to his knees on the grass, a bout of pain taking the strength out of his legs. Sarah was beside him at once.

"Let me," Alvise said gently. He gestured to Micol, and she sat on the grass in his place, taking Niall's head on her lap. Alvise kneeled beside Sean, and undid Sarah's makeshift bandage. Sean groaned, his forehead covered in a thin film of sweat. Sarah was horrified. The wound was deeper than she'd originally thought. The laceration was an ugly gaping hole, and Sean's T-shirt was soaked in blood. How could he make the journey back? Sarah trembled inside, but didn't show anything on the outside because she didn't want to upset Sean. Silent words were exchanged between Sarah and Alvise as their eyes met over Sean's head. The Italian man closed his eyes and rested his hands on Sean's abdomen. Sean whimpered softly and tensed as Alvise touched him, but then he too closed his eyes, his features relaxing, smoothing. A warm golden light, similar to Lucrezia's iris, began emanating from Alvise's hands.

Alvise took his hands away. Sarah gasped as she caught a glimpse of his palms: they were full of blood, and lacerated, but the tears in his palms started healing at once. Alvise's face relaxed as the gashes closed and disappeared, leaving only the faint ghost of a mark.

"It doesn't hurt any more," Sean said, amazed. A puckered, raised scar, whiter than the rest of his skin, had taken the place of his wound. "How did you do it?" he asked.

"This is my power," said Alvise. "Healing."

Sean gazed at him in silent awe. Of all the gifts he'd seen in his many years as a Gamekeeper, this was the one that amazed him the most.

"What happened down there?" Micol interjected.

Sean climbed to his feet. "It's a long story, Micol. I suppose all you need to know for now is that the King of Shadows is dead."

"What happened to Nicholas?"

"He's gone," Sarah said. "We'll tell you everything ... as soon as we make it out of here." She looked at the scorched earth and the boulders in the middle of the clearing behind them, the ground black all around. Even though the blue lightning had stopped and everything was calm, she didn't want to stay in this place for one minute longer.

"I kept mental notes of how we got here. I think I know how ..." Sean began.

"Sean? Sarah?" Niall had opened his eyes.

"Hey ..." Sarah crouched beside him and helped him sit up.

"Am I alive?" he said, patting his chest in disbelief. "I thought I was dead."

"You were very close. Alvise healed you," said Sean. "And he healed me too."

Niall stared at Alvise. "You *healed* us?"

Alvise nodded, smiling. "That's what I do," he said.

"Well, I owe you one ..." Niall said in his light-hearted way, but the look on his face betrayed his emotion.

"Come on. We'd better go. It's a long way back," said Sean, offering Niall his hand.

"There will be no journey back," Alvise whispered. He raised his hand. The spiral imprinted on his palm was glowing. Golden ribbons began twirling in front of them, opening a rift in time and space for them to step through.

Lucrezia was calling them back.

56

The End of Shadows

And all that happened will be forgotten
The years of waiting, the years we lost
When you stand on my doorstep and say,
"This is our time."

It took Sarah a few seconds to get her bearings after the passage through the iris. She emerged head first, falling on the floor with a painful thud, spat out by the spiral as if the journey to the Shadow World was never meant to be. Her head spun and spun, and waves of nausea hit her one after the other as she tried to steady her heart and her breathing. She kept her eyes tightly shut through it all, not wanting to see what was already making her world spin. When she opened them, the first thing to come into focus was a high, frescoed ceiling, and then two bright eyes encased in dark, creased skin, staring at her.

An older man, tall and proud, and dressed in black. Beside him was Alvise, his quiver still strapped to his back.

"Sean?" she called, and her voice sounded funny to her

own ears, like it was coming from far away, or like someone else was talking.

"I'm here." Sean appeared at her side, and wrapped an arm around her waist. Sarah breathed in relief.

"Is this Palazzo Vendramin?"

"Yes. We are safe," Sean whispered.

"Sarah!" called a voice she knew. A silver-haired girl, Winter, opening her arms to embrace Sarah. Just at that moment, Sarah felt a current of air behind her and heard a *thump*. She jerked around to see Niall crouching in front of the golden spiral, his head in his hands.

Winter ran to him at once. A long, deep feeling of relief bubbled up from Sarah's toes and swept through her body as she watched them entwine, sobbing with happiness and relief and fear of what might have happened, but didn't.

Sarah got to her feet, swaying, looking for something to hold on to. She nearly fell again, but Sean righted her. Her ears were ringing, everything was turning and happening in slow motion. "Elodie?" she managed to say.

"She's here. She's fine," Sean whispered, gazing briefly towards the far corner. She followed his gaze.

Elodie was standing calm and strong, her lips blue and her eyes fixed on the sumptuous, silk-covered bed sitting in the middle of the room. There was a girl lying on it, her face as white as mother-of-pearl, her eyes open, the same blue as Alvise's, shadowed with purple, and hair the colour of pale straw gathered in a side braid.

"Lucrezia," Sarah murmured.

And then something happened, and it was like everyone in the room took a deep, collective breath, sucking all the air in: Lucrezia opened her pale lips, and she *spoke*.

"Yes. I am Lucrezia Vendramin," she said hesitantly, as if she weren't entirely sure of her identity, and somehow saying it made it true. It looked as if shaping her mouth and her vocal cords around the words took a real effort, because she hadn't spoken of her own will for a long, long time.

In a moment the older man – *Lord Vendramin*, Sarah thought – was on the floor beside Lucrezia's bed, his face hidden in her hair, his arms around her reclining body, murmuring her name over and over again.

Alvise stood immobile, tears streaming down his face, until finally he spoke too. "*Sorella mia*," he whispered. *Sister of mine.* Lucrezia Vendramin was awake.

57
The End of Dreams

She dug out the seeds of destruction
One by one, down to their roots
And she realised that rebirth
Felt a lot like death

Lucrezia's skin was still white and her limbs thin and fragile, but there were two spots of pink on her cheeks. She leaned against her pillows, too weak to sit up after many years of stillness, but her eyes studied her visitors through half-closed lids.

For the Vendramin men, having their sister and daughter back was like a dream come true. And still, they were shaken, unsure. It was as if they were holding her by a slender thread that could break at any time, and she could be gone again.

Alvise held both her hands, almost as if to keep her tethered to them, and their father had a protective hand on top of her head. Micol stood at the foot of the bed, grinning.

Sean, Sarah, Niall and Winter looked on, overwhelmed

with emotion, all nearly unable to believe that they'd come back in one piece, and were witnessing Lucrezia's miraculous healing. Elodie stood slightly apart from the others, aloof, as if part of her hadn't fully returned from the Shadow World yet, as if part of her had been left there.

"How . . . how did it happen?" asked Sarah. "How did you wake up?"

"I don't know," Lucrezia replied in her hesitant English. "I went inside your mind, and I called you. The Surari stopped me and I tried again and they stopped me for the second time. But I called you again and you heard me, and you listened to me. Then there was a terrible voice in my head, and fire burning my brain. It was very strong. I could not hear you, Sarah. I did not know what happened to you. Then my mind—" she looked for the words to explain "—exploded. Yes, it exploded," she repeated, freeing her thin hands from Alvise's and bringing them to her temples. "There was fire everywhere . . . and then there was silence and everything went black. I was so sure I was dead. All those years of many visions and voices in my head, all the time, day and night. Every second. I could never rest . . . But now they had stopped. I could hear nothing and see nothing. It was so peaceful. To be dead was a relief, because all these years were so hard. But I wanted to see you again," she said, eyes resting on her father and her brother. Guglielmo Vendramin caressed her face and Alvise held her hands once more. "I floated in dark and I felt no pain. I wanted to float forever. And then I heard your voice, Alvise, and I was awake."

"*Grazie a Dio!*" Alvise blurted out, drying his cheeks.

"*Figlia mia,*" Vendramin murmured, his voice breaking.

Micol was shocked to see the old man, who was always so

proud, so reserved, unable to contain his feelings. She leaned across and placed a hand over his, and for a moment their eyes met in mutual understanding.

"*Mi sento debole*," Lucrezia whimpered.

"She says she's feeling weak," Vendramin explained to Sarah and her friends. "We should let her be."

They rushed to leave with a small chorus of apologies. Only Elodie stayed silent. Niall and Winter walked out, hand in hand, then Sean and Sarah. Micol placed a kiss on Lucrezia's forehead and ran out, her joy unable to be contained. At last, Elodie stepped beside the bed.

"You are Elodie," Lucrezia said.

Elodie stopped and looked at the girl with her still-black eyes. "Yes."

Lucrezia studied her face for a moment, but she said nothing, and the French girl walked on without a word.

58
When All the World Is Calm

Out of dreams comes
A new life

A week later

Sarah walked in first, a wet smudge of black on her cheek.

"Got it?" Niall asked. He was perched on an armrest beside Winter, who was curled up against soft silk cushions.

"Oh, yeah. When we left, it was very dead, I can assure you," Sarah said, raising her blackened hands.

"Could not have been more dead."

Sean stepped into the room, Alvise by his side. A small, triumphant smile danced on Sean's lips. Elodie smiled back. That was Sean, the way he used to be, reckless, mischievous, loving the hunt, a Gamekeeper through and through.

Elodie was sitting on an ottoman, her long blonde hair on her shoulders, and her eyes, though shadowed with blue, were back to their natural chocolate hue.

"Thank you," Alvise said to Sean and Sarah, freeing

himself from the quiver and resting his bow on one of the sofas. "For agreeing to help us before going home." Conte Vendramin had asked them to help destroy the Surari that had seeped through to Venice during the rift between worlds. They had gone hunting every night for a week with Alvise, while Micol and Niall tackled the water Surari in the Grand Canal.

"Any time. But this was the last one for a while now. We need to get home," said Sarah, and her eyes met Sean's. He held her gaze, unspoken words passing between them.

"Yes, we need to get home," Sean echoed, and Sarah's heart skipped a beat. Would they go home together? Live together? They'd been back from the Shadow World for a week now, and they had slept in separate rooms. That was what they'd been offered, and neither of them had complained or asked to change. Not that there had been much sleep anyway, with the intense hunting they'd done. Sarah had focused on the hunt, frightened of the moment they'd have to decide what to do next. Would he tell her what she feared the most, that they were going to part ways, that he would go back to New Zealand, or to Japan to look for Mary Ann, or to France with Elodie? Would he tell her that after the culling of the heirs, it was her duty to breed powerful children with another Secret heir?

"I can't wait to be home," said Niall. Since he'd been reunited with Winter, Niall had had a constant smile on his face. He and Micol had seen to a particularly vicious kind of demon-eel, five of them let loose in the city's canals. But whatever else had seeped through was for the Vendramin to take care of: Niall and Winter had plane tickets to Dublin booked for that night.

"Wow, Sarah, you look shattered. You need a holiday," Niall said mischievously.

"Niall!" Winter scolded him gently. "Don't listen to him, Sarah. You look amazing," she said. Sarah's cheeks had filled out again and her hair was lustrous and shiny once more, the effects of the Shadow World washing away with every day spent back on the human side.

"Are you going back to Edinburgh, then?" Elodie asked Sean. Sarah looked at him, holding her breath as she waited for his reply.

"Yes. If Sarah puts me up for a bit." He grinned, but there was a hint of vulnerability in his eyes. Sarah studied his face for a moment, trying to read his intentions. He was going back with her, but it didn't mean that they would be anything more than friends, or comrades in the hunting. She sighed inwardly. The night they'd spent together at Nicholas' castle kept playing in her mind; unbearably sweet memories teased her and confused her.

"Please come with us. At least until you decide what to do," Sean said to Elodie.

Elodie seemed pretty much back to her old self, but both Sarah and Sean were worried. Once back in the human world her eyes had regained their old brown tones and lost the otherworldly obsidian of Nicholas' eyes. She'd been given a clean bill of health by the Vendramin physician – no trace of the Azasti was left – and apart from being very tired and a little pensive, she'd been all right. The night before, Sarah had woken up thinking she'd heard Elodie scream in her sleep, but as she lay awake in the darkness, she didn't hear anything again. She decided she'd dreamt it.

"Thank you, Sarah. But I must go to the mountains and

look for Aiko Ayanami. Something tells me she's still alive. And after that ... well, I think I'll go back to Annecy. Start again. The Brun Family is not finished yet."

"No. The Secret Families are not finished," Alvise intervened. "We need a new Sabha. We need to find out who survived and get organised again."

"But with Nicholas in the Shadow World, the Surari won't come through any more, will they?" said Micol, looking for reassurance. "I mean, if we get rid of the ones who are here already ..."

Elodie looked down. "I'm not sure it's entirely up to Nicholas. I think the separation between the worlds is not watertight and never will be. There'll still be gaps. Things will go back to the way they were before, I think, with Surari drifting in every once in a while, to be dealt with by whoever is left of the Secret Families and the Gatekeepers."

Sarah thought of home, of Aunt Juliet and Bryony. She thought of the Midnight mansion in Edinburgh, and her garden, of her cello in its purple case, waiting to be played again.

Sean slipped his hand in hers. "Fancy a walk?"

"Sure," she said, and suddenly, irrationally, she felt cold with apprehension. What was he going to say? That he had no powers, and therefore they could never be together? Would he raise the same wall between them, still unmovable, unreachable? Sarah's stomach knotted up and her mouth went dry all of a sudden.

"Sure. I'll just have a quick shower. Down in twenty minutes," she said and went to step out of the room. Suddenly, she felt the impulse to turn back for a moment. She wasn't sure why. She gazed at Elodie. Her hand was resting on her belly, and there was a look in her eyes that made Sarah's heart flutter. Elodie felt her watching, and their eyes met. She didn't move her hand away from her belly, but she didn't look down.

Sean was already gone, Niall and Winter were absorbed in each other, Micol was shuffling songs on her iPod. Nobody noticed, but in those few seconds, in that look, Elodie spoke to Sarah.

No, the Brun Family wasn't finished.

59
Love on the Water

All the time in the world
For us to see
That life is what we make of it

Venice sparkled under the winter sun, the air freezing and the sky pure and perfectly blue. Sean and Sarah wandered along the *calles,* hand in hand, until they got to a little *campo,* a small square, surrounded by beautiful buildings with arched windows and stuccoed façades. Schoolchildren and tourists with cameras and old ladies carrying groceries hustled all around them, busy and unconcerned with their conversation. *Strange,* Sarah thought. *My whole life is being played out, here, and nobody knows, nobody suspects.*

"Sarah . . ."

"Please don't say it," she blurted out, her hands raised to form a barrier between them.

"Don't say what?" he smiled.

"Don't say you're going away. That I have to marry a Secret

heir. That you'll look after me, you'll never be really gone, but we won't be together. Just don't say it."

"Sarah, Sarah, stop!" He laughed, and held his own hands up too, braiding his fingers through hers. "Oh. Maybe I should have asked before doing this," he said.

"Doing what?"

"Touching your hands. In case you try to kill me. You did that before." He laughed again.

"Don't laugh!" she said, looking down. She was getting really flustered. He seemed to be playing a game while she consumed herself waiting to hear what he had to say.

"Okay, sorry. Listen. I—" He drew a deep breath. It wasn't easy for him either, to put his thoughts into words. "I . . ."

"Picture? Take picture?"

Sean blinked and stared as a Japanese woman stood in front of him, camera in hand, a big smile on her face. "Picture, please?" she repeated, gesturing to Sean and then to the man and child behind her.

"Of course. Of course," he muttered, taking the camera from the woman. Sarah tried not to roll her eyes so as to not seem rude, but she sat rigid, willing the tourists to go.

"Thank you! Thank you!" the Japanese tourists repeated over and over again, and they even bowed slightly before walking away.

"So, yes. Where were we?" said Sean, sitting on the stone bench again.

"I don't know where we were, Sean. I don't know where we *are*. I don't know what's going to happen!" Sarah blurted out, finally out of patience.

"I'll tell you what's going to happen, Sarah," said Sean, suddenly serious. He cupped her face in his hands. "You were right all along. I've seen the effects of inbreeding among the Secret Families. It's time for a new era and a new generation whose blood is strong again ..."

Sarah's eyes welled up and she smiled between her tears.

"I don't want to see you crying ever again," said Sean, and dried a rogue tear that had rolled down her cheek. He stroked her hair, then took her face in his hands again and kissed her.

Sarah closed her eyes and let happiness flow through her. They were going to be together. After all the pain and fear, and the lies and the reconciliation ... and all the times they were so close to death they could feel its cold breath on their necks ...

They were going to be together.

It didn't seem possible.

Sarah's mind went back to the first time they'd met. She'd heard his voice before seeing him. His deep, warm voice with a hint of a New Zealand accent, and then she'd stepped into view and took him in, those light blue eyes, impossibly clear, and with a warning in them: *Don't come too close*. Now the warning was gone, the barriers had fallen, and his eyes were full of love.

"Does this mean you're coming back to Scotland with me? As in ... you'll live with me again?"

"Of course. And Sarah ..."

"Yes?"

"I just can't wait to hear you play your cello again," he said, and kissed her again, the warm Italian sun shining on them both.

60
When You Return

My hand in yours
The end and the beginning
Of a butterfly life
Fragile and brief, so brief
But beautiful and ours
To keep at last.

Edinburgh was grey and dreamy and blustery, and Sarah's heart leapt as she stepped out of the taxi. At last, the Midnight mansion was waiting for her. The lights were on and shone yellow in the lilac dusk. Aunt Juliet was on the steps, waiting for her. Sarah ran into her aunt's arms and held her tightly. She couldn't help noticing the jagged scars running over her cheeks and arms, from when the demon had clawed her nearly to death. Her fingers traced Aunt Juliet's scars, her eyes full of sorrow.

"It doesn't matter. I'm alive and it's in the past." She fixed her niece with a direct gaze. "I won't ask you what happened,

Sarah. I just want to know one thing. Are we safe now? Is it all finished, whatever was happening?"

"Yes. Yes, Aunt Juliet. We are safe."

Her aunt smiled and held her again. "And Harry ... welcome home."

"Sean. My name is Sean Hannay."

"Right," said Juliet, looking at Sarah with raised eyebrows.

"Long story . . . ." she began, but stopped midway through.

Because on the pavement, with a mane of red hair, bright-blue eyes and a purple dress – she always wore a hint of purple somewhere – was her best friend. She was holding a shoebox.

"Bryony!" Sarah called, racing towards her. They fell into each other's arms, negotiating the shoebox, tears streaming down both their faces.

"I was so worried!" Bryony whispered into Sarah's hair.

"I know ... I'm sorry I worried you. I'm here now."

Bryony handed her the shoebox. "This is for you." Only then did Sarah see that the box had holes dotted all around it, and there was a soft towel folded inside. She pulled the lid of the box off. Within the towel, curled up asleep, was a little black kitten. For a moment she couldn't speak.

"I thought ... with Shadow gone." Bryony stumbled to explain.

She hugged her friend. "Thank you. Thank you so much!"

"It's a girl. What will you call her? I was thinking maybe Moonbeam?"

Sarah and Sean shared a look. The fleeting image of the moon-demons, skeletal and translucent among the trees, danced between them.

"Er ... I think there are much better names," said Sean, scratching the back of his head.

"I'd go for Sunshine," said Juliet. "Not very Sarah, but it's cute."

Sarah smiled. "Sunshine is perfect," she said, caressing the kitten between the ears. "I need to know, Bryony. Did you get into the School of Art?"

Bryony's face broke into a smile. "Yes!"

"Oh, I'm so happy for you!" Sarah squealed under Sean's delighted gaze. It was amazing for him to see her so happy at last, so carefree. He watched as Sarah, Sunshine and Bryony entered the house.

When he and Aunt Juliet followed, they couldn't believe what they saw. Sarah had taken her shoes off and kicked them aside, and hung her jacket on the peg hurriedly, like it didn't matter if it hung straight. Was the old Sarah really gone, the one who would have a panic attack if her shoes weren't lined up, if her coat didn't hang perfectly even? The girl who had to dust and polish every surface over and over again before leaving the house?

Juliet's smile just got bigger. "Now, you must be hungry," she said, trying to suppress her joy at seeing Sarah so ... careless. "The cupboards and fridge are full. All the beds are changed and the place is gleaming. I had everything ready for you."

"Thank you so much, Aunt Ju ..." But once again Sarah's voice trailed away. She'd seen a letter on the table, one that Aunt Juliet had set aside from the pile of bills and brochures that had arrived while she was away.

Sarah knew what it was.

She took a few slow steps towards the table. "I want to open this alone," she said, lifting up the letter with shaking hands.

"Of course, sweetheart," said Juliet, and they watched Sarah step out of the kitchen.

She went upstairs to her room. So many memories were there, all her things that had lain in wait until she returned: the silvery-grey walls, the long, white voile curtains, the freshly made bed on which Aunt Juliet had placed a sprig of lavender from the garden. Her cello in its purple case sat against the wall, waiting to come back to life. She wanted to play so badly that her fingers hurt with desire.

Sarah sat on her bed. Her hands trembled so much that she struggled to open the envelope. Her eyes scanned the text, looking for "we regret", or "unsuccessful" ...

Tears were streaming down her face as she walked back to the kitchen, slowly, deliberately. Sean, Aunt Juliet and Bryony looked at her, expressions of encouragement but also worry visible on their faces.

A smile of pure happiness spread across her face as she showed them the letter offering her a place in the Royal Conservatoire of Scotland.

Finally, they were alone. A sliver of moon was shining white and pure on Sarah's garden as they strolled hand in hand, unafraid at last.

"Look. I kept this all along," Sarah said, lifting the white and scarlet opal to the palm of her hand.

Sean took it from her, rolling the stone between his fingers. It was smooth to the touch, and cold. "I wonder if it's just a stone now, or if it still has a piece of your soul in it."

"I don't know."

"We can't run the risk, I suppose. If part of you is inside here, we need to—"

"Keep it safe."

"Yes."

Sarah stopped and stood in front of him. "Will you do that for me? Will you keep a piece of my soul?" Sarah's green eyes burnt in his, full of tenderness.

Sean shook his head. "I won't. Your soul is your own, all of it. I love you, but I won't own you. Not even a piece of you."

Sarah smiled. "In that case, I know what to do with this."

She led Sean towards Anne's herb patch. Memories of her mother were everywhere. She could see Anne planting and digging and pruning, her black hair down her shoulders, the same raven hair as Sarah.

She kneeled on the damp soil and started digging delicately under the thyme bush. That was where her mother had concealed her magical diary, buried for Sarah to find. The opal went into the ground, interred deep, safe in the heart of her home. Sean looked above him. A few stars were visible in the cloudy night sky, the sky of home, so different from the harsh, vivid sky of the Shadow World and its sea of stars. The new moon above them was a maternal, tender face – not the hunting goddess of the Shadow World.

Sean had often thought that Sarah was like the moon: white, luminous, distant. Untouchable. But not any more. She was with him. And all the world was calm.